ROXANNA SLADE

BOOKS BY

REYNOLDS PRICE

REYNOLDS PRICE

ROXANNA SLADE

SCRIBNER

SCRIBNER
1230 Avenue of the Americas
New York, NY 10020

SCRIBNER and design are trademarks of Simon & Schuster Inc.

Set in Electra

Manufactured in the United States of America

1   3   5   7   9   10   8   6   4   2

Library of Congress Cataloging-in-Publication Data
Price, Reynolds, 1933.
Roxanna Slade / Reynolds Price.
I. Title.
PS3566.R54R69   1998
813'.54—dc21   97-39167
CIP

ISBN 0-684-83292-5

FOR
FRANK HIELEMA

ROXANNA SLADE

ONE

Every time somebody calls me a saint, I repeat my name and tell them no saint was ever named Roxy. They know of course I was seldom called Roxy, though back in my childhood I tried to persuade my family to call me Roxy instead of the Anna which everybody chose but my brother Ferny. He'd call me Rox at least half the time and was my big favorite. For practical purposes Anna Dane was my maiden name. I never enjoyed it. Even now after so long it has never seemed to be me. Roxanna means *Dawn* or *Daybreak* which is fine, but my family never called anybody by their whole name.

So through the years I've consulted several child-naming books in hopes of discovering some good luck in Anna. But they just say the name is an English version of the Hebrew Hannah and that Hannah was the name of the prophet Samuel's mother and also Christ's maternal grandmother. Both women were likely saints, and I never felt the least kinship to either one. There was a popular song years back called "Hard-Hearted Hannah, the Vamp of Savannah, G.A." I've wished more than once she could have been me. But not one person who's ever counted deeply called me any more than nicknames, no one that is except a tall boy named Larkin Slade. And he died young, leaving me off stride for the rest of my life.

In a way Lark's death was the start of my life which is strange to think of. I was grown when he went, just barely grown. But I've given that odd fact a good deal of thought through the intervening years. Whenever I've heard about people's childhoods—how urgent they are to future health and plea- sure—I've always felt that my childhood scarcely amounted to more than a dream, a pleasant enough dream with no grave fault, no hard stepmothers or beasts in the night but a made-up childhood all the same, certainly nothing real enough to cause the bitter pain I've since known and am bound to have given.

I had kind parents with no bad traits except my mother's tendency to put on flesh and the plug tobacco that my father chewed as neatly as any horse chews hay. They never had a great deal more money than it took to get from one day to the next. Father ran a store with groceries and dry goods that ranged from gingham to plow points but was always in dutch. Still none of us children ever went to bed hungry or lacked clean clothes sufficient to the season, and we were respected on every side.

In the kind of town where I grew up, few distinctions were made on account of money unless you were outright redheaded trash. Truth was, you were either white or black. In those days we said *colored* if we meant to be courteous and not hurt people, and the color of your skin pretty much said all there was to say. The Bible forbade calling anybody *common* (Acts X:15, "What God hath cleansed, that call not thou common"). So even if they were the sorriest white skin ever conceived, the worst you could call them was *ordinary*.

There were four Dane children in my generation, counting me—two girls, two boys. It was not a big family for that day and age. I and my sister Leela were the second and third children. There was one brother two years older than I and one who was younger than both us girls. So Leela and I came very close to raising the boys once Muddie's kidneys began to fail. Muddie was our mother. That failure took long years but always kept her unreliable for bearing serious weight and pressure.

Still my brothers were good boys in those days, just normally wild before they grew up and left home naturally. How they fared after moving away is a long grim tale that may not belong here, depending on where my story leads me. Both of them perished in sad circumstances well before they deserved, one of them leaving a wife and children that I've scarcely known. But I can see each of them in my mind's eye, fine as they were in their fortunate days and prone to gentleness till they each found some drug to lose their minds for—money in one case and pills in the other.

For instance it was through the good will of my younger brother Ferny that I met Larkin Slade and loved him on sight. Ferny had met Lark the summer I was nineteen when Fern went to work for a bachelor cousin of ours named Roscoe Dane far up on the Roanoke River, a cranky old bird who smelled like bacon and tried to cultivate rented land with insufficient help or truly good sense and was always in straits, though all of us liked him. His nearest neighbors were a family of Slades.

There was old Major Slade who'd lost half a leg and several fingers in the Civil War, his second wife Olivia who was far more beautiful than any woman since, and numerous children of all kinds and ages by each of the wives. Most of the young Slades had grown up and left with very little trace of themselves like children in old-time pioneer stories who bid you farewell and cross the far hills to vanish forever.

The Slade place had been up there way more than a century, just above the flood plain of the Roanoke when the river was wild. And though it was only eight miles from our home, Ferny stayed gone forever till Roscoe's cotton was sold in late September. When Fern got back to us in time to start his last year of school, he was browner than any walnut chair. And very nearly all he could offer by way of memory from a long summer's work was praise for somebody named Larkin Slade.

Lark Slade deserved all the praise he got, as I soon learned thanks to Ferny's good-hearted descriptions. My birthday falls on October 8th, and on the year in question—1920—I was blue for several causes as the date drew near. My sister Leela had fallen out with me for fairly normal sisterly reasons having to do with a blouse we shared. We'd spent too many years in each other's faces, and Muddie had taken my sister's side as she generally did. In those days in any case there were so many souls in every family that you never made much of any birthday even if you were well off, so I had no great hopes for my twentieth.

Then on October 7th when Ferny had been back at home for a few weeks, he walked in from the post office with a card addressed in a strong man's hand and called me aside to whisper a plan. "Let's give this whole bunch a big damned surprise." Fern always called our family *this whole bunch*. Then he said we could "borrow" Father's car before sunrise and motor up to Larkin's place for the day. Tomorrow would be Friday. Ferny had shaved Friday off more school weeks than not, and I didn't try to object on those grounds. Anyhow he flashed the postcard to show me Lark's signature. It looked like the map of splendid distant mountains.

I recalled Father never used the car on week days. Muddie couldn't have driven a goat cart in a crisis, much less a car. And since nobody then paid a scrap of attention to a driver's license, Ferny stole the car several times a year. He could start the Model T under water if called upon; and he'd run off with it and two especially ordinary girls the previous spring, staying nearly a week and requiring a hunt by the sheriff to find.

"It'll drive them all crazy," Fern said to tempt me. He was smiling down strongly at Lark Slade's postcard. By *them* Fern meant our family of course, and of course he was right. He and I were mostly the troublemakers, though the troubles were slight by comparison with any family's now.

I doubted Fern knew my birthday was coming that very next day. I chose not to tell him. I just nodded and smiled and said I'd be ready.

I could still make choices at a moment's notice, and seeing two things had made me say Yes—the mischief in Ferny's bright copper-brown eyes and the sight of Larkin Slade's whole name in his own rushing hand. Old as I was, and more than half of all girls near twenty then were married, I ought to have smelled the danger before us. I was old enough not to join my brother's foolishness and trick our father, a peaceful soul. I very well knew Ferny always overreached. But even a girl about to turn twenty—me, an earnest creature who took duty seriously—couldn't sense death coming on a cool fall day.

At the last minute before Fern and I crept out in the dim dawn to start the car, I pictured three family faces at breakfast—Muddie and Father and Leela of course. (My older brother was long gone, living in Shelby with a dreadful wife and an unloved daughter with a neck as long as any wet week.) They wouldn't know where on Earth I'd gone or whether I'd departed with a mean grudge against them.

So I took a stub pencil and left a quick note on the kitchen table to say I'd asked Ferny to take me off for a birthday outing. I needed the air to improve my low disposition which I knew had been getting on everybody's nerves. We'd be back by supper (in those days *dinner* was the midday meal). Again I knew they wouldn't be needing the car. I meant for the note to spare Ferny's hide. Our parents had never laid a hand on me or Leela; and if we were late, as I hoped we'd be, I could always say we'd had a puncture or another small mishap which Fern had handled miraculously.

When we got to the main road, Fern stopped the Model T and faced me broadside. Turned out he'd seen me leave the note, which I thought was secret. Of course he'd intended to make harmless mischief, and I'd ruined his plan. For the hundredth time Fern said to me "Rox, you going to be a damned saint all my life? You can do it on your own time, but don't go shouldering stuff for me. I've borrowed this car for my own reasons. You're along for the ride."

I asked him why, if he was so upset, he hadn't just reached back and torn up my note.

Fern looked at me long enough to draw a long breath. Then as he moved us back onto the road, he said "Please just try to live on the *Earth*. You'll get to Heaven in time." He really wasn't mad but his skin had blotched red. And though the morning light wasn't truly that cold, his breath smoked from him like blue incense.

I said I had no expectation of Heaven, which even then was partly true, and that I was sorry.

Fern said "Don't be. Never be sorry again in your life or my life anyhow—I'm living forever." By then he could grin.

But I knew he was serious. I told him I wouldn't; and when my brother moved us both on down the bright road, I believed myself. I was not the cause of anything harmful yet done in my life. And I never would be, or so I hoped in my belated innocence and virgin folly.

The trip took us longer than we'd expected, mainly because back then most roads were narrow and cut by deep ruts with treacherous sandbars. We had one puncture that took awhile to mend. You couldn't cross the yard in those days without having at least one flat tire. And Fern stopped three times to show off his skills to boys we passed, his old school mates who'd abandoned school at the legal age which was then fourteen. I'd climb down and wait in the shade while Fern gave them short dusty spins. With the last boy, the oldest, Fern managed to tip the car onto two wheels. I watched it happen, not at all sure we'd ever go home intact again, not as children worth claiming by honorable parents. And it was close to eleven in the morning when Ferny paused us in sight of the Slade house and pointed toward it.

In its deep grove of oaks and hickories, the house was two unusually tall stories high with full-length porches upstairs and down. And it rambled considerably like a lot of houses then as families grew to a dozen or more; and aged relations, plus bachelors and spinsters, came home to die. If the pine

siding had ever known a trace of paint, it showed none now. It was weath-
ered to a likable shade of bone gray, and the tin roof was numerous shades of
rust. No trace of antebellum glory in other words but no ruin either.

This was plainly a sensible working home, the well-kept refuge of people
with no big sense of self-importance. It was plainly fit to withstand all but
fire and cyclone and a slave revolt. I recall that the first time I glimpsed the
Slade house was the first time it ever crossed my mind how odd it was that
no Southern home had ever been built with any notion that the slaves might
rise up and attack with scythes and pitchforks. By the time I'd registered that
much, Fern had killed our engine there a quarter mile off down a long alley
of cedars and oaks that looked very much like the road to somewhere final.

I was fairly well dressed to meet decent people, so I asked if we couldn't
move a little closer.

Ferny shook his head. "They've got awful dogs and Major Slade may
well take some shots with his old bird gun if he's had a drink yet." He was
half grinning but his voice sounded earnest.

I said "Then thank you, I'll wait for you here. Run say hey to Larkin;
then carry me home please."

Ferny took in my whole face and upper body as if I were suddenly some
territory he'd never guessed at. He finally said "You'll wait till dark" and
moved to get down. I didn't know he had expectations of an escort coming
to guide us in.

So I was worried but when I looked ahead, a wide pack of hounds was
legging out toward us with a tall boy behind them.

Ferny said "Luck's improving. Here's a birthday present." He nodded
through the glass toward everything coming.

I was too busy looking to notice that Fern had recalled my birthday.

The hounds reached us first, small old-time beagles with the kind of country noses that could find a lost child through miles of thicket, not to mention a fox. At a distance I hadn't noticed one peculiar dog at the head of the
pack, the first one to reach us. It was thoroughly different from the twenty-
odd others. Before or since I've never seen its like—not ferocious or ugly
but not a member of any dog clan from our end of the world at least. It was
so short haired it looked truly skinned, the tannish yellow of antique piano
keys with a thin wolf's muzzle and cat-green eyes.

When it got right to us, it came to my side of the car and met me head-on. I was still seated. It was still on the ground. But the way it fixed on me, I all but expected it would say "I bring you this urgent message, woman. Listen close. Your life hereafter hinges on it."

My guess proved very nearly right. My life hinged there as the day would reveal before midnight. The dog didn't speak of course, not then anyhow. In a few more seconds it was swamped by the other dogs, all glad to see Ferny who had stepped out among them. We were white at least. All white peoples' dogs back then were prejudiced against colored skin and many still are.

Ferny was squatting there, kissed by hounds, when the tall man caught up and scrubbed Fern's scalp with the knuckles of the biggest right hand I'd ever seen.

Fern stood up beaming a half mile wide. He was never given to worshiping people and generally offered them as little as he could. But this new boy plainly drew at him powerfully. I'd never yet seen Fern this glad to be breathing. The two of them stood there grinning in silence. Fern's shirt was precisely the color of the sky, a celestial blue.

So finally I had to lean out and say "I'm this young scoundrel's sister Roxanna."

The new boy blushed a furious red, the only dark-haired human I ever saw blush that deeply. And not only blushed but met my eyes with eyes of his own that were Wedgwood blue, another trait I've never seen elsewhere yet would later notice in people of Irish and Welsh extraction. Big and shining under all that black hair, he barely looked older than Ferny's seventeen. But the first words he said to me were "Happy birthday. We're the same age now."

Had my birthday suddenly become world news? Where on Earth was I?

In the face of the shock and grief that were near at hand, it would take me days to recall the new boy's words and to realize that somehow he and Fern had planned this escapade—by mail it turned out—and that Fern had filled Larkin with the expectation of meeting a lovely possible bride. On the spot that instant, I just felt mildly stunned and dusty. But the air had warmed nicely and when Lark put out his huge hand to help me, I climbed down carefully into the bright day.

I said "I feel a lot older than you." I meant to say I *knew* I looked older. But it came out differently if not really wrong.

Whatever I felt or thought I knew, I was sure of one thing. I'd never seen a boy or man as fine as Larkin Slade.

Till then I'd spent very little time or energy noticing men or dwelling on them. Leela my sister thought of precious little else and was eager to wed the first boy that paused to smile, which was part of why she and I were moving back from the closeness we'd shared. I well understood I'd also likely marry some man and raise my own children. The human race appeared to do that. I also knew, and had heard others whisper, I was dying on the vine with no immediate prospects at twenty.

It hadn't bothered me more than three or four seconds. Not till here and now on a dry country road near the Roanoke River, surrounded by dogs and my pitiful brother (pitiful years down the line from that day) and his good friend who was grand to see as the darkest rose on a wine-red bush you find somewhere you were not expecting roses. Facing Lark Slade now I felt alone as a snow-covered alp.

But then Lark said "We've made a plan. Hope you like it." He'd looked from me to Ferny as he spoke.

Fern had never stopped smiling. He turned it on me. That open honest face and neck, set in that blue shirt against that sky, looked very much like an angel messenger—*telling me what?*

I'd loved Ferny Dane all his life, so what could I do but hold out my arms—I was carrying nothing but a plain gray parasol—and try to speak enough to show I was living? Somehow I said in Lark's direction "I'm a captive guest." It didn't hurt to say it, I'm glad to admit.

Lark laughed, came forward again, gave me his version of a courtly bow and said "We keep our prisoners happy—well fed at least."

Without a word or sign from Lark, the hounds moved back and went utterly quiet.

The peculiar short-haired yellow dog had gone apart to a thicket of blackberry briars and was stretched out panting, facing nothing any human could see.

Larkin was extending his left hand toward me, inviting a shake, though his right hand looked strong enough at his side.

That seemed as odd to me as the yellow dog, but I gave him my own left hand. When I felt the dry surprising heat of his rough-skinned palm, I said "Boy, you're about to burn *down*."

All Lark could do for a while was nod. Then he said a little fiercely "I *have* been waiting—"

I was honestly scared to ask him what for, though off to the right Ferny

bent over double and gave in to a long seizure of laughing. Of all the children I've ever known, Fern laughed the earliest in life—at three months
old—and right from the start he laughed in full silence. Just opened his
wide mouth and held it there silent while his eyes shut for joy. He was
silent now and he hung back to let Lark walk me toward the house. Wild as
the woods looked on every side, there was a clean walk straight on to the
porch through the great dark alleyway of old cedars.

Larkin, like Fern, barely said a word till we got to the foot of some sway-
backed steps that might have been salvaged from Adam's first hut on the far
side of Eden. And when Lark spoke it was not to me. He said "Father, why
don't I marry this lady?"

The Slades were famous for harmless craziness across several counties,
so I charged Lark's remark up to that family trait. Then I noticed who Lark
had spoken to.

At the farthest edge of the porch, looking half trapped in thick English
ivy that was overtaking things, a short stout white man sat on a rocker.
From his right knee downward, he wore a peg leg with bright brass hard-
ware. And he looked a lot older than any ruined house, though his jet-bead
eyes were live as hot beetles.

I'd glimpsed old Major Slade years before at somebody's funeral. So I
knew this was he, too wild-eyed surely for early in the day. He was dressed
head to toe in one color of brown—shirt, necktie, trousers—and he
grabbed at his chair arms, trying to rise.

But I laughed to stop him. "Please keep your seat, Major. I'm nobody's
bride."

I have to admit Major studied me slowly with those eyes that would scare
most grown grave-hearted men. They were keen big eyes but pickled in brandy,
long years of homemade brandy strong enough to embalm any pharaoh.

In any case I've never been prone to fear, so I met the swimming eyes
head-on.

Then the major said "I'd marry any face fine as yours."

Another voice laughed, a woman's voice but low. Then the woman
stepped out through the wide front door. She'd heard our joking and was
smiling down on me.

I'd seen handsome women in our town and at the movies which were
then called picture shows. But none had prepared me for the sudden

appearance of this much beauty in one face and body. I felt I ought to curtsy or kneel to her eyes alone. They'd clearly been the cause of Larkin's eyes, that same color of a pure spring sky devoted to joy.

But she didn't pause for any such foolishness. She said "The major was married last time I heard, and more than once—I'm his second wife Olivia. I was born a Venable. I'd know you anywhere. With that clear brow you're bound to be a Dane." She stroked at her lovely eyes as if they required frequent clearing. "Never saw a Dane without a fine forehead. And you're Fern's favorite sister."

"I'm his sister Roxanna. He's never said a word to me about any favorites."

She shook her head No. "Fern worships pretty things. I knew you'd be pretty."

Through that I'd heard Ferny come up behind me. He was quiet as warm dust under your feet.

Miss Olivia said "Dinner won't be till noon. But if anybody's faint I strongly suspect we can scare up some makeshift rations meanwhile."

The major pointed hard at the house-front behind him and said "Damn house *full* of food, sinking *down* with the weight."

Fern of course said he was next to perishing.

Miss Olivia waved him past her toward the kitchen, then invited me up to sit on the porch next to Major. There was an old swing hung from the ceiling on rusty chain, and a few more rockers were spaced wide apart.

But Larkin said "Let me show you the river."

The major said "Seen any one river, you seen all the rest."

I lied and said I'd yet to see one. It was true I'd never seen the Roanoke, just smaller streams like the Endless and the Deep. Then I came to my senses and thought of my age. Girls my age—grown—were still not considered free to wander out with any young man unrelated by blood. So I figured I should hold back till Ferny rejoined us. But it troubled me to think that shy a thought with Larkin at hand. Outlandish as all this marriage talk was, I'd watched Lark enough in the past quarter hour to think I'd give a good deal to know him well. Still I faced him and said "Let's sit in the shade till Ferny can join us."

Lark plainly understood and shared my regret, but he dropped his question and handed me on up the steps to the swing.

I sat there and swung a few gentle arcs. Soon I realized I'd be dizzy shortly, and I stopped the movement.

By then Larkin had sat in a rocker some six feet away and tilted to face me. It left him with his back toward the major.

So after a quiet minute, the major said to me "Look him over hard now. He's a fairly good boy."

Despite my knowledge of the Slades' reputation for original behavior, for a real minute I sat there thinking I'd fallen through a floor into some kind of crazy house I'd never encountered. It seemed like a world that had known about me from the day I was born and that had firm plans for my every step. Who in the world—in the United States even that long ago—had ever heard of sane-looking strangers walking up to you on a clear fall day with marriage plans and a groom standing ready, a highly acceptable groom at that?

Well I looked at their groom, this boy beside me. I've mentioned his hair and eyes, his high healthy glow. Now I thought of what the Bible says about young King David before he was king—that "he was ruddy and withal of a beautiful countenance and goodly to look to." I've also mentioned that I'd reached the age where girls were more than likely to be married and have one child at least if not more. I'd admired several boys in our town and had spent considerable time with one. But he later went to Newport News, Virginia and ceased correspondence. Still in my mind, boys had never come anywhere near meaning what Leela and some girls my age thought they meant—the end of creation and my purpose in life. They never would quite be that for me in all my years, but that's a later story.

Here this morning in early October, and maybe it really was owing to my birthday, I saw Larkin Slade as a different proposition. It wasn't his looks. I honor good looks as a gift from God, especially when the looks endure long years which means that the heart behind them is sound. But I'm also drawn to numerous people as plain as dry rice when they concentrate on causing sweet laughter in those nearby or when they truly need me. This Slade boy though wore a curious close glove of light all around him. It was a cleaner light than the actual sun and a lot more active, though it was somehow troubled in the way it seemed to toil and shift with his movements, even when he was still in his chair.

In fact the longer he sat there beside me, entirely quiet with his wild old father dozing beyond us, the more Lark Slade began to affect me. As I said

I'd had brief crushes since I was maybe nine; and while I'd never lost my head, I'd cared sufficiently for one slim boy that vanished north so I mourned in earnest, though nobody knew why I lost flesh that summer. But here seated next to a boy I'd known for less than an hour, I swung on in silence and felt my body undergo a change I'd never known nor heard of elsewhere.

The best I can recall it now, the change consisted of the powerful certainty that my whole being had begun to expand. My body stayed completely quiet, but slowly it seemed to grow lighter and larger and a good deal stronger till my two arms could fold Lark in like a needy soul. And once I had him held safe with me, I went on growing, adding circles around him as if I were a tree till he was rocking deep inside my new mind and chest— no risk of harm or loss, not to him anyhow. Understand, he didn't shrink at all or become a child. He stayed his full long masterful size. It was Roxanna Dane that had grown to preserve him.

I have no idea how long it lasted, and all the rest of my life I've never known anything similar. I've wanted of course to protect my family, my husband and children and every other child on the planet. But I've never again had the actual power to shield somebody, and I've understood the reason—I failed Larkin Slade on that first occasion. As I held him inside my powerful mind, I began to think that I had no right to capture his being. I was kidnapping him against his will. So slowly as before I turned him out of my head and chest and left him rocking in the world again. That would be his doom, and it's gone on being a hard part of mine.

Lark had been watching the road through that as if other girls might follow my lead and stream up the alley. But the road stayed empty and as distant looking as Greenland anyhow. So Lark turned back to face me, seeming to know what I'd just accomplished in saving him and then setting him free. He spoke up at last. "Are you all right?"

It shocked and shamed me to think that what I'd imagined might really have happened or that Lark had felt something anyhow. I managed to tell him that maybe I was thirsty, and then I stood.

The major's eyes opened and cut my way. "You leaving, are you?"

I said "No, Larkin's going to get me some water. You thirsty too?"

Major said "Mighty thirsty these past sixty years, but I can't say I ever thought of curing it with water." His face found nothing funny in that.

But Larkin laughed heartily and offered me his arm. "Let's go indoors. Plenty water in there."

Something told me *Don't go*. I know I partly dreaded seeing Ferny, my beloved brother, with all his recent teasing about boys and all this peculiar talk about marriage by relative strangers. Fern had to be responsible for the whole strange tone this day was taking. But then I thought Miss Olivia would be present, feeding Fern's face back in the kitchen. She'd seemed like a source of useful knowledge or strength anyhow. So I took Lark's arm and said "Let's find your mother. I'll bet she's feeding Fern."

The hall we walked through was darker than Egypt, and both walls were covered with framed family pictures—big old oval frames with bowed wavy glass and faces as firm as any rock slab. I naturally thought they were Major's forebears; they looked sufficient to bear many majors.

Yet Lark passed by them with nothing but a wave and four quiet words—"Mother's people, all Venables."

Little as I knew her, it didn't surprise me.

Turned out I'd guessed right. The kitchen ceiling was the only low ceiling in the entire house—maybe lowered for warmth and the hope of brief comfort—but there still seemed space for several hundred people around us, great empty volumes of air and sweet smell. And indeed Lark's mother was still at the stove making fresh corn cakes for Ferny and another boy older than Lark. They were the good kind of cakes you never see now, light as cool air but buttery and filling.

An old black woman, more than half baldheaded, was working at something with her back turned to us.

She didn't look toward us even when Lark said "This young lady's parching." He was smiling at me.

Miss Olivia faced me. "Of course you are—how negligent of me."

The Slades were miles off the route of the traveling ice man, and I seriously doubted that they could harvest ice from the river in winter and keep it year round the way people did in the old days. But still without a word, the bald black woman took up a glass, limped to an oak chest, opened it, chipped a sliver off a big block of ice and poured water on it from a tall china pitcher. She moved like the oldest creature surviving from Bible times. She'd plainly gone past the need to talk if she still knew how. But she offered the glass out slowly toward Larkin.

And he went to get it, saying "Thank you, Coy."

I thanked her too—it was excellent water with a slight taste of iron which I've always needed—but Coy wouldn't look up. She pointed to the table where she'd been working and gave a deep moan.

Larkin said "Oh fine. Many thanks again, Coy." People in general didn't thank black people that often back then. They could cook and clean and make every bed for a household of twenty, and nobody thought that was anything amazing to earn the world's thanks. It was just assumed black people did what you told them to do and were compensated for it like willing plow-mules with food and the chance to rest a few hours in something approaching a dry warmish stall. Mules had Sunday off but very few blacks did. I wasn't all that grateful myself, but I registered Larkin's ongoing strangeness as one more welcome fact to know—he'd thanked a creature for a generous act.

What Coy had done also was pack a considerable amount of food in a long rush basket, a bountiful picnic.

There was an old wide-faced school clock on the wall behind the stove. If the clock was truthful, it was going on noon; and I actually felt the beginnings of hunger. Sick as I've been many times in my life, I've seldom lost my appetite for more than a day or two. So words slipped out of my mouth unintended. "Is anybody else as famished as me?"

Miss Olivia paused in the midst of the room. I hadn't realized till then that she wore a dress from—what?—thirty years ago. It was heavy gray wool, full down to the floor and with tight long sleeves. She was holding the pan with the next corn cakes for Fern and his friend. She laughed and said " 'As famished as I'—nothing wrong with you, Anna. You two go on with Coy's basket. These stuffed young gentlemen will follow you down."

That somehow made me unusually bold. I said to the strange boy on my brother's right "I don't know you. I'm Ferny's older sister."

The boy stood up with a serious face. And when he was up, he was no boy at all. He stood there taller than anybody I'd ever known, way past six foot; and in what felt like the next ten minutes, he couldn't speak. His face flushed hard but no words came as his eyes narrowed down and a slow smile won its way on his mouth.

Since nobody else spoke to fill the silence, I wondered if the poor boy was somehow afflicted and possibly mute. So I nervously said "Please call me Roxanna."

He finally did. His voice was normal, pleasantly deep.

Then Ferny said "*Anna*—people all call her Anna except for me. I call her Rox, like rocks in the road." To me Fern said "This is Lark's oldest brother. Everybody calls him Palm."

Palm said "No they don't. My true name is Palmer. I'm Palmer Slade."

For whatever reason I turned back to Larkin. He was facing his brother, looking almost proud. He said "Palm's the oldest by less than a year."

Palmer finally smiled for one bleak second. "Lark's the beauty, no question. I'm the one with the *mind*." He tapped his skull hard between the eyes and everybody laughed. Though Palm was far from being homely, that day at least he lacked the signs of heat and the will that were Lark's high points—the eagerness to load you by the moment with blessings that only Lark knew of and longed to share.

Palmer thumped his skull again. This time it made a whole new sound, a literal *thunk*. And everybody stopped laughing at once.

Then Coy spoke—she who was blacker than any deep summer night and her voice was clearly the boss, in this room at least. She pointed to Lark and said "Listen to your mother. Take this mess and you and your little friend go on your way."

Your little friend seemed to mean me, and Coy clearly had the last word. I'd seldom been called *little* in recent years. In fact I was tall for girls in those days, even down to today though I've shrunk with age—nearly five foot ten. Yet strange as it sounded in this strange place, I said to Lark "Please lead the way."

He was glad to do so.

And though I followed with no reluctance, as soon as sunlight struck us again, I said to myself *Watch everything closely. Save all of this. Time will never taste sweeter than this.* A lifetime later it turns out I was nothing but right, about that one thing anyhow.

The river is dammed up now, a filthy lake. But in 1920 the Roanoke River was one of the wonders on anybody's map. It had supported a whole sweep of country for hundreds of years of buffalo, Indians, white and black people and the ghosts they became. To be sure the river flooded time and again and drowned a world of livestock, chickens and poisonous snakes. My father knew people who had dug their houses back out of the mud a dozen times in the course of a lifetime, and everybody knew of at least one child

or elderly woman who had been borne off on that broad torrent and seldom found.

But on this October noon with Larkin, at my first glimpse I caught my
breath and thought of the gods—the gods we'd studied in school, Greek
and Roman. When I was a child (and still to this day), their stories often
made better sense of real folly and pain than anything I'd ever heard of at
church. Nothing else but their hard chancy power seemed fit to explain
the life of that deep surge of water as it poured past the wide bend northeast of Lark's home; and I tried to think of the names of gods—Apollo or
Neptune, even warlike Mars, all of them male. I went so far as to turn to
Larkin and, laughing to show I wasn't quite crazy, I asked him "Who is the
god of all this?"

He didn't pause an instant. "My eldest brother Palmer—you just met
Palmer." He pointed behind us toward the house, that silent rangy impressive young man with few words to say whom I'd met in the kitchen.

And I actually turned, expecting Lark's mother and brother and Ferny.
But the house had disappeared behind bushes, and no one was coming.
The sight of Palmer was clear in my mind though as if I'd drawn it and
must look at it always.

Lark said "Palmer can all but *walk* on this river. He's more than half fish
when it comes to swimming. Nothing wrong with young Ferny's strength
either."

I said "I'm sure it's way too cool today." The idea was already strong in
the air—Lark was somehow longing to swim, to show me he could. We
hadn't yet had the first frost of the season, but nights had been cool, so I
tried to discourage him. "You'd die of pneumonia."

Larkin smiled. "Don't count on that." Then instead of offering me his
arm, he reached for my hand.

I let him have it gladly.

And it was the better part of an hour before we realized we were still alone.
The others hadn't joined us. The whole time, understand, was innocent as
birds too young to fly. But it's in my memory still, minute by minute. It
seemed that, back before the Civil War, the major had built a long pavilion
for watching the river and meditating on history and whatnot. Major's own
father had remembered when buffalo still came down from the woods to
drink. But Lark said that, since the day his father surrendered in the war

and walked home from Charleston, he'd literally never set foot here again. He couldn't stand to watch river traffic somehow nor think of the past.

Lark didn't know why. He was more than three decades from being born when the major's lost war ruined most of this world—in the major's opinion. So the trellis roof and sides had rotted and been hauled away, but the wide brick floor was still in place under three oak benches that looked like relics from the Tree of Good and Evil. After we'd walked to the edge of the water and Lark had cupped up a warmish handful for me to touch, he led us back up to a V-shaped bench and we sat there, near but facing each other.

After two or three awkward moments of silence, Lark started to speak and went on as clearly as if he'd written it days ago and memorized every word perfectly for now. It was the tale of his entire life or as much of that life as he could pass on to a grown girl he'd only just met. Truth to tell it was not what you'd call a hair-raising adventure. Lark suspected that he would be punished in the afterlife for killing as many wild things as he had, right down to the speechless oysters and mussels. He had often held grudges against his parents and especially Palmer.

He'd pushed on Palmer harder than anybody. He thought everybody he knew was too hard on blacks (the first white person I ever heard say as much, though Lark called them Negroes which was still polite then). Stranger still was the open stress Lark laid on his body as bare needy *skin* that was permanently lonesome. He said that much straight toward my eyes in words clear as posters.

This was back before even the boldest young men would speak freely on any such subject to an honest woman as young as they, even their wives; and it interested me very deeply, then and there. One of the reasons the men couldn't talk more freely about the human body was that so many young women were literally ignorant of any answers to give. So few of us had any clear idea of what was involved or the names of the vital parts and actions.

When Larkin sat there in the October sun and told me his body was all but dying of not having touched some girl he could love, of being far past the age when he should have found his mate and started his world, I had only the vaguest notion of his meaning. I do still recall one sentence he said. He met my eyes at a foot and a half of sunlit distance, and he said "Sweet girl, you could use me up—to the last dry dregs—and I'd never say 'Quit!'"

In those days of course and in a small town with farms nearby, you lived in closer view of the animal kingdom than now—turkeys, chickens, hogs, horses, packs of dogs, foxes, snakes and every known insect—so you had to be blind not to get some general sense of how the world propagated itself. And girls would hear occasional rumors from one another, or from the black women that cooked and cleaned, as to how human beings resembled the livestock. Even the movies weren't that much help. People clutched each other in dim silent rooms and sometimes fell back deep into darkness, but no certain acts were specified.

Still the matter had intrigued me, the little I knew. I was ready for further information but had nowhere to turn. I'm not at all sure that—faced with a creature as rare as Lark Slade—if he'd asked me the largest question of all, I might not have just said "You lead the way." Every sign he gave of a young man's beauty, strength and gentleness was calling me onward. I doubt I'd have even been scared of the chance that his family or my brother might come out to find us involved in whatever Larkin needed to do with his skin and mine.

And for more than a few minutes, in October air that was lighter and purer than anything since on this burdened planet, it felt like we were heading that way. We were instants away from whatever leaning and mingling of parts this man might need. There were dense woods and thickets to left and right. And somehow the whiff of destruction between us—Lark's eyes now were far more ferocious than Major's—was part of the powerful *draw* I felt.

Lark even reached the point of saying "Do you understand me?"

I more than half lied to say "I understand." I'm still not sure of just what he meant or might have requested if I hadn't been so backward.

By then anyhow Lark seemed ready to stand, but my pale answer stopped him. He looked away from me to the river and, for whatever reason, fixed on a spot that seemed to be on the far bank, the north side. It was more than a hundred yards from our bench; and as far as I could tell, Lark watched a round patch of full sunlight. He finally said "I could get Major's boat and row us over." He pointed to the sunlight and finally stood up close beside me. The spot did look a little magical as if the air in that one place was dusted with something especially valuable, gold dust or purified radium maybe.

But—God knows why—I said "I feel like I'd better wait for Ferny."

At first Lark's eyes were as disbelieving as if I'd claimed that the Holy Ghost was set to light on my knee any minute, issuing general pardons to sinners, and that I'd better stay put to welcome the landing. But then he laughed a long bitter laugh, took up the picnic basket and aimed for the dry ground nearest the edge of the water. He planned to eat there. I could join him or stay. The moment when I'd been his main fascination had ebbed away or was ebbing fast.

I went on toward him then as fast as I could think my way clear of all the reluctance that had been drilled into my skull since birth. On my way downhill I managed to think *Roxanna, you're crazy. This boy could be the mad rogue of the ages. At the least he comes with a very strange family hung round his neck. Be polite but head home as soon as you can.* I may have taken a minute to reach him and was nearly back to normal when I came up behind him.

But Lark looked round from where he was seated in grass that was somehow green this late in the dying season, and he said "I felt like you would never get here." He didn't look relieved exactly, but I still seemed a part of some hidden plan he'd yet to unfold. Then he turned back to watching the river.

I suspect I sound like the soul of ignorant crossroads innocence; but to this day now—me into my nineties—that sentence is still the finest I've heard, the one that spoke straight into my heart. *I felt like you would never get here.* I don't think I answered him. I was that full of so much unaccustomed feeling. But I know for a fact I leaned down behind Lark and, touching him only with my dry lips, I kissed his broad neck.

Lark actually thanked me. Then he said "Can you stay?"

I said "Beg your pardon?" I was truly uncertain of what he could mean. Nobody had ever asked me for more than washing a dish or fetching cool water.

Lark said "Near me. Will you stay with me?"

Strange to say I asked him "How long?"

He still hadn't turned but was facing the river.

And I half wondered *Is he talking to that, just a few sweet words to a broad stretch of water?*

But he finally said "Roxanna Slade—how does that sound?"

I laughed. "Well at least it sounds easy to spell."

Finally Lark faced me.

He was too good to watch for more than three seconds. My eyes nearly flinched.

Lark shut his own eyes and whispered the rest. "Then add one more easy word please, lady." With his long forefinger he spelled it on the air like a slow schoolboy—"F-O-R-E-V-E-R-M-O-R-E."

In the very little time that we had left, I'm proud to say I whispered "It's really two words. But all right. Yes."

I don't think either one of us knew what we'd done. It was some weeks before I fully realized that he'd proposed and I'd accepted and that both of us were near voting age—legal adults—or so it might have seemed to our parents or other sane grown people. And when I finally knew that truth, I was changed for good by it, though far too late.

When the other Slades and Ferny got down to the pavilion, some time had passed. Larkin and I had eaten a sandwich and a hardboiled egg ahead of the others, and that was as far as we ever strayed from the strait and narrow path. At the sound of the major's voice calling for food, Lark rushed to stand and say "I forgot you were still on the Earth." But he laughed anyhow. We repacked the basket in a matter of seconds. Then as naturally as any leaf opening to daylight, Lark reached for my hand and led me up toward them. By then they seemed a familiar destination but I was puzzled. Hadn't I just heard Larkin claim that the major hadn't been down here since the war ended fifty-five years ago? Surely my birthday couldn't be the occasion to break such a habit.

Major anyhow was watching me closely as if we'd never met. In a way we hadn't, so I went up to him and said I was Sim Dane's daughter from Garland. In those days women didn't just thrust out hands for their elders to shake. Still I half offered mine.

The major made no move to take it. But again his old eyes searched up and down me, not in any indecent way but as if I were ground he'd lost in a skirmish.

I was about to laugh in self-defense.

But Miss Olivia said "Major, you recall Simmons Dane."

"I do not," he said. But he finally grinned and slowly leaned, not to take my hand but to touch very lightly the side of my waist. Then he said "Young lady, I've waited for you." His voice was fifty years younger than his face. The face seemed made out of patches of skin from different creatures, all colors and textures loosely stitched.

You didn't exactly know where to look or where the major *was*, so I looked down at his one long foot. It was in an ancient tan cavalry boot.

Miss Olivia stroked her eyes again, that peculiar way, as if clearing spider webs from her sight. Then she said "Major Slade, you calm yourself.

This is just a picnic, and everybody here is just a human being—no angels of light. Anna and Larkin, Palmer and Ferny, you and I and the clear sun himself have got plenty time before night falls."

And though Miss Olivia was smiling as grandly as the day itself, I've always thought that—from that moment on—she'd half foreseen what I failed to note. It *was* a picnic in honor of my birthday, requested by Ferny and planned by the Slades to please mainly Fern. All the rest so far was kindly teasing except for Major. He was way past clear in his mind by then, being well over eighty and from a long line of people famous for premature confusion.

Palmer and Fern had hauled even more food down, and they sat some way off from us and ate when we did. It was not till we'd all but finished the chicken and sandwiches, ham biscuits and pickled okra, little brown-sugar pies, cold tea, lemonade and peppery cheese straws that for some reason I missed the dogs. What had happened to that pack of hounds that met us this morning at the car, not to mention the peculiar yellow dog off on his own? To have something pleasant to say to the major, I asked about his pack. Was somebody hunting them or since the day was turning out fine, were they off by themselves in the woods?

Major looked up again with those wild eyes that had seen more than his share of six hundred thousand boys die in four years. By the time he spoke, he'd managed a smile. "Not a dog on this place for twenty, thirty years."

Nobody denied him or bothered to try. And when I looked to Miss Olivia for the truth, her eyes wouldn't meet mine—she was watching the river. In a while she said "Anybody tried the water?"

The river was as brown as the dirt all around us. I couldn't imagine anybody testing it this late in the year.

But Palmer said "I swam it last night when I couldn't sleep."

Miss Olivia said "You'll be catching your death." Her voice was firm as if there were no room for doubt.

"The river's warm as my bed," Palmer told her. "You rest your mind."

It had been unseasonably warm here lately, but I'd have thought the river would be chilly.

Then Ferny stood up and unbuttoned his cuffs. "I'll race you Slades to that sunny spot." He pointed to the circle of bright sunshine on the opposite bank. For all the time that had passed since we got here, the sun had stayed brilliant in that one place.

For some odd reason, unlike most women I'm a good judge of distance and could find myself, blindfolded on Mars. I calculated the far bank itself was a hundred and twenty yards from me, and I was a little uphill from all three boys.

The major had barely said two words since he ate his first biscuit, but he roused up then and said "No such thing. After all this rain that current'll be running way too strong."

It hadn't rained that much, but I didn't say so. I kept my silence.

It was Miss Olivia who'd brought it all up, and she wouldn't quit now. She said "Lark and Palm, you take Ferny's dare?" Her eyes had gone surprisingly hard, and her mouth was set in a dead straight line.

Lark looked back to me and said "Ferny's too young. I'm not a fair match." He fixed on my eyes to give me a chance of calling things off.

But before I could think, Ferny said "The hell *you* say." By then he was already down to his underpants.

As shy as girls had to be in those days—bound head to foot like desert wives in layers of swaddling—boys were free to strip off at will, though generally once a girl was past sixteen, boys turned their backs to her as if they'd grown monster heads in their groins and could turn her to stone with the briefest glance. In any case I'd seen everything my brothers had to show from crown to heel, a thousand or so times before I was grown. The major had seen many dead boys naked. I was uncertain about Miss Olivia. She came from an older world than this with her dark beauty and the shiny dark hair.

The unbecoming hardness was gone from her face when she said "Palm, don't let a Dane from Garland shame you."

I noticed she'd left Larkin out of her message.

But Lark stood in absolute rhythm with Palmer, and silent as thieves they stripped to their drawers to match my brother. They looked, at the same time, two completely different ways—both well made and pitiful, pale as they were and hugging their shoulders like orphans at a funeral. Not one of the three ever turned full to face me. So I never saw all of Larkin or Palmer, not that day. But both their behinds were firm as boiled chicken and sat high on them.

Lark reached out both hands left and right and took hold of Palmer and Ferny by the wrist.

Major Slade said "Do it without my blessing—"

When none of them faced him, Major said again "Oh God, stand near."

I've never known why but I thought *Say please, Major. Say please to your God before it's too late.* Of course I didn't speak it.

And still not looking back, the three boys trotted straight to the mighty river.

More than ever to me, it looked very godly and I said a silent prayer like Major's.

Then Larkin looked back. I've always thought he was focused on me. Before he could speak though, or even wave, Palmer and Fern were diving beside him. So he had to join them.

Miss Olivia said "Oh Major, there—*look* at your sons!"

I turned and Major Slade had covered both eyes with his wounded hand, the one that lacked two fingers.

Miss Olivia was laughing and I had to smile at her, but then it dawned on me *Major knows something bad.* I looked toward the swimming boys to check; and they seemed fine, though hard to tell apart. They were still close together. One was thrashing the water so wildly I thought he'd soon be exhausted. I guessed that was Ferny who was never an athlete. But with all the flailing, Fern was leading the others.

The one in second place was riding high and pale in the water. You could see his long body plain as if he barely skimmed the surface and was halfway flying. I guessed that was Larkin.

The one I figured was Palmer was all but out of sight, as deep in the river as a long dark seal or some mysterious creature that lived here and nowhere else on Earth. They all seemed to have every skill they needed. And soon I was feeling nearly at ease, though somehow I needed to turn away and watch something stiller—a sycamore tree at the edge of the river that must have been more than a hundred feet tall.

The major's hand had come down from his eyes, but his eyes were still shut.

Miss Olivia had picked up all our scraps and the various dishes and stowed them silently back in the basket without me hearing. As my eyes met hers, she said "Tell Palmer or Ferny to bring this back when they're dry and dressed. Lark can help lead the major. I'm going to the house."

I thanked her for staging this handsome party on my behalf.

Important as she looked with those eyes that seemed the source of all goodness, she said "No trouble at all. We do it all the time." Not a spot on her face was worried or even concerned with the boys. And then she walked off, though she paused in a second and said "Major Slade, Lark'll help you home."

The major gave no sign of hearing.

So she faced me again and said "Happy birthday, child."

Nobody had actually said it till then. It almost shocked me and, yes, *child* did grate on me a little. I was never her child and could never have loved a mother as sure and splendid as she.

But she said it again, took two more steps and pronounced the name "Anna" before she was gone, clear and deliberate as if this were school. As long as she stayed in sight, climbing slowly, she left a visible wake on the air like motes of some bright metal—maybe copper—in the merciless sun.

By the time I turned back toward the river, Ferny had landed, Lark was on all fours at the edge of the bank and Palmer was three or four strokes from landing. That was mildly shocking with all Palmer's size and the praise that Lark had heaped on his strength. The real surprise of course was Ferny beating both Slades. His terrier body had a good deal more in the way of power than I'd ever dreamed. It would be years yet before I realized that my dear brother had burnt up the best of his strength in that one race and its aftermath—burnt it forever. He'd never be whole again.

Fern couldn't foresee that either. And as if to prove it, Fern stood in the absolute center of the bright place and gave a slow wide wave toward me. If anybody here was in danger, it had to be Fern. He was swamped in sunlight, head to toe.

I smiled broadly toward him but kept my arms down. Something new again was opening in my mind, a big quiet flower with velvet petals like a purple gardenia if there were such a thing. This second opening didn't feel new as it had on the porch when my mind reached out and folded Lark into my care and shielding. It felt old as anything buried inside me—the hope for fine days, the dread of falling—and it centered this time, not simply on Larkin but on Fern and Palmer likewise who were standing beside him.

Every way I've tried to express it through the years sounds lunatic, so I've told nobody but I'll try again here. What I slowly felt, sitting there long yards from three well-made boys (one of whom I firmly know I'd loved for the past two hours), was a wide sense of privilege. Wide and tall with no roof on it and no side walls. When I asked my mind to name the privilege—what was I being given?—the answer that came was something as plain as *Being alive here now this moment*. When that seemed common and insufficient, I asked again and then understood that *Life, in the world I occupy, is an adequate blessing—whatever pain may bear down on me from the skies or elsewhere*.

Fit as I'd always been to be pleased by the smallest good luck, the briefest meeting or an unblemished leaf that fell to my lap from any tree, something at the heart of my seeing those three young men at that distance, breathing the air of a perfect day seemed to show me the point of my life hereafter. I would be a person who worked at proving, to however few doubters through the hardest times or easy days, that the actual world is worth all your strength.

Never hold back a cent of all you own and bear inside you, spend it all, die empty-handed. Any trace of stinginess is worse than dying young. Every one of those three boys was worth all I had—they were that fine to see. And I hoped to touch Larkin wherever he felt the need of comfort till I died beside him long years from now, having used him *up* as he said I should.

My hoping that must have reached Lark somehow. Far off as he was, he also looked straight at me. And though he didn't wave, he gave a solemn bow and then repeated it even more slowly like a genuine gentleman from centuries ago.

I waved, I'm glad to say, and beckoned him back. Nothing in the day or my mind was promising a turn for the worse. I thought of calling out, loud as I could, and urging Larkin to win this lap. Thank God I didn't. I just waved again.

With that Lark took Fern and Palmer's arms, and they came toward the river.

I looked back to see if Major had blinded himself through it all, but now he was looking.

I said "Sir, who are you pulling for?"

He didn't quite face me, but he said "Never bet on a human creature."

I didn't and haven't in all the years since. I stood up though to see the race better.

All three seemed to be neck-in-neck in the water. By their slowness this time, I could see the current had strengthened a little. Or they were tireder than they'd been. They were being slowly drawn downstream, nothing serious-seeming. Then the one that I could see was Larkin speeded up and outstripped the others with very little pains.

A voice kept hollering "Whoa, whoa, boy!" It was bound to be Ferny.

But Major Slade chimed in behind me, though he was barely whispering. "Oh son, draw back. Don't tax your heart." When I faced him, the major said "His heart's been murmuring all his life."

Till then I'd never heard the term *murmur* applied to a heart and I actually smiled. It sounded that harmless and I wondered what it said.

The major frowned and said "Don't play the fool," to me not the boys.

And that's when my own heart chilled and clamped down. *Lark is aiming toward some kind of trouble.* Ever since I've asked myself why I thought he was *aiming.* From that time on I've never felt it was accidental or even God's will but a plain choice of Larkin Slade's in full possession of his faculties on a perfect day, having just met a girl he claimed to want.

There in the lead he was riding even higher in the river than he had been. That was decades before anybody I knew had water-skied, but it really seemed Lark might be on the verge of standing up and running toward me on the thick brown surface.

I was standing too so I got the first glimpse of him going under. He plunged out of sight like an iron statue. But as sudden as it was, I told myself Lark was playing some trick on Ferny and Palmer. He'd reach land fast as a real torpedo and say some word I'd never imagined, better than *undying love* or *faith*. Whatever life Lark and I would live to enjoy could start from that instant.

But Fern and Palmer had stalled where they were and bobbed upright in the water like decoys. Their faces looked baffled or maybe just miffed to be outstripped so effortlessly by Larkin who'd barely seemed their match till moments ago. But in a few seconds more of mutual frowning, they began to dive in place where they were. They seemed to know something nobody else knew yet, and their frantic diving went on for a long time.

When I looked to Major Slade for a sign, he had got upright on his peg leg and cane. But his eyes were downward and streaming tears.

Not raising my voice I asked him who or what we should get—meaning more strong boys or some other form of rescue.

Major's head stayed down. He didn't seem to hear me.

When I checked the river, neither Fern nor Palmer were visible. So I'm afraid I cried out to Major Slade "You're standing here letting all of them die."

It at least made him face me. His old eyes were open and he nodded his head slowly time and again to tell me *Yes, that's happening here. One more time.*

It didn't quite happen, not to all three boys. But Larkin was gone. Ferny and Palmer nearly drowned themselves in the hunt for Larkin. Before my eyes they were swept downriver more than four hundred yards. And when they fought their hopeless way to land, they were not just all but dead with exhaustion, they were also cut and bruised from rocks and snags they'd struck. They stopped on the bank to let the sun dry them a little. Then they put on their drawers and came up toward us.

At first I thought Fern and Palmer were being too cruel, slow as they were. But now I realize they were in shock. Larkin truly was gone. Not a sign or a trace according to them, and I knew they were honest. The pain had cut into both their faces. Nothing to do but head back downstream in an old rowboat and wait till the body floated itself or came to rest somewhere they could reach it, if that ever happened.

I've always been very slow to respond to possible danger or grievous news. Somehow I barely believe in trouble at the time it's happening even down to this day. So it takes me awhile to admit to trouble. As they left I said in a voice so calm I can hear it still "You ought to take the hounds." I don't know which way I thought hounds could help. But I know I pictured that yellow-haired dog and thought for an instant it might have some brand of unearthly powers.

Ferny and Palmer didn't even look back, though Palmer said "The hounds are far gone in the woods."

All I could do was stand in place and watch the river separately. After a blank and chilling wait, I felt the lightest touch on my arm.

It was Major Slade who'd somehow made his way downhill, stumping along on his peg leg and cane. He'd got his tears dry and was offering me his arm, though he couldn't speak. He pointed behind him to the house, the homeplace. By then his patchwork face had been so torn by his failure to save Lark, he was barely recognizable.

I thanked him and said I believed I should stay there at least till Ferny and Palmer were back.

That freed him to say "They may be gone for days or longer."

Someway I started to argue with him. "They've got no change of clothes or a scrap of food, Major. They'll be hungry soon."

He thought that over carefully and said "The world's full of chickens and shoes." Then he took the first hard step up toward the house. Slow as he was, he never asked for help.

To his back I said "There must be hands all over this place that could come down and help us." I meant black people and any white overseer or foreman to help us comb the river for Lark. Country people who lived by rivers always had rowboats at the very minimum and nets to drag.

The major kept going at a crushed snail's pace. But he clearly said "Not a sane man left above ground here now."

I said "Palmer and Ferny—"

But he moved out of sight, leaving me as desolate as I'd ever be for many years more.

I sat on a bench in the old pavilion, thinking Miss Olivia would be there soon. In a minute I realized I'd yet to pray for help. So I got still and tried. Even in those days prayer was hard for me. I felt, and still feel, God goes his own way and is not all that susceptible to change. But to let him know my hopes occasionally in some narrow strait, I'll say a word or two—mostly just *Help* or *Please, kind sir* (though the *kind* is mostly a form of politeness).

What else in the world is there to say that isn't as pointless as those long church prayers that mention the grass and leaves and birds which plainly survive, whether I pray or not? Very little of what I've watched and been forced to assume as God's own will has seemed steadily kind, though Jesus appears to promise that's the case. I don't blame God. The human race has got to be more than discouraging to work with, Roxanna Slade included.

So that October afternoon for what felt like days or weeks again, I sat there watching the current and saying "Help" or "Pardon" every time my mind repeated the new fact, the one that was just beginning to sound true and unchangeable. *Larkin Slade and I only met this morning and loved each other in some real way, and now he's been swept off by the single hand he couldn't refuse.*

Miss Olivia turned up in the midst of that. It didn't surprise me that she'd already changed the dress she wore for the picnic and was now in black, a plain black cotton all the way to her shoe tops. She might well have come from a battlefield long years ago with the burial crew and the flocks of crows. These people were on close terms with death. Anyhow she never said why she'd returned.

But the first thing I could think to ask her was what time it was. Women then very seldom wore watches. They did their chores till the chores were finished or they fell over dead, whichever came first.

She knew to the instant. "Not but quarter till two." Against her black dress those blue eyes burned like Larkin's own wherever he was now, facing his death or a transformed life. Miss Olivia gave a sharp nod, walked alone to the river and looked a long time. Nothing about her tall broad back invited me to join her. But when she came toward me, she could manage a thin smile. "You need to lie down. Let me take you to the house."

Far as I knew up to that point, nobody but Major had shed a tear. I suspected Ferny was as sad as anybody. But he and Palmer were still downstream well past the bend. So my eyes shed a few hard drops, one of the few times in my life when tears have come at the same time as real loss. I generally weep long after the fact when the bruise has worked its way from my skin down into my heart and begun to scald me.

At the sight of my tears, Miss Olivia's own eyes filled.

I've already mentioned that Lark had her eyes, but it occurred to me to wonder if Lark was truly her son. Maybe his mother was Major's first wife who'd died long since. I actually asked her.

Miss Olivia said "Mine. Every grain of his body was made by me." Her tears continued, though silently.

So I said again "There's got to be somebody on this place that could go out and help them." I pointed downriver and suddenly thought "Our cousin Roscoe is just over there." I pointed to the bend.

Miss Olivia also thought that through. Then watching the water, she said "Oh Anna, Roscoe's in Petersburg with one of his whores. There's nobody else on Heaven or Earth to help Larkin now."

It was the first time I'd ever heard the word *whore* said aloud, and I wasn't entirely sure what it meant. But that wasn't what struck at me so hard. Even then long before there were ambulances and rescue teams with helicopters, I could barely understand Miss Olivia's desperation. I'd never come up against bedrock before.

She seemed to understand but what she said was "Never let a child die before you do." She had now lost three and later confessed to me more than once that she was just part of the person she'd been before standing watch by those three bodies when the hearts had ceased.

The thing I couldn't know at my age was that the thing she warned me against this day would come down on me four years from now. Still I recall how that same moment I felt for the first time since I was born *You don't want this. This costs too much. Get out of this now.* By *this* I meant *life*, and many times later I'd face the same choices before I took action.

Strangely I managed to sleep like a child flat out and abandoned like a bat on the ground. Miss Olivia had led me to a little room up in the eaves of the house, a squat walnut bed with a mattress full of sweet pine needles. It must have been past three o'clock in the afternoon when I lay down. I didn't know another thing till well after dark when somebody sat on the edge of my bed and touched my shoulder. The air was pitch dark when my eyes opened. All I could see was the slightest flickering from somebody's oil lamp and the dimmest outline of what must be a man seated beside me.

I was still cloudy-minded but something about the man's clean river smell and the shape of his head—tall skull above the ears—made me know it was Larkin. I lay back still looking up at the shape; and "Oh," I told him, "I dreamed you were drowned." I more than halfway thought I was dreaming. Whoever it was he was holding a lamp, a ruby-red small children's lamp from the true old days.

Then the dark boy near me just said "I am. I'm drowned for good."

In that many words I could hear it was Ferny. And knowing my brother as long as I had, I could estimate he was missing Lark more than half as much as I was. So I never blamed Fern for his brief deceit. I've always thought Lark's spirit was in him that whole long night. Anyhow I let us both go silent till I nearly dozed again. Then I knew I'd have to ask sooner or later. I said "Has anybody laid eyes on Larkin?"

Fern said "Eyes and hands. We finally caught him."

"And he truly is drowned?"

Fern's head seemed to nod.

I asked him shouldn't we head home now.

I thought he hadn't heard me, he took so long. Then he said "You got to let me stay here tonight."

I realized Muddie and Father wouldn't know what had happened to us once sunset had fallen and we weren't home. They'd be sick with concern, and of course there were no telephones for miles. But all I asked Fern was "Just tell me why."

He said "You're bound to know."

I found his hand. "I don't."

Fern said "You loved him too, didn't you? I'm fairly sure I saw it."

I said "I knew him three hours give or take twenty minutes."

Fern took that in silence.

So I had to say "I *did*."

We never said anything else about leaving, and he never had to ask me again what Larkin Slade had meant to me in the few bright hours I'd stood in his light. Nor ever again did I choose to ask what Lark had actually meant to Fern. Back then you didn't just ask sane people, even your family, to lay out their inmost feelings solely because you were curious to know.

When I'd washed my face in the bowl of water Fern brought up for me, he came up behind me and touched my back. As I looked around he was holding a narrow blue box out toward me. I said "What's that?"

"The remains of your birthday." Fern looked as sad as if he'd caused the whole horror.

In the warm lamplight I took his blue box and opened it, genuinely scared of myself. Would I break down again, whatever this gift was? It was something I'd asked for all my life and had never yet had. A perfectly plain no-nonsense pocketknife, good steel and mother of pearl on the sides. I couldn't think how but I told myself *This proves you'll have a life to come.* Then and there I felt Fern had saved my life, and I knew I'd have to tell him so when I felt strong enough to talk. I even have that knife to this day, and it's served me well.

Anyhow by then Fern's own tears could flow. So we two sat back on the edge of the bed till we felt we could face other people, looking strong.

To compose myself I stopped at the wash stand one more time before we went down. In the mild light my own face shocked me. Till that bleak moment I'd thought of myself as average-looking with trustworthy brown eyes, a good-sized straight mouth, firm jaw and clear skin but nobody's beauty by any means. Tonight though, high in this sad old house, a whole new fire had lit inside me and was striking as foxfire. I rubbed both my dry hands over my eyes and down to my neck. I had to be wrong; I was just Roxanna. But I turned to Ferny and said "Am I changed?"

Fern took a long look through the dim air between us. Then he finally nodded and said "No question." He didn't say whether for good or bad. But as he moved to lead me downstairs, his own face gave almost his last smile. It stayed till we heard Major's voice say "No" from the kitchen.

All the Slades were back in the kitchen with black old Coy. Miss Olivia, the major and Palmer were round the long dining table. Coy was sitting on a bolt-straight green chair small enough for a baby. It was back against the far wall but as far-off seeming as the last moon of Jupiter, and Coy was wearing a long black shift that might have been a shroud. Somehow I wanted to see only her. She was that far out of my whole little world, and her face was as blank as a virgin tombstone.

Coy seemed to feel the pressure from me and to understand it. She spoke before the others. "You got to eat something or *you* be dead."

Fern was behind me. I turned to him. "I'm staying, I guess—"

Fern nodded. "Got to."

Miss Olivia said "No way on Earth I could let you set out on a night like this."

The night itself appeared to be calm, no wind or thunder. But I figured she meant the dangers of driving on country roads in something as fragile as a Model T Ford. I had this sudden picture in my mind of Ferny dead in a ditch and me watching helpless one more time.

By then Palmer had drawn up two more chairs, and Major Slade pointed Fern and me to them.

Coy had understood fully. I was starved as any dog. So we ate the cold remains of the picnic in virtual silence before Coy opened the pantry door and brought out a caramel cake she'd made for today, my twentieth birthday. We'd been meant to eat it with strong cups of coffee in late afternoon before heading home.

The sight of it clearly surprised Miss Olivia. She'd either never known of its existence, or it shocked her now. All she said though was "Coy, please don't light a single candle. I doubt we could bear it."

As I said we were eating by kerosene light. The whole room was dim, but I understood her wish for darkness. I've mentioned that she'd now lost three children, though I wouldn't know that for some days to come. Still grim as we all were, we ate the cake—Coy included, back in her wall chair. I remember the delicate taste and feel on my dry tongue as if I were chewing it here this moment seven decades later.

Then Major said "Let me take you to see him."

Even at my age I'd seen a lot of dead people. Funeral parlors were scarce as money which meant that—as is normal for the human race at large—the women in a family washed the corpse and dressed it, and the men built the coffin. So it seemed not only natural but urgent that I should go see Lark.

Miss Olivia said "Major, you keep your seat. You've strained your heart. Palmer, lead Anna in there."

I got up and asked Fern to come with me.

But Miss Olivia said "Ferny's torn up, Anna. Let him rest here for now."

Ferny nodded blankly as if that were true. Right or wrong I've always believed that Fern not only tore but *broke* that long fall day.

Palmer took my elbow and led me onward.

The Slades' front parlor was darker still, only one small lamp. And Larkin lay on an old leather nap-couch that had the upper half of his tall body propped. He was in a black suit, a white shirt but no necktie. The shirt was open at the collar to show his strong throat, a column that still looked too strong to fall. And while his eyes were shut in the dimness, they seemed on the verge of opening again at the sound of any kind voice.

For one long moment I was truly scared to speak. I didn't know Lark well enough to call him back from death. I was honestly simple enough then to think that, but also I was very near distraction. I'd barely known him well enough to use his first name, but it beat in my mind like a terrified bird in a cold dark house—*Lark, Lark, come home*. I tried to keep still and think out the meaning of all that had happened since I left my parents' house this morning. I'm someway still convinced that acts have meanings.

Believing that is nearly the same as saying God goes insane off and on when you least expect. Otherwise what could I ever hope to do with the sight of this poor boy drowned forever at the simple end of a girl's birthday—a normal girl that he'd claimed to love? At the very least this had been the strangest day of my life and while I hadn't quite blamed myself for the tragic event, I couldn't help thinking for the first full time that, if Roxanna Dane hadn't fled her home for her twentieth birthday, one promising boy would still be alive and likely to last a good fifty more years.

Palmer finally spoke but in Lark's direction. "He's playing a trick—" His voice seemed to fail him.

It made me half think Palmer knew of a plot. This was all a long joke, this whole long day from the strange dog till now. Any instant Lark would shift his legs to the floor and stand up to say some further thing about his feeling for me. Again as before at the edge of the river, I wanted to hear some version of *Our lives are now twined* in his voice only. I even spoke my feeling aloud straight at Palmer's eyes—"Looks like he'll talk to us, any minute maybe."

But Palmer had got his own voice by then. "Not a chance on Earth," he managed to say and broke up sobbing. Men were brave enough then to have real feelings on any subject and to own them in public.

By then my eyes had opened to the dark, and I could half see that except for Lark the room was otherwise empty of all but a wide old low piano and a broad array of still more Slade ancestors' faces hung on the walls. Just the sight of their long-gone stern-eyed glares in so much shadow braced me oddly. *There are still people left.* These few anyhow had made it through lives a lot harder than mine. To that point I was almost surely right. But of course I was scarcely more than a girl. So I took the first move to lead Palmer back to the remnants of his family still waiting with Ferny and Coy in the kitchen a million miles off.

They all looked toward me, but again it was Coy that said the first words. "You never get over this if you live till Judgment." When I nodded to her, she seemed to laugh behind her hand. Nobody heard her but me very faintly. Three years later Coy went truly crazy, and they had to retire her to a house on the place and hand-feed her every last morsel she ate. Still that hard evening she was nothing but right.

Wild as it sounds I very much needed to laugh then myself. I'd come from a family that tended toward pleasure and happiness, that had good reasons from our past history to expect calm seas and welcoming harbors. But in one day the world had turned this strange in my hands. I stayed on the kitchen doorsill and choked the laugh down while I heard my inward mind tell me all I'd learned today. *You find your path, and a person to walk with and, before you can so much as focus your eyes and take the first step, they fade right before you—dry empty air.* Turned out I was right.

TWO

I waited—we all did—through a year's mourning. And very little of that long year snagged deep enough in my mind to last. I've never been someone who thinks time itself has much real meaning. People I've met in gloomy elevators for three or four seconds have meant more to me and my good memories than some of the people I've lived with forever. From my long past what I've mainly dwelt on when I looked back for consolation are six or eight instants when I learned a thing I badly needed to know for survival or when I glimpsed a lone child or adult performing some act of open-hearted grace in no hope at all of the smallest reward.

I almost think the main part of my life has passed in my mind, hid even from me, though I often overheard it or watched it move in flashes. For instance with all I've told so far, the clearest picture left from those days is altogether different. To this very moment I can call back every quick breath and the sights I saw in the moonlit dark when I woke far into the night of Lark's death.

Ferny and I had stayed over in the country to help the Slades out. It says a good deal about how crushed we were that neither of us thought to mention the worry we were causing our parents. By bedtime that night they were gone from our minds. I was sleeping on a cot at the foot of Miss Olivia's bed, and I woke up suddenly to hear her breathing far gone in deep rest. Behind her sighs though, regular as hammer blows, a voice in my mind said clearly three times "Palmer Slade needs you." It was not my voice, though it may have been a woman's. Yet strange as it was and shocking with its news, it struck me as somehow a happy arrival.

I rolled it over and over in my mind till I finally gave it my answer "All right." I wasn't all that clear about what I meant. What did I know about what a man needed—or a woman or a child? But my ignorance didn't scare me. With all the sadness of the past day and evening, I had still moved into some new calm that would last for years. I shut my eyes and slept hard till dawn. When Miss Olivia touched my shoulder and asked me to come down and help Coy with breakfast, I already knew this family was mine. Some way or other I'd yet be a Slade. How could I think of parting completely from people I'd hurt as badly as them?

How or why that bond would lock itself into place didn't occupy my mind at first. Once breakfast was done on the morning after Lark's death, Ferny and I drove home in our dank clothes and got through the straits of explaining our absence to Muddie and Father with a lot less damage than I'd expected. The sad news of course helped cover our story. That and the fact of Ferny's grief. After the sudden closeness Larkin and I had felt, I was stunned, as I said. But it wasn't till we were back at home that Ferny broke down.

It was at our family's own supper table the same warm evening. Father had already volunteered that Muddie and Leela, Ferny and I should drive back out to the Slade place tomorrow for Larkin's funeral. As ever Leela was chattering on about what she'd need to wear for the trip—how bare her wardrobe was of mourning clothes, how she'd have to dye one of her hats black, which one did I recommend?

It irked me and when she kept picking at it, I finally said "You can wear your *face*, Sister. That'll cause general moaning." It was the worst thing I'd ever said to her, it was thoroughly untrue, and the memory still shames me.

Muddie and Father actually smiled (though Leela was his favorite). It was Fern though who brought up great booming laughter that threatened not to stop.

After ten seconds Muddie covered her ears.

And Father said plainly "That's enough for now, Fern."

Fern quit in the midst of the deepest laugh. And while each one of us sat and watched, hot tears poured out of him too big to stop.

Nobody said a word. We all understood in our own way that Fern was the finest of us all in his feelings, and I knew I needed to follow his lead and free up the strangling grip on my heart. But with Muddie and Leela there, I *held on* as I'd done and would still do all my life. I somehow generally manage to think *One person here has got to stay upright, and I'm the one chosen.* Chosen by whom I've never been sure.

Muddie said a strange thing that we all knew was wrong. "Ferny, Son, this won't happen but once."

Ferny managed to answer her just as strangely. He nodded his head with a scary fierce speed and he said "I'll see to that, yes ma'm."

Father was genuinely angry by then, a thing that happened less than once a year. He looked at Muddie with very near hate. It was shocking as thunder. "It'll happen every day for the rest of his life." He was pointing to Fern whose tears had not stopped. Then Father told him gently "You can go to your bed, Son. I'll speak to you later."

Fern looked to me.

I had literally nothing left to give him—and after that moment I never would, not anything that Fern could use—but I managed to nod and confirm Father's urging of rest.

So Fern got up and left. His room was the low dark room behind the kitchen.

Father didn't leave to speak to Fern though. He and we women ate our buttermilk pie in silence. Then Father got up, put on his coat and hat and walked out the front door. That was decades before white people started walking for their health—most sane people thought it would kill you, and I tend to agree still—but Father had discovered exercise privately in his boyhood. Once I asked him why every so often he'd strike out and walk as much as four miles. He didn't crack a smile when he said "I walk just to keep from killing people," and I didn't ever mention it again. I did, though, reflect that with his full name—Simmons Augustus Dane—he sounded like a long-striding soul.

I don't know when Father got back that night once Ferny broke down but after clearing the supper table, I left my mother and sister in the kitchen and went in to Fern. I saw it was my turn to recompense him for his gift last night, my new pocketknife.

Fern was facedown on his narrow bed but was watching the single floor-length window. In the last red light, despite his strong body he looked as frail as he'd prove to be in the hard years to come.

I sat on the edge of the bed by his knees, and I rubbed at the small of his back, lean as iron.

He shut his eyes and gave a soft high hum through his nose. I'd forgotten how he'd do that as an infant if you rubbed a lucky spot on his skin. It had made me think he'd be a musician, but again I was wrong.

So I said "That knife you gave me—many thanks. More girls ought to have one."

Fern opened his eyes but still wouldn't face me. "You owe me at least a penny, girl."

I asked him why.

"Every boy knows that. If somebody gives you a knife or a blade of any sort, you have to buy it from them with a penny. Otherwise it'll cut your love in two."

I'd been to the post office late in the day, and I had some change tied up in my handkerchief. I undid it slowly, felt for a dime, kissed it to my lips, then laid it in his open left hand.

His fist closed on it and he nodded acceptance. A whole dime then was no small sum.

I said "I don't know much more than you, Fern. But my guess is both Muddie and Father were right just now. Life is apparently steady hard times, but Larkin Slade is the worst loss you'll take. Very likely the worst."

"You too," Fern said. Then he rolled to his side and met me dead-on. "Lark had loved you for months since I showed him that picture."

I couldn't imagine what picture he meant.

"The one I stole from you back before Christmas."

"The one of Leela and me in Raleigh at the fair last fall?"

Fern nodded. "I cut Leela out. It was just you standing there looking forlorn."

I had to laugh. "Oh Lord, I *was*. You didn't show that awful likeness to Lark?" I'd worn a washed-out cool cotton dress and an old straw boating hat with hard fake cherries, and my face looked as grim as I felt after following Leela for a whole fall day.

Fern said "You looked all right. Calm down. No, I *gave* it to Lark—he liked it so much."

Partly to keep Fern talking this calmly but mostly to feed my own aching mind, I said "Tell me everything Lark said about it."

Fern gave it some thought but finally shook his head. "Lark wouldn't want that. He swore me to secrecy."

So I sat there silent, my hand on my brother's back, thinking my thoughts. Full dark was nearly on us before I knew what to say. And what had come to me was as heavy as anything I'd ever felt, but I had to go on and let Fern have it, or I'd have broke too. "I plan to love Larkin Slade the rest of my life."

Ferny said "Me too."

I've always suspected Fern kept his half of that plan far better than I managed to. It was part of what killed him, so young and distressed. But that fall night with Lark's funeral facing us tomorrow noon, I felt I'd been mowed down way below my knees and could never think of rising.

In that same night not long before dawn, I woke in mine and Leela's room and had the first vision I ever experienced. It offered no angels or soft light and music, no sign of Christ or God or demons. And far from being a dream or a hope, it was clearer than scratching your eye on a thorn, though it brought no pain. It was broad warm day at the height of real summer, the sky was the main view, and I was walking entirely alone in a light pale dress toward the edge of a deep wood—woods even deeper than those in my girlhood before every live tree was marked for cutting or poisoned by the air it tried to breathe.

I was feeling strong but with no big purpose in mind at the moment. Then as I got twenty yards from the thicket, a body stepped out and stood still before me—a young man naked as God ever made him. I've mentioned seeing my brothers naked all through my childhood—none of the Danes were especially modest; we didn't think we were that fine to see—so what surprised me was not the bare skin but the suddenness with which Lark was there so near me, the look on his face and the feelings he caused in me at first sight.

I didn't realize right off that it truly was Larkin. I'd only seen flashes of his body in the minutes before he drowned. But to keep from concentrating in a way that would have seemed rude, I fixed on his eyes. They were not exactly Lark's eyes—not at first, not the ones I'd known. I've always assumed I was seeing Lark in what Saint Paul called our "spiritual body" raised from death and restored, and that sort of body is generally changed for the better in most ways. Or so people claim who've had more acquaintance with the risen than me. (I'm not making fun. I believe in resurrection.)

But I held my ground and faced the dream-Lark pleasantly. After a good while he said "I died recalling your name. But remind me now." It seemed fair enough, with all he'd endured, that he'd lost my name.

I told him "Roxanna—you'd only just met me."

So he said "Roxanna, I'll thank you forever."

My eyes were filling with glad tears by then. But all I could think to ask was why people rose from death stark naked. Even I wasn't fool enough to say as much. Still I think Lark read my mind.

He said "This is how you'd have liked me most."

I told him I hadn't got that far yet. "I'm still a maiden child." It was true but I laughed.

Lark laughed for a moment and then held a hand up to quiet us both. In his own fine voice, the one I'd known that single last day, he said "Palmer may well need you now." Before I could ask if his was the clear mysterious voice that woke me last night saying very nearly the same few words, Lark turned slowly with both arms out as if to steady himself in a stream or to take flight now. He didn't swim or fly though, no more than if he'd been still alive. He stepped on forward into those thick woods and in ten seconds was gone for good. I never saw Larkin alive again, not even in dreams, though I long hoped for dreams with some glimpse of him and wouldn't refuse that chance tonight long decades later.

Again that same night after I'd slid on back to sleep with daylight just beginning to break, my body had a kind of vision of its own. No pictures or sounds and nothing I've ever known how to describe in words alone but since I'm aiming for the whole truth now (so far as I've encountered it), I can say it amounted to the fullest pleasure my skin and mind had ever felt till that moment. Since today in America anyhow most people seem to think that bodily gratifications are the finest available, I'll say that what I underwent was bodily, yes.

It started near the front of my mind just above my eyes in a spot the size of a silver quarter, and it poured slowly out from there down my length till it rested where my legs join together. Then it seeped on slowly away through my feet and I never woke. Every bit of it happened to my skin, understand. My mind was just the trigger. Not only did I sleep on through it, I didn't even make any sound you could hear. Leela would wake at the sound of a feather, but she slept soundly right on through my first taste of a grown woman's pleasure.

It left me, not only soothed in my sleep but utterly clear on one last point that proved important for the rest of my life—I was now a woman. I must live like one or like what people in general thought a woman was in those simpler days. Again I saw no pictures of anything, no human face or any other creature's, no memory of Larkin Slade's rangy body or endless eyes nor any other man's I'd seen.

Yet strange to say it didn't surprise me, didn't shock or shame me. And though it happened so long ago, I can bring the heart of it back even now, if I can get quiet enough in my mind and am well-intentioned toward myself. I've never doubted it amounted to the cause of what I did next.

At Larkin's funeral on the 10th, a Sunday, I'd found myself concentrating on Palmer to steady my nerves if nothing else. Palmer seemed that strong in his own black suit that left him looking a whole head taller than his normal great height. And his eyes seemed set on some distant point, far past human vision, that he'd discovered in the wake of his brother's sacrifice. Without seeming worn or in any way tarnished, he aged some twenty years in a day. I think it was why I could never call him *Palm* again as his family did. It looked to me as if he'd earned his full name.

He got his old father and Miss Olivia through the burial with the quiet command of a battlefield veteran. The family graves were east of the house some hundred yards in the midst of a field of stripped cotton stalks. A black man I'd never seen before rolled Major down on a homemade kind of wheelbarrow cart. Miss Olivia of course walked swift and upright as any young captain on parade. The black man got Major upright as well but on two canes today and with eyes so baffled it might have been his own execution he stood there expecting. Clearly Major scarcely understood what was happening. But he kept his gaze on Palmer's face and wept throughout in absolute silence, letting his man all but bear his weight once the preacher's voice started.

Miss Olivia, who'd been as staunch as an oak beam suddenly broke into scraps at the grave. Her whole heart seemed to heave up in her throat. And when she'd moaned but couldn't shed tears, her legs slowly buckled till she sat on the ground before Palmer reached her.

Muddie touched my arm and said to go help her but I knew better. Miss Olivia had never found a trace of solace in me; she couldn't start now. I just faced the ground till Palmer reached her and sat her on the rock wall that guarded the graves till the preacher got his few lines recited and Palmer and two other black men could lower the coffin.

The black men waited with shovels beside the open hole till all my family had walked on ahead—Major Slade was waving for us to go first. As I passed through the gate, the major looked toward me with the blankest eyes. But he put out his right hand and snagged at my arm till I nodded and bowed. As his hand went down and I took the next step, Miss Olivia faced me and said clear as any diamond scratching through glass "You were here at the start of this, Anna. Weren't you? Say you were. Stay on please and help me."

She hadn't quite said I'd caused Larkin's death, but I heard her that way and so did my mother.

Muddie barely met my puzzled eyes before she smiled like a petted dog and told Miss Olivia "Gladly. She'll help as long as she's needed—won't you, Anna?"

Since my own mother took me apparently for an underaged child, what was I meant to say but Yes? I just managed to nod.

That wasn't sufficiently courteous for Muddie in these circumstances. Her eyes went hot as pokers. She met my eyes dead straight. "Thank Miss Olivia—deeply—for the privilege."

I was twenty years and two days old. I could have been married at least four years and have had three children, more if I'd had a set of twins (twins ran in Muddie's family). And while I'd never been known for independence—Leela was our rebel—I returned Muddie's heat. For a dignified change I called her *Mother*. "Mother, Larkin's parents know my feelings far better than you."

Miss Olivia nodded and the major reached out for me again, but by then I'd stepped ahead and aimed toward the house.

Within three steps Fern was there beside me. I knew not to look at him right that instant—my knees might have failed me—but he fixed on me, and we went a good ways before he said "I'm staying here with you."

"Father may need you, Fern."

"Rox, Father can kiss my rusty ass."

I knew Fern loved Father in his own way, so I didn't blame him. I forged on forward thinking I could help old Coy spread dinner. No way on Earth we wouldn't all have to sit down now and eat our path through a big hill of food.

We did exactly that. The Slades as I've said had no near neighbors. But people of every kind and color from the darkest ebony through browns and tans and high bright reds to the palest white somehow heard from miles away—Larkin was cherished far and wide—and food had come in by horse, goat cart, car and foot. The goat cart carried a single old white woman; and when she got out to deliver her bacon, she couldn't have stood more than four feet tall. But none of them tried to stay for long.

So by the time the seven of us took our places, and Major had blessed it in his peculiar way (saying only "Lord, we accept these rations"), the table was burdened with smoked ham, chicken cooked every way known to humans, plus one baked guinea hen, a platter of fried streak-of-fat-streak-of-lean, eight or ten different strains of home-canned vegetables, the last of Palmer's summer tomatoes (he was the gardener and had a cellar still full of the green ones he'd pulled before the first cold spell).

Even harder to believe there were ears of corn he'd somehow managed to keep till now. Also biscuits, hot rolls, cornbread fried in small thin pones with lacy edges and a dish of delicate spoonbread the size of a growing baby's tub. Pickles and relish of every description and eventually six kinds of cake and endless pies. Likewise iced tea, spring water, several wines made from the local fruit and the cut-glass tumbler of strong apple brandy that nobody touched or drank a drop from but Major Slade.

It has been a minor but strange fact of life that since childhood, however down and deep blue I get, my appetite has mostly stayed healthy. I'm no kind of glutton, and I've never gained more weight than I could carry easily. But fresh and thoughtfully put-together food has been one of life's unfailing pleasures down to this day when I eat alone. And sitting there at the Slades' wide table with Lark no more than minutes underground, I swallowed what calmed me far more nearly than any known drug.

Which is not to say that for one cold moment I failed to know what we'd just done, what I'd just lost and might never replace. That still didn't keep me from studying Palmer the best I could without seeming rude. I had clear memories of the two different voices that had said he might need me. So the rest of that day I worked at the sight of his face and eyes, his tall strong body, and wondered what I could mean to him in days or years to come.

Ferny dropped out of school and stayed there till Christmas. I stayed two weeks. I'd have gladly stayed longer if that had seemed fitting. One of the really hard problems for girls in those days—white girls whose fathers had at least decent incomes—was *idleness*, pure bottomless idleness in a quiet house in a quieter town that offered you nothing whatever to do that you didn't personally think up and carry out.

Whatever foolishness any politician or TV preacher tries to peddle today about human *families* as the peak of all striving, the highest of every human achievement, let me tell you plainly that in my youth and young womanhood, the families of many people thought to be decent as bands of angels were nothing but factories for driving souls crazy or still more evil than their hateful mothers or fathers.

And that big claim—but dead earnest—doesn't even mention the brothers or uncles who could use their younger kin like side meat. And even if all your people were saints, the lack of anything solid for young white respectable women to do would leave a girl so bone-shattering bored that she might easily turn out a demon of world-sized meanness, just for something to *do* with the endless silent hours of frost or broiling swelter.

Everybody who had two dollars a week to spare for a cook had a good one in the kitchen. The cook also helped out with the heavy housekeeping. Every morning she'd sweep the indoors and often the yard. (Almost everybody had too much tree shade to grow any grass, so yards consisted of packed dirt or sand with occasional ivy and rosebushes.) She'd make and change beds and empty the slopjars first thing every morning.

My parents went to their graves with no trace of indoor plumbing. That was not necessarily a sign of poverty on anybody's part. Many well-off respectable people didn't want "that dirty stuff" indoors. So the "garden house" would stand fifty yards off through the open backyard. At night or in bad weather, we used white china slopjars in our rooms, otherwise the privy.

What was left by way of work for the housewife and any young daughters of the family was fairly slim. You could make up your own bed if you really insisted; you could take your sweet time getting sponge-bathed and dressed. Your hair alone could take half an hour to brush, comb and plait. Then you might have, as I did, a little light daily duty.

Mine was to gather all the kerosene lamps that had been used the previous night and clean them. That involved wiping down four or five fragile glass chimneys with old newspaper, then trimming the dirty wicks, drying any oil which had dripped down the sides. That could take three-quarters of an hour for four or five lamps if you got them as clean as Muddie expected.

Once they were spotless, though, your daily chore was finished. You weren't expected to handle the oil itself. Father insisted that he fill all lamps just before dark. He'd seen a black girl catch on fire in his childhood, and he had a great horror of it happening again. Depending on what their mothers knew and wanted to teach, some girls learned sewing or other handwork. But Muddie could scarcely thread a needle, so Leela and I never tackled much more than darning a sock or anchoring a button.

Anyhow once you'd done your morning chore, then you were free for however many hours were left till preparations started for that day's dinner. Dinner as I've mentioned was the midday meal, the main event. You might have no job at all in the kitchen with the cook and your mother doing the work, or by ten or eleven you might need to undertake some modest task such as shelling peas and stringing beans or brewing tea strong enough to half dissolve the spoon. Then you'd eat with the family and—if you were normal for your time, place and color—you took off your dress and had an afternoon nap, or you sat upright in a padded chair and snoozed a few minutes, or you walked into town for some small need like hairpins or stockings.

Then you had the shank of the afternoon to survive till suppertime dawned. Supper was mostly a matter of dinner leftovers or cold food in summer, and the black cook would stay on to lay it out attractively and wash up afterward. (She could generally take the remnants home for however many children, and that constituted a genuine supplement to her slim pay.) Leela and I frequently volunteered to help with the washing, not so much because we were filled with pity but again to move the clock onward toward bed.

Evenings you spent playing cards with the family if they weren't fanatical Baptists or Presbyterians scared of a blistering eternity in Hell. From late March till early November, you passed most evenings on the porch in the dark rocking aimlessly and listening to talk—mostly older people talking but sometimes entertaining harmless boys who might stop by and every so often invite you to the picture show. Or if all else failed, you'd maybe read old ladies' magazines off in a corner like some wretched hermit that nobody cared to know.

You also kept up a ferocious correspondence with practically every distant person you'd met. The postal service really worked in those days, so you'd write most every distant soul you knew with detailed accounts of the family menus, the weather conditions, not to mention excruciatingly detailed reports on any man that had so much as breathed your name. And all that of course with the world outside—even our tame town—full of sickness, hunger and desperate loneliness that you might have set your mind to relieve in whatever small way.

We were *Christians* after all, or so we told ourselves every Sunday from ten o'clock till noon. But no, not one of us ever did anything more actively charitable than feeding some former cook on her deathbed or sending old clothes to a burnt-out family. My eyes were very slow to open on the full extent of black people's suffering and the dreadful poison of our neglect. And I confess, with grievous shame, that I never did one kindly act to an actual stranger—black or white—before the Depression when tramps turned up.

Leela had a more active brain than mine. She read a good deal and would tell in agonizing particulars the plots of stories she was reading or dreams she'd had till you were forced to think up some fake emergency and leave the room. Still I've always known how wasted her keen mind was in our circumstances, and I've never forgot that it was Leela who said "Every woman who's kin to us talks about nothing but food and family."

And though I never had Leela's smartness nor her quick wit (in time she'd do me a lifesaving deed), I often shared in silence her bone-deep fatigue from hearing the same two topics explored in endless variations that meant less than nothing in the scheme of things. I mean for instance Muddie and any of her women friends could talk nonstop for three-quarters of an hour about the proper way to slice a tomato, though it was the cook who did more than ninety percent of all slicing. They could likewise retell for the nine thousandth time a story of some obstetrical mishap or outright tragedy from forty years past that they'd still not drained the interest from.

To be fair of course I can say that few men had more interesting work or conversation, though they did have jokes and local friends outside the family. My father sold dry goods, plain men and women's clothing and farm machinery every day of his grown life but Sunday. Neither of my brothers ever did a week's work that challenged the excellent minds they possessed. And it wasn't the fault of any man I knew. My brothers' problems with work came later as I think I've mentioned, though with more education they might have done better.

Almost nobody in our part of the world, men or women, attended college. Doctors and lawyers were the main exceptions, though the older lawyers had often just "read law" with some old attorney, then put out their shingle—well trained or not. Even the white and reasonably paid men had by no means all finished high school. It was no shame then. Whole parts of the county were literally out of the reach of possible schools, ten or fifteen miles off when children had nothing but their own two feet or an old blind mule.

So unless men were geniuses sent by God and fully equipped to lead boys to battle or compose church music or experience angels back in the woods and take dictation that proved they were prophets, they seldom fell into interesting jobs. The main advantage men had over women came in two simple forms. They could leave the house every morning and stay gone till sunset or after; and so far as I know, not one of them ever had to bear or nurse a baby.

Also more than a fair share of men were the holders of the family purse strings. When it came to rest or spare time to think or the slow backwash of love that a mother may get from most of her children, men in general were sadly worse off. They wound up showing it too in midlife—the toll they'd taken in the outside world—and they went on showing it ever more gravely if they lived to get old. Then they tended to sit and turn quickly to stone, bent shattered stones with no word to say for all they'd seen and likely tasted.

In my two weeks up by the river with the Slades, I didn't have all that much new to do. But I offered my help right on through the day, and Coy or Miss Olivia or Major seemed glad to have it. The strange part of course was being there in the heart of Larkin's life with him gone for good. Little pieces of him were everywhere—objects, small things he'd used every day or prized. Again I hadn't known him long enough to feel as deeply bereaved as I privately thought I ought to be, but I did slowly move into a kind of dreamy feeling he'd reappear any day now, and then we'd decide if we meant what we'd said on the edge of his death.

Beyond that the best thing that happened in those two weeks was having my first substantial sight of a grown white woman's life that looked worth living. Miss Olivia had impressed me from the start with her looks, her power over everybody round her and a curious absolutely frank whiff of mischief that could sometimes turn into very near malice. But I watched her like a hungry child through the days and nights I was first there with her. No question she spent the biggest part of the day and night on household business.

Major was plainly long past running an operation as complicated as a wide river farm with three or four tenants, five big families of the Slades' ex-slaves and more than a few square miles of timber that were only just starting to be sold off to the stinking paper mills that had opened downriver—so near you could smell them on any warm evening. I was not wrong then in seeing Miss Olivia as herself a manager of military stature.

With a few more like her, the South might have done a lot better in the war, though I've never been one to wish we'd succeeded. From the time I turned eleven years old, when the Civil War was not far behind us, I'd silently figured out—from people's stories of Southern glory and fame and starvation, not to mention worse—what an idiot waste of everything it was. It didn't take a genius to recognize the wrong, just a watchful child with a child's sense of fairness.

But with all the duties that kept her moving from before dawn till bedtime, Miss Olivia had the rare ability to use little scraps of time that other people treat as pointless waste. She'd have half an hour in the midst of the morning and would go through the yard to the separate building that was Major's farm Office and sit there reading a scene from Shakespeare or six poems of Shelley's. Or she'd work at memorizing miles of verse by Tennyson or James Russell Lowell. Then she'd say it back to us in the evening after supper when everybody gathered by the big iron stove.

That fall was colder than fall mostly is. And in the long evenings we tended to sit together talking aimlessly and listening to Miss Olivia roll on in her rich voice, holding us close by sheer force of will, her great dark eyes and whatever story she chose to tell. They almost always involved bloody death or cold starvation. And often as not, she'd add the perfect recitation of some Scotch ballad of cutthroat revenge or some ghost story she claimed to have witnessed face-to-face by way of illustrating her power and the claims she made to deserve our attention.

She could also pause if she had eight minutes before her next duty and play the boxy old parlor piano, finer music than I'd ever heard in those quiet days before home radios and nearby concerts. Her style was old-fashioned—she strummed all her chords—but it showed deep feelings on any matter of love and death. I've known her to sit ten minutes at least in utter silence at the stained keyboard, her eyes shut firmly. Then she'd raise her beautiful hands from her lap and play some melody she'd just composed. Or so she claimed and I had no cause to doubt her. I've never heard any of them played elsewhere and can still hum the tunes to three of the finest.

Miss Olivia was also known, so Palmer told me, to keep a diary every day of the year. It was locked in a cupboard in the separate Office. More than once I caught her gazing at something—a hawk in the sky, the major's peg leg stretched out before him or often the side of Palmer's face, even Ferny's eyes. And once alone with her out on the porch, I asked what she did with what she *stole* through her eyes (I'd even caught her watching me closely in quiet moments).

She laughed very pleasantly to hear it called theft, but she gave my question some actual thought and finally said "I write down every fact about life in a book I keep. I've kept it since girlhood."

I said "What for?"

And kindly still she looked down at me like the saddest lunatic she'd ever met. "Oh to exercise the mind God gave me, and maybe some child or great-great-great-grandchild a century from now will find my thick book of endless work and learn something new about the roots of his blood."

I truly didn't know so I asked her on the spot. "You and the major have grandchildren now?"

Miss Olivia said "Major does by his first wife. They're all grown and scattered. But I'm still bereft."

It slid out of me as natural as breath. "Put your hopes on Palmer." Then I almost literally died of shame to have offered such private advice to an elder.

And for ten seconds Miss Olivia looked shocked and mad. But then she gave her pure laugh again. "I'm actually banking great hopes on you for a whole tribe of children."

Under the fire of my blush I kept quiet.

"You and Palmer," she said. "In matrimonial circumstances to be sure." She was watching the side of my face as closely as if it were her last map to bliss.

Children had more than crossed my mind of course, children with Palmer. The voices I'd heard in the night and my vision had led that way. But through the two weeks I'd been with the Slades, Palmer had said no more than a hundred words to me till the night before I was due to leave. Up till then he'd have already left in the morning by the time I was up, and often he didn't come home at night. Sometimes the dogs would have disappeared with him, so I assumed he was hunting in the woods. But he never brought home any game he'd killed. And when finally I asked Miss Olivia where he went, she said "That's a question I never ask a man. Not since I got good sense anyhow."

By then I was frank in wanting everything Miss Olivia would tell me. I said "Why not?"

"Well first because it's a need men have to wander in secret with the trust at least that nobody's looking. And second maybe because I've had occasion to ask and be cut to the bone by a truthful answer. I'm not necessarily speaking of Palmer—I have no notion where Palmer takes himself when he's left my sight. I'm referring to other men further back in my time. When I was a girl even more than now, some white men spent a share of time with black women. The second year I was married to Major, I asked him once where he had been when he hadn't showed up for two nights and three days. He didn't need more than two hot seconds to find his answer and pitch it right at me—'I've been out gorging on what I don't get here.' "

The words came to me as strange as Spanish. I'd literally never heard such meanness before even at second hand, not at home or in school—meanness or honesty—so in my confusion I gave a high laugh.

Miss Olivia had never looked more in earnest when she said "It burned out my curiosity, I tell you. And once the burn scarred over and faded, I've gradually accepted being happier than most, most women I know anyhow."

To this late date still I've never recalled one lie Olivia Slade ever told me or one foolish claim she made in my presence. There were numerous hard words and gestures from her when I'd let her down as I did more than once, and there were the terrible times after my marriage that I'll tell about, but otherwise there was never sufficient cause for complaint—not from me, not ever.

And even today with a world of women in outside jobs and flying to Mars—doing things no women from my time could dream of, much less perform—I've run across no one single woman who gave me Olivia Slade's sense of power, not even any First Lady on TV. It was less than steadily *merciful* strength but strength all the same, a force that would never pause in its course to hear you say the word *No* or *Maybe* to any serious need of hers.

That particular conversation took place the day before I was planning to head back home. So it was fresh in my mind when Palmer turned up at noon to eat dinner. He'd been gone since sunup with most of the dogs. I don't know whether it was some kind of spite or just a form of ignorance in me, but there at the table in sight of his mother I asked Palmer what he'd learned since breakfast. I think I meant it jokingly. What was there to learn in a world he'd explored every square inch of already?

He took his own time, then looked right at me and said "Well I finally achieved my purpose."

By then I'd realized the ground was shaky, so I asked nothing else.

But Ferny said "What would that be, O Wise One?" Fern liked Palmer well enough but without the worship he'd felt for Larkin. Since we'd been there Fern had spent his time driving the major down back roads the old man hadn't seen for years. Fern said they were reliving Major's young life, and he thought that was easing the old man's sorrow.

Palmer never let go of his hold on my eyes but he answered Fern. "The Wise One has finally discovered a perfect place to show Miss Anna."

It startled me a little. I wasn't even sure he'd ever called my name, so I broke his gaze and looked to his mother. If anything was wrong or too strange, I knew her face would show it at once.

But she was smiling slightly toward Palmer. Then she said one word— "Montezuma?"

Palmer nodded.

Major said "That's too hard a trail."

Miss Olivia said "Not so. This girl's tough as leather."

I wasn't entirely flattered by that, but I tried to keep smiling.

Palmer looked to Major. "Too hard, I'm sure, when you were a boy. But that was eight hundred years ago." He didn't mean it harshly, and he half grinned to prove it.

By then Fern was grinning too.

And Major gave his paralyzed laugh that sounded like somebody bringing up lumps of coal from his belly.

Palmer pushed back his chair to stand, and he faced me again. "Can you be ready to ride a horse in under ten minutes?"

I had no riding clothes of any sort and couldn't remember being on a horse in recent years.

Miss Olivia faced me. "I can fit you out with something decent." Her calm was no more reassuring than all the male grins. She turned to Palmer. "I can have her ready in half an hour." From the set of her firm mouth, you might have thought she had a set of Joan-of-Arc armor to strap to my limbs.

*   *   *

Admittedly this was not 1860. But as far off the main line as we all lived, respectable girls seldom got much farther than the front or back steps with an unmarried man who was not close kin—*blood* kin with a certified reputation. Having brothers all my life, I was hard to shock. Still it set me back a good many seconds, hearing Miss Olivia and Palmer cook my future between them—and my own brother watching with no word to slow them.

Ferny was doing nothing by then but helping the major rise and leading him out for his nap.

When I looked back at Palmer, his eyes were waiting for me, all but certainly kind. He said "It's nothing that could harm a crippled flea—the site of an old gold mine in the woods about three miles off by a beautiful plain."

Miss Olivia faced me and said "You'll be back in good time to help me with supper. Meanwhile you'll wear a pair of Palmer's old trousers, won't you? The sidesaddle's ruined, out there in the stable." She pointed toward the back of the house, the way people still do to objects that are dead or sorely missed. You might have thought her ruined sidesaddle would repair itself and float in to meet her in the next ten seconds.

I said that I guessed I could make do somehow. Then as I watched Miss Olivia's face, it gathered with what seemed the start of dread. I asked could I bring her some spirits of ammonia or an aspirin maybe—she often had headaches that she forged past like boulders in the road.

Miss Olivia said "No, it's just that you're leaving now we've all learned to love you."

Nobody in my life, except in those few brief hours with Larkin two weeks before, had said a more welcome set of words to me. Awkward as I was, all hands and feet, I had the sense to thank the great lady I knew her to be. And as I left her and climbed upstairs to wait in my room till she brought me the trousers, I knew the very words themselves would likely form another link in whatever chain fate was hammering out for me and mine before my eyes.

The trousers swallowed me. I was the first white woman for miles who'd wear men's pants till Katharine Hepburn started in movies nearly twenty years later and slacks were invented. Anyhow the comic picture I made eased Palmer and me into his odd and apparently sudden plan for the trip. His horse was Alec (pronounced *Ellik*), a well-made chestnut gelding. Mine was a sweet old plug named Arabel that I'd already met in pasture walks.

I've mentioned not being on any kind of horse in recent years—five years at least. But one of my uncles had kept riding horses when I was a girl, and I'd gone through a normal girl's spell of being in love with the whole idea of sitting atop the world of a gentle mare's broad back and surveying things from that safe distance. I'd never once been thrown or run away with by any horse; so with Palmer beside me, I set out with no substantial fears. If there was a slight dread, it was dread of all I didn't know about Palmer Slade.

And that was everything except his height, his being a little older than Larkin and the steady strength he managed to keep at a smokeless burn somewhere deep in him. It didn't surprise me that he scarcely spoke in the first three miles. We stayed on the dirt road—all roads were dirt but some were impassable—for most of the way. And Palmer chose to ride ahead of me, saying Arabel liked to follow his horse. That was fine by me. The sky was nearer gray than blue with a cool nip in the easy wind. And in under a mile, my mind had reclaimed its old enjoyment of an elevated seat and the clean contagious reassurance of even as worn a nag as mine.

Then not looking back Palmer held up a flat hand and stopped his Alec on the sandy shoulder just in my path.

Arabel stopped right up against him. Alec was her son. I pulled back on her but she wouldn't budge.

So Palmer laughed with no explanation and then said "The hard part starts just into these woods."

I said "You told me there was no big danger."

He waited what felt like at least ten minutes, then said "I may very well have told you a lie."

"Miss Olivia agreed—"

"I'm her favorite, Anna. She works for me, on my behalf anyhow."

But nothing in his face was alarming, and those were days when you didn't expect every man you met to rape you or batter your face to pulp if you wound up alone together ten seconds. So I said "Lead on whenever you're ready." I did have a slight suspicion Palmer had more plans than he'd told me. But again—being who I was, where and when—my mind offered me no scary prospects.

It turned out the hard part was as easy as falling. What Palmer had meant was a stretch of thicket and deep fallen leaves that concealed a few holes and traps in the ground. Arabel watched her son closely though and we never stumbled. After what felt like more than a mile, Palmer and Alec stopped again a few yards short of the sheer side of a fairly tall hill. It looked like a miniature stone cliff from far off. I'd never seen its like except in books, though it looked real enough. Palmer got down and came to help me. But I beat him to it, a little dazed to be back on the Earth again and thus so very much shorter than he—my eye level fell in the midst of his chest.

He took the reins of both horses and silently led them on toward the cliff. I assumed I was meant to follow and did. It was not till he'd tied both of them to saplings and walked on closer still to the cliff that I saw an opening surrounded by a wilderness of dead tangled vines.

In another few steps Palmer stood beside it and turned back to me.

I had to ask "Is this Montezuma?"

He nodded Yes.

"Where's all the gold then?" I meant to be funny. Miss Olivia had said that the mine was long abandoned.

But Palmer stood there thinking it through as if we faced a serious mystery. At last he said like a boy reciting in geography class "Every mineral known to science has been found in the state of North Carolina. That's a fact you can count on."

I told him I would (turned out he was right when I checked years later). Then it was I who had to say "Can we go inside?"

"You want to?"

I had to say "Isn't that part of the trip?"

And for the first time since the day we met, Palmer blushed furiously as if I'd thrown berry juice all down him. Seeing a grown giant that abashed, I broke down laughing in a way I hadn't enjoyed for months.

Palmer didn't join me but waited till I finished. Then he made a stiff gesture toward the opening and said "I think I can almost get you through safely." As I stepped forward he took the butt of a candle from his pocket and lit it to flame.

I didn't sufficiently note his word *through*. I thought we were dealing with a dead-end shaft. So when we'd walked a completely uneventful fifty yards through near full dark, half-stooped and with rock walls pressing close in on us and occasional wood piers and falling-down beams, I said "Maybe now's a good point to turn back." My face was covered with spider webbing, and my left hand was holding the back of Palmer's belt. He'd suggested that as the best arrangement for leading me. Then when he didn't stop, I came to rest against him and his arm came around me. That will sound like a silent movie from those same ceremonious years. It was silent all right. Neither one of us spoke.

And Palmer's arm was the only thing that moved.

I could sense his breathing near to my face, but we didn't touch elsewhere than at our covered waists.

He finally said "Is Larkin truly dead?"

I knew what he meant. Knowing my grammar was wrong, I still said "Not now nor never."

Palmer said "I know that."

I said "All right." And that appeared to be all he needed or at least enough to live with for now.

He held in place another few seconds. Then his arm went down. And he turned to lead onward, not back toward the entrance.

For all I knew we were bound for Hell or a billion dollars—it *was* a gold mine, however deserted. The path was downhill steeply from there on and seemed to get darker despite the candle. It may have been trust or mere desperation—who else could help me?—but for whatever reason I followed Palmer with no further question. And if there were doubts, I don't recall them. I wonder still—was I that trusting a youthful soul or just the local idiot?

After thirty more steps (I was counting anyhow), I began to feel light seeping in ahead. I felt the light before I saw it. The weight of it on my forehead helped calm me. For all I knew we'd exit on the place where Larkin waited, gilded and winged. I clearly recall I thought of that chance. Maybe this is where Palmer had been the past two weeks, hunting the way to the brother he loved. Or did he truly love him? The thoughts weren't entirely childish but almost—a final lunge by my fond hopes.

No, nothing that fanciful. Nothing that happy. But once my eyes were steadied, I could see we stood on a low rock ledge maybe eight or ten feet above a plain as flat as your hand so far as I could see with only a few low spindly pine trees at lonely intervals and pale scrub bushes. It had to be the plain that Palmer had mentioned. I'll never know why but what I said was the first thing I thought. Strange as it was it flooded my mind. I said—in fact I all but shouted in some kind of joy— "Oh Palmer, the sea! Thank God, the sea."

I'd never even called the ocean the *sea* before as I well remember. To the best of my belief that instant, we were looking eastward at the roaring sea. But the sea—the Atlantic Ocean anyhow—was more than a hundred miles off, due east. Someway, undistinguished though the actual view here was for beauty or strangeness, I had this overwhelming sense of the actual ocean, which I'd never seen except in dreams and occasional pictures.

Palmer's eyes narrowed as he studied the view. He grinned at some thought he didn't express. But when he finally looked down to me, he said "Shall we dive on out there then?"

To the day he died a lifetime later, I never asked him all that meant— diving into what and heading where? I doubt he could have told me, though I still think he meant it.

Nor could I have told him what I intended by saying "Yes" to his calm gray eyes, earnest as any dying child's.

He took it for what it appeared to say. Not then and there on the edge of the plain but not long after. First we sat on the ledge beneath us, and Palmer began to talk more freely than he'd done in my presence. In many ways I felt I was back in my first and only day with Larkin, Larkin and I alone by the river before the others came out for the picnic. Like his younger brother, Palmer told me his whole life story. In general it seemed as uneventful as Lark's or my own—a few more hunting trips and scrapes in the deep woods than I'd yet managed.

Palmer plainly had a craving for nature and wild things that Lark hadn't mentioned, but in those days that was not strange at all for a boy from the country. And Palmer gave me no hint at all, not then, of being trapped in the kind of starved body that Lark had complained of with so much long- ing. Neither did he offer a word to explain the places he went to, or whom he visited, in all his hours alone in the sticks.

I returned his confidence with my own recollections. My story was a good deal shorter than his, not because I was slightly younger but because back then I had absolutely no sense at all that anything I'd ever thought or done was of the slightest interest to the world, even my loved ones.

Palmer took it all in, though, as if it were actual shining ore from the dead mine behind us. He'd already told me the mine was abandoned when the Civil War ended. The dumb old Confederates mined it out to the last small nugget for all the good it did them in the late starving days. And when I'd brought Palmer more or less to the present by saying "And here I sit, twenty whole years old and knowing less about running a life than when I was ten," Palmer said "Don't let that slow you a bit. Somebody else can run it for you. Happens all the time under every roof." Again he faced me with those big eyes and held on as if he could sit in silence and stare at me till the sea really did rush into our plain and leave us on beachfront property, effortless, holding the deed.

By then my mind or my heart anyhow was leaning his way. Not leaning exactly, no way he could feel, but starting to burn with a heat I could feel as new and welcome.

Two more things that mattered took place before I went home the following morning. First at supper that night with everybody listening and old Coy beyond us, Palmer talked at the table—a surprise to all, I could see at a glance. And they listened to him like God at Judgment. He described our ride in the kind of detail I'd seldom heard—peculiar rocks he'd seen in the road, strange galls on tree trunks, a clutch of wild turkeys, none of which I'd seen and he hadn't bothered to mention.

He described our every step through the mine, stressing a fact he'd never told me—how dangerous the shaft was now, how likely a cave-in was any day on some luckless prowler or *loving couple* (he used those words). And then he told them what I'd said the moment we broke out of the mine onto daylight and my first view of the plain. When he'd mimicked my voice near perfectly, he quoted the actual words I said. Then he looked to his mother and said "*You* tell her, Livvie." He was all but smiling.

Miss Olivia said "Palm, you may call me Livvie if we meet in Heaven but not before."

Major Slade laughed again, an event as new as anything yet on a day of novelties. By the look on his face, laughter still pained him. But he went on and gave in to it at length.

That clearly pleased Ferny.

Then Miss Olivia turned to me. "You didn't climb down and examine the ground at the foot of your ledge?"

"No ma'm, we didn't."

"You'd have found sea shells and black sharks' teeth as big as the palm of your right hand ten zillion years old at least."

The major and Fern were nodding as if this were well known to all.

I said something vacant like "It surely was lovely—"

Miss Olivia tapped the table hard with a finger as if I'd slid off to sleep in school. "The point is, Anna, you had a real vision. Where Palmer took you, from the foot of that ledge for thousands of miles on eastward toward sunrise, there once stretched an ocean in prehistoric days. Unimagined monsters swam those deeps where black snakes crawl today and red ants." She paused and studied my eyes as slowly as if she'd never seen me till now.

Then before she stood to start clearing plates, she made her curious gesture of sweeping webs from her own eyes; and she said "I *thought* you had special powers from the moment I met you, girl. I was right." The fact, if it was any kind of fact, didn't seem to please or disturb her though. Her face stayed calm as she left the room, and the set of her shoulders was still strong enough to bear whole planets if the need arose.

The second thing waited till deep in the night. Father had said he'd come to get me at seven in the morning so he could get back to open the store. That was no trouble since, like any country family, the Slades were always up and busy before daybreak. Their early rising had meant I seldom got enough sleep for a young idle person, and I'd been trying to turn in by nine. In the two weeks I'd been there, I'd slept in that low narrow cubicle up in the eaves. It was normally Palmer's bedroom, as far off and private as he could get. But his mother had made him sleep with Ferny in the separate Office out in the yard while I was visiting.

The bed was narrow and the ceiling low. Even I could sit upright on the mattress, a deep feather mattress, and touch the downward slope of the roof. Of course I had a kerosene lamp to help me go to bed or rise without fumbling, and Miss Olivia had given me an ancient child's night light (a single candle with a porous white porcelain screen that showed the Good Shepherd guarding his dazed silly flock). But I used neither one of them much, being scared of setting the bone-dry pine walls and ceiling on fire and killing everybody. As a rule at bedtime I undressed in the dark and fell straight to sleep. That was never hard to do in the cold pure blackness.

So when my eyes came open in the night, in the midst of a thoroughly peaceful dream, and saw the Good Shepherd shining gently beside me, I knew right off that something had happened not of my making. I wasn't scared though. Being in this house, I thought first thing that Major had died or had another stroke. My head raised up off the pillow and looked round all the space that the Good Shepherd reached. Nothing, nobody to the best of my knowledge.

But somebody had to have lit the candle; and it must have been recently—no Jesus anyhow, not this time, not revealing himself nor any other raised soul. I could still smell sulfur from the match that was struck. Was Ferny playing some joke on me by way of farewell? No. Fern was no longer staying in the Office but had lately been sleeping in Major's room at the foot of Major's mattress on a trundle bed, and Fern was still too sad to think of a joke.

I propped myself up higher on an elbow and blinked my eyes to search again. By then they must have opened enough to the chilly dark to see a shape just past the light, apparently kneeling at the foot of my bed. Susceptible as I've always been to what seem like brief meetings with the dead (in my mind, understand—not ghosts in chains), I thought it might be Larkin again. That truly warmed me. Better Lark's ghost than nothing at all for nevermore. I meant to set him at earthly ease, so I said "You managing all right where you are?"

He said "I was hoping you'd ask me nearer." It was not quite Larkin's voice but close.

Recalling the night just after the drowning and Ferny's coming to me in the dark with a sound like Lark, I thought again it had to be Fern. Honest to God, I didn't think of Palmer. And I don't know why—I was generally sore in my back and legs from the afternoon's ride. I must have been unusually confused. Anyhow I said "Come as near as you need to."

In the gap between my words and his moving, I must have lain back and dozed on off. I'm still a deep sleeper, old as I am.

When I woke the Good Shepherd light was dark, and I could feel the close heat of a body. So I rolled to my left side and reached out an arm. It touched the warm flesh of a big hand and wrist. Only then did I think I understood. I said "Is it Palmer?"

He waited. "Is Palmer who you want it to be?" He was whispering but clearly.

I took a long moment to run through the possible harm we could do. By then I knew that, whatever came, nothing would prove to be more discouraging than turning my back on a maybe last chance. I rolled to my right side, slid over to the far-wall edge of the bed and lowered the covers. Then I said "I think I want it to be you, Palmer—yes, thank you."

So it proved to be. He entered the warm space where I'd been with a silent neatness almost as if he had no body but was all mind and heart.

When he'd settled, though, I could guess he was lying on his left side facing me. I was likewise almost sure he was bare from the waist up anyhow. Still I was not scared and, to my surprise then and there, not excited. After all I'd spent many nights in the same bed with near-grown boys—my brothers whenever we'd have extra company and beds ran short. The main difference now was that I felt as if something which had been coming at me from very far off, the whole length of my life, was finally arriving. No drums or trumpets, no rose-colored fountains or phosphorus flares.

Yet nothing in my pitiful training nor all my highest expectations of grace and blessing nor any rumors that I'd heard prepared me for what to do or say the next moment. So I said something true that Palmer would nonetheless laugh about forever, just between him and me. I told him I was sore as a bad thumb from Arabel's trot. We'd trotted a good part of the way back this afternoon.

Palmer said "Well I'm told this might hurt the healthiest body on Earth if it's her first time. You want me to leave?"

I told him I didn't.

He said "It's my first, I want you to know."

I could just believe him, just barely believe him—I wanted to of course. For part of an instant, my mind heard Miss Olivia and what she'd mentioned about white men and their secret black girls. I well knew Palmer had been around black girls, in some way or other, all his life. I guessed he could have pretty much what he wanted if he only said the word in the right dark shack or under the stars. After all, white girls were scarcer than polar bears this far in the sticks. But that moment passed. From then on, I just believed his claim; and I told him as much.

Then he waited so long in the total dark that I kept sliding to sleep beside him. He finally started to lift my gown and feather his fingers up and down me.

I hadn't been touched in any such places by man or boy since Father tried to sponge me and Leela down when I was five and Muddie had gone to bury her sister two nights away—innocent sponging, I'm speaking about. My father never moved a finger to harm us, not that I ever heard of.

Anyhow after many minutes of light brushes and lingerings, Palmer moved onward to his main purpose.

＊　　　　　＊　　　　　＊

The first few minutes hurt, yes, a lot. It may have hurt well beyond the start, but pain has never been frightening to me. And as later, with the pains of childbirth, I likely forgot any serious suffering. Again growing up in a sizable family with boys and men of assorted ages, I'd luckily had no cause to think that anything a man might want from me could leave me bereft or even worse off than I'd ever been. Then that first pain stopped eventually, and my mind eased down. Young as he was Palmer moved slowly, and I gradually understood that a decent young man was way inside me searching for something I apparently had in my power to give.

Considering who he was—whose brother, whose son—and what I'd learned about him today, I chose to try giving Palmer what he was after, whatever that was or might prove to be. I was far from knowing. And not that I knew a thing about the simplest skills in stroking a likable man to his ease. Simple as I was I guessed it was up to my mind to help him toward his goal.

So in my mind's eye then, plain as anything I'd ever watched, I saw myself as taller than Palmer by at least a hand's breadth, holding him firmly by his left wrist and gently tugging him on down that rock ledge we'd been on today and into the sea. I've mentioned not ever seeing the real sea except in a silent movie or two. But the idea of it—waves and surf and a merciful undertow—seemed appropriate to me as a place to lead him.

And I got him there. Palmer had thanked me and drifted off into silence which may have been true sleep before I thought the next idea. It came as a boiled-down message to myself in six words—*Roxanna Dane, you're a mother now.* I knew it as surely as I knew I was leaving this boy not long after daybreak and going home to my parents' house where in nine months' time I would give them a grandchild. They were yet to have one.

In the weeks to come, I'd learn I was wrong. It was Leela who told me that every time a man and woman join doesn't necessarily end in a child. I hadn't been altogether clear on that point. But for those long weeks as fall got bleaker and winter hove in, I had all the thoughts I'd have in later years, making real children in my actual body.

When I woke into that last morning at the Slades', Palmer had left my room at some point without another word to me. As I washed in the chilly water from a pitcher I'd drawn with my own hands at the well yesterday, I asked myself how much of the night I'd dreamt or hoped into being. There were signs on the bedding that something had happened which involved more than me, but my lower body didn't look too different or feel truly changed.

My mind was clear on what it thought had happened, but it had no other tangible proof. I went so far as to get down and look in the curls of dust beneath the bed for any string or burr that might have dropped off whatever clothes Palmer wore when he entered, if he did. And all I found was a single dime that might have belonged to anybody. I still have it somewhere.

Finally as I combed my hair in the scabby old mirror, I studied my face and eyes as closely as if I might be a vicious stranger, some creature who—for mysterious reasons I'd never met with on Earth before—intended me harm or death itself. Plainly I wasn't any such person now. But to me all the same, I looked unquestionably changed and new, even stranger than I looked the night Lark died—so strange that I felt an actual fear of heading downstairs and having the major and Miss Olivia see a person so altered they'd scarcely know her at close range. The difference involved my eyes entirely. They were opened now on deeper places than anywhere I'd ever been.

But nobody mentioned the change when I walked down into the kitchen. Miss Olivia was drinking coffee at the table, the major and Fern were drawing some kind of map of their plans to wander, and Coy was pounding a huge piece of round steak to batter and fry. As I said country breakfasts in those hard days were serious business. No sign of Palmer but that was not new with all his lone-scout secret ways.

His absence though did feel a little cold. Of course I'd have no more mentioned him than I'd have stood there and told my story from the dead of last night, but oddly Miss Olivia took her first look at me and said "Palmer Slade expressly told me to give you his thanks when you left." She often spoke of members of her family by their full names.

So I took her lead and said "Where is Palmer?"

"Oh riding the wind on a homemade glider for all I know." Miss Olivia actually looked to the window as if he might fly by in the clouds.

Coy said "No such a thing. Gone to get my medicine."

Miss Olivia said "You out of that medicine this soon again?"

"Run out of it once a month," Coy said, "—every month of the year on the very same day, and don't nobody but Palmer remember." Coy took frequent teaspoons of some black syrup for her rheumatism, and the nearest drugstore was long miles away.

So in case I'd worried about embarrassment, I wouldn't have to lay eyes on Palmer today. That chance at a calm pause might have relieved me. To the contrary though I felt, like a grievous surge in my throat, the bitterest taste I'd known till now. Some vital part of my mind and body was not here near me, and I felt cold fear to be leaving without it.

But when Father and I reached home before nine that same cold morning, Palmer had already stopped by the house and left me a small package wrapped in white paper and tied with green string. The moment Muddie put it in my hands, I knew it was Woodall Drug Company's wrapping. I didn't ask her who had left it, and she didn't volunteer the name or take the chance to tease me at all. That made me wonder if Muddie could see the change I'd noticed in my eyes and face.

If so she didn't allude to that either, though oddly she did take both my hands and open them palm up to study them closely. Whether she saw anything, I never learned; but nobody on Earth ever knew me better. At the moment Leela had walked into town to fetch the mail; so I was free to go to our room, shut the door and open the package in that brief privacy.

It was a big box of Jordan Almonds which I remembered telling Palmer were my favorite candy. I searched the box itself and the wrappings but found no card, note or signature. So when I'd sat there and eaten two almonds to sweeten my throat, I was forced to hide them way back in the chifforobe while I unpacked my few worn duds and got myself ready to face my sister and Muddie again.

For whatever reason they were kind and welcoming, folding me back into my old place and my round of chores as easily as if I'd never been gone. There was not one syllable of teasing or probing and, oddest of all, not a single mention of Palmer's visit with the candy box. Even when Father came home for the noon meal, no Slade was mentioned except Miss Olivia and the pitiful major.

By the time night came and Leela and I undressed together for an early bed with no word of Palmer, I'd begun to wonder if he'd stopped by at all; or were the almonds just a welcoming gift from Muddie herself or somebody else? That began to seem more and more likely. Yet no other member of my family but Fern had the slightest knowledge of what had passed between Larkin and me on the day he drowned nor surely of anything between me and Palmer these past two weeks.

*   *   *

In the following days then—with no word from Palmer and nothing but a letter of thanks from Miss Olivia—I began to turn inward and dwell on myself, always a grave mistake. After their original lack of talk about Palmer and the other Slades, Muddie or Father or occasionally Leela would mention the family and wonder how they were. Ferny wrote us less than no news except to say that the major was paying him now for his time. That was meant to assuage Father's growing sense that Fern had abandoned him at the store and for no gainful purpose.

But again nobody touched on my feelings, and nobody seemed to notice what I could feel—that I was beginning to pick up speed in the long process of sliding down into a siege of the blues. It had been a tendency with me since childhood. I'd forge ahead strongly through trouble at school or a spell of bad weather and deep bronchitis. Then one day when I seemed better off, a sudden cloud like black ink in water would burst on my mind. And I'd be left half blind in spirit with no other hope or visible help than the sense that I was bound for death and must fight my way free. Since nobody among my family or friends had ever mentioned feeling anything more than *blue* on occasion, I had nobody to tell my failing to— nobody, God knew, to ask for help.

This time as always I was baffled to know what had flung me down. Of course I'd lived through Larkin's death, then two weeks in a sad cold house, Palmer's visit to me that final night, my wrong conviction that his child was in me, his refusal to contact me by mail or pay the briefest visit. But no single item from that sizable list seemed sufficient to be the weight that crushed me.

I'd realized in my first few days at home that I'd misunderstood about the child—my monthly came on normal schedule. In the calm at home I'd realized that much of what I felt for Larkin was just the excitement of meeting a likable face and limbs on the edge of vanishing. Palmer's late-night visit—for all my training in morals and manners—had never felt like a wrong in God's eyes, much less my own. And it was surely his right— Palmer's, that is—to disappear into empty space if he had nothing left to tell me or ask me for.

But down I went and again nobody noticed. Once Muddie paused in the front hall, looked at me for maybe three frowning seconds and said "You might need a fall tonic, darling." *Tonics* in those days, spring or fall, generally meant some thunderous strong dread laxative. Free bowels were the absolute secret to health for all my forebears. I just told Muddie No and went my way.

So from then on I managed to have a nervous breakdown and hide the fact, a common enough skill in those old days when you could find your normal-acting aunt or your quiet brother hanging dead by the neck from the stable loft—self-killed and nobody understood the reason—or what was more likely, sitting on the front porch and facing the road without a murmur for the length of a whole long blistering summer till they finally turned your way and said "It's a cooler day, praise God" or stood up and walked downtown for the first time in maybe ninety days.

I stayed clean and well combed, I did my light chores, I never burst out into public tears nor otherwise complained nor tongue-lashed a soul. Whenever I lay down though for an afternoon pause or walked into town for a spool of darning thread, I realized in lone-wolf silence how utterly gray the world had turned in every particular and how entirely beyond belief it was that I was expected to live on here for fifty more years of this much numbness. What had swamped me was not pain exactly but a lack of feeling so complete as to hurt worse than any kind of death I'd witnessed anyhow.

I got so bad—but still in secret—that when Muddie and Leela began to plan for a big Thanksgiving weekend with my elder brother and his wife back home, plus food for thousands, I gave the first thought of my life to an *ending* (the ending of me by my own hand). In those simpler days suicide was well known even in small towns. There was lots of rope around as I said. Every kitchen had its can of Red Devil lye or other strong poisons, every master bedroom had a loaded pistol on the mantel, every house had a deep well of endless water for anybody with the will to jump.

I could sit by a window, and did more than once, in a really hard afternoon and plan my ending to the last small detail as painlessly as you might plan a trip to return a library book overdue by no more than a day. I finally settled on the Monday morning after Thanksgiving. I'd rig a strong rope from the loft of the stable and be hanging quiet, with no drop of blood, when Father found me by dinnertime. I thought so long and precisely about it that even today I could paint you pictures of how it would look and tell you every word they'd say at the sight of my corpse. The nearer I got the righter it felt. And so it still does in memory now.

*   *   *

What stopped me was Ferny's last postcard before the late November home-coming. It asked could he bring Palmer Slade back with him. They'd sleep on pallets for a night or two, help with the company and leave late Sunday. Miss Olivia was forcing them out of her way since some of the major's descendants by his first wife were threatening to visit, and she wanted them to see old Major at his frailest since they'd all but deserted him in recent years. I collected the card myself from the post office on that morning's first mail, and walking home with it I thought at first I must speed up my plans and not have to face Palmer after his silence.

But by the time I neared the house, God himself or some branch of grace had flashed a beam toward me, and I'd remembered my dark night with Palmer as clearly as if we'd been in warm sunlight beside a real sea. At first it failed to touch my stunned feelings. But just as my right foot took the first step up toward our back door, I heard Palmer's voice in my head again as it spoke the final sentence before I gave him permission to join me bare in the night—"You want me to leave?" I knew that I didn't. I wanted to see him, and I somehow knew he'd ask for my life.

With the card in my hand, I opened the kitchen door at last on Mud-die's energetic voice. And as shy as I've always been of calling anything a *sin*, I thought what a sin it was to let such a small thing drive you crazy and then let another thing as small as a postcard haul you back from the far edge of death. But as my mother reached to take the postal news from me, I said the word *Thanks* once, aloud in the room.

My older brother arrived on the late Wednesday train for Thanksgiving. Ferny and Palmer came early Thursday morning in Major's car. And the weekend went more smoothly than expected by anyone, though we all over-ate like hogs in Heaven and despite three or four of the usual sharp exchanges and sulks that every family reunion inspires if it lasts any more than fifteen minutes.

Palmer and Fern spent a good while riding around town or walking off meals. When they were indoors Palmer was pleasant-faced but mostly as silent as in his own home. As I watched his hands particularly, I came even closer to wondering if I'd dreamt the whole night of our joining together. Had those enormous powerful hands really ever touched me in curiosity and need, really reached my *quick*?

        *   *   *

My elder brother left at three on Sunday afternoon. Our liberation from that many hours of his talking wife and peculiar daughter felt like the end of centuries of slavery. Ferny had mentioned earlier that he and Palmer promised to be back up at the Slades' by sundown. So when time got on past four-thirty and Palmer had still not said a word to me in privacy, I told myself I'd go back to being my lone-wolf self again any minute now and to get ready for it—not to slide once more down as deep as I'd gone. I told myself *You learn to be single or cut your throat quick.*

But at that same instant, the boys were drinking coffee in the kitchen. I was washing the white turkey platter, bigger than West Virginia on the map, when something made me turn and take a last glance at Palmer's hands. And something about their healthy color, the warm blood in them, told me at last *You didn't dream a thing. Palmer Slade came to you.* When I looked up at his face, his eyes caught me and I must have flushed scarlet.

As I finished the platter, he came up quietly behind me and said "Let's get a quick last breath of fresh air." *Fresh air* in those days was thought to be the finest medicine available so long as you didn't partake it at night. Night air was lethal from the instant of darkness to the first streak of dawn.

Muddie and Father were in the front room. Leela was somewhere else as well. So I met Palmer's look and said "You think it's worth doing in the short time you've got?"

He thought and then very gravely said "I do, yes, lady."

I told him in that case I was game.

Palmer chose our path and we walked into town, took a turn round the courthouse tree that had stood there for three hundred years (so Father claimed) and headed back without having said more than thirty words each. We'd even passed the Methodist church which my family attended, and home was in sight before Palmer stopped and moved so close to my face I could smell his characteristic odor like distant vanilla flavoring, a favorite of mine.

He said "I'm apologizing in real shame, Anna."

I told him he owed me nothing on Earth.

But his broad hand waved me silent in no uncertain terms.

"I've treated you harshly with my long silence, and I want you to know exactly why before I let Ferny drive me home."

I said I'd listen and stood while he braced himself.

At that instant a smile was as far from his face as the tigers of Asia. But he finally said "I've waited this long to be sure I could speak the real truth to you. And I know I can now." Our hands were separate at each of our sides. He seemed to reach out for my left wrist, then abandoned the try. What he said was "Could you forget Lark ever breathed and just live with me?"

I said "No sir."

Palmer said "Why not?"

I said "See, Larkin was kind to me. And we all watched him die that sudden clean way. No, Palmer, I'll see Lark's face till I die. That's all there is to it."

Palmer thought about that. "But that's truly all? You'll just see him sometimes in your mind's eye?"

I suspected it might be halfway a lie, but I nodded and said that sounded right. "My mind's eye, yes."

"Will you marry me then?"

It occurred to me that I'd given Palmer everything else I owned that somebody else hadn't got claims on. And that was no more than the duty to love and help my parents, my sister and brothers if they should need me down the long road of the future we'd get. That felt as normal as the mist I was breathing out in the cold air. I could still be married and do all that. So I said "Yes. When?"

It was Palmer who said "My mother asks us to wait till we've passed the first anniversary of Larkin drowning."

That also was normal and perfectly acceptable given the way families mourned back then, never less than twelve months. I said "October 9th then—1921?"

Palmer nodded, still solemn. Finally he took my wrist and made a curious little figure in my palm, round as a ring. But he offered me no engagement band. The jewelry stores of America hadn't yet made that a compulsory part of being betrothed.

I wondered plainly inside my mind *Will we live to turn that circle he made into actual gold?* But I said the word "October" again.

And Palmer thanked me before I could say any thanks of my own.

So I wished him many happy years to come and asked if he would keep it a secret till I'd got my own feelings under control. I'd mentioned being under the weather here lately, but I'd never hinted at the depth of my blues.

Palmer said "That sounds fair at least, but Mother will want to know as soon as possible."

I told him I'd write him in no more than ten days and give the signal for him to tell his mother. Then he could come back here before Christmas and get my father's permission and Muddie's. When Palmer nodded his acceptance of that, I felt entirely different from how I'd ever felt in the past except for maybe once—those very few minutes I'd sat with Larkin Slade by the Roanoke River in fall sunlight. I thought it was happiness. And I guess I still do, though I've known my share of happiness from numerous creatures in the long years since.

Standing by the church where I trusted we'd marry, Palmer also looked like a whole new person. I searched what I could see of his face for the source of the change. But apart from heavier brows and eyelids, a sign of maturing, I could find no novelty. Then it occurred to me that the change lay somehow in the sudden freedom he was plunging into at this keen moment. Maybe for the first time since Lark was born, with his special gifts of face and voice, Palmer had struck out on his own life—no trace of a brother to steal his light, no finer head and shoulders near him to blank his goodness. And he did look all but splendid as I watched him take me by the elbow now and guide me home, a path I knew like the hills and very dim valleys of my mind.

THREE

Neither one of my parents objected at all, and even Leela seemed ready to celebrate what appeared to be her sister's good luck. I teased her and said she was only glad I'd be leaving the room we'd shared so long, giving her all the space for her endless wardrobe. That made her eyes water, and she told me something I was pleased to hear for the first time ever. She claimed that I was the person on Earth she admired most, and she said I was good right down to the core of my mind and soul.

As I mentioned I'd heard that claim before, but with utter sincerity I didn't hesitate to tell her that any such idea was as far off target as she'd ever got. I meant it too and time proved me right. More than ever I knew where the ruts and cracks ran through my being. And I understood what a big proportion of my deeds and words was meant to strengthen my own frail hands in grasping the world.

I've said that, according to Palmer at least, Miss Olivia and Major approved the marriage plan. Miss Olivia wrote me a single kind letter, saying she looked expectantly toward the day when I'd be back with her. And Ferny's rare postcards kept repeating how often Major asked for me— *When is that girl coming?*

Palmer and I had never discussed where we'd be living. But from the start I had high hopes that we'd be on our own right away. We'd have our own house or a few rented rooms with several miles of distance anyhow from each of our families. In his visits to me, Palmer still never brought up the question of where. And I didn't feel it was my place to barge in and start making rules. One thing I did though—resisted all of Palmer's invitations to go back up to the river and spend a few days at his homeplace again.

I told him I'd like to wait on that till we were truly married. He didn't object or ask for more reasons, and Miss Olivia never wrote another word about needing to see me before the wedding. It crossed my mind that she might already be subject to feeling like a mother-in-law. After all she'd never yet surrendered a son to another woman. Palmer would be the first live child she'd risk losing hold of, and every fact I knew about her was proof in advance of how she'd fight the loss.

In those days where I lived anyhow, the weddings of normal white people were nothing like the Roman circuses you see on every church corner today. It didn't seem all that huge an event—two people deciding to live together till one of them died way down the road or week after next. That was pretty much what you expected to get, that and the children that generally come in such circumstances. Surely no cause for bankrupting Father and driving Muddie to nervous collapse just to do what humans have done for several million years. So as we got on down to August 1921, Muddie had to remind me that she and I ought to see the dressmaker soon and speak to our pastor about which day would be convenient for the service.

The seamstress was well known to be a little *off*, as people used to say. Nothing loud or raving but slow in the comprehension department and unnaturally kind, though a wizard with her fingers. Even after you'd picked your pattern and fabric, you had to keep dropping in to remind her of your expectations and the date beyond which you couldn't use the dress except as a shroud for your eventual grave. She'd done a fair amount of sewing for Leela's various dances and long house parties with friends elsewhere, but she'd scarcely tightened a button for me. Yet I liked her immediately and took every chance to call at her house whenever I thought she might not mind a visit.

Her name was Betsy Magee, an old maid maybe sixty or so. Not only a spinster, she had no visible kin of any sort but lived alone in half of a four-room house no bigger than a rich child's outdoor dollhouse. Like ours and most of the houses around us till the 1940s, her house had no electric power. So all her fine work had to be done in daylight. If the sun was shining—summer or winter, boiling or freezing—Betsy would sit on her porch and bring the cloth right up to her eyes for hours on end. She was near blind as well. When I'd stop by she'd say "Let me tell you one long good story. Then you go your way and leave me working." And while she told it, she'd go on stitching with the satin or muslin touching her nose.

Then she told me a story that I'd heard parts of but never entirely. It involved the death of a distant cousin of mine, Arthur Straughan. He'd left home young to pursue his musical talents in Baltimore. A lonely soul who never married or found a mate of any description, so far as was known, Arthur came home the summer he was thirty years old, sat up every night till nearly dawn playing "not very attractive" music on the piano and harp and was heard to have frequent shouting matches with his dope-fiend brother. So on the noon of July Fourth, he walked across a bare field to Betsy Magee's, took a piece of green chalk out of his pocket, drew an outline of his body on the front porch floor, thrust a pistol into his mouth and blew off his head.

With the clean precision of a master musician, he fell straight backward into the plan of his body in green on the floor and landed inside the line at every point. No one ever knew how he managed it. Betsy had been rolling the edges of scarves at the time (summer scarves in silk) and when she heard the one shot fired, she took an eight-foot-long white scarf to the door and looked. When she saw it was Arthur—and saw his brother running toward her over the field—she threw that white silk over Arthur's ruined head to spare family feelings.

When Betsy got that far in the story, she looked up at me and said "You run on home now. Your dress'll be ready before you are."

I stood but paused one moment to ask her "Why did he do it?"

Betsy knew at once, her version at least. "God cut him off at the root, the dry root." Then she beamed a wide smile.

I said "But on your porch—how cruel."

Betsy's smile barely faded as she said "Wait'll you taste how cruel God can get."

And when I was almost out her front door, she called again after me "Maybe he knew I was tough enough to take it."

I've never been sure whether *he* was Arthur Straughan or God. In any case I told Betsy she was very likely right. And all the way home, I said a plain prayer asking only that I never taste pain in any such quantity and that my roots stay green long enough to branch into some life better than mine or Palmer's even.

The final weeks at home went as smoothly as I could have hoped. Palmer's visits every second weekend were calm and welcome with his usual sparse talk and long rides and strolls. Like my father—and long before the country went wild on the subject of exercise—Palmer had figured out for himself that whatever pressed his mind or body could best be eased by onward movement through the clean open air. And while it meant a good deal less to me, I was always ready to join him just to watch his face clear up like a gray sky late in the day as it purifies itself for sunset.

But far as we went and deep as we often were plunged into privacy, miles from others, Palmer and I never touched in earnest again in all the months of our engagement. I wouldn't have stopped him if he'd felt the need, but he never mentioned any such pressure. And I took the chance whenever I could, with Leela and two other girls and with our cook, to find out anything more I might need to know on the subject of what men's bodies required of their wives and how to respond.

It would scarcely be possible for young people now to imagine how hard it was in my day to get any clear and reliable advance word on sex in general. And with all the conflicting stories I'd heard, I was left half wondering if Muddie would offer me any guidance. She was having a good spell of health and was loving her duties, but she sailed through every opportunity at maternal instruction till she realized I was having my final monthly as what she assumed was an untouched maiden, ten days before the wedding.

It was too wet and chilly a day for a walk, so she came to mine and Leela's room where we were resting after dinner with the shades pulled down. She set a straight chair in the midst of the floor halfway between our two single beds. Then she took her seat, looked to us both and said "This is mainly for Anna with marriage so close. But since I scarcely know how to say it, I'll do my best here once for all and give each one of you the little I've gathered on a matter nobody ever coached me on, not for so much as two quick seconds."

Of course Leela and I had vague ideas of what might be coming. But with this sudden arrival of the unexpected, it was more than Leela could easily bear. First she gave a high laugh, followed by a real moan. Then she flipped onto her stomach and sank her whole face deep into a pillow.

I faced the ceiling to spare Muddie's eyes meeting mine as she spoke.

She took a long pause and said "I'm fairly certain both of you have understood, from the Bible and maybe some magazine reading, that men and women must unite together before God's purpose for all can be fulfilled."

From her pillow Leela said "*All?*" Despite her concern for clothes and hair, she'd often said she was giving much thought to an old maid's life.

I had to laugh too.

Muddie had the grace to join me.

Then Leela chimed in again.

So when we'd all composed ourselves, Muddie skated on through the rest of her speech at a breakneck clip. "You'll see all the signs that men are truly hounded by their need. There seems very little they can do about it. Your chosen husband will demonstrate on your wedding night, or soon thereafter if you're too exhausted and he's sympathetic, what's natural and expected. Don't be alarmed when he shows his parts in an urgent condition, generally reddish. They're as natural to him as your eyes are to you. And above all try not to be too scared when you feel a sharp pain. Don't yell or weep if you see a little blood. It's all God's will, give or take a few blunders if he's young too or has been drinking recently. And if you're a cheerful cooperative mate, it will only bind him to you tighter in bands strong as steel."

Leela sat up, propped on her left arm. "Muddie, what exactly is rape?"

Muddie said "Well to the best of my information, it's love gone utterly wrong. But don't give rape so much as a moment's thought, not in *our* world—it can't happen here—and don't scare Anna."

I told them both they couldn't scare me. It hadn't occurred to me that the legal transactions of sex might prove delightful—interesting, yes, but hardly delightful—yet I was at least on the verge of seeing how funny this whole concern of all creatures was, though it would take me years more to confirm it.

Leela was far from satisfied and held out for further clarification. "How does any girl know when that border's crossed—I mean, if God includes pain and bleeding in his will?"

I half rose as well. "*You'll* know," I said.

Muddie said "Anna, hush. You're out of your depth."

To have told her I wasn't would have shocked her too hard. So I took the rebuke and lay back flat.

As Muddie left the room, she touched my arm. And when I looked up, she was streaming tears.

I said "Is it worse than you've told me?"

Muddie's head shook slowly and this time she whispered as if to spare Leela. "For me, never, no. Your father's an angel."

With the slender knowledge I possessed from my one night, I could see viewpoints from which that was laughable—angel visits in the dark, not remotely mentioned in scripture—but I kept my own counsel and thanked her sincerely. I couldn't recall a prior time when Muddie had tried that hard to be of practical help to her only daughters, and I know Leela got none when her time came.

The date we'd set was November 8th, a Saturday. After giving Palmer the early date of October 9th, I'd come to my senses and realized what a rush that looked like—twenty-four hours more than a year since Larkin's last breath—so we postponed it a month. But I'd been ready since late October. Miss Olivia was due to arrive on the Friday to help me and Muddie. Ferny and Palmer would come on Saturday morning with the major and old Coy. The very simple service was meant to be at five in the afternoon. We'd race back to my house, change our clothes, hug our families goodbye and climb on the six-thirty train for Washington, D.C. Palmer had not yet made thorough plans for where we'd live on our return.

I'd asked him if we couldn't rent the spare bedroom and tiny kitchen at Betsy Magee's till we got our breath and he could decide on his long-range hopes in a neutral place but not far from our kin in case we were needed. He'd come near enough to saying Yes, so I'd asked Betsy to hold the space till I knew for sure. She'd said it was ours any day of the year, which was plainly not true since she needed the rent to live her life and usually had some old man in there whom she was nursing.

That uncertainty had me worried since more and more I'd come to feel very serious indeed about that fact that I couldn't easily stay for long as a married woman in my parents' house or even the Slades'. Meek as I'd mostly been in my past life, the whole idea of marriage in my mind felt like a new and desirable freedom—a clearer leaner life than I'd ever suspected I wanted, though I craved it now. Even today, far more young women than would want you to notice seem to think of marriage as a quick shortcut up the alley to freedom. Well shame *on* em, as older women would have said in my youth and with bottomless wisdom.

Miss Olivia arrived as planned on the Friday, well before noon on the shoo-fly train. My father had been introduced to her once long years ago and told everybody far in advance how handsome she'd be. Muddie had only laid eyes on the woman at Larkin's funeral, before Miss Olivia stepped down off the train and shaded her own eyes to find us in the brilliant light. From the puzzlement on her face, you'd have thought she'd traveled eight thousand miles, not a simple eight. But she seemed glad enough to meet the family. Then to our surprise down stepped old Coy in a long black dress. There had been no warning that Coy might come this early in the plans.

So at once everybody's brows furrowed deeply, trying to picture where she might sleep. With my elder brother coming and his poodle wife, we were full-up with white people not to mention other tints.

Mother winked to me and mouthed the words "She can sleep at Edna's." Edna was our cook at the time and lived fairly nearby.

But Miss Olivia headed us off. "Coy decided late yesterday that I couldn't travel on the train alone. She can sleep on any kind of cot beside me. She's clean as a river rock"—all of which was said with Coy standing there pretending she was deaf.

Any such arrangement was so unheard of in those days, north *or* south, that Father and Muddie went pale as sheets. Leela managed to catch her laugh before it started; and I said "Surely. Welcome, Coy."

Coy called me "Miss Roxanna" for the first time and handed me a little parcel tied up in what looked like a clean handkerchief. "For your teeth," she said and pointed to her own. Then she said "Tear it open. You ain't going to like it."

It was several twigs of sassafras wood trimmed clean at one end—old-time country toothbrushes. I hadn't seen one since I was a girl and had made them myself. You chewed the clean end into near pulp and scrubbed at your teeth. I told Coy that on the contrary I liked them very much and that I'd take her gifts to the nation's capital for their first long trip. That seemed to please her.

Coy nodded. "I'm looking *forward* to you." She was in new shoes, men's brand-new hightops, stiff tough leather big and black enough for gunboats.

I told Coy how much I admired her footwear, but I understood her to be assuming that I'd be moving with Palmer to the country. It raised my dander and, right there surrounded by all my elders, I said "You'll be welcome wherever we are."

Miss Olivia smiled. "Coy's never been more than two miles from the river in her entire life."

Coy said "Don't need to. Nothing else worth seeing."

I was going to try to answer her, but by then Father had Miss Olivia's grip and Coy's cardboard satchel in hand so we headed home.

*   *   *

Though I walked along beside Miss Olivia the whole half mile and talked to her easily, in my head I couldn't make myself believe what I suddenly knew. *Tomorrow this woman will start to matter as much in my life as anybody else walking here beside us. Palmer could say we have to live with her. Any children I bear will be part hers. Strong as she so plainly is, she could crush me soon just walking past me down a dark hall or reaching toward me to take my child.* I've never known where I got such feelings that far in advance of close contact—maybe because the mother I'd known was soft as down feathers and helpless in the world—but the future would prove that I wasn't far wrong.

By the time we reached the front steps of my home, Miss Olivia had noticed something grim in my looks. She leaned and whispered as she took the first step—"Don't give it a minute's worry. You can do it."

To this day I've never been sure I understood her—what she meant by *it* and the promise I could do it. Had she read my silent mind that quickly? Or was it just something you were always safe to say to a bride? I've never known the answer, so I still can't say if I managed to do whatever she promised or whether I failed in one more expectation fixed on me by people far stronger than I was then or ever became.

The rest of that last day was calmer than anybody had expected. The weather went on bright and warm. Miss Olivia and Coy joined Muddie and Edna in the kitchen preparing the food they'd serve friends tomorrow after the service while Palmer and I raced to catch our train. The soft-pitched weave of their four voices presiding over tasks they'd done forever but still tried hard to bring to perfection was steady as the sound of a rocking chair from my early childhood.

That complicated music plus the thought that every motion they made was meant to result in human pleasure of the simplest most disposable kind—from palate to belly—was likewise consoling to me in light of how eager I'd always been to leave as few tracks as possible behind me in human affairs. I say *consoling* but in honesty I already knew in the cold of my bones that these four women had reached a goal I'd never reach—a tame contentment or maybe surrender, valuable as platinum but closed to me for whatever reasons.

*   *   *

Shortly after we were back from the depot, Leela withdrew to our room for a cause that mildly surprised me. When I looked in on her after she vanished, she'd peeled to her slip and was lying in genuine sorrow under the afghan I'd made her.

I could tell in an instant when Leela was pretending, the same way she could pierce any lie I told from a thousand yards in the dark. She was plainly sincere now. So I sat beside her and asked how I could help.

She said "No way except stay *here* beside me, turn the clock back ten years and freeze it there."

I knew exactly what she meant and leaned to whisper that, more than a little, I wished I could walk out now and *obey* her—call the whole thing off and live on at home.

Leela thought I meant it more than I did. And through her tears she said "You *can*." So I had to tell her I could but I wouldn't. That's always the hardest thing to hear, but now it was true.

She had the grace to nod and try to grin.

Then once I kissed her, I had to go back to packing my bag for the fortieth time and checking my eyes again and again in Muddie's big mirror to see if I could find any trace of a reason to think this marriage was a wrong committed on Larkin or God or Palmer or anyone else live or dead. I honestly had to conclude from appearances that No, I wanted to stride right on into Palmer's hands.

Once my elder brother and his wife had come in safely on the evening train, I felt I not only could but should withdraw for the night and pray if not sleep. By then Leela had recovered herself and was fascinated by our brother's wife and what Leela thought were her stylish skills as a milliner—she made her own hats, and I'll have to grant they looked homemade.

So I went back to our room alone. And once I was under the covers and the light out, I managed to say the first half of the Lord's Prayer before I slid off into sleep like a plummet and was many miles gone when the door came open and Father stood there in the dark with a lamp.

Lit from underneath as he was, his face was as different as in our childhood when he'd tell us ghost stories, leaning to the lamp to look weird and ghostly.

Not entirely sure it was him, I said "I went to sleep in my prayers—excuse me. I must have been exhausted."

"You can sleep again in just a minute, but can I have a second to tell you something?" The voice was Father's beyond a sane doubt.

I told him "Surely" and moved to the far side to give him room at the edge of my mattress.

He set the lamp on the floor, turned to check that Leela was asleep, then took a seat beside me. Before he said a word, he gently stretched his whole length down outside the cover, lying on his back. Like that he waited so long in silence I thought he'd dozed away.

I took the opportunity to look toward his profile and study its line with the lamplight behind it. He was fifty-five years old and a little overweight. But lying down as he was, his face slimmed remarkably and he looked very little older than the parent I'd always known. Known and loved if love has any meaning in this present time when family love is so suspect and tarnished. If my father ever did a vicious deed, I never heard of it, though I well know of course that—like all white men of his time in our world—he accepted the local view of black skin.

I'll break my story here to write down something that has mattered to me. If white men in my day did badly by Negroes, white women did worse. Even Muddie, kind in most ways, would ruffle her feathers and rush out hard-eyed at any hint of what she called *insubordination* in any black soul—male, female or child.

Like most white women of her place and time, our mother patrolled that single boundary sleeplessly. White women in fact ran the whole dark boat of racial hate. They stood at the wheel anyhow. Or was it racial *fear*? Fear would feel like a stronger candidate to me if I'd ever heard in all my years one single threat any black person made to any one white. The fact that from childhood I silently disagreed with my people's views on most everything connected with color was no great credit to my white soul. I had just been helped and loyally befriended by so many black people, all ages and kinds, that by the age of reason I took their side.

Of course I may have been touched then, as a few other times, by God's own grace far past my deserts. If so I'm compelled to add that again, and to my permanent shame, I took the sizable gift in silence and barely hinted by so much as a syllable how wrong I thought my dear family were, how close to Hell fire not to speak of our church, our teachers, all our kin and every white friend we had. Not that my one voice would have made the least difference to people who'd *lost* a long war on their own home ground with their empty children watching.

Still a person who feels compelled to judge those older times, from these years later, might ask him or her self what normal-seeming acts of the present—acts we perform with slim sense of blame, like fouling the Earth with the waste of our lives and making more children than the Earth should contain—will look years hence like felonies and evils. Every soul alive is, right now, engaged in some dark offense against goodness and life but is too blind to see.

So that night, back in mine and Leela's old bedroom, Father seemed to be what he still is in my memory, a cause for gratitude in my heart. And it seemed entirely natural to ask myself in that silence whether I ought to leave him or not. When he still didn't speak there dim beside me, it's what I finally asked him. "You ready for me to go my way?"

He waited longer. "My darling, you very *sure* it's your way?"

The truth was "No" and I said it plainly.

That set him off on another long silence. Finally he said "You know you've asked me to give you away. How can I do that when you're not sure?" He hadn't turned to face me yet, thank God—I might well have broken.

I said "I'm the one that must live with what I do." Then I half turned to face the line of his forehead, nose and mouth. "Don't you see it that way too?"

He nodded but still didn't turn.

I said "We know Palmer Slade's a fine boy."

Father said "He's a man. You're clear about that?" When I didn't answer Father said "Your mother has explained things to you?"

I knew what he meant. But I couldn't say Yes, though the last thing I wanted was for him to explain now.

Father said "Palmer Slade will be taking from you a thing that you can only give once. You better lie here all night if necessary and convince your-self you want him to have it. If you don't find that you can answer him Yes with a peaceful heart, then tell me at daybreak. I'll call this business off and clear these strangers out of here in no time so you can start over with the life you want and the people who love you."

I had to ask if he could just turn and face me.

He slowly did but then we both were in pitch dark. The lamp that he'd set beside us on the floor was stroking the ceiling but with no reflection onto him or me.

Eventually I spoke to where I guessed his eyes were. "I'll love you more than anybody still."

And he said "Please do." In another dark minute he changed that slightly. He faced the ceiling and again I could see the side of his pale honest features as he started to say the last thing he knew. "I know it's no longer my right to say it, but you please love me as much as you can." Then he got up and left.

I think I may have slept a total of thirty seconds the rest of the night.

Just after dawn on the day itself, I was offered again the chance my father had held out to me. I was awake in a normal housedress drinking coffee back in the kitchen with Edna, Coy and Muddie. Father was out attending to chores, and Miss Olivia was still in her room. We expected Palmer and Ferny to drive in with Major Slade by ten o'clock. But just before seven old Coy was the first to hear a noise in the yard. She said "Some news coming here. Everybody get braced" and pointed through the wall. By then we'd all heard a loud engine close by, then the sound of it strangling.

I stood to go see, but Muddie stopped me—"You can't meet the public." She went toward the front door, and I stood waiting just inside the kitchen to hear what I could. I somehow knew a big dark door had opened or shut in all our lives, and here were the messengers.

They were two young boys—one white, one black, neither one more than twelve. They'd driven the Slades' car right through our yard and stopped at the porch. The white boy was Austin Waring. The black boy was Coy's great-grandson Doncey, or so she said. She tended to think everybody was close kin to her someway. Muddie got to them before they knocked. I recognized them by the sound of their voices and could hear every word. As straight off the mark as a bullet from a gun, Austin said "Major Slade has passed. They sent us to tell you."

Muddie was stunned but finally said "What exactly do you mean by *passed?*" Everybody on the continent of North America knew what *passed* meant.

But Doncey said "He gone, lady. *Gone.* Cold as ice in the bed when they found him this morning."

I looked back to Coy.

If she'd heard she didn't turn or pause in her work. Edna was stirring hot milk at the stove and shook her head in sorrow at me.

Coy was still unmoved, surely deafer than I knew.

So I stepped on out into the hall to see better. By then Miss Olivia had heard the voices and, in her bathrobe and long nightgown, come up beside Muddie. Miss Olivia's unbraided hair hung well below her shoulder blades in premature mourning, and her pale lips opened but then couldn't speak. So Muddie faced the white boy and said "Say it again."

Austin said "You tell em again, Doncey. Talk *plain*."

I couldn't imagine any word plainer than *gone*—is there one?

Doncey said "Old Major dead in the night. They sent us to tell you."

Miss Olivia said "Had to be another stroke."

Doncey said "They saying it was that. Your boy and Ferny told me."

Miss Olivia said "Why didn't Palmer come here to tell me—Ferny or Palmer?"

Austin said "They're all broke up. It surprised em in the night. They're needing you now."

Miss Olivia turned then as if her eyes had seen me backward through her skull. I was ten yards behind her. She faced the boys, pointed back to me and said "This woman is due to get married at five o'clock today. The last thing Major Slade would want is to stop her now."

She'd never called me a woman before, I was almost sure. I wanted to tell her "Oh no, I'll wait. You go on home." But no sound came.

Miss Olivia stood for a good half minute till she knew her mind—no sign of embarrassment that we were there waiting for her next word. When she knew her mind, she turned back to me—me not Muddie. And over that dim long space between us, she said "Nobody down here knows but us and these two boys. We'll keep our own counsel till you're safely on the train and halfway to Washington. Major Slade would have it no other way."

I pointed behind me. "Edna knows too."

Muddie said "I'll speak to Edna."

To Miss Olivia I said "But Palmer is all upset quite naturally."

Miss Olivia said "I'll send Palm a letter by these boys now. He'll be here on time."

I remember repeating where I stood *This strong woman means to steer my life from here on out*. At the time it didn't feel all that hard to bow and accept her. She was so fine to see even there in her nightclothes. And I think I very well may have made a shallow bow before I went on back to my room where Leela was sleeping still, sunk deep. I lay down flat on my bed and felt the shape of my life growing up and around me in the chill air. Something as natural as the tilt of my mind and as hopeless as the will of others to plan my course was running my fate like a child's snow sled on a vertical chute.

As ever the thought didn't feel like something I ought to stand and try to fight down. If you'd asked me then, I'd have probably said "Isn't everybody's life carved out by the hands of a thousand others, not to mention God?" If you mentioned free will, I'd have probably told you what I thought I believed, though I'd been reared Methodist—there was no such thing. Your only choice is whether to tuck your head and bear what the wind blows toward you or to meet it head-on and still feel your spine snap and all your best features stripped off clean as any peeled green stick of wood. Yet none of that left me any less ready to live through the future and face Palmer Slade if he chose to appear.

Who appeared right then was Miss Olivia. She gave a light tap on the door and stepped in. With Leela asleep she sat on the edge of my bed and whispered "You're not shaken, are you?"

I told her No but I'd miss the major.

She said "When Major was a boy in the cavalry, he learned to step over his best friends blown to bits in his path and do his next duty."

I said "You weren't even born that early."

Miss Olivia decided not to treat it as an insult. "You're right as usual but he told me ten thousand and fifty times."

"What did you tell Palmer in that note you sent?"

"The same as I'm now telling you. 'Let the dead bury the dead.' "

"Miss Olivia, that could sound very cruel to some ears."

She said "Of course it could but the words are from Jesus, not Olivia Slade. I've had to live my life against all doubters. My son is marrying you this evening. It means that much."

"To whom, please ma'm?"

Miss Olivia knew, as she generally did. "Every soul under this roof here and mine. Maybe to the angels in Heaven and the demons." She ended smiling but I saw she believed herself.

"What if Palmer refuses?"

She said "Palm never refused his mother one thing in his whole life, not till now at least."

By then I'd wondered if today's peculiar events didn't mean that Palmer had lost his courage and was using the major's death as a pretext for stalling and slowly letting me down. But would Ferny have cooperated in the plan? I even said it aloud to Miss Olivia.

Again she spoke like a grand campaigner surveying the line and counting her losses. "Ferny loved old Major more than us all. He'll be genuinely crushed. They'll be here though by midafternoon. You watch my word."

I watched and they were. At a little past three, Miss Olivia met Fern and Palmer in the yard, instructed them not to mention the news and led them on indoors to see us. Leela and Father were in the living room with me, still not knowing of any change, when I faced Palmer. I figured we weren't meant to show any sorrow. I'd got my own eyes under control.

And aside from looking a little drawn, Palmer seemed natural—he was always quiet enough for any setting but a mob. He came and kissed me lightly on the cheek.

I pressed his hand where no one could see.

He shut his eyes hard and nodded once.

It was Ferny I was worried about. For the second time in a year, Fern had lost somebody that mattered to him—somebody who'd chosen to lean on him. Ferny had always longed to bear great weight. More than any boy I've ever known, he wanted to carry his load in the world. Even as a child he'd volunteer for tasks that were rightly mine and were hard, and I'm sad to say I used him too often—hauling tubs of bath water and wood for the tin stove in mine and Leela's room.

Coming on behind Palmer as he did this day, in an old black suit of Lark's that Coy had cut down to fit a smaller frame, Fern looked like a bar of silver so cold it might conceivably burst into blue flame and blot us all out. I took both his hands, and yes they were icy.

I smiled and said "You been to the North Pole?" He didn't smile but he said "Yes ma'm. I'm still up there. Can you bring me home?"

I told him I'd make every possible effort.

Neither Father nor Leela took any hint from that of the death we were hiding.

And the two boys went on back to the kitchen to feed the hunger that follows real sorrow.

I thought it was time I went to mine and Leela's room and got my mind into whatever shape would prove necessary at five p.m. when I'd undertake to change the life I'd always led into something entirely different and longer, a grown woman's job from that hour till death.

Everybody said that Betsy Magee had outdone herself on my long dress. I could see it was lovely, and I bowed to Betsy to say as much as I came up the aisle. But I've always felt that it outdid me too. I've mentioned not considering myself a beauty. And dressed to the nines in solid white, I felt a little like a piece of live bait still twisting on the hook. *Take precious me. I look so fine.* Even I wasn't spoiled enough, though, to let it interfere with what I wanted and managed to do in the next few minutes. For the first time in my life to that point, I listened closely to the marriage vows; and they sobered me up considerably (not that I'd drunk a drop of spirits).

Those were times, to be sure, when no normal people had the outright gall to write their own private vows, taking or leaving whatever part of the customary words it suited them to say in the face of God watching and with some long-haired boy strumming his guitar by way of wedding music. Without a trace of visible doubt or silent reservation, I honestly think, Palmer and I said the old hard words. First we said *I will* when the preacher asked if we'd *forsake all others and keep only to each other as long as we both should live.* Then we each recited, like far and away the most urgent speech we'd ever make in life, *I take thee to have and to hold from this day forward for better, for worse, for richer, for poorer, in sickness and in health to love and to cherish till death do us part, according to God's holy ordinance.*

Long years of time would prove, I think, that we kept our word, give or take short fits of selfishness but no enduring unrepented betrayals so far as I learned. Yet to this very day I don't understand precisely what I was wondering about at the end of the service when Palmer and I walked down the aisle leaning on each other with me thinking only *What were we supposed to mean when we said to* have *and to* hold? *What's the real difference between* have *and* hold? And could I manage my end of that bargain? And what would Palmer Slade have to say on the day of his death about such a promise of having and holding?

God knows he held my body that night in our private compartment on the Washington train. (Weeks before he died the major had given us money for what was then called a *drawing room* on the train.) Considering how more than a year had passed since our first touch, and that we had strictly kept to ourselves through the time of mourning, I was still surprised at how little time we spent *drawing* in that tiny room and how much Palmer hurt me, though nearly every minute he was saying "I'm sorry" or "Pardon, oh pardon."

I still think I was more or less right in believing that all his feverish strength poured straight from his father's death and the pressure on him of hiding that sorrow from most of my family and every wedding guest. So I never cried out or let him hear a word of complaint. And dark as it was, he couldn't see my face.

I did understand that, for this time at least, my body and I were just an occasion for Palmer to calm himself from a shocking loss and maybe a heartbreak. But since I'd known from an early age that people are called on frequently to be the *occasion* for this or that—to be the mind or body somebody leans on to satisfy a thirst in their head or to bank off of into what comes next in their own fate—I didn't take even the worst of the pain as a personal grievance. I was young enough to be mildly honored that I was the chosen occasion for now. And I won't deny that, whatever Palmer Slade was doing and whoever I was in his mind that night, I was *interested* right through the whole wakeful darkness.

I'd been half in favor of delaying our trip and burying Major. But Palmer and his mother both said No, if we waited we'd never cut loose and travel, not any time soon. We must go right then while Miss Olivia sent for two truckloads of ice from an ice plant miles away and kept the old gentleman chilled in the smokehouse until we were back for the actual funeral. I accepted those reasons, though I knew full well it would mean us coming back in a week and settling in at the Slade place for days if not much longer.

But in the meanwhile we had our week in the nation's capital which neither one of us had seen till then. Again we traveled on the handsome gift the major had given us, and we stayed at the first-rate Willard Hotel which had slept the likes of Abraham Lincoln years before—not that Major would have liked *that* distinction. Among the small-town girls of my time, I was not so peculiar in never having stayed in a public hotel. And I'd had no experience of cities bigger than Raleigh and Richmond. Here so many years later, it may sound hopelessly countrified; but I can't help saying that, as long ago as 1921 with just a week's exposure to what was after all no giant metropolis, my young mind predicted the present fate of our pitiful country.

Understand first that I had a grand time every day of that week, as good a time as any week since. But in the midst of all the new pleasures, I did learn one thing most people still seem not to know. The human heart was, and is, not built to live in crowded quarters with more than one or two other people unrelated by blood. Ganging strangers together in cities like termites hiving or stacked like logs is asking for just what we have in the whole world today give or take the odd prairie—runaway madness, murder, rape, hatred, unthinkable cruelty to children and hundreds of thousands of souls who wind up sleeping unshielded the whole year round in the snow and rain.

I have few illusions about family life, and I'm no big defender of the deep rural world as a better form of perfection either. But I know another thing that follows from the first—thick swarms of people will one way or other be the cause of whatever end the human race undergoes. So those two certainties came from our honeymoon, not that I've offered sermons about them down through the decades—not that they proved useful knowledge at all. What are people in cities to do—all die? In any case that entire week was an odd and I'll have to say thrilling experience for me—being watched by an endless supply of strangers in the hallways and lobby of a fine hotel and then being locked entirely alone with Palmer Slade in a room that had no memories of anyone we'd known.

It was still a time when women—and honest men for that matter—didn't grow up on a daily diet of movies, books, TV stories and whispered rumors of romance or raw love. They can't sell toothpaste on TV today without the bald assurance that your sex life and chances for wealth will improve dramatically with regular use of the featured brand. The mostly pitiful silent movies and books in mine and Leela's girlhood could have left you believing that men were driven occasionally to clutch Mary Pickford closely to their heaving chests which produced sudden fainting in Mary and emergency treatment to stand her back on her feet in time for the sure-to-follow delivery of a baby and an ensuing lifetime of diapers and endless sieges of cooking.

Despite growing up in a world like that—the world of "well-brought-up" white Southern girls—I've mentioned being raised in a house with brothers on hand not to mention a father. So I was not exactly a moron on the question of the principal facts about men. Yet still, alone in a distant town in a big hotel with a man I knew very little about when it came to details of his heart and mind, I asked myself many times each day whether this was where I was meant to be and whether I'd set the course of my life on the right road to follow for fifty-odd years.

Strangely I'd really not asked such questions till now. And except for short prayers, I knew no way to answer myself but to watch the boy I'd chosen *till death did us part* and see if I could imagine who he'd turn into as time rolled past us. Could my own twists and turns match his? Could I feed his hunger? Could he stand and lift me through any more plunges that I might take into hopelessness?

In between long visits to the Capitol building, the national zoo, the old Smithsonian and the White House itself, I observed the following traits in Palmer. He was wide awake the instant his eyes broke open in the morning, no slowed-down vagueness. The high rate of burn in all his doings required that he eat a good breakfast no more than half an hour after rising from bed, that all our meals be precisely on time and that—if he'd engaged in strenuous work of any sort—he must eat a small portion of something sweet; or he'd suffer a headache that might last for days.

Considering the frequent exertions he was driven to make on my body that honeymoon week and for months thereafter, he ate a good many slices of pie and squares of fudge to spare himself pain. From then on, at all hours, I took silent care to have some good sweet available to him. And to be honest here, I never felt burdened by what Palmer required of me that early in our life. I continued relishing the sense of helping him win some ease. Truth to tell I gained my own ease from him more often than I had the grace to mention and I regret that stingy withholding of a fact that might have pleased him.

Palmer didn't want me or anybody else to ask him more than one or two sizable questions a day, questions that called for serious thinking on long-range decisions. And if he didn't answer you for whole days to come, sometimes for weeks, you were well advised not to ask again. He hadn't forgot you, he was taking his time, you'd get your reply from the depths of his soul when he knew what it was. Palmer dreaded making an error of judgment more than any other human I've known. And he made very few in the years I knew him, though he suffered for some and made others suffer—a relative few as far as the husbands I've known are concerned.

The public things he loved were harmless. I've alluded to his infinite walks in the woods, his willingness to watch some natural process as slow as a glacier walking down a mountain and learn pleasure from it. He loved every animal he ever encountered, even the creatures most people dread such as snakes and grinning pink-eyed possums, screaming hawks and stinking red-necked buzzards full of filth. He loved black people's voices and words, the eloquent meanings they made out of lives as low to the ground as a highland turtle's, though of course he was capable of tearing the throat out of any shirker as I'll have to relate here later on.

He'd trust any Negro man or woman on sight, and for him that was not at all true of white people. Furthermore he said he was never deceived. No black person ever let him down badly with money or honor. And while our children were young and growing, still open to life, Palmer could sit on the porch in the evening and watch every move they made in the yard—running for lightning bugs or playing dark tag—as though each step were as splendid with promise as the solemn orbits of the farthest stars or the nighttime movements of unwatched flowers.

And he worshiped my body at the very least for a good bit longer than any woman has the right to expect. I'll have to describe one time when he strayed, but I've mentioned that he told me before we ever joined that he was pure. And when he touched any other human in that final way, he never bore a trace of that act which even the keenest cat could have sensed and surely not me. I was born too far back and have lived too long to lay out any more secrets of his and my joined minds and bodies than are strictly needed for the story I'm telling. Enough to say that Palmer Slade gave every sign but actual words that my bare body could serve for him as an adequate site for whatever private needs compelled him. And he almost never left me feeling merely used like an object or a rented hand. In far the larger share of the times we joined our flesh over thirty-three years, I knew I was honored and cherished in silence by the man there above me who was Palmer—no question.

Of course nobody back home had a telephone, not till the midst of World War II. So we couldn't call Miss Olivia or my parents from Washington. We could have sent telegrams, and they could have answered. But with no prior plans, we kept our peace and they kept theirs. We knew they'd beckon if the need arose. In fact I can't recall that Palmer ever mentioned his father's name or spoke of his death in the whole week away, not till the last day—I know I didn't. I was gliding along for most of that time on what I realized was wafer-thin ice.

Yet the gliding itself kept me more excited deep in my soul than I'd ever been. By the time we stepped off the train in Washington, I'd convinced myself I had chosen right or that God had chosen for me. I believed I'd been set down in a groove like a needle on a brand-new gramophone record and would play happy music—contented music anyhow—the rest of my life. And I feared that any sight or mention of what we'd left would send me crashing through ice into deeps I might not survive.

Then on our final afternoon when we'd eaten our midday meal and paused in the room for Palmer to take his pleasure again and a short nap afterward, he woke up and asked if I'd like to go with him to a "really sad place."

I didn't even ask what place he meant but told him Yes.

He said "Then we'll walk out to Arlington cemetery and pay our respects to Major Slade's memory."

I said I thought Arlington was a Yankee cemetery.

And Palmer laughed, laughed long and free, for the first time in days. He said I was right but that Arlington House at the top of the hill above the graves had been General Lee's home before the war. The Yankees had confiscated it from him when he chose the Rebel side and rode off south.

That seemed good enough credentials for Palmer. So I was dressed and ready shortly, though part of my mind was dragging back strongly against the whole idea of ending our week in a flock of dead soldiers to honor somebody who was now far gone and was anyhow the relic of a time I'd always secretly despised as I mentioned. Odd as I was for my day and age, I'd always known that fight was lunatic, though I kept my mouth shut. Imagine a war, costing six hundred thousand lives in four hot years, over no cause saner than whether or not white people could buy black people like *cars* and work them for the rest of their lives in no better conditions than a white-tailed deer might hope to find in the Carolina woods far into hard winter.

Near the hotel was a small florist's shop. Palmer turned us in there and bought a crimson rose—no request for advice, no coaching from me. And then in fall sunlight gorgeous enough to flatter the saddest sight on Earth, we walked across the river uphill toward the Lees' old mansion and all those acres of plain headstones.

We stayed and wandered through grass and graves till just before sunset. The graves that seemed to interest Palmer were not from the Civil War but the ones from just recently, the many young men who'd died in France no more than a short three years ago. I was silently glad of their presence. It kept me from any disrespectful outburst about Union soldiers and the missing even crazier Rebels, many of whom were kin of mine. We were still moving slowly down rows of fresh stones when a guard walked up and informed us he'd be locking the gates in another few minutes.

Until that moment Palmer's deep red rose had stayed in his hand and hadn't wilted at all. As we walked downhill to the black iron gates, I said the first whole sentence I'd said since we came in sight of those huge columns on the house—one more thing General Lee lost and could never reclaim. I said "You're forgetting to leave your rose."

Palmer didn't break stride and didn't face me. He said "How could I forget anything that's covered with thorns?"

I said I thought he'd bought it to leave in memory of his father, maybe on the steps of the Lee house itself.

Palmer said "You don't think I've lived many seconds of this whole week without missing Major?"

I hadn't thought any such thing, no. And it pained me to hear it there at the end of a honeymoon that had seemed satisfactory to him and me. I said "Major lived a long full life," meaning of course that I didn't see any cause for long mourning in such a bloodless calm departure.

We were through the gates by then and almost at the edge of the river. Palmer stopped at last, looked down at me earnestly and finally said "I bought the rose for you to remember this day forever." He held it toward me.

A sick surprise bloomed up in my chest. As clear as the plunge of a needle through the hand, I knew what was coming and I couldn't take the rose.

Strangely Palmer knew what I felt. The hand with the rose went back to his side. He walked me across the street to the river where he paused us on the bridge and waited till we'd watched the water for a minute. Then he flung the rose out downstream beyond us and said to me "You know we're going back to Mother's place, don't you?"

"I do, yes sir."

He almost smiled. "You got any questions?"

I said "For how long?"

"What if I said the rest of my life?"

I said "I'd stay with you. But against my will. Very much against my will."

"Didn't you surrender that the day we got married?" The hint of a smile had left his face. I'd never seen him more serious.

I said I'd probably surrendered everything. "But so did you. You took the same vows."

Palmer thought that over as a boat came toward us.

A tall young woman was standing in it, dressed in a handsome coal-black dress—neck to ankle. The boat had a little red-roofed cabin, but I couldn't see a soul crouched inside. The woman appeared to be alone on the broad Potomac and bound against the current. As she got just below us, she looked up suddenly, found my eyes and gave a slight wave. She got as close as twenty feet from me, no way to mistake her eyes meeting mine.

It flew through my mind that she had some big meaning that would dawn on me soon—*Was she someway the rest of my life coming at me?* Even at the moment that seemed too foolish, but I still waved back to her sadly.

And Palmer said "You know her, do you?"

I shook my head No. No meaning had come. She was one more creature on her own private rounds.

After she'd gone on under the bridge and vanished from us upstream against the whole Potomac, Palmer said "She might well have been your other sister."

I'd noticed a likeness in hair and eyes but not much else—she was older than me by maybe five years. Still with her there on the river alone, I did feel close to her plight at the moment. No pity, no fear but the knowledge I was still in the world alone and bound upstream. Palmer had said she might have been my *other* sister. So I said "I don't have another sister except for Leela Dane." I could hear how childish that sounded, standing there. And I felt tears coming. So I turned my back to my young husband and took the first steps on toward the hotel.

I didn't hear Palmer's steps behind me. But when I'd gone a cold twenty yards, he said plainly "Roxanna Slade, look here."

He'd never said my whole new name before.

And God knows I hadn't said it over and over to myself as some girls did months before they were married. I stopped all the same and turned to face Palmer. I wasn't sure I even liked the sound. A *Slade* and a *Dane* were surely two different things. Maybe for me the new name was just a lie. But when I held my eyes on Palmer for a whole long instant, I liked his face. For that moment there it looked as nearly forlorn as it looked when he came ashore for that first awful moment after Larkin went under in the swift Roanoke.

Palmer didn't speak again now, but he came on forward.

I held my place till he got right to me. Then I took the wide tough hand which was what he had to offer.

As mine was to him.

Our train tickets put us off at my home—the depot at least and Father's face there waiting for me with a new kind of transparent shield across his brow and eyes that no one but me would ever have noticed. I thought it was there to brace him at first against the sight of me as a woman and to hide from me what he felt about the loss. I'd have had to go back home in any case and pack sufficient sensible clothes for life however long at the Slade place.

I'd told nobody but Leela about my powerful hopes to live in Betsy Magee's rented rooms for a while. I'd let my parents make the normal assumption for those times—that, with Palmer being the sole man who could manage Major's tenants and timber and guard his mother on to her grave, we'd be living up by the river in the old house or somewhere in range of Miss Olivia's voice. So at least I didn't have to eat crow in public, though I did have to take steps to hide my disappointment when—after a quick two days in the only house I'd ever known well—I had to set off for one I dreaded.

I let Palmer know my continued feelings in a few silent ways. I sat quietly while Muddie ran on at supper the first night about her plans for getting the wedding presents packed and sent on to us wherever we'd be. Then I told her I'd let her know when we knew our permanent whereabouts. And then on the morning when Ferny drove down to fetch us to the river, the last thing I said to Muddie—in Palmer's presence—was how we were looking forward to Christmas with her and the family and to keep all our china and silver till then. We'd use it for the feast.

Palmer never flinched but smiled in his sly way and hugged everybody appropriately. And that helped me through the long cold ride and the moment when we broke out into sight of the Slade place and those same dogs tore out to meet us as if a hard year hadn't rolled by and Fern and I were condensing out of the bright day itself to pay a harmless midday visit to a pack of hounds.

Within an hour of our arrival when I was already helping in the kitchen with a big hot dinner, Palmer entered and stopped in the doorway. When Miss Olivia looked up, he said "Mother, Anna and I will be taking the Office for our private quarters. I'll move our things over there right now and bring any private stuff of yours back here to your bedroom."

He hadn't said so much as *By your leave,* and that cheered me up more than I'd expected. I turned to watch Miss Olivia's response.

She worked the better part of a minute as if she hadn't heard him.

Meanwhile Coy was grunting away like a cornered boar at the stove — "*Uh-uh-un.*" Whether she meant she approved or disapproved wasn't clear, or maybe she thought the world would end in the next few seconds.

I'd heard her say more than once last year that we were living "in the Last Days." I had no evidence to prove she was wrong. It wouldn't have surprised me in so much silence if angel trumpets had sounded doom.

But by the time Miss Olivia paused in her task and looked toward the door, Palmer had already left on his purpose. I'll give her this much — she looked straight at me and burst out laughing. Then she said "I guess I'm learning my place in the new world."

I know I blushed like a hot fire truck. But I said "Palmer's got his own mind all right."

Miss Olivia said "I'm glad you noticed" and turned back to work. Her smile hung on for several more minutes like the sign of a pact she was offering between us — *We can handle this fool if we join hands against him.*

But I gave her no sign I accepted the deal.

When she asked me to call the boys to table, I ran into Ferny in the front hall staring out the open door cold as it was.

Fern looked a little better than he had at the wedding. The shock of Major's death had faded, but he showed how much he'd aged in the year we'd all survived since Larkin's last day. He was drawn around the eyes and cheekbones. The skin was paper thin, and all the color in his lips was gone.

That lone sight of him pulled on me strongly. From behind I put a hand on his shoulder. "You got enough to do here, friend?"

Fern didn't look back. "What does that mean please?"

I said I only wondered if, with Major gone, time wasn't growing heavy on his hands.

Fern said "You want me to leave here today?"

I told him that was the last thing I meant.

Then he turned to face me. And though there was a curious curl to his lips, a chilly smile, he said "In another few days you'll be glad I'm here."

It was my turn to say I was baffled now.

Ferny looked out the door again. "I'm staying for you. You may need me."

I laughed a little but figured I shouldn't press him further. He'd always been prone to scaring people for no real reason. I told him Miss Olivia was ready to eat.

So he turned and walked right past me toward the dining room.

I asked where Palmer was.

Fern didn't pause but pointed behind him. "He's in the Office clearing out mess. Asked me to help him but I declined."

I stepped out into the cold midday light, blank as any chemical fire, and trotted to the Office.

I'd scarcely ever been in there, no farther than the doorsill. But when I gave the door a light knock, nobody replied. I turned the knob and took a few steps in. The room was bigger than I'd expected, bigger than most of the rooms in the main house. It seemed perfectly square with a pine-board ceiling that rose to a peak and a cast-iron stove in the midst of the floor. The floor was beautiful heart-pine boards at least a foot wide. Even I knew there were no such trees left alive in the world. And the only furniture I saw at first was a big old roll-top desk with a thousand stuffed pigeonholes. If this was the only available private place Palmer knew of, it could be made to serve. It looked as emptied and long abandoned as any ship ransacked by pirates and left adrift in the midst of nowhere.

A voice said "I hope you know how to make curtains."

It startled me and I couldn't find the source. So I froze in place.

To be sure, it was Palmer—but Palmer *changed* in the past quick hour as much as Fern had changed in these recent months. And like my brother, my husband seemed a full decade older. He was half laid back on the dark brown blanket of an old brass bed. A shotgun was lying across his thighs.

Somehow it seemed normal. Guns were as much a part of country life as they are of the public schools today. Maybe Palmer intended to hunt after dinner or finish off any squirrels or swallows that might have invaded the premises. I looked at the only two windows, tall and glazed with wavy panes—no trace of shutters or curtains. So I said we could tack up old bedsheets if his mother had any. And then I could probably sew something better, awkward as I was. When I looked back to Palmer, he'd laid the gun on the floor like a low wall between him and me. I said "I trust that thing's unloaded."

He said "No, sorry to disappoint you again. That's all I do."

I could see Palmer was in some mood I'd never found him in till now, distant and edgy. I told him "This far, I don't have big complaints." It was true enough to let me smile.

That seemed to free him or jog him loose in the feelings that held him. He extended his long right arm straight toward me.

And I said "What?" though I guessed I knew.

In the times that Palmer had brought me to him, I'd come to think I knew all he was. But in that next quarter hour in the Office he'd swept clean for us—with us open to view by any passer and his mother's huge meal chilling on the table—he labored on me with a kind of wild purpose and aim that were freshly revealing. I still can't say what exactly was revealed. His face continued to look like Palmer. The heat of his body and hands were the same, even in that unheated room. But the charge that was in him, the voltage itself was as high as sheet lightning.

And it clearly ran him, not vice versa. For the first full time, I was totally excluded so far as I could tell from Palmer's eyes which were open but elsewhere. He was solving in his way some equation that had blocked his mind. And working it out caused him obvious pain, though once he was done and had caved in on me, he felt like every tired child I'd held.

Just at that moment I guessed he'd hacked a path through the recent sadness of Major's death and his own regret to be chained back down in his old rut here, his mother's servant. But he never said that, not then nor later, and I may well have been describing myself. I know anyhow that, with all the hard times we endured between us in years to come, from that time onward I mostly knew I mattered to Palmer in the direst way. Who else could he have found on Earth, in our sparse corner of space at least, to take calm part in the secret plays he staged in his tall crowded skull?

*   *   *

When we'd stood and composed ourselves, we went to the house in perfect silence. If you'd been watching from a reasonable distance, you might have thought we were fifty years old each and that speech or touch was as unnecessary to us as to oxen in a field. But I at least didn't feel that separate, and apparently no one in the main house thought we'd parted enough to bear the insertion of the thinnest blade between us. They smiled to greet the sight of our faces.

And it turned out that they'd held the whole hot meal. Not one question was asked, then or ever, about where we'd been or why we were late. And it was only midway through the food before Palmer for the second time called me the full name I was so seldom called.

When Miss Olivia made some mild remark about wishing I'd get more rest for myself—that my eyes had looked tired ever since the wedding—I said "Miss Olivia, there was one long week you didn't *see* my eyes. I'm as rested as the sunrise."

Palmer turned on his mother and said "Leave her alone. Roxanna's a thoroughbred saint. She lives round the clock. You let her be." Everybody drew one long deep breath, startled or scared. Then everybody laughed, thank God, as I still do just to recall it. A saint, by Palmer's and most folks' meaning, is just a person who never blocks your path but grins and yields all paths to your will.

It went on more or less that way for a year and two months. I made us some thick curtains fast, and gradually we turned the Office into a fairly pleasant room. The main house didn't have running water either, so we didn't feel especially deprived. But Palmer cleaned and polished the iron stove, and that took the chill off the worst days and nights. Of course we ate most meals in the house, though occasionally Palmer would come in at dusk wet and cold from estimating miles of timber and ask me if I could just bring our supper out from the main house and we'd eat alone by oil light.

Movies hadn't yet made lamplight romantic, and I remember it mainly for the smell and the chimneys to clean and the danger to hair and clothes. Still I think my husband and I took pleasure in staying close inside a small hoop of soft light with nobody else anywhere in view. And oil light did show Palmer's face at its best—strong as a great head carved by a sculptor in search of the image of patient strength.

✳   ✳   ✳

The population of the Slade place went down in late February when Ferny announced one evening that he'd be heading back home in two days. Did anybody have last chores for him? Truth to tell there'd been no genuine work for Fern once the major was buried. For a while he'd invented small jobs for himself—there's always plenty of ruin around a country house—but Miss Olivia had told him she wouldn't be able to continue the modest sum Major had paid him for help and company. Fern knew that wasn't stinginess.

The Slades were no more wealthy than most people up in the north of the county back then. It would take more than a hundred years, not till the 1970s and eighties, before that part of the world had even half recovered from the slavery war. And by that time of course, you couldn't persuade a smart young person to live anywhere but in a town of at least fifty thousand with numerous malls.

Furthermore I knew that our father was pressing on Ferny to come back down and help him in the store. So nobody felt any shock at his leaving, though I knew how much I'd miss his presence. The morning he was set to leave, Palmer had driven to Roanoke Rapids to pay off various merchants he owed. Miss Olivia was busy with her duties.

But I was as idle as any stalled car when Fern didn't knock but walked right through the Office door with no prior warning. I must have been dozing because his footsteps brought me upright from the bed where I'd lain down after breakfast, feeling not only tired but bored to distraction and halfway reading Dickens' *Tale of Two Cities* for at least the third time. I smoothed my hair and got to my feet.

Fern took a chair and said "Rest on. You need to. But I need to tell you one or two things before I go." He motioned for me to lie back, but I declined and took the other chair.

Fern had never had trouble saying what he meant, and he started right in. "I know that you and Miss Olivia are both too big to live together—"

Lean-framed as I was, I had to laugh at the picture that suggested.

But Fern waved me silent. "I'm thinking in terms of your minds, not your bodies, girl. So I want you to know that I told Palmer yesterday how soon he'd need to move you out of here. I couldn't have told him if I hadn't already seen how restless he was in these old tracks of his. He told me he was watching for the first good chance to put the Slade place in some good other hands and move you and him to somewhere better."

What I said next shocked me as much as Ferny. "The main chance," I said, "would be Miss Olivia dying." I tried to cover it by laughing again.

But Ferny was earnest as any good butcher knife. "That would do it," he said. "But Palmer's too kind to hasten her on, and she could live another forty years."

I asked if he had any clear idea of Miss Olivia's age. I've never been good at judging age.

Fern said "I know, to the month and day. She'll be fifty-nine on the first day of spring."

That was younger than I'd guessed. She could easily see me into the grave.

I said "Well with Palmer and me out here in the separate Office, things could be a lot worse."

Ferny's head shook hard. "A year from now if you're not out of here, you'll be near dead if not insane." Fern was the only member of my family who'd ever discussed my hard times with me.

I almost wondered if he'd lost his mind in these sad months, but I didn't bring it up. I told him I felt as strong as I'd ever been.

Fern looked up and down me. "You look it but you're already pregnant."

This will be hard to take in modern times. But while I technically understood the connection between adult love and oncoming children (and though I'd imagined being pregnant the year before), it had scarcely crossed my mind since marriage that I might have started a baby this soon. Palmer hadn't mentioned it nor anyone else. And I'd been so involved with learning the way my husband thought and felt and fending off my own creeping boredom that it hadn't grown into a fear or a hope yet. I'd likewise had no physical sign I could recognize. So I told Fern he was out of his mind. Where on Earth had he got that notion?

He said "I can see it."

"I surely can't."

Fern pointed to the smoky mirror behind me. "Take a good long look."

At first I laughed but my brother's seriousness finally made me get up and look. I've mentioned that mirrors never meant much to me. I only used them to comb my hair or to check on any sudden blemish. I probably hadn't spent a total of fifteen minutes with this particular mirror since the honeymoon ended. So I told myself that the hazy strangeness across my eyes and the firmer cheekbones were nothing but symptoms of ongoing time. I was aging steadily like the rest of the world. Still when I turned back to Fern and said "*Wrong!*" I found myself smiling deep inside at the distant chance he might have stumbled on amazing news.

Fern stood up then and just said "All right, I'll see you at Christmas." I'd promised Father we'd come home for Christmas.

I gave him a kiss on his fine broad forehead and stood in the door to see him go. He'd got all the way down the steps and was walking fast before I whispered loudly to call him back.

Twenty feet away he paused and waited.

I asked him again where he'd got his idea about my condition.

He looked behind him toward the main house before he spoke, and then he whispered too. "Larkin told me last night in a dream."

I knew by his face he wasn't joking. Yet I didn't believe any such thing could happen, so I was left wondering again if all these months of sadness and country idleness had confused my brother for a while or forever.

Fern held in place for a silent moment and fixed on me like a book or a set of vital instructions he meant to memorize.

I let him look and I tried to search him almost as closely. Just in those few minutes in the Office, his brown eyes had darkened and clouded further. And the few yards between us seemed a desperate distance we could never reclaim. I well knew that, even in our narrow world where families tended not to scatter, Fern and I were changed forever and all because of him trying to give me a birthday surprise when I turned twenty.

Lark was long gone. I'd made my choice of Palmer Slade and didn't regret it, and Ferny Dane was out of a friend and his first employer. I knew he was young enough to start a grown life, and I honestly thought he'd do that now. But even so it was painful to watch my good brother turn his back then and head toward a world that soon turned out to hold nothing for him—nothing that could save him.

In another ten days Miss Olivia found me alone in the kitchen and asked me the same thing, politely and gently. *Was I expecting?*

I told her she was wrong but didn't ask why she suspected as much. I honestly thought I was telling her the truth. So it was not till the first day of spring, that I really began to know for myself. My monthlies had never been all that reliable. And I hadn't paid much attention to their lateness, even in the face of recent suspicions.

But then we got in sight of Miss Olivia's birthday, and Palmer asked me one evening if I'd like to ride with him into town the following day to buy his mother something. I took the chance gladly, to get a little fresh air and maybe see my family. We managed to do both. The day was bright and warm. The drive was easy and we got there in time for dinner with Muddie and Father. Leela was visiting friends in Halifax some twenty miles east. Ferny was off on a trip to Raleigh hunting a job there. He and Father weren't working well together.

As we left Muddie caught me alone for a minute and asked if I was "bearing up." It would turn out later that Fern had told her he was sure I was expecting.

At first I didn't hear the hint in Muddie's question, and I told her I had seldom felt stronger. Though I'd heard that kind of concern all my life, I was somehow unable to hear the worry in her and Miss Olivia's questions. Older women back then often looked on pregnancy as a hard dark tunnel of sickness and pain maybe ending in death for the woman, her baby or both at once.

That common dread was not unrealistic if you looked back at the old bloody record of hemorrhage and sudden overwhelming infection that were common as head colds and killed young mothers like flies, a fact that's all but forgotten today in America at least. One visit to any old cemetery will show you how many men's graves from those former times are surrounded by two or three dead wives whereas today many dyed-blond widows spend hours a week tending several husbands' graves.

I'd gone to school with a number of children whose mothers had died the day they gave birth or within a week thereafter. If you listened to any one of them closely, you could hear their belief—for the rest of their lives—that they'd killed their mothers. Imagine what it did to sons and husbands. If a man had an ounce of sense or conscience he had to realize that, every time he took his pleasure with his wives, he might be tripping a process which would kill that mate in under a year. Maybe it was fate itself which kept me from sharing such a common sense of fear, but why was I ignoring the plain natural signs?

Anyhow Palmer and I pushed on that bright March day and bought a few nice things for Miss Olivia. It wasn't until we'd finished our errands that Palmer said it might be a good idea if he dropped by Dr. Rogers' office and let him take a look at the felon that had formed on his thumb and wouldn't turn loose. The thumb didn't look that bad to me, but I went on with him and sat in the dingy old waiting room till the doctor came out with Palmer lanced and bandaged, and stepped across the room to me—the last person there.

When he was a new young doctor, he'd delivered me and Leela and treated our simple complaints through the years. Ever since a crazy man in the backwoods had shot him in the chest ten years ago (the man imagined Dr. Rogers was having an affair with his moron wife), the doctor had seemed far older than his years.

After we'd exchanged a few pleasant words, Palmer suddenly said "Doctor, while we're here how about checking on Anna's health?"

I laughed. "No such thing! I'm strong as a bear."

Dr. Rogers said "I can see you are. Step in though and let me check your heart and blood pressure."

I tried to decline but Palmer said "Be sensible please."

So I followed the doctor. And to shorten the story, within a quarter hour I was more embarrassed than I'd ever been. Dr. Rogers thought I might well be pregnant. And Palmer's eyes were burning like searchlights. It made him that happy to my unending surprise even now.

We didn't mention the change to anybody for several more weeks. I could tell Miss Olivia was watching me like a dynamite stick and calling on me for fewer chores, so I had even more time on my hands to think of how my life might change and what Palmer might feel about who I'd be. By early April I was fairly sure the suspicions were right. So I agreed to ride in again and see Dr. Rogers, still asking Palmer to keep our secret as long as I needed.

My mind had not been responding normally to the possibilities—or what I thought was normal. It might have been the even emptier hours and days that were gathering round me in the Office. But I felt myself drying out at the edges, the way I'd first felt in those bad weeks after Larkin's death when Palmer was out of sight in my life, and I spun downward nearly out of control into serious blues.

Yet once Dr. Rogers made a full internal checkup—the first I'd ever had, which was normal enough back then before there was a gynecologist at every supermarket—we knew where I stood. I was well on my way to bearing a first child. The physical signs indicated I was healthy. And as Palmer and I drove back to the Slade place through endless woods that were greening fast, my heart began to give off a silent emotion as new to me as the tender leaves. Strange as it was it felt mainly happy, and it felt big enough to take over in me.

Palmer kept his word about guarding the secret. We hadn't stopped by to tell Muddie and Father when we left the doctor's office. We didn't tell Miss Olivia that evening. Ferny and I were corresponding weekly by then; I didn't tell Fern. Palmer and I just held it between us like a sizable wreath or a handsome tray that would soon bear a gift for the world at large. Not that we felt any softening of the brain, any sense that a child would prove to be the answer to whatever lacks or sadnesses we'd known, not to mention other people's. Such carrying on about babes in the womb was not a part of our world or any world I'd read or heard of in my young life.

Children were, beyond question, acts of God. In starting and bearing one, you and your mate were doing a share in keeping God's orders to thrive and multiply. But back in those days anybody with two working eyes and two grams of sense could see what tragically many people are blind to now when, with all the modern drugs and doctors, reality turns out to be much the same as it's always been—that many children are born maimed and agonized, that many mothers suffer thereafter and die in poorer darker places, that many healthy children grow up under hails of meanness and unthinkable outrage from the people meant to love them, not to mention how many marriages crumble under the weight of nothing more urgent than pure human selfishness. So both of us kept a careful silence, seldom discussing it even in private.

Finally in early May, another fine day with a long peaceful evening, Palmer looked to me across the supper table and mouthed *Can I tell?*

In just that instant I felt it was right. Coy had just walked up to the table with fresh hot biscuits that no two angels trying hard could have made in Glory. And I whispered "Go to it."

Palmer took up his knife and tapped on his water glass.

It was the first time I'd ever seen anyone call for attention that way.

Miss Olivia looked up sternly as if he were nine years old, and she said "That glass was my mother's, Son. Kindly don't crack it."

But he had her attention which had never been that easy for him to get. So he told her my news. (In those days married people didn't think about a baby as "ours." We were just being honest, both of us knowing that

Palmer's part in starting a child had been no more than a matter of minutes. Mine would take a lot longer.)

Miss Olivia turned to me, no trace of a smile. "You lied to me, didn't you?"

It nearly floored me. I flushed blood-red but I had the guts to say "No ma'm. You asked me long before I knew."

Her splendid eyes didn't blink for a minute but held onto mine. Then her head shook slowly side to side, and her eyes welled full of tears that wouldn't flow. She rang the little bell for Coy to clear the dishes. Then she stood up gravely, whispered "Good night" and was gone like a ghost or a terrible bird that might still lurk in a room's dark corner and seize your face in powerful claws when you least expected.

For the rest of that dark night with all Palmer said—in trying to explain how sad she'd been, how much she'd lost—I lay on my side facing the wall and wished my womb would spasm once hard and cleanse itself and me both, light and free again in my father's house.

Palmer had to leave for work before daylight. I stayed in bed and prayed just to vanish, just to shrink up inward till—by evening when he'd climb our steps—there'd be our stale sheets and my folded clothes but no trace or recollection of me. I hate to tell it, but it may help someone if anybody reads this. I even reached my right hand down and entered myself as far as I could with my strong nails in the hopes of damage. I didn't even bleed. And by the time I'd tortured myself back down into some kind of sunrise rest, there came a light knock at the only door. I had no choice but to answer since Palmer had never yet managed to mend our lock.

I was halfway composed and ready to stand when the door opened wide, and Miss Olivia walked in with a tray.

Before I could think of who I was and whose place I was in, I said straight at her "No, no ma'm. You take that back." It was not morning sickness. I was still shocked and bitter about last night and what she'd said.

But she held her ground. The place was hers undoubtedly. She set the tray on the one small table. There was a pot of coffee and a covered plate of something. She poured a cup of coffee, creamed and sweetened it and set it by the chair at the head of the table. When she faced me she was still not smiling. But she said "Anna, I beg your pardon. I can try to explain. May I sit down in peace?"

What was I going to do but agree? I put on the black kimono Muddie gave me on my last birthday and walked to the table. The room was warmer than I'd realized. Palmer had opened the curtains when he left, and the sun was already powerful. I sat by the coffee. And when Miss Olivia stayed upright, I said "Rest your feet."

She thanked me, took the other chair, uncovered the plate of eggs and sausage and set it before me.

Half mad as I was, I didn't refuse it.

She had the good sense not to try to touch me but kept her hands together in her lap. When I'd taken the first mouthful of coffee, she said "I want you to know I was not myself at supper last night. I was maybe more stunned than I've ever been since Lark drowned at least."

In my final few months at home, I'd sunk into telling Leela and even my mother exactly what I felt about something they'd said or done. As the words would come from me, I could literally hear them like a stranger's voice. It never sounded mad or cruel, not to me, just new and impressive. And at first that scared me. Was some demon in me, or was this who I was meant to be as I grew on up? Still not knowing, it spoke in me now straight at Miss Olivia. "I was as stunned as you, maybe more."

"You accept my apology?"

I told her I did.

She said "I don't know how much Palmer has told you, but I lost three children long before Larkin."

I told her I'd seen their graves at Lark's and Major's funerals—little statues of lambs turned to face each other with the names and dates, brief stretches of life but long enough to seem like people torn from you by God.

Miss Olivia's eyes were wide and dry, but she said "I know you've suffered real losses. Your own child though, no more than an infant—"

I told her I had no doubt at all that nothing on Earth could equal that.

She nodded hard. "*Four* of them now. None left but Palm." I nodded as well. It felt as if I were watching a teacher in grade school standing at the blackboard proving a problem in plane geometry. I could see how perfectly right Miss Olivia was. But she raised no feeling in me, not this bright morning. Even in my deepest troughs of the blues, I'd cared more than this. I thought if I forged some half normal gesture, it would trigger my sympathy. Her left hand was laid down near me on the table. I moved to cover it.

She drew it back from me but slowly, not as if I'd burned her. After she'd studied my face a long time, she finally said "You know I've got no grand-children yet? These next months will be very hard on me."

A laugh flew up in my throat but I stopped it. *Whose child is this? Who's making it right this instant inside herself? Try saying Roxanna and you'll have the answer.* But all I said was "I hope I can ease things for you some way. I may need to leave here, Palmer and I that is—"

Those words struck her across the eyes like a rawhide thong. Then she calmed herself. "That truly might kill me."

Again my laugh rose and half escaped. But my face stayed calm as I said "Miss Olivia, I'll do everything in my small power to see that you survive this, grinning."

By then she seemed on the verge of leaving with no clear winner in the struggle we were staging. She got upright to her feet very slowly, turned toward the door and said "Monkeys grin—monkeys and skulls."

I said "Miss Olivia, I just meant *smiling*. I hope all of us are smiling by the time this child gets here."

That brought her back. She retraced her steps and sat again and told me straight as if she felt no reluctance at all. That's kept me wondering all these years if she'd planned to tell me her final story, her big trump card, or if I shook it out of her somehow. In any case she told it so plainly that her worst enemy couldn't have doubted the truth of one word. She said "What you don't know—what Palm doesn't know—what nobody on this place knows but Coy is the fact about me."

She paused and reached toward a spot on the table, a small dried stain from some old meal at my usual place. First she tested it with a fingernail. Then she took that finger back to her lips, wet it and set out to scrub the stain. When she quit it was gone. And it almost seemed she'd changed her mind. She looked to the door and seemed to think of leaving.

But I likewise touched where the stain had been and said "My house-keeping skills are slender."

That settled her somehow. She sat back a little and said "They'll grow." Then she took my face with her eyes as surely as if she'd reached through the four-foot distance between us and clamped me to her. "I'll do this fast. You need to know but it hurts me to tell you. I was born two years before the war ended—1863—and in my girlhood east of here in Weldon, there were very few young men left alive. One of the last results of the war that nobody mentions was a million old maids, no boys to marry. I got on up to being seventeen, eighteen. And still no young man had showed any interest in me and my famous eyes (famous in my house at our dinner table). It pained me a good deal, the prospect of lonesome barren years and an old age of begging a dark back room from some luckier cousin with a life of their own.

"So when I was eighteen, an older man took an interest in me—a lawyer who hadn't served in the war. His heart was weak, so weak he fell over dead one evening at my parents' supper table. But not before he got me pregnant. I lived on at home barely stepping outdoors for the whole long ordeal. For those long months I faced my father and my helpless mother by the moment and saw their heartbreak not to mention despisal from my younger sisters—and then I had a still-born boy on the loveliest day of a beautiful spring. I survived someway. I lasted through nearly twelve more years of agony fit to grind strong bones to dust.

"Everybody in Weldon knew my story. By then I'd become the trusty but luckless woman you hired to sit with dying relations or crazy old men. I was recommended to Major Slade when his first wife was dying slowly of a dreadful cancer deep in her vitals. I'd never laid eyes on any of the Slades. But I packed my satchel and came here to live and tend that woman through weeks of howling, justified howling. There was nothing we could do but pour morphine into her like water till she finally died. Through even the worst of it when her entrails putrefied so badly you could hardly stand near her, the major never laid a hand on me to ask for any kind of consolation.

"But when we had buried the few pounds of bone that were left of his wife, I had to ask him when I'd be free. Major held his place, his usual chair out on the front porch; and he said 'Miss Larkin, you'll never draw one *free* breath again if I have my way.' Then he smiled and here I've been ever since. I was thirty-one years old, and here I sit—not one free breath in all these years."

She plainly thought she was finished at that point. I'd believed every word. But since she meant me to be moved and changed by what I heard, I needed to know at least two more facts. Mean as it sounded at last I said "You mentioned two more dead children once. I've seen their graves."

Miss Olivia's eyes acknowledged my hardness. They clamped nearly shut. Then she said "Three years after marrying Major, I bore him dead twins—two little girls. He'd never had a girl. When we buried them Major asked if I didn't want him to fetch my 'other baby' from Weldon. I'd never been sure he'd known that story. So I thanked him and said that would be a real kindness. He had my first child dug up and brought here, and he paid for the stone with no trace of complaint. Then two years later Palmer was born. That seemed like an end to my curse. Or so I thought till the day Lark drowned."

I could see that her whole face, still turned on me, was only meant to be telling the truth I'd need to know to live on here. I wouldn't bear that. Even with all the pity I felt in the wake of her news, I said "Miss Olivia, I didn't kill Larkin."

I'd never said it to a soul till now.

She waited to hear all I meant by that. Then she finally rose to her feet again and left me in silence.

I ate every scrap of Coy's good cold eggs.

Predicting a baby's arrival in those days was more of an art than a definite science. Dr. Rogers and I had pretty much concluded that I'd be due in the Christmas season. Since I'd long since promised that Palmer and I would spend Christmas in my home, I made early plans with Muddie to go there at least a week before Christmas and wait for the child. I and Leela and our two brothers had been born in that house—so had Father before us—and the nearest real hospital was twenty miles west. In any case back then many well-off white women seldom chose to bear children in a hospital. The chance of deadly infection was greater in a hospital than at the hands of a country doctor and a Negro midwife. So home delivery was a normal expectation, so normal that even Miss Olivia couldn't seriously object.

What she did though, right through summer and fall, was to go on wringing her hands in worry about my condition and the oncoming labor. I never got used to it—the idea of this woman, strong as a buffalo, scared by a process as normal as tree bark. What was she scared of? She'd seen plenty deaths, anybody could die, it was no hard skill. All the same in the summer months when I could see that she was entirely sincere in her worry and was not just trying to upset me, I didn't let her get me down.

Blistering hot as that season was right into October, I invented slews of jobs for myself—writing letters to every soul I knew in the outside world to keep up my spirits, mending everything broken I could find, reading Miss Olivia's diary (which she said I could read, "just not the past two years' worth, starring you") and taking walks in the cool of the evening when Palmer got home. Exercise then was mostly looked on as fatal to a pregnant woman, but neither Palmer nor I believed that. We'd watched enough black women toil in the field till hours or minutes before they delivered, and they seldom died from it.

Then when I was about to scream from the tense air around me, a rescue arrived. It turned out Coy had a simple-minded child who lived down the road with a blacksmith husband and could sew very beautifully entirely by hand. Her name was Castille, like the soap. And for whatever reason she had no children which was probably a blessing. All you had to do was buy Castille a pattern, cut the cloth for her; and she could put it together overnight. Coy said she'd literally sit up whole nights working by oil light. Most mornings also Castille would come to the Office. Then she and I would work together till mid-afternoon pausing only to eat. We made maternity dresses for me, shirts for Palmer, long skirts and shirtwaists for Miss Olivia and baby clothes sufficient for a set of quintuplets.

Maybe because she was barren herself, Castille had peculiar ideas of what children did inside the womb. And day after day she took great pains to see I understood all her hopes and fears. She thought for instance that it was good to read aloud to unborn babies—the Bible of course but also other future information that might prove useful. Though she couldn't read a word herself, she brought me her husband's old remedy book, an almanac with the phases of the moon and a startling pamphlet which claimed (with pictures) that Abraham Lincoln hadn't died of his wounds but was still alive somewhere in Tennessee planning to start the war back up and finish the job of freeing black folk.

So while Castille bent low over her sewing, I'd read aloud to her and me, plus the growing baby and any birds that flew past the window. There were times, I think, when we both expected Mr. Lincoln to knock and step in on us tall as any old pine and terribly scarred but kindly as ever.

I at the very least learned a good deal in our working hours, especially the old-time remedies for everything from strokes to floating kidneys. Castille seemed to enjoy the listening. As to my child and the course of its growth in the deep dark within me, only time would tell. But any honest and harmless relief from Miss Olivia's air of doom was as welcome to me as bathing my swollen ankles in the creek that ran between the Slade place and Castille's. I'd walk her home some days. And on my dusty way back, I'd wade some distance up the snaky old creek watching for any sight of a cop-

perhead or cottonmouth moccasin. Whenever one appeared I'd halt and
warn it of my condition. They always showed me dignified respect. I think
well of snakes.

Unfortunately for me by early November, Castille and I had made all the
clothes any child could need. And I'd fairly well scoured the Office and the
main house for manageable tasks that could use my plain skills. That, with
the weather closing down, was when Miss Olivia's concern really bore
down on me. Not that she told me anything I hadn't already learned from
watching the live world of women and babies. But by the time I got too big
to move with any ease, my mind began to dwell on the dark side.

Those were also the days when perfectly sober friends and kin could sit
and tell you to be very careful about what you watched, heard or dreamed.
Any undue powerful impression could *mark* the child. See a snake and the
child might arrive with a scaly hide, that sort of folly.

But as days shortened drastically and the cold nights settled, I had mischievous empty hours to think of such foolishness and worse. Even today I
seldom meet a young pregnant woman who doesn't have nightmares or
secret worries about delivering a damaged child. But back when I started,
public institutions for the deformed and unfortunate were scarce. So the
average person came into contact with many more tragically damaged
children than now.

All the more reason then to wind up in bad hours, sometimes whole nights
long, when I pictured myself giving Palmer a monstrously misshapen son or
daughter. There were dreams he'd wake me from all but nightly—me sobbing
in my sleep—that were so real and awful, I kept them dark secrets.

Still I made it on down to December with no bodily problems worse than
swollen legs and a sorely burdened back. Miss Olivia kept asking me the
date of my departure for home. I'd long since told her December 18th but
she'd forget it. I'd patiently tell her "one week before Christmas," and she'd
ask again the next day. So I was looking forward to the 18th like my personal salvation. Then late on the morning of the 16th well after Palmer had
left for the woods, I was in the kitchen with Miss Olivia and Coy. And Miss
Olivia said "I still can't believe you and Palmer are going to shut me and
Coy out of this coming business."

I tried to control my voice. But I said "Miss Olivia, listen. It's my mother or you in this coming event. I believe it's customary for a woman to go home to her own mother at such a time."

Coy plainly said "That's *right*."

Miss Olivia said "This is *Palmer's* home. The child is Palm's, isn't it?"

I had no idea then what bombs were really like. But I'd heard of them. Anarchists were something people talked about even in the country, and again World War I was barely behind us. I recall standing there in the face of that question and saying to myself *In an instant now you'll fly into pieces and kill this woman.*

Coy had turned to watch me, and I tried hanging onto her eyes in the hope of steadying myself or laughing anyhow. But all Coy did was give her long repeated groan.

So I ran.

I'd never fled from anyone till then. I was no bull terrier, but I generally tried to hold my ground if I knew it was mine. Yet that day I surrendered on the spot without a peep. Even now I'm not sure why Miss Olivia managed to break me with six normal words. By the time I'd slammed the Office door shut and fallen on the bed, I thought she might be saying that somehow my child was *Larkin's*. Had she lost her mind? Lark had been underground for more than two years.

But hadn't Fern told me how in a dream Lark informed him I was pregnant? That was crazy too, though not with Miss Olivia's cold meanness. By then I was dreading she'd turn up any minute to beg my pardon or pursue her purpose, *which was what*? Was she killing me by seconds and inches? Was she driving some wedge between Palmer and me, to get him back?

I lay there dry-eyed but sick at heart, wondering over and over again how I was meant to wade through a whole life if life was like this. No answers arrived, Miss Olivia didn't show up, in a few more minutes I'd stumbled onto sleep. And I didn't wake till awhile after noon. When I did I was lying on my right side, and I knew straight off that something was new. My hand went out and felt the quilt.

It was sopping wet. At first I couldn't look. I thought it was blood, still warm. But no, it was water. My "waters had broke" as old women said. My next thought—honest to Christ, my next clear thought—was *Kill yourself right now. Don't have your baby in this hateful place*. It seemed as sane as anything else I'd lived through lately.

My bag had been packed for several days. In case of emergency Palmer could drive us home at once, and I'd be safe in a kind place. But Palmer was gone now well past reach till sundown at least, and with no telephone there was still no way to call for help. I sat up on the bed to try to clear my mind. There had to be a way to get out of here and bring my baby to life in a calm house that wouldn't just blight his eyes from the start (I'd been hoping for a boy). Before I could rise to my feet and get balanced though, the door opened quietly—no previous knock—and Coy was with me.

From my first day at the Slade place, I'd never been sure if old Coy liked me, resented me or scarcely noted my presence. She kept her mysteries as closely as a rock beneath your foot that silently plans to outlast you by trillions of years. Coy took three steps on into the Office leaving the door half open behind her.

I was scared to stay, but I halfway sat up.

Coy's filmy eyes looked up and down me as if I might or might not be a person.

I was never sure what she could see. So when she didn't speak, I said "I think my waters just broke."

Coy nodded. "Did."

"What does this mean?" I said. I'd raised my voice knowing Coy was deaf.

But now she damped both her hands on the air. "Talk quiet," she said. "I ain't deaf yet." But she stayed on silent.

So I said "Am I all right?" I was whispering.

"If you asking me," Coy said, "I say you all right."

"I'm supposed to be at my mother's, aren't I?"

"You been saying so, yes. Course women has babies in the ditch if they want to, has em drunk or sober."

I can't imagine where the thought came from, but I was so desperate I said "Have you come to take me?" Coy wouldn't so much as climb into a car. She'd only travel on her own two feet, not even on trains except to my wedding.

She thought about it though. Finally she shook her bald head again. "You ain't going nowhere till Palmer get back."

"Then will you stay with me?"

"I ain't no midwife now," Coy said.

"But there's one down the road?"

"Old Mamie? She been dead three or four weeks; went to her funeral.

Must have forgot to tell you. Mamie rose up and preached in the midst of us all, had to bolt down the lid of that coffin to stop her."

You never knew when Coy had drifted out of her head, when she was joking or bringing a true report from a world not much like your own. Miss Olivia had told me she believed that Coy was older than the major which was hard to imagine, considering how Coy worked seven days every week with no sign of weakness. Anyhow the news about Mamie, true or false, was hard to take. I paused there trying to see my way out.

Coy finally pointed behind toward the main house and said "Nothing to do but call Miss Olivia, mean as she be. You want me to?"

I said "You know it's the last thing on God's Earth I want."

Coy nodded. "Last thing."

"But you can't help me out here on your own?" I was somehow dreaming of doing it myself.

"Coy too old," she said. "Might kill you and that baby both." When I paused for a moment, she actually turned and took a step to leave.

What could I say then but "Fetch Palmer's mother please, and you come help her"?

Coy did all that.

By the time Palmer got back just before sunset, I'd had the boy with nobody's help but Miss Olivia's, Coy's and my own strong mind. When Miss Olivia got to the Office, I begged her pardon for any mistakes I'd made on her. But I also said in the briefest words that I meant to have a healthy child and would she please not try to alarm me now or ever again with her constant worries if that's what they were.

She nodded once.

And from then on I was not scared a minute. Once the pains began and settled into waves, I bore down hard as an old cotton baler. Oddly that went on for fewer hours than it usually takes with a first-round mother, though it must have seemed like a year to me. Like the memory of my first night with Palmer, my wedding night and other painful times, any memory of my labor pains is long since faded. Anyhow the child, with all his parts in place and looking normal, gave his first howl in late afternoon.

Coy said she'd never known a heifer to deliver so fast.

Even Miss Olivia managed to praise me in roundabout terms. Still I took the boy from her as soon as she'd let me and held it close through the nap I took before Palmer walked in. Even when I heard Miss Olivia say to Coy "You know what they plan to name this child?" I kept my eyes shut.

Coy said "No. But it's hers to name."

And the child slept on beside me. So far I was too flat exhausted to feel an automatic love. Those were days before *bonding* was invented. What I know I thought, in one of the instants I was awake before napping again, was *I'll tear the head off anyone or thing that touches this boy to take him from me.* I'd scarcely killed fifty houseflies till then in twenty-two years, but I knew I meant what I thought precisely.

I let Palmer decide on the name. Of course we'd already talked in private about likely names for a boy or girl, but we'd never come up with anything certain. And we skirted the biggest question of all—which kin if any we wished to honor. So the first time we were alone that evening, I took pretty much all the strength I had and said "Name him, Palmer."

He looked down at me, and I knew what was coming. I didn't know what I'd do when he said it. He was gentler than I'd guessed, and he asked me first. "How would you feel about him being *Larkin?*"

It came out automatically. I said "Oh God—"

Palmer said "Don't worry. Can I name him for Major?"

I looked to the boy himself for any guidance. He was nursing my breast, and his eyes were turned up at me as if he could see the first puzzle float past in his world, but he seemed to have no preference whatever when it came to names. So I said to Palmer "You were right the first time. Can I just put my own father's name in the middle?" Father's given name was Augustus, which led to the boyhood nickname *Gus* that all his life he refused to answer to.

So Palmer said it all straight out with a waving bow that touched the floor— "Larkin Augustus Slade, welcome here." Then he broke into the nearest approach to a wide smile he'd ever experienced in my sight at least—Palmer, I mean. "Let that be it" was the last thing he said that I could still hear.

Tired as I was, I was satisfied with that.

From that critical day I well understood what a brave soul Miss Olivia was to accept my terms and lead me through those straits in safety. I mean she took that child from the fork of my body, cut the cord, tied it off, saw the afterbirth pass and buried it past the reach of the hounds—all before she and Coy cooked supper.

When Dr. Rogers came out the next morning to check on the aftermath, he said he couldn't have helped me any more with his own hands.

And Miss Olivia told him it was the sixth child she'd delivered in her life not to speak of her own. Couldn't he finally issue her a license?

He told her no license was necessary for anybody with her plain skills.

All the same, two nights later when I was still weak as water but clearer minded, I turned to Palmer in the midst of the night and said "Understand—I've got to take this baby and go to my home. Your mother has done all she could to down me. I've fought all I can. That's not in my nature to keep on doing, and I can't keep winning. She's too strong a fighter. She'll kill me soon. So once I'm strong enough to stand, I'll take young Larkin to my family home and treat him like your much-loved son till you finish up here and move down to join us in a place of our own."

Palmer had known for months of my hope to rent Betsy Magee's back rooms. But the roots of my hair actually rose at the risky sound of my voice declaring my will. I'd never heard of any woman saying such things and lasting the night. I half expected my gentle silent mysterious husband would strike my mouth and be justified.

He didn't, though for longer than ever he held me waiting to see what he'd do. Dark as the room was, Palmer took my face in both of his hands and held it steady. Steady and so firmly that a little more pressure and my skull might have cracked. For the longest time he kept his silence, looking at what I couldn't imagine in the near black air. So far as I knew, there was nothing in his line of sight but my stark face in the chilly dark. At last he said "You understand how much this will complicate my life?"

I told him I did.

"You know I could stop you."

I said "Palmer, you could kill me this minute with a snap of the neck. You could kill my baby even easier than that."

"I thought this baby was *between* us, Anna."

I told him it most certainly was, but I also told him I thought it was *our* life we were talking about. However complicated his life might get, *our* life would stand a chance of lasting if I struck out of here and he followed suit as soon as he could. I knew not to mention the marriage vows. I'd irked him more than once by harping on those.

He was bound to hear me, but again he was silent as the air between us. Then in a minute his hands moved down a little on my head; and he gave it two fairly strong turns, left and right. A third turn might well break my neck—he was always that strong. But when I kept quiet, his grip eased a little and his hot forehead came down and leaned on mine. What he said was "I won't try to stop you. I'll see what I can do beyond that."

I told him that any question of *us*, this new young family we'd apparently started, was in his hands.

Palmer said "You're goddamned right it is." But when he seized me hard again, I could tell it was more than half mock strength.

And then I knew that, with any luck at all, we'd have a life for better or worse. When Larkin Augustus woke in his basket a quarter hour later, I whispered for Palmer to bring him over and let me feed him. Respectable white women were not supposed to set foot to the floor for at least ten days after labor.

Palmer didn't move.

I could hear his slow-paced sleeping breath, but I lacked the will to wake him up. So I slowly inched my way through the room, lifted the child like a ticking bomb, went back to the bed and fed him there up against his far-gone good-hearted father.

FOUR

The problem in trying to tell the story of a human life is easy to state. People's lives—from the wildest lover's to the bravest scout's—are uneventful for way over three-fourths of their length. If you don't believe (and I know I don't) that every instant in a life is urgent to that person's fate, then you could write a satisfactory life of the busiest man or woman who ever lived in less than two pages, often on a postcard. Most things that happen to a person leave no more trace than last month's raindrop.

Like most people, wherever they live or travel, I've been engaged in little more than a drab-colored village event—certainly not the official state fair with charming lights and music and giants. All the same I'm almost convinced that, if you can tell the absolute truth about the five or ten moments that mattered in any one life, then you'll have shown how every life is as useful to the world and to the eyes of God as any president's or pope's. Or so I've believed and I doubt I'm lying. If I hadn't always trusted in that unknowingly for most of my time, I'd have died by my own hand long since. To make those moments understandable though, you're forced to surround them with the bones of what caused them and what *they* caused.

In any case after Larkin Augustus was born, Palmer and I seemed to step fairly quickly into that new plan I knew we should make. The baby and I stayed beside Palmer in the separate Office for another month longer. When I'd been stopped from going home in time for the labor, my mother got Miss Olivia's permission and came up to stay near me and help with the boy. Muddie slept in the main house, and some nights she took August with her and let me have some unbroken sleep. I had so little breast milk to give him that we'd started right off feeding him bottles when he cried for more.

Muddie and Miss Olivia managed to be civil despite the fact that Muddie called the boy *Augustus* from the first minute she held him in her arms. In fact I noticed in a very few days that Miss Olivia was following suit with apparent content. Even Palmer didn't try to change the practice, though I would sometimes hear him say the word *Lark* as he played with the child. I thought at the time that everybody silently realized how painful it would be to say the name *Larkin* many times a day, so we all just quit. I was the one who after a week or so shortened the name to simple *August,* and that caught on with everyone but Muddie for the rest of his life. She insisted on *Augustus* to keep Father's name alive.

I'd asked Palmer to prepare Miss Olivia for mine and the baby's move down to my home, and he said he'd already done that with no comment pro or con from her. In mid-January then in a terrible freeze, Muddie and I with August and our luggage went out to climb into Palmer's car. We'd seen Miss Olivia at breakfast, and I'd just assumed she'd come out to wave us off when we left. People always did back then if they had two legs and could walk ten yards. But no, Miss Olivia stayed inside the house, plainly visible behind the parlor window.

When Palmer took the baby from Muddie so she could climb in, he thrust the boy high up in the air to give Miss Olivia a last little glimpse.

She refused to take it. Or at least she didn't smile or wave. But her eyes which had kept every volt of their power stayed on young August till the final instant.

I suspected she was thinking *That's the last time I'll see him.* I blew her a kiss against my better judgment to say she was wrong.

She was right for nearly the next four months. Palmer stayed with his mother by the river, claiming he couldn't just leave her in the cold. And when winter broke in time for planting, he stayed on to be sure the tenants got it right. Of course he visited me and August almost every week but still said nothing about moving down. So I chose May Day as my deadline, and then I wrote him to say I'd rented Betsy Magee's set of rooms and would he please send Betsy the first month's rent? It was partly a bluff. I hadn't moved in, hadn't even told Muddie. But when Betsy sent me word that her latest aging bachelor-roomer had been found cold dead in the midst of a nap, I asked her to give me a one-week option which she readily did.

To my great relief Palmer sent the check by return mail and a letter to me. He asked me to move on into Betsy's rooms, saying he'd join me by the middle of the month. He felt he owed his mother two weeks' notice. In my answer I didn't point out that he'd had four months to get her prepared. But I certainly said we were looking forward to his arrival. Then Father helped me move a few things plus August of course. And we experienced a curious two weeks, the boy and I. I'd felt drawn to him from the very start. He never had that awful drawn-up boiled-red spider look that so many newborn children have for the first few weeks, and he cried so little that Palmer asked me if something was wrong with the boy's vocal cords.

Not at all as it turned out. He just saw no cause to howl for his food or companionship or a change of position in his crib. He had good sense quite prematurely. By the third or fourth day if August needed something he'd lie still and make low talkative noises as if he fully understood the idea of conversation and was practicing up with throat exercises till he knew sufficient words. It was in that two weeks that I actually came to love young August past the natural bond of motherhood, and the reason was something I've never told till now. It lay in the things I was fairly sure he told me, young as he was, in our days alone together.

The late spring days were warm and long. At Betsy's I had very little to do but talk to her while she sewed clothes and get the baby through his few duties — the feedings, his complicated daily bath and numerous naps, then the walk to Muddie and Father's for supper every evening. So lonely and idle as I was, I'd lie down most afternoons with August beside me on the big bed all nested in pillows. And we'd sleep soundly, waking maybe if Betsy knocked and offered us lemonade and one of her peculiar desserts or whenever the late sun struck my face and let me know it was time to dress us and head for Muddie's.

It was in those slow long afternoons that August actually spoke to me. I know I was sane. I well understood no child that young could begin to talk. I may just have been undergoing some phase of the illness I'd known before in the form of melancholy, the deep dark blues that would haunt me till something worse eventually replaced them. If the *baby blues* were the problem, this time they made me subject also to real streams of joy.

And that fresh happiness came always when August and I were alone together. I'd wake up as I said, and beside me there would be August with his ebony eyes fixed on me like the magnet he was compelled to obey. I'd offer a smile, a touch on his cheek, I'd call him sweet names. He'd never break that locked-on stare of his, so I'd go silent and take the message I all but knew he longed to press toward me.

It always came as some form of the words *Swear to me you'll never leave* or *Swear you'll save me from every danger*. Sometimes a stormy frown would gather around his eyes as if my answer which was always Yes had failed to assure him. And then I'd actually say the word *Swear*. That would mostly calm him, and he might smile very briefly as he broke his stare and turned aside from me to express delight in the way infants do—by surrendering their whole bodies to a brief muscular spasm that straightens their arms and legs.

I understand that a similar message is what most children say to the world, or to their parents anyhow, from the moment they're born till the moment they know they need to cut their own path away. Or at least that's what I understood for more than half my life. In recent years of watching the news, I've been forced to conclude that a great many children have monster parents and are terrified every minute they're awake till they're old enough to flee or die from the knowledge.

Nonetheless I've never doubted that the fact of those long afternoons, with that first child my body had made, turned into one of the two or three most urgent things I tried to do in the following years. Though I'd had a perfectly safe childhood, I still felt the need to swear to August that he'd have at least that much safety if I had my way. Also in silence I swore to give Palmer Slade everything I had that he needed, providing of course he chose to join his child and me on a permanent basis. All that was left was to vow to myself that I'd somehow stay peaceful and strong enough to keep the other pledges I'd made right on to the grave.

Palmer kept his word, the word I'd pressed out of him. In the third week of May 1923, he drove up at Betsy's just after sunset. I'd had a siege of sadness all day—no reason but the prevailing silence of recent months and too long a separation from normal adults that could speak my language. Being that moody right on into the afternoon, I'd sent word by a passing boy to let Muddie know that August and I would skip supper tonight and stay quietly at Betsy's. I should have known that any such message wouldn't just be *received*.

No, in under an hour here came Leela dressed for a palace with our supper in a basket, food enough for a family of twelve. So while I was sorting through all the dishes, Leela sat by August's crib and read him a story. He'd seldom lie still for more than ten seconds with anybody but me and Leela—he loved every word that came out of her mouth whether it came from her own mind or just from the Bible-story book Miss Olivia had given him at birth. The book had belonged to his Uncle Larkin and had Lark's childish drawings in the margins.

Leela was there then when Palmer arrived, and I plainly recall she showed him more welcome than I could manage at first anyhow. I was too stunned, I guess, and too relieved to grin and jump as a young wife maybe should have. Not till I saw his fine long head and the far-back smile in his eyes did I actually believe that the man I'd married had kept his promise and was still mine for life or tonight anyhow.

Shy as he'd always been with me, Palmer said the thing most mates dream to hear. He set his suitcase down inside our new private door that had its own key. He kept a distance of four or five feet, but he offered both hands and said "Your wandering boy is home."

At least I had the sense to say "I couldn't be gladder" which was simply the truth. It surprised me to hear it.

It seemed to surprise Palmer Slade even more. For an instant his face went blank as paper. I thought he was showing the hurt he'd taken from his silver-tongued mother when he left her alone as a crow on a dead tree, but then his eyes closed, and he launched the best laugh of his life to that point. Or so I felt.

And August actually laughed out loud in Leela's arms, very likely the first laugh he ever gave us and one of the rare entirely happy moments of any human life, even one as open-armed as his.

In the final days Palmer lived at the river place, he had bought a small truck, coal-black like all cars in those days and one of the first mechanical trucks in our part of the world. It had cost more money than we had to spend. So Palmer was buying it on time which I've never trusted. Still he had to have a reliable way to get to his duties on the Slade place and all the extra jobs he did, finding and estimating timber for several lumber companies and the paper mill. As we settled into life together at Betsy's, he was spending six days a week dawn to dark on the road or out of my sight anyhow.

That was normal enough. Most men, white and black, worked similar hours or longer. Women did too of course, though we seldom left the yard and we worked till bedtime—some women till long afterwards if they had repulsive husbands. Anyhow slim as everybody's income was, Palmer kept his chin shaved, wore a clean shirt daily and took every chance for a small piece of work in addition to his Slade-farm duties. Pay was that scarce and paltry.

One good thing for him, me and August—Palmer generally got home clean at night and was not too exhausted to be himself beside us through supper till often he'd nod off helplessly by nine o'clock upright in his chair. Almost always from his days in the pine woods, he'd come in smelling of pine sap or rosin, a welcome odor. And the worst he had to show for his lonely treks through the underbrush were occasional scratches, chigger bites and in summer the ticks. I can't recall that we feared ticks then. Maybe spotted fever hadn't traveled east yet from the Rocky Mountains. All the same I hated to see their bodies, swollen pale blue with his blood as they sapped Palmer's waist and back, deep into his warm groin and privates and down both his legs.

As soon as he walked through the back screen door, I'd make him strip, hand me his clothes; and I'd put them on the porch till I had time to check them. Then I'd ask him to walk straight on to the tub. Betsy had put a great copper tub in the bedroom corner. I'd have hot water ready on the stove in a kettle. I'd test it first in the crease of my left arm so as not to scald him. Then I'd slowly pour it from the back of Palmer's neck all down his body till every tick—he'd be studded with them—turned loose and died. After that I'd soap him good and scrub him.

Only when he'd stood up, dried himself and let me be sure I'd got every tick would I feel free to go back out, examine his clothes and decide if they'd need to be boiled tomorrow in Betsy's outdoor iron pot. It was maybe more work than was strictly needed, but my mind demanded it every time. I felt I was not only saving Palmer but August too. To the best of my knowledge, August never got bitten. But just the thought of their yielding up their blood to those blind little mouths was a horror to me. And it still is today, though Palmer at least is safe now beyond all harm this world can offer.

By late in the summer, I'd begun to think we three were charmed in a safe broad circle made out of our care for one another. No miracles happened, Palmer worked hard as ever, August grew naturally with no worse problems than occasional colic or a little heat rash, we ate a good many suppers with my family; but otherwise I was learning to cook simple dishes that Palmer liked. Toward the end of July he mentioned his mother for the first time in weeks. He said she'd appreciate the chance to see her grandson. Why didn't we drive up with him this coming Sunday? We could take a picnic and eat by the river.

I hadn't seen Miss Olivia or corresponded with her since I returned home. Still if I'd needed a reason to refuse Palmer's idea, he'd handed it to me. I thanked him politely and said he could take young August on his own. But no, I couldn't see the Roanoke River ever again for any reason.

Palmer let my few words settle in the room like a fog. And then he said very calmly "I'll take the boy then. Please have him ready."

That was long before American fathers volunteered to take their children off the mother's hands for as much as five minutes much less a day's excursion. But I well understood, or thought I did, how much Palmer loved August. And I knew Miss Olivia would know what to do if the child got sick or difficult. So I had the boy not only ready but splendid on Sunday morning in the newest outfit Betsy had made him, a white sailor suit edged in navy blue. She refused to charge us a penny for his clothes. She liked him that much and sometimes called him *July* or *September*.

When they left after breakfast, I watched them off from the little back stoop. Palmer had kissed me lightly as he picked up August. I'd brushed August's fine hair one last time. And all the way to the car in his father's arms, he kept those two dark eyes right on me, no hint of a smile. I thought *I won't see them again.* Somehow I thought they'd wreck the truck and both be killed. At once I knew that was hardly likely to be the case. I'd had no prophetic powers till now. But the rest of that long day, I moved in dread every step I took. Time would eventually show I was right, though about the wrong threat.

At eleven that night they were still not back. I've mentioned that nobody had telephones, Betsy had no car, I couldn't imagine waking up Father or hunting for Ferny and asking either one of them to drive me to the Slade place, I couldn't even tell Betsy how scared I was when she checked in with me at her early bedtime and asked where on Earth "the boys" might be. I sat in a straight chair trying to read a book of Palmer's about how Stanley discovered Dr. Livingstone deep in Africa, but what I felt by the literal instant was an agony unlike any I'd known.

I understand it will shock good people if I say I've always felt to this day that I understood what Christ endured that terrible night when the disciples ran off and left him to face his tortured death as lonely as any green tree in a desert. But I felt my own desertion that deeply, and I won't claim I didn't.

At nearly midnight I went down the back steps silently and walked around to the shallow front porch. There was plenty of moon, and I actually stood there staring at the place where poor Arthur Straughan had sketched the true outline of his body, then blown off his head. Palmer owned a pistol. It was in our bedroom right then on the mantel. If I'd stayed alone another half minute, I don't know what I'd have been strong enough to do to myself.

But the truck turned in and threw lights on me, and the boys were back. I followed them inside. August of course was long since asleep in his same white suit that was scarcely soiled. Palmer looked entirely like himself, though I thought his eyes had gone slightly wild. He went straight to the crib and laid August down. When he turned back toward me, he stayed in place and watched me closely but offered no word.

I don't think angels with scorching swords could have stopped me asking where in God's name he'd been with my child. The *my* was hardly out of my mouth before I regretted it.

But Palmer ignored the claim I'd made. He answered my question about where they'd been by saying "I don't have to answer that." His voice was polite but the meaning was so unlike his nature that I could hardly hear him. Till then we'd never had one serious quarrel, though he'd occasionally frown and go silent.

So I was on thoroughly new ground now. I said "Have you seen a clock today?" I pointed to the clock beside our bed.

He said "Yes, lady. It's past midnight. I'm going to bed. Some of us work tomorrow." Then he did just that.

I had to undress August and clean him up, all of which the child slept through. It was only then that I saw the thin ring on his plump right hand. Babies with little rings were not unheard of in those unsafe days. This one was gold, scarcely more than gold wire. Since Palmer was already breathing the rhythms of his normal deep sleep, I couldn't ask him about the ring.

I was forced to assume that Miss Olivia was the source, and I wanted to ease it off right then and hurl it away. Instead I leaned to August's hand and forced myself to kiss it. Then I slipped into bed without affecting Palmer.

His silent presence felt like the North Pole at very close range.

I think I may have slept three minutes before day broke, and all those hours I was mainly thinking my life had ended and could not be renewed.

But in the morning as Palmer finished the normal sizable breakfast I'd cooked, he broke silence finally and said "You ever seen the ocean?"

"Just Chesapeake Bay which doesn't really count," I said. "I've been to Norfolk several times to see Muddie's brothers." All her three brothers had moved there years ago to work for the Navy; but with Muddie so susceptible to sunlight, we'd never even got out to the beach.

That made Palmer smile for the first time in at least twenty-four hours. He said "No, I meant the Indian Ocean."

I was still too worried about last night to join in his fun whatever he meant—if he meant fun at all. I had a child yet to bathe and diapers to wash.

Palmer said "Would you show it to me and August?"

"What is *it*?" I said.

He said "Norfolk."

I told him I couldn't think of one thing in Norfolk he needed to see not to mention poor August.

Palmer didn't miss a beat. He said "Then Wilmington, North Carolina."

I told him he'd need another guide for Wilmington. I'd never been that far south in the state.

Palmer said "Then let's ride down next weekend and breathe a little salt air."

I said "There's not enough time in *two* weekends to drive from here to Wilmington and back." The roads were that bad still.

"Punkin, I'm talking about the train." He called me *Punkin* when I acted dumb.

I had to sit back down to believe him. People of our sort—men especially in the crop-growing months—barely ever left the land. And money. Where would Palmer get the money, strapped as we were? Where would we stay? I didn't know a soul in Wilmington, and he'd never mentioned friends. But something told me this crossroads was crucial to the health of our future. I thought I could see a fork in our road, two ways I must choose between—being Palmer's wife or just his partner. So I stood up again and warmed his coffee. "I'd want to leave the baby with Muddie and Leela."

Palmer nodded. "That's very much my feeling too."

That single sentence felt to me like water poured out on a pavement that had long been scorching my feet, and I was compelled to bend and brush the back of my husband's powerful neck with my cool mouth.

The trip lasted a full five days, one whole day on each end just for the trains. And with all that would come to light soon after, I still know they were our best days, mine and Palmer's as man and wife—better than the honeymoon or any calm pleasure of our later years. I still wonder why. How much of the memory is just my delusion, fed by my hunger, and how much is true to the hours as they passed? I'm not the best judge obviously. But in my opinion what flowered on that simple excursion was the absolute heart of Palmer's good soul, what kept me beside him as long as he lasted, give or take the bad hours and days.

He had never looked finer than in that old town among those live oaks draped with ghost-gray moss in that sea air as clear as salt could make it. I'd been watching Palmer's face for nearly three years. And just that weekend it somehow cast off the boyish husk that had guarded him maybe. The full-grown face was a great deal stronger; yet at the same time, riskier. It seemed freely offered to the passing world for whatever it chose to fling his way. Other people's looks have always mattered more to me than to women in general, the women I've known anyhow. And though that concern tricked me on more than one serious occasion, I've never been able to purge myself of the birthright instinct which steadily tells me that anything beautiful is bound to be good.

And goodness or at least open-heartedness and boundless patience seemed to pour straight toward me from Palmer's mind and heart every minute I was near him that weekend, and I scarcely left him for anything else but the call of nature. We reached our rooming house near dark on the Friday, a dry warm evening with all windows open and the white curtains moving in a merciful breeze. We cleaned ourselves up and went out to find a bountiful supper of soft-shelled crabs which I'd never had and much enjoyed. (I've tended to bite my fingernails in worrisome times, and soft-shelled crabs have always seemed to me like a fingernail-biter's ideal food.) Then we took a long walk through the cobblestone streets—nobody to scare you, though a few drunk sailors yelled compliments at me which was by no means a common occurrence in my young life—and we came back tired for an early bedtime.

If truth be told, and it's my sole warrant for telling this story of an uneventful life, I had looked forward to an opportunity to please Palmer's body on neutral ground with no chance of August calling for notice. And Palmer had hardly locked our door before he stood in the midst of the big room among shed clothes as bare as God made him. After the way he'd looked in the sunlight, I was fully confident he'd look more splendid still in nothing but his skin by soft lamplight. And he did look good enough to stall the hand of the cruelest accuser.

What was unexpected somehow was how subject to ruin—malicious damage or acts of Fate—his whole muscular frame would look once he stood near me naked. For the first few instants, I had to restrain my wish to snatch a bedsheet and throw it around him—some form of protection however frail. But the band of extreme seriousness across his eyes, as he faced me so watchfully, held me in place. At last he broke free and moved to the window behind the curtains to stare at the street.

For the first time in my life, I was bold enough to stand where I was and strip myself not quite entirely but down to my slip. So far as I know that simple act was a novelty for good girls of my era. When Palmer didn't look back, I finally said "I owe you a lot of thanks for this." By *this* I must have meant the whole day and his idea to free us up and bring us here.

At first he didn't seem to hear me. Then he turned and took me in in one unblinking look. He said "Dear friend, you earned every minute."

That sentence is the kind of thing you wait for Heaven to send your way. Many never live to hear it, but it came to me in Wilmington at age twenty-three. Without looking back I took short reverse steps to the bed and sat on the edge. I plainly figured my husband would join me there and take my lead.

He stayed in place another long moment by the window, watching me. Then he gave a slow nod and circled the long way round to the bed, the opposite side to where I waited. When he'd pulled back the white spread and laid himself down, he said "This is one *whipped* boy—excuse me." Then I heard him turn over.

When I stood to swap my slip for a nightgown, I saw he'd turned toward the distant wall away from me.

Which is how the night passed. When I turned out the light, it was just past ten. I must have lain there wide awake a handspan from him till midnight at least. I recall the voices of more clumps of sailors down in the street. I finally heard a single boy's voice sing a whole verse of "Home on the Range," a truly fine tenor with a lot of Irish in it. I know when the boy got to *Seldom is heard a discouraging word*, I clamped my eyes shut in hopes of flushing out one tear at least to ease the swarming weight of my mind. I felt more alone than I'd ever been, even at the instant Larkin Slade disappeared. Tears would have been a welcome companion. But nothing would come, no tear at least, though sleep finally folded me in like a coal-black blanket, old heavy rough wool.

Yet that next morning, Saturday, Palmer woke me up by stroking my hair that was loose on the pillow. I turned and looked. He'd shaved and dressed right under my sleep like a seasoned thief. It bothered me almost worse than last night, but he leaned to kiss my forehead and say he was hungry as any moose. Neither one of us had ever seen a moose; are they usually hungry? I never mentioned the strangeness of the night. He looked that well and rested again. So I sponged myself off and dressed in a hurry, my coolest housedress. The air was already close and damp.

After a breakfast that would have braced an army, Palmer had still said very little. But once we'd made a brief stop in our room, he asked me if I'd ever ridden a trolley. I had to remind him that on our honeymoon we'd ridden every trolley in the District of Columbia. That seemed to set him back for a while, forgetting so soon. But I managed to rally him, he took off his necktie, and off we went on a trolley to the beach. In no time under a lemon-colored sunlight, the dampness lifted. And the first sea air I'd encountered in years seemed to fill my head like a huge bright bowl that might drift away. It lasted till night.

And all that long day, we stayed at the beach. Not that it was anything like what people mean now by *beach*. It was just a broad stretch of the south Atlantic coast with a very few tall old gray-shingle houses and some fishermen's shacks, maybe two little modest cafes serving seafood and a deep shoreline of bone-white sand as clean as the floor of a well-kept church. At first Palmer rolled up his seersucker pants, I took off my hot silk stockings and we walked a total of maybe ten miles both north and south, still in the strong but breezy lemon sunshine.

Every few minutes I'd think to myself *This is surely farther than I've ever walked. My legs will quit soon.* But they didn't. I kept pace with Palmer, barely speaking a word but trying each step to hoard every sight and sound, every feeling, for some later day when I'd have less to see and might need some cheer. Despite the presence of the whole Atlantic crashing toward us with shells and driftwood, seaweed and gulls, the thing I worked at storing most truly was Palmer's profile, his whole lean body and striding legs and the dry close grip of his hand on mine.

When I gradually realized that no, I wasn't about to faint or fall down exhausted, then—again in silence and with some fear to think how dangerous it might be to call a moment *happy*—I began to admit to myself that all day yesterday and today were building toward some peak of contentment that might well never be matched again, however long I lived. If that sounds strange or sad or pathetic to any young woman of the present time, then she needs to recall or learn for the first time that not one single wife of my time was ever encouraged by *anybody* to question her husband's lion's share of the rights in a marriage or to doubt that he—in all his soul and body—was the only target of outright physical and mental devotion you were licensed to aim for.

I'd been trained in that world. I wasn't a genius or a praiseworthy scholar, but I had fairly good sense and responded accordingly. So here and now I must also add that I didn't even question then, and still don't today, that Palmer Slade was a qualified goal for all the love I could feel and show— all that wasn't shared with our child and reserved for later children. What else could I have done with my existence, then or in the years that came after or here in this all but empty room I inhabit in my ancient dotage? And why did I never tell that plainly to the goal himself, an ordinary boy who became a good man after some detours?

After our trip up and down the sand, we ate a big bait of boiled shrimp and crabs at the better-looking of the run-down cafes. And once we'd finished Palmer finally said "You know how tired I was last night?"

I told him "Of course."

Then he said "But I'm healing fast. I think I just need one more thing."

I thought that *healing* was an odd word to use, but I said "What thing?" I thought it might mean lemon pie or more of the bitter boiled coffee he'd drunk.

But he said "Swimming—let's both get wet."

I surely hadn't swum since well before Lark's death. So far as I knew, neither had Palmer. I didn't mention that though. I pointed out how we both were dressed. But when his face fell, I said "You strip to your underdrawers, and I'll wait out on the porch for you." The cafe had a small shaded porch facing the waves.

Palmer looked disappointed at first and shook his head to decline my suggestion. But when I urged him, he paid for our meal and asked the man who ran the place if he'd get in trouble for swimming in his underwear.

The man, who must have weighed three hundred pounds, said "Sport, you could strip and turn your whole hide wrongside out. Not one soul out here would tell you *Nay*."

We laughed, then stepped out onto the porch. Palmer peeled in an instant, gave me a wave and ran toward the breakers.

As he hit the water, I actually said the word "Goodbye" more for insurance than the fear or certainty of harm. Then I sat still for a long half-hour in occasional short prayers, watching my husband demonstrate again and again how ready to live and how nearly unsinkable he was and how I wished he'd at least pause once in the shallows and look my way which he never did.

Finally after I'd tried and failed to hail him in, he did stand up in knee-deep surf facing Europe and slowly lift up handfuls of water and pour them down from the crown of his head, scrubbing himself hard with just his palms. Then he came up toward me smiling with an ease I hadn't seen on him in many months.

Yet when we got to the rooming house in late afternoon, I'd barely drawn a cool breath before Palmer shucked his clothes again, fell across the bed and was out in two seconds till well past dark.

After lying unused beside his slack body for half an hour, I went downstairs to the little bleak lobby and read old magazines till Palmer woke up and sought me out near nine o'clock, saying he was starved. Well of course he was. But since it was late, where—even in an active port in those days— were we likely to find a place to eat without razor fights and ladies of the evening on all sides of us?

Palmer just held out his hand and said "I know."

Though he told me he'd never seen Wilmington till now and though I'd been gravely confused by his failure to reach out toward my body, I followed him out.

What he did didn't take a college education. We walked half a block till an old black man passed, impeccably dressed in a white linen suit and both his arms stacked full of corn—ten or twelve ears of fresh-picked corn still in the husk. With some difficulty he tipped his cap.

So Palmer said "Old cap'n, where can I get some supper? This lady's failing fast."

The old man looked us both up and down politely but slowly, and then he laughed deeply. "Follow me home two hundred yards, and I'll boil you this corn. Got a cooked ham too and some biscuits I made at sunrise today—make you see your grandmammy!"

That was an old expression for bliss that I hadn't heard since I was a child, so I laughed too and Palmer met my eyes with a quizzical look I didn't understand.

Thinking my laugh gave him leave to accept, he said to the old man "Lead the way."

It surprised the man as much as me. His face went solemn as any costly horse.

I felt peculiar but not so much as to make an objection.

And the old man stood astonished for one long breath. Then he said "My name is Marcus Patterson. Lived here all my life in Miss Patsy Yarborough's yard." He pointed beyond us toward a tall dark house with the pillars and iron work that crowd all Wilmington. Then he gave a graceful beckon with his chin, and we followed him home.

By eleven o'clock in Marcus Patterson's two-room house—clean as your hand and all but sizzling from the little iron stove he boiled the corn on—we pushed ourselves back from a good many bare cobs, a bowl of country butter that we'd raided severely, a cut-glass salt cellar and the crumbs from a dozen or more ham biscuits. For all the kind black people I'd known since a black midwife brought me into this world, I'd never eaten a meal in a black home—or been asked to eat one—until that night. Sadly it goes without saying that no black person had ever sat down in mine or Palmer's dining room, however much work they'd invested in every bite we swallowed.

So while I'd been a little off balance in the past two hours of Marcus Patterson's attention, I sat back feeling both pleasantly filled and immeasurably grateful. It would be decades before, looking back, I could fully comprehend the dreadful rigging of the scales of justice that made such an evening's gift both graceful and somehow—once it was offered—so easy to take and deeply satisfying and yet so depressing.

Why would this almost surely never happen again in mine and Palmer's lives? (It never did and hasn't to this day with me in a house lived in by only one other human, a fine black woman.) Even at the time though, July of '23, I stumbled to say some version of the rich gratitude I felt. I said "Mr. Patterson, you have *made* our trip." I'd never heard a white human being address a black man as *mister* and wouldn't again for many more years.

Palmer cut his eyes around on me, not harshly but keen. He wanted me to know he was clocking my feelings as they moved into words way beyond any depth I'd waded before. He even said a calm "Amen" to my brief speech. And when Marcus Patterson got up from his chair beside the stove—he'd watched us eat, not partaken himself—and deftly gathered up our plates, Palmer leapt to his feet, took the plates from him and carried them over to the galvanized tub that seemed to be Mr. Patterson's sink.

I doubt that Palmer Slade had carried a single plate but his own for more than three inches in his whole life till now. When he'd set them down, he reached in his pocket, brought out a silver dollar, held it out slightly, said "Much obliged" and laid it on the nearest shelf. A dollar at that time was more than handsome payment even for the ample amount we'd eaten. You could buy a week's worth of groceries for a dollar.

Marcus Patterson's face went grim as a hawk's. Then he smiled and said "Don't ruin it now, Son."

Palmer took back the dollar and gave a low bow which sweetened the air.

So with all the mystery of my young husband's not touching me still there in my mind, I told myself again to remember to thank God or Fate for this high watermark in my life. I don't know why I thought God hadn't been reading my thoughts by the fascinating instant, which He's famous for doing in my Bible anyhow whatever's the case in the actual universe.

At maybe four o'clock that night, two hours before dawn Palmer turned toward me and laid his broad right hand on my hip. I'd been deep asleep and when I came to, what surprised me most—it actually rushed up in me like shame—was the realization that till that moment I'd scarcely thought of August our son in two whole days. So when Palmer's hand stayed there heavy on me and made no further immediate request, my throat filled up with bitterness. And I finally said "Palmer, if you need Roxanna Slade on a regular basis, please find a way to say so. Or send her home where others can use her."

He was quiet a long time. Then his fingers moved on up to my waist, and he pressed them slightly inward on me. I was still a little slack there from my first pregnancy. Then Palmer said "I haven't felt good enough for you. Not always clean enough for someone fine as you."

I said "I thought you knew me better than that. I keep secrets badly. If I didn't feel you were more than sufficient, you'd have been the first to know."

He said "All this day I've thought about Larkin—Larkin that last afternoon in the river."

I said "Me too. But Palmer, swimming was your idea, not Roxanna's. And you came through fine." I still felt as if I had nothing to give him here and now, but I offered him one more plain true sentence. "You were good to watch."

He said "Good as Larkin?"

I said "Beyond a doubt," and I knew I meant it.

That tripped something deep in Palmer's body. He rolled to his own side facing my back and touching me down the length of my frame.

I could feel his readiness growing against me, and I had to ask myself if I could stand whatever he chose to offer me next. Then I thought *You lie still and let him ask.*

But he'd never asked in words before and he didn't now. He was slower and gentler than in the past, but he pulled me over to lie flat beside him, and then he went about taking again his almighty need.

I've mentioned how you couldn't turn on TV in those days and get free instructions on the most private skills or read any one of a thousand books on the subject of how to please a mate. But by then I wasn't exactly a fool on the vast dark subject of freely giving another body a joyful moment and taking your own sweet pleasure in that. And there in our white room in Wilmington as day broke on us—the day we'd have to retrace our steps toward home and our duty—I discovered I seemed to know as much as any seasoned whore we'd passed on the streets of this seaport.

I also thought, when Palmer was calmer and snoozing again, that tonight in the hours with Marcus Patterson, my husband had shown me a mystery I'd never seen so clearly—a welcome ease with all the world or all

I'd seen him encounter till now. By the time dawn seeped through the waving curtains, I felt again that I was lucky. We'd reached a real peak and could never deny it.

That was late July as I said. The rest of the summer and early fall went peacefully. The baby thrived and Palmer spent even more time than usual working at his mother's or elsewhere. I stayed busy just keeping up with a growing child, keeping our tiny apartment in shape and doing whatever I could to help Muddie who was showing more and more signs of the ailment that would bring her down soon, some apparent kind of slow kidney failure.

Part of the trouble started in late August when Leela suddenly decided that maybe she truly wouldn't marry after all—nobody was asking her—and that she'd better give thought to training herself for some paying job other than childbearing and cooking forever. In the weeks when she was contemplating the actual move to a teacher's college for the two years of work that would give her a license, she took more than one occasion to hint that *public instruction*—which was what she called *teaching*—was in every way a nobler calling than wife and mother.

I told her in no uncertain terms that *my* chosen career was at least as hard as coal mining (and was more confining—miners can generally sleep through a night) and that it required the mind of a general, a nurse and a saint, not to mention other needs. Anyhow Leela departed with the luggage of an infantry division for her teacher's college in Greenville. That left Muddie alone in the house too much of the time brooding on her health and what she'd begun to think were her failures of love and devotion to her husband and children.

So I'd take August to visit most afternoons and play two-handed bridge with Muddie or let her tell me what occupied her mind. Right to her deathbed she never stopped telling the stories I loved and would ask her for. I sometimes felt I was witnessing my mother bleed to death—she'd have that much stored up in her mind that needed to pour out even if I'd seen her the previous day. (Ferny had found a job in Raleigh, at the State College Library. And Muddie didn't see him nearly often enough. Nobody did, not at home anyhow. My older brother was all but officially a lost sheep now, and it pained Muddie greatly. Ferny did as well, though at least she could see Fern occasionally however far away he'd seem, even right in the chair beside you on the porch in reach of your hand.)

*   *   *

That way the month of August crept by and all of September. And it wasn't till the night of October 5th that Palmer quietly mentioned after supper that, if I could find it in my power, he'd like us to visit his mother on the weekend of the seventh and take the baby with us. I well recalled the pain he'd administered the last time I failed him; and the eighth of course would be my twenty-third birthday, the third anniversary of Larkin's drowning.

I hadn't laid eyes on Miss Olivia since August was born and I left the Slade place, and I had no desire to see her now. It was not just the common chill that lies between wives and their husband's mothers. No mother-in-law elsewhere in my vision approached Miss Olivia for bristling strength. But I'd vowed "for richer, for poorer" to Palmer. So sure, I told him we'd make the trip with him. I told myself we'd all be on our best behavior, not to mar the memory of as fine a boy as Lark.

And it very nearly worked out that way. Palmer's original idea had been that we'd drive up on Sunday the seventh, spend the night and be there for the anniversary as well as my birthday on the Monday. Since it didn't much matter what days of the week Palmer did his work, I told him that I wanted to disrupt August's schedule as little as possible. And I made the one condition that we not spend the night. We'd go on Monday morning and come back that evening. Palmer agreed to that a little slowly. And I planned accordingly with a growing dread that I tried to conceal. The fact that, on the night of the seventh, we had the earliest frost I recall—a hard killing frost—only deepened my apprehension.

But the drive went as smoothly as drives could then. August slept through all the bumps and was in a calm mood when we got to the Slade place in time for the noon meal. By then the boy could sit up in the old highchair that Miss Olivia told stories about. It had seated children since before the Revolution. Or so she claimed. She'd make the same claim for an old brown bottle she found in the yard too that everybody knew was six months old. But nobody ever corrected her. Things seemed easier for Miss Olivia to bear if she thought they were old.

Anyhow we were all but finished with Coy's chess pie when we heard the sound of a car pulling in, and Palmer went to the window to look. It took him awhile to recognize the driver, but then Palmer turned back to me as if I were responsible for who it was. "It's Ferny Dane," he said. "Do you know why?"

I was at least as surprised as Palmer and said as much.

It was Miss Olivia who finally told Palmer "I assume he's come for the day itself. We all know how much he prized your brother."

Palmer flushed dark red which he seldom did. But for the moment Miss Olivia had silenced any other complaint he might have. The pressure was high though.

And I was left wondering what was so wrong about Fern turning up? If he'd managed to get a day's leave from his job and driven all the way up here from Raleigh, then of course it was right for him to be here—as much as me anyhow. Fern had known Lark longer and better than I. But whose was the car? By then I'd gone to the window too, and could see Fern walking alone to the house.

He opened the front door without a knock, and I watched Palmer grit his teeth at that. By the time Fern reached the dining room door, everyone in the room was tensed and braced in varying degrees.

At the sight of Fern's smile, Miss Olivia said "You're an answer to prayer."

Palmer gave a deep grunt that we all ignored.

Then Fern stepped in to kiss Miss Olivia. Next he turned to August in his highchair. "Boy, you have *grown*."

August laughed outright for the first time that day and threw his spoon halfway toward Fern.

I was still by the window, but I blew a kiss toward him.

Fern looked exhausted from the trip and older still, but he blew me a short kiss back and beamed his best smile.

Palmer was standing near to me—no smile at all, no welcoming step.

As Fern stooped to get the boy's spoon, he looked up at me.

Like a great fool I could only think to say "Who'd you steal the sporty car from?" It came out sounding stingy hearted.

Fern caught the sound. He rubbed the baby's spoon dry on his pants leg and laid it on the table. "I bought it Saturday to see you today. Happy birthday, Roxanna."

Palmer had said the same words at daybreak, but Miss Olivia and Coy hadn't made any reference to my birthday. I must have blushed too.

That sent Palmer further down the slope he was on. He said to Ferny "Where'd you get so much money?"

Easygoing as he generally was, Fern clearly felt Palmer's new sharp edge. He smiled his best smile. But he said "Since you're so much richer than me,

I don't mind telling you. Your own dear daddy gave me a piece of money just before his last stroke. I hung onto it and it paid the down payment."

I'd never known that and assumed Palmer hadn't.

But he said nothing then.

Miss Olivia said "Ferny, you earned every penny. And you don't owe *anyone* a word of explanation."

Nobody spoke for the longest time, so I tried to break the lock by taking up the last thing Fern had said to me. I told him "I've quit having birthdays now—an old married woman with a thriving baby."

Fern nodded. "I'll try to forget it hereafter. Yes ma'm, you are moving on, beyond a doubt."

For whatever reason that fanned Palmer to a quick high flame. "We're moving through life with little help from you, Slick." *Slick* then was not a complimentary nickname. And it was also the last thing Fern had ever been.

Miss Olivia said "Palm, I think you need air." When he stood on pale in his place by the window and said no more, his mother said again "Go walk up the road. It'll settle your food."

Palmer went, still silent and quiet on his feet as any black cloud. Even the loud old heavy front door made no sound at all when he shut it behind him.

Miss Olivia stood, pointed Fern to his place at the table and said "Come on, Anna. Let's feed this guest."

As I passed my brother, I bent to the crown of his head and kissed him. He smelled as clean and good to know as in his young boyhood when I'd wash his hair. I whispered that Palmer was under a lot of strain—not knowing what I might mean, just hoping to save the day.

Ferny said "I think I know." Though he had his arm out holding August's left hand, Fern's face was as bleak as when he looked up at me in the first crisis of that long day three years ago with Lark just drowned a few moments beyond us.

As I moved toward the kitchen, those words felt odd and harsh in my mind. *What on Earth does Fern think he knows?*

In the kitchen five minutes later, Miss Olivia left me alone with Coy while she took hot corn fritters to Fern. So I had a minute to tell Coy again how much I thanked her for her help with August's birth and what a satisfactory child he'd been from the start.

Coy nodded at the stove but never looked up to speak.

In the face of her silence, I drifted on with stories about how soundly the boy slept, how well he'd been, how hard he was already trying to talk.

Coy kept on nodding and finally said "He bound to be smart with the blood he got."

I couldn't tell if she meant my blood as well as the Slades', but I laughed and said again "I couldn't be gladder that the little fellow's mine."

That turned Coy around. Her big wood spoon poised in the air before her. Then she shook it at me like a preacher's warning. With her free left hand, she wiped her top lip that was shiny with sweat. Then she whispered to me with fierce deliberation, "You hang on to August. You need him this minute and the rest of your life. Need him *bad* right now."

I'd heard enough craziness from Coy in recent years to think this was normal foolishness from her. But once I'd laughed and started to tell her I was fine on my own, I saw Miss Olivia framed in the doorway.

She was nodding agreement to Coy not me.

That bit into me worse than the freeze that had killed every leaf and vine last night, every moth or squirrel pup caught above ground and insufficiently shielded.

I went back to the dining room, picked up the baby who snoozed off at once and sat while Ferny ate his meal.

As ever he ate like a pack of hyenas with excellent manners, though he hadn't put on a pound of flesh since he turned sixteen.

I sat still beside him, enjoying his eyes in the moments alone.

Miss Olivia had stayed back with Coy in the kitchen.

Ferny asked little trifling questions about my days and doings, about Muddie and Father. He was still on awkward terms with Father for leaving his job in the store and going to Raleigh, so he hadn't seen our family in recent weeks, and he plainly missed Muddie and Leela anyhow.

I was so haunted by the way he'd changed that in a few minutes I'd lost any sense that something peculiar was loose in this place. Something *against* me was here in the air like an ill-meaning bird, but what I mainly noticed was my sadly changed brother.

Ferny was still only twenty years old, yet the older strangeness that I'd seen in his eyes and the shape of his face since Larkin died had quickened its rate. Even in a peaceful situation like the Slades' dining room, Fern looked on the edge of total exhaustion. Every cell of his face, on the backs of his worn hands, seemed to be silently calling for care—some detailed affectionate outside attention from another human being that could ease his mind and refill a heart that was draining fast.

To my real sadness I knew I couldn't be Fern's salvation. I had my own needy souls in Palmer and August Slade. But I hoped my brother could find some kind girl and not stay alone which he was doing then. What I didn't know—didn't know for years—was that Fern had already found the drug that would make him a slave, and a solitary slave, for the rest of his short life.

When he looked up smiling from his empty plate, I asked what turned out to be the wrong question. Remember, I brought the roof down on myself. Ferny hadn't come all this way to harm me. I said "How about I put August down near Miss Olivia, and you and I walk down to the river while the sun's warm?"

Fern nodded. "I was hoping you'd feel strong enough."

I told him "Oh yes," then realized how hard I'd dreaded the river till now. It had to be a reflection of how sad Ferny looked that I'd thought of a walk toward the water again. Anyhow I stood up to settle young August in the midst of a box made of big feather pillows on the wide brass bed in Major's room that opened off the kitchen. Palmer was nowhere in sight or hearing but the way I felt then, that was no burden.

For all the frost from the previous night, the sun was very nearly too warm. And on the way down, Ferny took off his black coat and left it on a low tree limb.

I said "Some bird may mess on that."

Fern laughed. "That would just about put the lid on it!"

"What lid on what?" I said.

Fern said "The tin lid on this day—all that's been wrong with it and is getting worse fast."

I made a quick choice not to press him on that. I forced my brain to concentrate on the ground I was covering, the actual dirt that Larkin and I had walked on—very nearly the last piece of Earth he would ever touch alive. I kept expecting the place itself to draw tears from me. But we got ourselves, both thoroughly dry-eyed, to the major's long old brick terrace.

Fern even led us to the V-shaped bench where Lark and I had sat, and we settled there to watch the great river go its endless way. For a long time not a word was said. I was thinking *I ought to say something for Lark, maybe even tell him my baby's name.* But no words came and I didn't hunt them.

It was maybe five minutes before Ferny spoke. He said "I think I'm about to hurt you."

I thought he meant by recalling the past. I said "Don't worry. I made my peace with Lark way back. He was living his fate."

Fern waited again, then finally said "What I know has nothing to do with Lark."

I turned to face him, but he wouldn't face me. I could tell he was watching that spot on the far bank where he and Palmer and Larkin had stood in the stunning light before they swam back.

I said "Is it true?—what you think you know?" Ferny had never harmed any soul but his own poor self. With all the strangeness in the air today, the last thing I expected was meanness from my younger brother.

But at last he turned and said very clearly "You don't know where Palmer is now, do you?"

"This minute, up here? No, he's walking off his temper. You know how he does. He'll be fine by dark."

"But you and August may not be."

I could literally see those seven words come through Fern's lips, and each one hit me like a slug of lead, but I still had no idea what he meant. I knew I shouldn't ask and I didn't.

So Fern said "Is your body in good shape?"

I told him "To the best of my knowledge." What on Earth did he mean?

"You're not by any chance pregnant, I hope?" Now he was watching the river again.

"Lord no," I said. "We're in no rush."

Fern said "Then before you even think of a new child, get Dr. Rogers to test your blood."

I honestly wondered if Ferny had somehow gone truly crazy in his weeks in Raleigh. These last three years had been hard for him every way. But I held my hands out palm up toward him. "See, my blood's red." My skin was pink, not purple or bruised.

Fern barely checked me before he finished the wreck he was building. He said "Palmer's screwing a Negro woman two miles from here. Has been for years. Surely hasn't quit now." Then at last he faced me full-blast in the eyes.

I'd never heard a man use any such verb in a woman's presence, and I felt my skull all but literally split in two. No maul or ax could have split it faster. I couldn't speak.

I must have looked so badly crushed that Fern tried to backtrack and help me a little. He said "I've known that was true as recently as when August was born. Palmer may be doing better. But if he's not, you're in deep trouble more ways than one." In those days twenty years before penicillin, white people were terrified of syphilis—not terrified enough though to make it disappear.

I'd already known that Fern's claim was true, known it the moment he made his first thrust. This try at throwing me a wet sugar-tit—that Palmer might be *doing better now*—was almost worse than the news itself. I got to my feet and said "Who else in the world knows this?"

Fern said "Miss Olivia. And maybe Coy."

"Is the woman kin to Coy?"

Fern could actually smile. He said "Everybody between here and Spain is kin to Coy." When I didn't laugh he said "Her daughter—one of them anyhow. Or so Coy claims; she claims six or eight."

"Not Castille please?"

Fern smiled. "Castille wouldn't trip Palmer's eye, would she—wall-eyed as she is?"

I knew at once that it had to be true, and I took eight or ten strides uphill toward the house. When Fern didn't follow I turned back and begged one final kindness. "Don't tell this to another soul please."

As Fern faced me then, he looked like the last angel Eve ever saw as she left Eden. He nodded Yes and raised his right hand swearing silence. And he kept that silence the rest of his short life.

All the way to the house, I thought—not just that my world had collapsed around a dirty lie—but that my favorite brother, a boy I'd loved since the time he was born when I was three, had forced the pain on me in the midst of a sad day and for no purpose but meanness, for anger at Palmer and somehow at me for being the innocent occasion of his friend Larkin's death. As the later years passed, I slowly came to realize that Ferny thought he was telling me urgent news for my good—not to end my marriage and leave me helpless but to make me deal with a tangled truth and thereby strengthen myself for the far worse trials I'd have to face later.

When I reentered the house through the back door, the whole place was hung in the thickest silence I'd ever heard. Not even the usual creak of old boards. I glanced through the kitchen door as I passed.

Coy was taking her usual nap at the scrubbed work table. She'd pull up her chair, lay her head on her hands and sit there upright but dead to the world for exactly however long she could spare till the time came to walk out back with her ancient ax and kill however many chickens she'd need to dress and cook for supper.

No sign of Palmer in the dim front parlor, no trace of life in the separate Office when I looked out the window and strained to see light or any movement. The need to hear some word about Palmer, good or bad, was rising in me.

So I managed to climb the narrow stairs without a sound and to pause in Miss Olivia's open door. She'd taken off her shoes and was lying, otherwise fully dressed, on her own broad bed with August loosely held in her right arm. They were both asleep. I stood there long enough to be sure of that. Then it struck me as curious that, so far into my life with the Slades, this was the first time I'd seen Miss Olivia so much as shut an eye on daylight. I'd have never disturbed her if I hadn't felt this pressing a need. So once I'd waited a long time, I said her name quietly, hoping not to wake August.

At once she looked toward me, but so did the boy. All three of us waited to know *What next?* Then August decided not to wail but to turn his attention to his own wondrous hands of which he seldom tired. So Miss Olivia rose with a minimum of effort, stacked pillows to either side of August and told him firmly not to move. Then she went to her mirror, stroked her hair back, cleared her eyes and turned to me. I don't know how I must have looked by then. But at the sight of me, Miss Olivia pointed behind me across the landing to the opposite room, and we both went there.

It was the small room that had been Major's before his first stroke. And it was still as bare as a tent—just a low single bed, a black leather trunk and one straight chair. Miss Olivia sat on the edge of the bed and motioned for me to take the chair.

I walked round behind it but stood with both my hands on the chair back. When all she did was watch me in silence, I finally said "Where is my husband please?"

With no visible sign of malice on her face, Miss Olivia first said "Who would that be?" It seemed like a genuine question to herself. But then she studied my meaning in her mind till she finally said "I can't guarantee it but I think you know."

In a hot quiet rush I told her I hadn't known a word about trouble till Ferny just now told me by the river.

She nodded slowly. "I asked Fern to drive up here today for that very reason. You had to know and I knew you wouldn't accept it from me." Her mouth seemed to slip from her iron control for too long an instant, and her lips made a quick smile.

I asked how long she'd known about it.

And then she waited a painfully long time, rubbing the flats of her palms on her knees, before she could say "Since two days after we buried Larkin."

"I was *here* though—"

"I said *two* days. Lark was buried on Sunday. You were with your family that Saturday, remember?" When I agreed she said "Palm vanished that morning and I didn't see him again till maybe an hour before you and your family got back up here for the actual funeral. Since he'd left me in such a terrible lurch, I demanded he tell me where he'd been. He tried to spare me, but I can smell a lie from miles off. I stood my ground, and then Palmer admitted he had a woman."

When Miss Olivia had paused for breath, she looked to her right side and pointed out the window. "She's that Pittman girl who lives up—"

I stopped her. "Don't *tell* me that. I doubt I can stand to know."

Miss Olivia said "You'd *better* stand it or else it won't stop. You must root her out by *name*, with details, this very day. Either that or you and that child are set for long years of the kind of misery I've known by the hour since I took Major's offer and entered this house like a fool even older than you are now and at least as blind."

Naturally that hit me hard. I don't know what I'd have said or done if I hadn't been virtually paralyzed for nearly a minute. My first thought is always to hunch down as low as a body can go and crawl through the hail till somewhere down the road I can stand up again and take my bearings. But we both heard a man's footsteps downstairs, and we stalled in place.

At last Miss Olivia walked to the landing and called down "Son?"

Ferny said "No ma'm."

And August broke into his rare alarming wail.

Before I went to him I faced Miss Olivia a final time and said "It's Coy's daughter, isn't it?"

Miss Olivia said "I've never been sure. Sometimes Coy claims her, sometimes not. See, Negroes don't think of kinship as we do. At times they claim everybody they know. Then they'll cut back to nothing and say they're alone as a hawk in heaven." Then she stood to her own full height. "Would to Christ we'd left every last one of them in their African homes. All we've done is use them to ruin our lives."

August wailed again.

So I went straight toward him. And I'm forced to confess that, at the sight of his wrenched helpless face, I thought very plainly *Sweetheart, I wish to Christ you'd never* been. *Then I could run.*

That was near mid-afternoon. Palmer walked through the back door at five o'clock, looking just like the man who'd left in the midst of dinner, only calmer. His clothes were spotless. He smelled like himself. The first thing he said was, since it was near dark we had to head back. So all we had to do was gather up August's things, hug Miss Olivia and climb in the car.

As I ducked my head to enter my seat, Miss Olivia called out to me from the porch "Oh Anna, hold on."

I thought she meant *Hold on in this storm.* And I tried to let her see that I would, just the strength of my face.

But she turned and actually ran into the house. What she'd meant was *Wait.*

Palmer told me "Stand there. She forgot to give you something."

So I obeyed him and, when Miss Olivia had trotted back to me, she held out the beautiful tortoise-shell comb and silver hairbrush I'd admired on her dresser so many times. She said "Happy birthday" and then her eyes filled.

Mine stayed bone dry but I took her gifts and truly felt for once in my life that I might yet earn them if, sometime in the next ten seconds or hundred years, my whole head didn't explode and spread in a thousand directions with killing power. We were halfway back before I realized I hadn't told Ferny goodbye as we left. He'd been out of sight, though his car was still there, and I'd flat forgot him. There wouldn't be many more chances for that.

Hours later back at Betsy Magee's, I wasn't altogether sure I *hadn't* blown up and destroyed everybody anywhere near me. It seemed that we'd made the trip in silence with August sleeping every inch of the way and then that I'd fed him again and laid him down while I put together a cold chicken supper for Palmer and me. We seemed to eat it anyhow, even I who'd felt I could never eat again.

After that I sat at the kitchen table and carefully turned the worn collar of one of Palmer's work shirts before he rose up from reading the paper and said "Bedtime." Every move I or Palmer or August had made in those slow hours seemed made by a ghost or a ghost in a dream.

It was only when I went in to undress and found my husband still awake, propped up and reading *The Life of Thomas Jefferson* (a book I knew he'd read twice before) that I fully realized all this was real. This whole past day with its grief and its news and what now felt like raw devastation was as real as the plainest average Sunday. The first symptom that stunned me was blindness. Actual blindness came on me. All I could see was a pure blank screen clear as any washed blackboard with no sign of an answer and, God knows, no map of where to turn. It scared me worse than anything in years.

Then in maybe a minute the blindness began to break up at the edges, and the first thing I saw was a snapshot of August beside me on the wall. From the start he'd been the keenest watcher of the world I've yet known. He'd turn those huge eyes on you and stare, then give a long blink as if to photograph what he'd learned. I glanced back to Palmer.

Cold as the previous night had been, tonight was much warmer. And Palmer lay on the top of the cover in nothing but his pajama pants—no shirt, bare-chested. He even looked up and offered his smile.

I faced the closet and wondered how I could manage undressing myself in plain view and pulling a nightgown over my sick head in the vicinity of this much treachery, not to mention the nearness of Palmer's skin that looked more awful in my eyes now than it ever had when covered with ticks from his days in the woods. The problem froze in place for a while till Palmer must have noticed.

In a level voice so quiet that August wouldn't be roused or Betsy through these porous walls, he said "Did Mother or Ferny upset you?"

That freed me enough, not to turn and face him but at least to peel to my slip, pull my gown on and finish undressing myself beneath it. Before I turned I answered his question. "They told me a good deal—I won't lie to you."

"And it threw you badly?"

I faced Palmer then through the ten feet of dim air moving between us.

I said "I don't even know if I'm alive." It was merely the truth, not one false syllable.

"You're alive, yes ma'm. We proved it last night right here in these sheets." Palmer pressed his whole left hand into the mattress.

I said "I felt alive but that was last night." Warm as tonight was I suddenly shook with a quick hard chill. "You felt like a human then too."

"And I'm not?" he said.

If Palmer had smiled or laughed at that, I suspect I might have turned, got the child and walked to my father's for the rest of my life. Awful and shameful as that would have been, I had that one choice available at least. I could have worked in my parents' kitchen and helped with the house till I outlived them both and lived on alone till my son, if he lasted, could store me upright in the County Home or bury my bones. I knew more than one girl who'd done the same thing. People—especially other married women—tended to be extremely hard on anyone else who made that choice. And if the quitter offered an alibi such as "He beat me time and again" or "He's got a woman that's taken my place," the answer was always "What did you expect?"

But Palmer didn't flinch at my wondering if he was human, and his face assumed its best grave expression.

So all I could do was keep telling my truth. They didn't have country music back then, not that we'd ever heard. So I couldn't know how poor-white common my thoughts would sound. I'd never been cheated on before, not that I knew of. So what came out was "You feel like a lying filthy dog."

Palmer said "That may not be unfair."

I said "Not if all I've heard is true."

He said "Maybe you better tell me what that is."

I still stood where I'd first turned to face him ten feet away. As I gathered my answer to his last question, I stayed in place.

But he slid to the farthest edge of the mattress, making the maximum room for me. Then he said "If you sit down here, I won't touch you, not if you don't ask."

I said "That's the last thing I'd ask for now." Then I knew I'd never asked for it before, not specifically. And I told Palmer so.

He couldn't deny it. But again he ran his huge palm out to smooth the sheets on my side of the bed. I'd changed them that morning before we left. They were clean as fresh snow.

And I went over and sat on the edge of the deep feather mattress, half turned away.

Palmer knew not to touch me. He was still awhile and then said "You're saying I've hurt you badly—"

I said "I told you I'm all but dead. Why not finish the job? It would save on words and questions at least."

He said "I asked you what you knew."

I met his face at last. It didn't seem monstrous now or cruel, just strange as if he'd landed from space with only the faintest resemblance to humans. I took that in, then told him carefully. "I know you've had a Negro woman that you've been using for some time now at your convenience. I know, for whatever reason you had in your pitiful mind, you picked a quarrel with Ferny today and went to that woman to shame us all. Ferny Dane never so much as scratched the back of your weaker hand. He's the gentlest soul in *this* world at least, and you tried to shame him when he nursed your father far closer than you. So of course Ferny told me—he's my blood kin. Then your mother confirmed it. They're *concerned* for me, Palmer. Some people respect me or did till today. Thank Jesus, somebody is looking out for me or I'd have stumbled along in the dark with a growing baby for months or years longer."

Palmer just nodded and watched me for more.

So I sat till I'd thought the whole mystery through again. This time my eyes worked, but my lungs nearly failed. I couldn't draw breath for nearly a minute like a child who falls from a high fast swing. Then I gradually thought my voice had returned, so I pushed on with what seemed the last question left—the only question now. "What am I supposed to do with my life here, mine and that boy's?" I pointed toward August in his crib beyond us as far gone as Mars and as close as my pulse. In that time and place, divorce was as unimaginable as a new ice age or lizards the size of boxcars in the yard.

At age twenty-three I'd yet to meet a woman or man that had been divorced, though—as I said—I knew one or two who gave up and came back to live with their parents or vanished forever. Only the men had a real choice to vanish, among the people I knew of anyhow. If men disappeared it was thought of as sad but far from abnormal. If a woman left with no for-

warding address she made the Whore of Babylon seem like Mother Teresa
on her finest day.

And that fact alone meant that I was sitting, on a bed I'd thought was my
marriage bed, beside this man I'd vowed to serve for all my life; and what I
was suddenly feeling was slavery. I was chained to what felt like the world's
grimmest master and the chain wouldn't break—not ever, not short of me
killing myself.

Palmer said "Can I touch your hand?"

I said "Please don't." Yet there I sat in reach in a nightgown.

Palmer said "Then you want me to leave?"

"When?"

"Now. This minute."

I said "You're paying the monthly rent, Palmer. I'm here at your pleasure. I'm the one to leave if leaving is called for."

"No," he said, "all you've got to do is ask; and I'll leave you, clean."

I said "For good?"

"I hope to God not. This is truly the one place where I've been happy
except for years back in the empty woods, no company but dogs."

Palmer's face looked truthful but hadn't I learned as the main fact today
that he could lie as coolly as the meanest cheat on Earth? I told him "I
can't understand a word of that."

"It's the truth," he said.

"Palmer Slade, you're saying that spending your days and nights here
with me—with August and me—and mixing your body with a whole other
woman is your idea of happiness? Happy for *who*? Maybe you and your
dick—" I'm fairly sure I'd never spoken that word aloud anywhere in his
hearing, though I'd heard him say it in private moments.

And it made him laugh, very quietly still so as not to wake August but
otherwise nearly out of control.

It actually pulled me in behind him. Against my strongest better wishes
I halfway smiled.

Palmer finally calmed enough to say "That's far and away the strangest
thing I've learned in my life, and I doubt you can believe it. But listen now.
This is a fact as true as sunset. I know I can love both you and our son like
God the Father on a silver tray *and* still at the same time see what you call
a *Negro woman* with no sense of shame or serious wrong."

I thought it through. "You're right about one thing. I can't believe that and, if I could, I'd still refuse to live in the midst of any such pure blind selfishness."

Palmer asked me the last thing I expected even back then. "Are you a Christian?"

At first I said "Of course I am. We married in the normal Methodist church. I read the whole Bible and won a free hymnal when I was twelve." I realized that didn't sound too convincing. So I said "Are you?" He'd been to church with me on several occasions but seemed unimpressed.

He said "I doubt it, though I'm not a heathen either."

"Then why did you ask me?"

He knew at once. "Because if you're any kind of true Christian, then you're forced to forgive me. Or did I hear it wrong?"

I said "What did you hear?"

"The Sermon on the Mount, I think they called it." He looked serious again.

That of course was long before religious TV, but I'd read enough newspapers and been to enough revival meetings to know that a great many "Christians" were about as likely to forgive the simplest sinner as they were to eat a live snake. I said "Well, the way I understood it is, you forgive people, yes, but then they change their path."

Palmer said "In what direction? You the navigator of this whole ship?"

"What ship?"

His arms made a great wide hoop in the air and swung all around. "Our whole damned life—everybody we owe one penny's worth of money or duty, attention or patience."

I said "I can barely steer this little rowboat for me and young August."

"But you want to steer me?"

I couldn't believe Palmer wasn't grinning now. He seemed to have drifted so far away from me and any relation to the ground we had to live on. So I tried to think, as quickly and keenly as I could manage, all I really asked for. And what I said was "Forsaking all others, yes. Till death do us part."

"That strict?" Palmer said.

"For my part, yes sir. And anyone I live with from this night on."

Palmer said "What other option you got?"

I said "My parents' house—it sheds rain anyhow. Some job I'll find. Honest single women that can read and act pleasant in public have jobs they can get." Then my voice lowered further. "Look, Betsy Magee has paid her way with two-thirds of a brain. I can match that at least."

He seemed to agree. Then he crossed both arms on his bare chest as if to take his skin and bones off the market for this final round. He finally said "I can promise you this much. See if you can take it—I'll forsake everybody else as long as I can. If I can't keep that up, I'll kill myself some orderly way back deep in the woods where you won't have to see my filthy eyes and mouth one final time." He faced me again with his eyes cleared now of a good deal of anger, though still not safe from the wilderness he loved so much in the midst of our world. He was waiting for an answer.

I said "I've got one more real question."

Palmer said "Bring it on."

I said "Who gave August that little gold finger ring he's worn for some time?"

Palmer waited so long I thought he'd refused me. At last he said "The answer would pain you."

"Say the name," I said.

"The last name is Pittman. Please leave it at that."

"But can *you*?" I said. "Can you leave it here and now and forsake all she's meant?"

Palmer said "I told you I'd try. That's a solemn promise. I'm not in the business of torturing people. I just got lonesome and acted on it with some-body I've known since early childhood."

I said "If you've been so desperately lonesome, it seems to me you've got company now—company you asked for, a wife and a boy."

He said "Anna, I've promised my best. Please take it or tell me to truck on home." It was plain he'd given all he knew how to give.

I knew we'd got to the final junction. We both knew which way the two roads led. As silence spread between us, and August seemed to drift on out of our reach entirely, I understood that the next speech was mine. Palmer had made his choice. What was mine? I took the length of a long half minute; and it felt as if I was moving upright through tons of hard concrete, looking for sun. But I said "All right. I'll see if I can take it. But do you understand I won't take but so much? You're not the only person in this mess who could die or vanish."

Palmer shut his eyes and slid further down on the bed, facing upward with his chest still covered. It looked so much like everybody's idea of a laid-out corpse that I thought he was trying to joke his way out at this last moment, but he never smiled again—scarcely smiled for weeks to come. And then he finally said "Understood."

I thought again of going to the baby and slipping that ring from his finger here tonight. But stunned as we'd all been by this full day, I slid myself beneath the cover like the thinnest knife, not leaving a trace. And to my amazement I was asleep in under ten minutes.

For weeks of long nights, Palmer and I lay down together on that same bed but never touched except by accident or in our sleep. Not that we treated each other with contempt or anything as unbearable as hatred. But for whatever natural or curious reasons, our bodies seemed to resist each other like two charged magnets. Even odder, though, is the fact that both of us slept like rocks in the ground. We'd douse the light and be gone in no time, at least I believed so.

If I happened to wake for a moment in the dark, I'd always hear Palmer breathing peacefully in his sleep. It was then in those brief wakeful spells that I'd pray hard to get just one more vision like the one I'd had of Larkin bare in the woods—stark naked and dead, smiling and aiming me toward his sad brother, Palmer Slade.

That consolation had poured so easily from Lark's clean death and had been so real that I've never doubted its genuineness. It came from another world, I'm utterly sure, with all the signs of a powerful care and mercy watching over me. So why wouldn't that same world help me now? In the fall and early winter months—faced with all I'd learned from Ferny, Miss Olivia and Palmer himself—I'd lie beside my mystifying husband and pray in the dark for useful guidance till I felt what seemed like actual drops of blood on my forehead. I'd even reach up and stroke my brow expecting to draw back fingers wet with my own blood. Dark as the room was, I can't be sure I didn't truly bleed.

I know anyhow that, even now seven decades later, I can feel the absolute dryness that lived inside me and all around me like some unfortunate prisoner bound to a stake in the midst of a prairie and left to bear the pounding sun till death seems more desirable than water or a kindly hand. But neither Palmer nor I ever mentioned the matter again, not in so many words. And so we each felt miles apart from offering one another comfort or pardon for the damage we'd taken. I had to believe that my husband loved me. The signs were there.

But I also had to acknowledge to myself that my young husband was sick at heart for the loss of his woman, someone he'd known longer than me. I scarcely ever doubted he'd kept his promise to me and had sworn off seeing her. And surely he saw how burnt I was through all my parts. In the teeth of that much—and despite the real danger that August suffered from both young parents being sick at heart—God or Fate just kept their own counsel and left it to us to heal and walk on or fail and die with hard results on our nearest bystanders.

About a month after the awful day up by the river, I decided to act on a postponed duty. When Palmer was at work and August was napping, I wrote short letters to Ferny and Miss Olivia. I wasn't sure what if anything I actually owed them for telling me the saddest news of my life. But I thanked them all the same, said that Palmer and I were working to repair our lapses and I asked them again not to mention one word of the problem to another live soul. To the best of my knowledge as the years went on, they kept their silence.

At least nobody ever mentioned the sadness in my keen hearing, nobody from the white race anyhow. What's more Palmer and I proved to be excellent actors. So do a great many troubled married people. With all my experience to this very day when divorce is as common as fleas on dogs, I tend to be overwhelmed by the news that a couple has quit—they've fooled even me.

Palmer finally turned to me in the dark on Thanksgiving night, and I very slowly found that I could stand his nearness better than I'd expected. I partly knew I was not the first woman alive on Earth to face such a problem, but it would be untrue not to say that his presence came back with a quiet kind of welcome all through my hands and mind. Still we abstained for another few weeks. Then around Christmas day I conceived a child and seemed to carry it normally right through till labor started.

This time I really did go to my parents' home with Palmer beside me. And there in late September '24, I bore a perfectly shaped little boy who never breathed. Nobody with me including Dr. Rogers knew or would say whether the boy had died at some point in my womb for his own reasons or whether he'd been suffocated in labor by my body's failure to ease him out in time to live.

I only know that he moved inside me till the afternoon before the first pain and that his well-formed limbs and skin were flushed with good red blood when they let me see him for one short moment before they told me that he'd expired. Even so I wanted to give him a name. But Muddie said if I named him the pain would last even longer. So he's buried in the Slade family plot with a stone that just says *Infant Slade* and the date, one single day. I insisted on the stone despite Muddie's urging, and Palmer gladly made the arrangements and wrote the check.

Through the months of that pregnancy, I'd taken some notice of the pressures on my husband. In those days intimate relations during pregnancy were thought to endanger the mother's womb and the child inside her. I'd tried to use my imagination and help Palmer bear that long exclusion once Dr. Rogers urged it on him. Palmer seemed to be grateful; and throughout the whole time he treated me with exceptional patience, spending every hour he could manage away from his work in the house with me or riding August around in the truck to use up some of the child's endless energy. And when we knew for sure that our second baby was dead, Palmer showed more visible grief than I. This many years later I think I recall that secretly I felt partly relieved not to have to face so soon again the big toll of motherhood.

All the same I was deeply blue for most of that winter. But as I said August was keeping me busy every instant of the day and for unpredictable parts of the night. My family including Leela were kinder than ever. And Palmer silently invented a steady stream of small gifts and pleasures to ease my mind. So I never took the fall or the plunge that I secretly dreaded— me out of my mind with blank depression.

I more or less got on with daily life. And though I've always secretly despised those women and occasional men who can never say *I* but must always say *we*, I can honestly claim that what I felt I was getting on with was truly *our* life—Palmer's and mine and August's with appropriate glances toward my parents, Leela and Ferny and of course Miss Olivia.

The main joy was August. When his brother died he was nearly two, sweet-tempered as a pup and as fond of me as I was of him. Palmer loved him steadily too. And to everybody's silent surprise, somehow from the day she first saw him Leela loved August powerfully and without much jealousy of me or his father. By the time we moved to Betsy's house, I was privately afraid that Leela's constant love for a baby (who after all belonged to his parents for a few years anyhow) was going to truly sidetrack her plans for education and a life in school teaching.

Her whole two years away in college, every week at least she'd mail August some attractive present—a small piece of clothing, a book, a set of colored pencils. However small, they were all chosen with care and arrived in time with the rate of his growth. On her home vacations she watched him almost as closely as I. And anytime I felt the need for a peaceful hour or the slightest help, there was Leela volunteering to serve if she was in geographical reach.

One afternoon when I'd seen her lay August down for his nap with a look that was plainly as loving as any human can manage, I waited till Leela came out to the kitchen for a glass of tea. Then I said the main thing I regret from those calm years. I said "Palmer and I are eternally grateful that you care for August as deeply as you do. But both of us feel a little concerned that our boy may stand in the way of your having a child of your own when the time comes for that." Once the words were out and I'd actually heard them, I thought *Oh Lord, she'll burst into tears and flee forever.*

But she didn't blink once. She drank a long swallow of her tea and then said, innocent as any day-old bird, "Anna, I thought the existence of babies called for the mother to have a *husband* or a man whose waterworks function anyhow." You could tell she'd been to college. They had more plumbing there than any other place she'd seen.

I allowed she was right.

So Leela gave a good laugh, no sign of pain. "You got a candidate for the job?"

I had to say I didn't, and then I had to backtrack and say that of course I didn't think men were the be all and end all of anything but their own swollen pride.

"Easy for you to say," Leela said.

And since I wasn't about to allude to mine and Palmer's past, I let the matter slide back into silence. And that was it for many more years till a decent man found and asked for Leela and she agreed.

Things didn't go so well for Ferny, and our older brother and his hag wife grew further and further away from us all till they were seldom mentioned as living, and we scarcely knew their raucous children. In those days even a fifty-mile distance between two families could be as wide as the whole Pacific if you chose not to cross it. That was regrettable with my older brother, but Ferny was gradually more than regrettable.

He was drifting toward deep sadness at least, plainer by the month. He worked on in Raleigh at his library job, and we never heard of complaints from that quarter. Apparently you can hunt and shelve books satisfactorily without the use of fully sober mental faculties. On Fern's rare visits home, it was clear to Palmer, Leela and me at least that he was doping more and more by the month, though his nature stayed as sweet as ever and his eyes stayed fine but increasingly older and truly unreachable by any of us.

I don't think any of us ever knew exactly what his poison was. By his smell we were sure it wasn't hard liquor. And of course in those days, there was nothing like the big drug cafeteria that's apparently waiting on any corner today. Occasional women did get hipped on morphine after childbirth. And while men in pain mostly dived into liquor, more than a few of them floated on paregoric (which was liquid opium, available over the counter) or the new strong sedative pills invented for veterans back from the First World War and still agonized with what was called *shell shock*.

All I'm sure of in Fern's case is that, one dazzling bright Sunday in March, he asked to take me and August to ride. Palmer was visiting Miss Olivia so off we went. It started as a perfectly normal outing. Then once we were deep into some strange thicket up near the river, I turned to study my brother's sad profile. It was still fine as any face on a coin. And courage rushed on me suddenly—or I thought it was courage, not blatant meanness. I said "Ferny, let me help if I can."

He smiled but didn't face me. "Help what, pray tell?"

"You. You're lost as any lamb in the Bible."

He drove a good mile apparently calm. Then he looked round slowly and showed me a face like some war picture—not the Great War or even the bloated faces from pictures of Gettysburg but twenty years ahead when we were suddenly shown in the spring of '45 those eyes and teeth of Hitler's leavings, even young children tortured past bearing. When he'd held on me long enough to near wreck the car, Fern said "Not even you, Roxanna, could remedy this."

I knew he was right, but still I said "Let me start, dear friend—"

By then he'd turned his eyes toward the road. But he put up his right hand, raised one finger and said "Long years too late. No fault of yours." The smile he seemed to be beaming ahead toward the road and bare trees was too good to lose, but Fern refused to face me again.

Ever since, I've known he was sparing me. And that was a time when you didn't tie men down and haul them to the hospital, church or prison for being heartsick from unknown causes.

Everybody else who was anywhere near us moved along as expected with exceptions. Muddie's kidneys were still unreliable, but she and Father held their own. Miss Olivia aged too but at a slow rate, and none of their minds were deteriorating yet. They were able to live in their own homes and do their jobs pretty much as ever.

Poor Betsy Magee was a lot less fortunate. After we'd lived in her back rooms for more than two years and had just begun to think of finding our own bigger place—Palmer was having better luck with money—Betsy began to show the first signs of an old Magee family affliction that we'd all hoped she was going to avoid especially in light of how she'd been short-changed in her mind. But there wasn't much doubt of what she had. And when Palmer took her to the specialist in Durham, the worst was confirmed. She was already well into Huntington's disease, a ghastly kind of severe jerking palsy that soon has you entirely crippled and then strikes whatever remains of your mind.

Palmer and I talked through it every way for several nights. Ought we not to tell Betsy that we'd stay put and see her through to her natural end in her own quarters? I'll have to say that, as much as I cherished her kindness and talent, it was Palmer who took the stronger line—yes, it was our human duty. He didn't say *Christian* for once and I was grateful. I had grave doubts that I could deal with August, who had just turned three, plus run an entire house and tend a woman in terrible shape. For obvious, maybe unjustified reasons, I'd set my mind against hiring a black maid to help me out. I told Palmer I'd do whatever he decided but that I was scared for the first time in my life that my own body and mind were way too frail for the challenge.

He'd learned from me and others of my past tendency to bouts of blank sadness, and he seemed to understand. All the same, three evenings after he brought Betsy back from Durham, Palmer told me he had no choice but to offer her our full care for as long as she needed.

With no grudging word I told him to do what his conscience required.

He walked straight to Betsy's bedroom that instant and made her the offer.

Back in our kitchen I could hear her voice, a long high wail such as I've never heard again in this world and pray not to. Then her voice plainly said "This is my Hell, Palmer. You and Anna don't deserve it, not yet anyhow; and I'll take it on my own."

Within six weeks, not telling us her plans, she arranged to enter the State Hospital down in Raleigh and to deed us her whole house free and clear. She wouldn't be stopped, wouldn't take a penny from us. And when the day came, Palmer and I and August drove her down and bade her a bleak goodbye.

She was dead in three months.

The day we got that news by mail, Palmer waited till we were both in bed in the dark and then said "Anna, do you want to live here?"

I asked what he meant.

He said "Do you want to live on in this house with the memory of Betsy plus your husband's cheat and the knowledge that somebody shot himself right on the front porch?"

It was the first time he'd used the word *cheat*, and it silently stunned me. I'd never been entirely sure of what constituted adultery. But I believed Palmer had changed his life, and I never heard the word or the deed mentioned by him or anyone else ever again. Similar thoughts about the history of Betsy's house had been preying on my mind ever since she'd left. But again I told Palmer I'd follow him wherever. I thought I meant it and likely I did. That same moment was when I knew for the first time that I'd forced Palmer to live three years in a house he all but hated. I couldn't tell him how slow I'd been to feel the situation his way.

But his voice was gentle as a safe child's when he said "Then I'll try to sell this place and find us something where we can breathe."

I didn't know how relieved I'd feel till he finished those words. I said "Find something that no one we know has ever set foot in." In such a small town, that was a near impossible task. But Palmer managed to find it fast— a house that was comfortably roomier than Betsy's, though surely not grand, and that served us well for long years to come as it's serving me still.

The owner had been an ancient bachelor hermit named Baucomb who had taught engineering in a school up north all his adult life and then retired here to his mother's birthplace to stay shut up and completely alone in ten spotless rooms for his last thirty years, seeing only mysterious gentleman guests from parts unknown, all of them well-to-do or so it appeared.

I loved it on sight. It sat close to the white sandy ground, and the one story rambled through a grove of tall sycamores and oaks with a wide creek down the backside of the little knoll we were on. The windows came right down to floor level and let in whatever light there was under so much shade.

Palmer and a black carpenter he trusted examined it meticulously, decided it needed nothing but a new tin roof, a coat of white paint and screen wire at the windows, all of which they promptly provided. The whole thing cost exactly thirty-eight dollars less than we got for selling Betsy's. The bargain would have thrilled her (she lived for bargains).

We moved over there in the early spring of 1926. Though it really was an entirely new surrounding for us—with no resident heirlooms, no left-over blood-kin ghosts to haunt us—it took us longer than we'd imagined to settle in. But we kept at it. And by the time cool weather came again, I realized that we'd turned the skin of the place into our own skin.

Palmer seemed to agree. His lifelong restlessness was gradually taming. He was twenty-seven years old after all in a time when that was middle-aged or very nearly. He shared with me most everything he did or all of his life that he felt I could handle, or I trusted he did, and he put every penny he made into one joint bank account that I solely managed. Any scraps of fear that I had—where he might go and who he might see when I wasn't watching—tamed down as well, and my days turned into days like most of the women's I'd known.

You got up with your husband in the dim dawn, cooked him and your child an almighty great breakfast, got your husband out the door for work, then spent however much time was required getting your child well bathed and dressed, then starting dinner and wondering what you'd cook for supper—I'm repeating myself; everybody knows the rest. All that was different for Palmer and me was that, with his kind of work, we never took a real vacation. That was no private curse. It was how our neighbors lived, and it was a lot easier than what we'd heard about the lives of our near ancestors only fifty years back, not to mention three centuries.

In our time if you got a weekend off every year or so to visit your kin or a nearby lake, you enjoyed the change, however complicated it was to pack for three people and face the dangers of unrefrigerated food on the road, the dreadful toilets and the very risky drinking water you met with in public places not to mention bedbugs and crazy landladies in the tourist homes available. In fact most days if you had twenty minutes in mid-afternoon to lie on the sofa and shut your eyes, you felt powerfully lucky.

The only women in my field of vision who lived otherwise were either the wealthy (in very short supply) who had many servants or the spinster women who taught school most of the year, then spent the penniless summers rocking on their parents' front porch or taking cheap short trips to some sight like Blowing Rock or Pilot Mountain. So I didn't have the shining example of a Madame Curie or Helen Keller to set me thinking restlessly. I kept my chin tucked and lived my life.

And for long quiet years after we moved, the line of that life was as unremarkable as most human lives, though if you'd asked me at any point whether I enjoyed my days as they passed, I'd have said that on the whole I did. I think I can swear that the same was true for Palmer. I might have gone further and said I considered myself a lucky human.

I certainly had no noticeable longing to write soothing hymns, design safe bridges or better wedding cakes or liberate a young man doomed to die for a crime he never planned. But then I'm fairly sure I had no gifts that might have aimed me at such worthy callings. Sometimes it's fairly slim consolation to notice how very few human beings of any sex or background are called to anything grander than dinner.

Or so I've generally felt through the decades. I've even tried to see my lack as a gift of another sort, not necessarily inferior, though I'll have to confess how unenlightened I've known I was and how sorry I often am of that fact. I'm even more ashamed to admit that I've learned more since television started up forty years ago than in all my other life. I've also known for most of a century that a working and occasionally rewarding marriage, with a man as generous and even-keeled as Palmer or a woman who hugged the ground like me, is surely the greatest good on Earth at the very same instant that it's also the hardest good to capture, not to mention *hold* for long. No flower on the finest day of summer has a frailer odor or dies any quicker.

FIVE

The time loped on as decades do when you and your family have got through the early trials of being under one roof, and Fate has chosen not to slam in on you with his world-famed fist—Fate *or* God. I've never decided if they're the same thing. And despite the likable hopes young women have expressed here lately that God the Father has a full set of female parts as well, all my experience affirms that he's *male* as the ancient prophets and kings never doubted nor the Virgin Mary herself in the song she sang once she'd been fertilized by God alone. (See the Gospel of Luke, chapter 1:46–55. Of course Luke was written by a man.) As far as I can see in fact, God's maleness is His most difficult problem. He seems to have far less patience than the universe He made requires of a loving handler which He claims to be. And his taste for vengeance is certainly eager.

I've known more than one man who slammed through the wall of somebody else's life just to prove he was hurting at the moment. And I've noticed that women can wait to take their vengeance. They can bear thirty years of beatings and broken teeth and then begin to poison their husband with arsenic laced in his noon iced tea, a process that may take numerous years if you keep the arsenic doses small enough so your husband can't taste them, though his hair and nails are falling out and his nerves don't work.

No man could dream of waiting that long to do his will. He'll shoot you by sunset or bring you a dozen roses from town, then wake you up from a short deep nap that very same night and beat your head in for somehow not seeming grateful enough. Don't men inherit that impatience from God?

           *　　　　*　　　　*

Anyhow Palmer and the boy and I lived on in the house we'd bought with Betsy's money. August grew straight as a poplar tree and stronger. You could spend whole hours—if he'd ever hold still—selecting the parts of his honest face which the Slade blood had formed and which came to him from my family, the Danes. He got the Dane nature, I'm glad to say—much milder than the fiery famished Slades—but while nobody ever claimed August was afflicted, he had a peacefully slow plain mind and has kept it till now. It hindered his school work but scarcely bothered him. He was good to his parents. He was crazy for baseball. And though he took to girls extra early at age eleven, he never burdened his father or me with problems of money or personal duty in relation to women. If he made mistakes he covered them neatly, never mentioned their names; and he went on his way.

Palmer did the jobs he'd found for himself in early manhood—locating and dealing in good standing timber—and timber supported us, not handsomely but well enough. Palmer kept his dignified looks and manners, and he stayed lean as ever in the places where most men take on flesh as soon as they're married (their waists and jowls). The only mark that time made on him was the gradual onset of deafness in both ears, a trait of the Slades unfortunately.

Palmer strained to overcome it. Until he was all but stone deaf, he tried to deny it. But by the time he was thirty-five, I could see he was slowly stepping backward from conversation and sociable laughter just because he couldn't hear the world. Women's voices were the hardest for him. I often wished I'd been a deep bass or at least an alto. I'd have kept him better company.

But the deafness and solitude seldom made him bitter. He read more books than ever before and listened to the radio endlessly with his ear cupped almost down to the speaker. All of the commentators then were male with good clear voices, and he could mostly hear them. So he haunted the war news once the Second War began. The orchards of France, the Russian snow fields, the bombed-out children of Britain were as real to Palmer as the meals I cooked and were far more important to his ongoing will to keep at work and to live on among us as some kind of partner and friend we could welcome.

I think I can say I strengthened through the time. I grew to trust our modest luck and my harmless family. Once Palmer and I had cleared the air around our duty to one another, I literally never worried again—not about my husband's faithfulness. Some gift of grace kept suspicion at a distance, and I served him every way I could think of as he did me (though he had a man's particular brand of attention; far-off things held Palmer more than close-ups).

I taught August every good truth I knew, I kept him clean and healthy, I punished him when needed but with only light switchings—no hard hand or belt. Palmer never touched the boy in even mild anger. Once when August was mad about some ruling his father had made, the boy took a key and gouged it across the whole passenger door of Palmer's truck. When I saw the deep scratch, I told Palmer he'd have to take the boy in hand this time at least. But Palmer shook his head mildly and said "Oh Anna, it's nothing but a truck. I won't be driving it to Heaven if I go."

With Leela away nine months a year teaching somewhere close or farther off, I watched my parents drift into age in a house far quieter than any they'd known before. When the Depression reached eastern North Carolina in the early thirties, it may not have made as deep a gash in an eternally poor region as it did elsewhere. But it led to some hard realities. Many banks failed with a lot of people's holdings. If you had good rich cotton land, you mostly couldn't sell it for more than a quarter an acre—and I don't mean a quarter of a hundred dollars. I mean twenty-five cents, an acre of fine land for one thin quarter. And Father was excessively easy on people, white or black, who ran up credit on groceries and supplies at the store.

Before long he was what was called *land poor*. He owned and owed taxes on hundreds of acres of cotton fields and trees, no crop paid him much, and he couldn't sell anything but his pine trees for cut-rate prices to the paper mills. Palmer made money on him—buying cheap timber, I'm sorry to say, and holding it for years—but Father understood that as normal business. He never grudged Palmer's slim success. If so I never heard him nor Muddie complain. What did turn sad and increasingly awful was Father's premature senility as it was called then. By the time he was sixty in 1930, he'd have occasional troubling moments.

I'd walk into his store with August in tow, August would yell out some loud greeting and Father would face us with a grin—but a baffled grin. I could tell sometimes that, for minutes on end, he wouldn't be altogether sure who we were. He'd address me as "Lady" to hide his confusion, and in fact he'd called me that in my girlhood, but he also used it for every other white woman halfway respectable.

Once August blurted out "Pa, what's my *name?* You ain't said it in weeks." His speech then was entirely controlled by school friends from deep in the county.

And Father just stood with big tears welling in his eyes. Then he tried to fill the gap with some joke, some comical name like "Fatty Arbuckle," though August was slender.

But the boy refused it and teasingly said "You don't love me. I'm your main grandson."

My mother had infinite patience with Father. And right to the end he never failed to recognize her even if he couldn't call her name. Oddly enough he also knew Palmer—long after Leela and I were strangers to him—and Palmer could almost always calm him when, in the early days, Father got furious at his limitations and started breaking things. I once saw him throw a huge plow point clean across the store and break a lamp just because he made short change for a colored child, and the child called him on it. He wasn't mad at the child but at his own mind.

Despite their spotty relations through the years, Father also knew Ferny most times when he saw him—Fern's rare visits home in his own last years.

One Sunday after a splendid dinner, I'd helped Muddie wash and dry every dish. And when she went to brush her hair down, I headed for the porch where Palmer, Ferny and Father were seated. As I stopped inside the screen door for an instant, I heard Father's voice as clear as an arrow shaft, aimed at Fern—"Young man, you look something like a son of mine."

Palmer didn't break his silence but left it to Fern.

And in time all Fern said was "Thank you, sir. I knew Ferny Dane way back in his prime, and I thought he was fine."

Well before that, Father had to retire and rent the store to a Jewish merchant named Pizer from Lynchburg. By the time I conceived again in 1938, Father had gone past Muddie's strength to care for him. At that point Palmer knew the right black man to help my mother with the handling (Father was a tall sturdy man to the end). The helper—named Masters Carlyle—was tall as a great oak, twice as strong and at least as gentle—and he slept in the back bedroom with Father till the slow end came.

When Father wouldn't even speak to Palmer beyond the two syllables of his first name, he'd talk to Masters in little light bird sounds that nobody else would claim to recognize.

But Masters would listen sometimes for whole minutes and then say calmly "I told you *no indeed*, Mr. Dane" or "You're likely to be right. We'll just wait and see." Whatever it meant—they had their own code—it mostly eased Father. And at the very end, the last two months, he got as peaceful as an ideal nine-year-old boy dreaming. Then he drifted off entirely.

That nearly killed Muddie. I truly wish it had. She'd spent every day of her life in the presence of Simmons Augustus Dane since she was sixteen, a youthful bride. And losing him now while she had a little strength left and the balance of her looks was like the great shutting down of a dark hand over her face. No light could reach her, no cool air to breathe. Yet she lingered expressly to help me out in my late third pregnancy.

I was two years short of forty when I conceived. In those prolific days women often had children on into their forties. But Muddie had always hinted to us that it seemed a little *ordinary* having babies so late like an old female dog loose in the underbrush and taking all comers. In any case she kept me company throughout those months that had more than their share of fear and worry for me. I'd lost the one child; could I have this one safely?

The first time I confided my fear to Muddie, she stopped at her kitchen sink, thought a long moment, then turned and said "This child is fine, it's bound to be a girl, you'll have no trouble whatsoever. Anna, I know what I'm talking about." As it turned out she did.

I went into labor in September '39. By then hospitals were more trustworthy in their cleanliness. At least I was hearing of fewer dead mothers. Dr. Rogers had got too old to be relied on, so Palmer drove me and Muddie to the clinic in Henderson in good safe time. August, who by then was nearly seventeen, stayed back home with Leela.

Early on the morning of September 15th with no more than forty-five minutes of pain, I gave birth to a healthy daughter. Muddie was proved right. Even before I could check with Palmer, I looked up to Muddie and said "We've named her Dinah after you—Dinah Dane Slade." We had never made any such decision. I did it on the happy spur of the moment, but Palmer never once complained.

And Muddie laughed then for the first time since Father died and said "Oh darlings, I was praying for that." Who she hugged was Palmer. She and I both knew that the Hebrew *Dinah* was an unhappy girl in the book of Genesis, but Muddie had seemed to thrive with the name, so we had slim fears.

I honestly think that Dinah Slade kept my mother alive for the next three years—Dinah growing up lovely and laughing as she did, that plus the sizable fact of Leela's long-delayed but sensible marriage in '41 and the birth of Leela's son Wilton in '42. Once Muddie had overseen that last birth to any of her children, she died on the front porch sitting in her rocker on a mild summer day, no sign of struggle, an open book untroubled in her lap. Her long kidney trouble was not the cause, though no doctor ever quite told us what was—a painless stroke or her heart simply stopped.

I was so busy, and Muddie had always been such a cool soul, that I didn't feel too sad—not at once. It took several months for the serious loss to bite into me. I guess that was owing to baby-busyness. It had been so long since August was born that I'd lost a few skills and had to relearn them. But there was another thing at work. Ever since September of '39 when Hitler started tormenting Europe, even Americans as far off as we were could understand that we'd be at war soon.

I deeply dreaded that Palmer would have to go and bear arms. He said a few things that made me think he wanted to serve especially in the Navy. But two more uneasy years passed. And by the time Pearl Harbor was bombed and FDR cranked up the draft, Palmer at forty-three was just too old, not to speak of being deaf. What was clear was that, assuming the war didn't end unexpectedly, August would go in a few weeks or months. He was nineteen and eager. But strange as it may sound, I didn't dread his going so much. He'd been such a lucky and healthy child, I had no reason to doubt he'd survive. And as Palmer kept saying, the boy would learn much more in service than we could buy for him at any university.

Like most every American girl, I'd enjoyed the First War. I was seventeen and eighteen, my elder brother went but never left America. And even our crossroads took on new life with War Bond drives and the fear of Germans. There was a settlement of German farmers—famous cantaloupe growers—way out in the county, and some townspeople were crazy enough to think those hard-working people were spies for the Kaiser. Spies on *what*, nobody ever said—pine trees and crows? The nearest Army base was sixty miles off.

But with the Second War from the very first week, President Roosevelt made us all feel we were actual soldiers even in our own kitchens. There were rationing books for clothing, shoes, beef, coffee, sugar and gasoline that housewives had to manage. Women were urged to can their home-grown food and I followed suit. There were national drives underway at all times to save scrap metal, scrap paper, tincans, tinfoil, even bacon grease—you name it; we saved it.

We were all in cahoots to wipe Adolf Hitler's name from the Earth. This country never felt more united and aimed one way in my life till then, and that meant the air had good-willed excitement in it such as nobody since has ever known. Even when caring for Dinah kept me from leaving the premises most days and nights, I felt like part of a righteous crusade for as long as I could stand it.

By the sweltering summer of '42, August had left for infantry training in deepest Georgia. And Palmer was spending more time than ever on his various war jobs. Farming was important to the effort of course, especially growing extra cotton and tobacco; and timber was urgent in many new ways. Palmer was also a member of the county draft board and had to meet several nights each week to hear the appeals from various boys to stay at home with a widowed mother or to claim that hay fever or mildly flat feet exempted them from service. So with my son gone and my husband scarce, more and more I was by myself with no one but Dinah. And while she was almost as good at age three as she'd been as an infant, she was still a moment-by-moment concern.

In fact her being a girl had made more difference to my mind and my feelings than I could have guessed. I'd be bathing her gently in the morning and find myself dwelling more and more on the future I thought I could foresee plainly for her, years from now—a life like mine or at most like Leela's. Till then I wouldn't have dared to think, not to mention tell the public, that I'd got any less from the world than I needed. And of course I never thought to ask any man if he was steadily satisfied with his lot in the world.

I'd never have dared to tell even Leela that Dinah's perfect but delicate body, enfolded and parted in all the normal ways, was any less than an adequate dwelling for the mind and soul she'd need in the world that would come hurtling at her once this slaughter was ended—once she'd be faced with choosing a mate, maybe one from a whole generation of American boys who had killed and maimed other men and occasional women and children because they were blond or had the black tip-tilted eyes of the Japanese.

When such thoughts struck me, I'd even pull back and tell myself they were foolishness. I'd had a blessed life. I still think I have despite a matter I'm soon to describe. And my body, with all its normal female woes in the waterworks department, was hardly more difficult to dwell in and use than Palmer's with his bad ears and an agonizing prostate.

By fall, an endless lovely fall, I was finding myself in tears too frequently. I was napping as often as Dinah would nap and rising exhausted and pale in the mirror. I'd fallen behind in plans to can every last garden vegetable, and Palmer had actually mentioned noticing that I seemed sad. Could I please tell him why? Had he let me down someway? Was I pining for Augustus? Maybe this was the famous "baby blues" he'd heard about?

I burst into tears and said I missed Muddie which was hardly the truth, just an alibi. I hadn't begun to let myself see that the low spells I'd had ever since childhood were deepening now into one downward trek.

When he'd cradled my head and dried my eyes, Palmer said for the first time in our married years that I might do well to take Dinah with me and spend a few days with his mother by the river. Miss Olivia was a year short of eighty by then. She'd scarcely lost a hair or a tooth since I entered the family. And while she and I would never be close, we'd buried our hatchets years ago and could manage civility when in close quarters. Palmer understood that or would never have made the suggestion of a visit.

And to my surprise I heard myself tell him "That may be a good idea." The fact that the idea failed to turn out well—oh far from it—had nothing to do with Miss Olivia's and my relations. Even now five decades later, the thing that happened seems nothing less than an act of God or idle chance. I still wish I knew which. I'd live to ask myself a thousand times in the ensuing years what wrong I'd done to deserve such a scourging. That one entirely unanswerable question was a heavy piece of what drove me crazy, but I still have no satisfactory answer and never expect to.

I suspect it was pure coincidence that again it was early October before we made the plans and Palmer drove us up. I left my own house in good order. Palmer would take his meals with Leela and Clarence, her husband. Their son, young Wilton, was three months old. But Leela had good help in the kitchen, so I didn't feel I was leaving my husband to a diet of cold canned goods. I likewise can't recall an instant's worry that Palmer would seek other company than mine in a few days of absence. That problem was surely buried way behind us. What wasn't safely out of the way was my scorched mind.

Here lately I've heard and read a good deal about depression and mania. It's as common on TV as syphilis or AIDS, though you catch those plagues apparently from love or love's various imitations. Who do you get depression from or the wild excitement of mania? Doctors and experts can talk forever, but no one's yet explained to me where strictly mental Hell comes from.

I'm led to believe that both of those nightmares have a physical cause as real as a virus. They begin with some degree of chemical confusion that's tripped by an outside event or by the built-in nature of your cells. Some flaw in your fabric is sent downward to you by your parents in the moment that you're conceived or by your unknown ancestors. Either way Hell comes on by slow degrees or occasionally fast.

I've started many a spring day in good strong spirits. And then at, say, noon I've paused to look out a clean window at hyacinths blooming in the sun and songbirds nesting. I'll know and even say to myself *Count your blessings, Roxanna*. But then I've felt a dark wind from the back of my skull press my eyes shut in under five seconds for no known cause. That wind can blow for a quick three minutes or for every instant of more than four years.

And what torments my mind to this day, though I've been spared now for a good long while, is *Why? And for what?* Though I'm no deep thinker and have never been a self-respecting Christian so far as church goes, I'm stuck with the faith that deeds have results, that no hard pain is entirely meaningless.

I've said it's a *belief* not an algebra problem, but the faith still grips me. I can't believe we're chemical recipes that some cook can ruin with the slightest swerve at the mixing bowl. Somebody or some *thing*—ourselves, our parents or mates or children or strangers or God—trips the dreadful switch. And if, as people used to believe at the time I was undergoing my ordeal, we either bring that suffering on ourselves in ignorance or laziness or the need to be noticed or God sends it on us in punishment, then the pain is equal whatever the cause. Or so I found.

Notice the fact that children mostly don't get it till they're in their teenaged years, not unless they lunge into drugs and other bodies prematurely. It can't afflict innocence apparently, or it chooses not to. That last possibility—a punishing God, a fatherly bookkeeper with a crushing hand—was what I believed had me in his claws. And I was very far from alone in *knowing* that. In fact if I could only have seen my fellow sufferers, I'd have understood I was one of a great crowd across the whole Earth of the living damned as I'd still be today if the hand hadn't lifted. Or been thrown off. I've never told a soul till now, but I may have finally thrown it off by a choice of my own.

That October day in 1942, as I saw the Slade place rise into sight, I honestly thought a change would help me. Miss Olivia would give me some relief with Dinah's needs. I'd eat the good cooking she'd always served. I'd get some exercise that consisted of more than lifting or bathing a three-year-old. I could walk up the road which was still unpaved and almost as deserted as ever, and I could strike a little way into the woods on the narrow deer paths and let myself see a world of things beyond the requirements of one girl child and the family propped around her.

By then in the forties, a few youngish women were wearing slacks for country living and Palmer had suddenly bought me a pair on a business trip to Suffolk. He'd often bought me clothes through the years—just something he'd see in a window and ask for, knowing my size. But when he'd showed me the navy blue slacks he got for me that very summer, I'd hesitated to wear them outdoors. He'd teased me mercilessly for my shyness and claimed I was aging way too soon. So mostly to please him and surprise Miss Olivia, I wore them publicly for the first time to ride to the river.

And Miss Olivia approved on sight. She'd seen us coming and was already down the steps trotting toward us when we opened the doors. Dinah had always loved her grandmother almost too much. Sundays, whenever we'd drive up for supper, we'd need to wait till Dinah was napping and take her out to the car asleep; or she'd cry inconsolably at parting from her grandmother.

Now they ran to meet one another. And old as she was, Miss Olivia leaned and scooped up Dinah like a light load of towels. By the time I'd reached them, they both were laughing. And Miss Olivia said "I like the britches, Anna. You look like a *sport*."

For that one moment my mind and heart lifted. I thought I might get through this present hard patch with little more trouble.

That hope survived through the next two days. My forty-second birthday and the twenty-second anniversary of Larkin's death had passed the previous week, so we had no special attention to pay to those mileposts. Miss Olivia, completely on her own without help, had mounted a ladder and painted the kitchen and dining room a pale lemon color that cheered the place. And with Coy too crazy to go on working, she'd found a treasure that was truly beyond price, a new young cook named Mally Shearin who had the kind of bone-deep sweetness that nothing explains but a saintly grace.

Mally's face and frame were as handsome as her nature, and her skin was the finest I've ever encountered—pure and unseamed as a length of the sheerest pale beige cambric. She might have been any age from the upper teens to the early thirties.

When Miss Olivia introduced us, she smiled at Mally and said to me "Would you ever guess this was Coy's grandchild?"

I had to say No, not this young woman as fine as a doe out of poor old Coy's bent crushed-down bones.

But so she was, though the first thing Mally said was "I barely remember Mama Coy." I've mentioned that Coy lost her mind not long after helping me bear August, and she'd died soon after.

Miss Olivia said "You missed an education—Coy taught us a *lot*. Didn't she, Anna?"

I couldn't imagine what I'd learned from Coy, but I said "Sure did."

That was on a Saturday morning. The plan had been that we'd stay six days, then let Palmer know if we meant to stay longer. Both houses had telephones by then. And Palmer had said that, at the least sign of friction with his mother or of me feeling worse, I should just say the word and he'd fetch me at once and take me to Durham for a thorough checkup at Duke Hospital. He didn't allude to doctors as a threat to keep me at his mother's, but in fact Palmer knew I dreaded doctors worse than death. So I took great pains to make those days go smoothly.

So did Miss Olivia and Dinah. Dinah slept with her grandmother, spent almost all of each day with her and barely leaned on me for anything. I'd brought a stack of magazines and the book of *Gone With the Wind*. I was the only live woman in the United States who still hadn't read it, though I'd seen the movie twice with Leela who thought it surpassed all human entertainment. I've mentioned that Leela read more than me in our early lives. But in recent years as life had grown calmer, I'd read more and more. It was mostly decent novels, occasional trash and as much about North Carolina history as I could find in the county library. I never ceased to be amazed and troubled by realizing how *near* the distant past was to me when to others it seemed like eons ago.

For instance Thomas Jefferson died only ninety-four years before I was born, the span of two not-very-long lifetimes; and he was talked about in school like somebody far off as Charlemagne. Yet my grandfather Dane was reared near Charlottesville, Virginia. He always said that, in his boyhood, he'd seen Mr. Jefferson ride his horse into town with streaks of auburn still in his hair. And Grandfather Dane knew me in my cradle.

Stranger still, people seldom mentioned the Civil War when I was young, though I'd been born only thirty-five years after General Lee's surrender which occurred not a hundred miles from my birthplace. *Six hundred thousand men* died in that war, a fact I still can barely believe. I heard a man explain on TV last week how, proportionally speaking, that would be the equivalent of killing off ten million boys today which is a good deal more than the whole population of New York City.

Even more terribly, slavery hadn't ended, not formally till thirty-five years before my birth. Former slaves were all around me in my early life. Some were still living in the 1940s, every one of them pleasant as your favorite old cousin. Yet I never heard one single person, white or black, allude to the awful fact of their bondage which was still in many ways unrelieved. Slavery and its leavings were like a slow dream too hard to recall much less dwell on but deep in us still. I always suspected that everybody I knew, of whatever color, had the dream of slavery every night of their lives. Either armed black men were coming to kill you, or white maddogs were tearing black children to ragged bits. But nobody dared to mention the fact.

We just convinced ourselves that local black people had all the blessings we took for granted—decent schooling, enough money—and any time they let us down (by politely declining to work on Sunday, say), we told ourselves we couldn't comprehend such ingratitude. Very little of that has changed an iota. Even to this day an honest person will have to admit that slavery's still with us and more vicious than rabies even here at the end of the twentieth century.

So while Miss Olivia and Dinah spent their days together, I'd sit on the porch and read about Scarlett O'Hara and her grit and gall. Then every afternoon when the others were napping, I'd walk up the road as I'd intended and into the woods (the Slades had long since sold off their horses). The leaves had only just started to turn, and the foliage and briars hadn't yet thinned themselves. The days were almost too warm for my slacks. But I wore them anyhow and felt a small but actual pleasure in getting to practice with nobody watching, a way to wear them with the confidence they called for.

In saying that much I'm sure that never for one quick instant did I want to be a man. I'd had enough time to see how men's lives were at least as full of trouble as women's and in many cases were much shallower rooted. No, what I liked about wearing slacks was the absolute *difference* from female styles. I'd enjoyed the women's clothes of my youth without quite going as far as Leela.

In recent years watching English TV, I've realized that what we wore was a country version of Edwardian style—long dresses, big hats—and we did look good for our part of the world. But the coming of pants in the 1940s was a new brand of leeway, all the odder because pants actually concealed your legs which dresses hadn't done for years.

Far better than any novelty clothes, my mind when I was on those walks seemed all but ready to clear itself. I was pretty well convinced that my blues were owing to Muddie's death, to August being drafted and the generally desperate news of the world. Everybody with eyes and ears knew of the awful heat of the fighting in Europe and the South Pacific. But nobody I knew had anything like a clear idea of the merciless torment underway for children abroad plus millions of old people, Jews, Gypsies and assorted other tribes of folk.

Anybody who read a daily paper had known for years that Adolf Hitler despised everybody who was not his brand of human whatever that was. But the cattle cars were his darkest secret from Americans on the home front at least. Word of them came in newsreels and magazines as ghastly shocks to people like me within a few days of the Nazi surrender in the spring of '45.

Though Gypsies and Jews were scarce in the South of my early life, I'd still had glimpses of their faces and lives. Gypsies were the strangest people we saw in our black-and-white world. They'd arrive in a line of old patched-up cars with no warning in even the smallest towns once or twice a year. They'd wear peculiar heavy clothes, knock at your back door, gaze at you with black hawk-eyes, then offer to sharpen your knives and scissors. And they sometimes had tough ragged dwarf horses or one of their battered cars for sale. Most people declined their services and used them only to scare bad children—*The Gypsies will steal you if you don't behave*—though nobody ever heard of a local child disappearing.

Jews in our part of North Carolina were almost as rare but were very hard-working, stationary, religious, civic-minded and kept very much to themselves in the evenings and on their Sabbath day. So there seemed to be very little feeling against them except in the usual starved-out fringe of pitiful Scotch-Irish white men who joined ugly clubs like the Ku Klux Klan.

I've mentioned that Father sold his business to a Mr. Pizer whose family had come from Poland years back. His daughter and two sons were strikingly handsome with their dark hair and eyes. The high school absorbed them with no sparks or fire, not that I ever saw. So I was spared in those quarters at least by never hearing people speak hatefully of any variety of human being except black people. And by the time August entered the Army, I was having what felt like night-long dreams of being a crippled old Jewish woman with numerous children entrusted to her. In her ruined body I was trying to flee from swarms of Germans and lead my starving children to safety through snow or dark water—savage nature, pitiless as wolverines.

—All that much then to say why, despite its entertainments, the Second War was harder on the minds of people who stayed at home than some other wars. It may also half explain why I'd just assumed the war would keep me low till my son was home again and Hitler was wiped from the face of the planet with his monstrous henchmen. Nonetheless on my first afternoon walks out from the Slade place, I told myself that the sight of nature in mid October—preparing both to die and revive before my eyes—was a sign for me that I had valuable work left to do and the power to do it. For eighteen years still to come at least, I must raise a strong and open-handed daughter. We'd raised such a son. And I must certainly ease whatever years or decades remained to my big-handed baffled well-meaning husband who had now retreated into silence and distance.

*   *   *

It was on the Wednesday after reaching the Slade place that I tripped a downpour which all but swamped me. I was walking farther than I'd ever walked on this old road. I was feeling as if I'd truly rounded some final bend onto, not a new world but a washed spruced version of the world I'd known. It knew my name and my modest talents. It wanted me back at full strength.

Five days ago I'd almost begged my husband to take me to Durham and let doctors strap me down to a bed and give me that new electrical shock which might wipe out the piece of my memory that was weighing me down or else burn out my mind entirely. Now as the fall air parted like water to let me forge on up the blank road, I knew I'd live for a long time to come.

That far I was right. It was five decades ago, but I'm seeing it still as sharp as it was the moment it struck me. What happened was, I rounded a wide bend. And after an hour of seeing no form of life but birds, I was faced with somebody standing in my path in the midst of the road. At first I thought it was a left-over tramp. During the long Depression years, even the sticks saw a great many tramps.

They were always men of various ages from twelve to ancient. They were generally white, surprisingly clean and they all were hungry. They'd knock on your back door, ask for food and I could never refuse them. But since they often looked woolly as bears, I'd say "You walk to the back of the yard where I can see you out of the window. I'll put you a plate on the steps right here and lock the door. Then you come get it." I'd always apologize for being scared of them. They'd mostly say they understood, even the ones with faces keen as any straight razor.

But this one today in the midst of the road had raven tresses of lustrous hair halfway to the waist. A few old white men wore their hair shoulder-length in those years, but hair like this was unheard of. I stopped in my tracks and thought of turning back but then realized the man was a woman and maybe a young one. What I'd registered as long dark trousers was a close-cut dress that raked the dust, and the cotton work shirt was loose as a shroud. The face that was set in that abundant hair had the severe cutting look of an Indian—high broad cheekbones and a long roman nose. The skin that I'd first thought was sunburned mahogany was clean and unlined and naturally dark. I spoke up finally. "Splendid day."

At first the woman seemed to hear no sound at all. Her black eyes went on consuming my face. Then her right hand came up, touching her lips as if to part them. She said "Splendid for *you*." She laughed a dry burst, then lost control and hacked away at the pit of her chest for a painful minute.

At once I thought *Tuberculosis*. It was common then as hives. All my life I'd heard such laughs as a sign of death, more nearly a cough or a dull little chop like a hatchet on hard wood.

Just that long laugh brought up blood. Bright as any sunset, a crooked line of blood ran out of her lips on down her chin and stained her blue collar. She paid it no mind.

I had no special medical knowledge, but I'd lost a high school friend to TB, so I said "I'm afraid you've had a lung hemorrhage. Can I help you home?"

She looked less likely to have a home than any dead fox. And she shook her head No. Then she said "Tired as me?"

"I beg your pardon?"

"You as worn out as Roebuck Pittman? Look like you are." She half turned away from me and took a few steps, then stopped again and faced me. Any normal person would have wiped at the blood, but she let it stream. We were still no more than ten yards apart.

By then I'd realized I was struck. No wide car swerving round the bend could have slammed me harder. Just the sound of that last name, the force of those eyes, told me I'd come face-to-face at last with someone I'd strained hard to avoid—avoid and forget. This woman had to be Palmer's woman from long years back. And though I'd prayed for her to vanish from anywhere near, I never once thought I might be wrong in this recognition.

She realized how much I knew. She said "You finally seen Roebuck, ain't you?" Her hand came up to her chin at last and scrubbed at the cooling blood.

I said "I'm sorry," meaning of course I was sorry to see her.

She took it as a request for pardon and said "Don't be. Too late. I couldn't hurt a *child*, much less old you in your new sporty britches." She laughed again. The blood repeated itself on her lips, and she drank it in.

From then on it caused me to feel cold fear, not pity or regret. Stunned as I was I wouldn't have offered to haul her out of the ditch if she'd fallen. I was even too shocked to comprehend how cruel I was. I couldn't speak.

She let me stand there utterly stalled by a sight that should have inspired no feeling in me but a dull recollection. Then she said "You living with my kin now."

I must have looked puzzled.

"My kin at Miss Olivia's house—Mally, that girl."

I pointed behind me toward the house a long mile off. "Mally's a Shearin."

Roebuck waited a long bleak minute. And then as she turned her back on me finally, she said "Mally got any *number* of names."

By the time she was gone, I was telling my hurt mind over and over *Don't let this sick witch ruin you now.* But my mind told me in no uncertain terms that Roebuck Pittman was no harmless girl and that I'd been damaged right down to the quick, the day I learned of her existence nineteen years ago and then forgot her. When I made my own turn back toward the Slade house, I knew I'd be compelled to pay every cent I'd owed this miserable creature through all that time. *Why* I thought I was in her debt, I couldn't imagine. But I knew I was—I and my children and Palmer Slade and every piece of the safe world we slept in.

I never told a soul, not the real story. But that night late—after Mally had finished in the kitchen and was gone and Miss Olivia and I were seated in the parlor, both sewing—I said "I've got a powerful hunch that Mally Shearin is kin to that Pittman woman you mentioned long ago."

Miss Olivia studied me like a red warning sign. She said "Anna, please don't push on that door."

I said "If the door is truly shut, I won't push, no."

Miss Olivia said "To the best of my knowledge—and I've had my eyes open—Palmer's kept his promise to you very strictly."

"But is your cook Roebuck Pittman's daughter?"

Miss Olivia nodded. "So I've always believed. Mally's offered no guarantees. Coy's long gone, as you well know; in her last years, she barely knew her name much less who she'd borne. And for years now Roebuck has been out of her mind. She wouldn't know whether Mally's a girl or a goose, much less who's her mother."

"Have you ever asked Mally?"

Miss Olivia shook her head. "That wouldn't be my business. Mally very likely couldn't know who her father is. The Pittman Negro that Roebuck lived with left her long years ago. He'd killed a fellow and fled the law."

I hauled my mind to the final jump. "Did it ever cross your mind she might be Palmer's child—Mally, I mean?"

Miss Olivia raised her endless fingers and made her web-clearing gesture again, the first time in years. Then a smile like a gash cut through her long face. She tapped her forehead hard and said "More things have crossed this mind, believe me, than the wide Pacific."

I managed to say I was sure that was true.

And I somehow managed to get through the whole planned visit as well and some days to come before I buckled. When I did, it came in the hardest way I'd ever known; and it came at home. It was late October, an afternoon of the kind of beauty that only the fall can show around here. The air was dry as parchment and the light a pure gilt that seems to be the last of some treasure all but squandered by the end of summer with these few last hours saved just for you.

Palmer had been at work since dawn. I'd done my usual chores with no hitch and had lain down at three o'clock with Dinah, meaning to snooze and then be up by four to start our supper. But I didn't come to till four twenty-five—the clock was beside me ticking loudly—and I realized that what had waked me was not my own mind but the gentle sounds of a voice somewhere beyond me in the house.

It was Dinah's voice, a three-year-old child's normal soft voice talking to herself in two or more tones imitating a mother and child in a long imaginary conversation. Dinah had more such conversations than any child I'd ever known. And while it had never troubled me before, I lay there a long hot moment thinking my child had somehow pierced my ear and was pouring in hatred through a clear glass funnel. With very nearly half of my mind, I knew the idea was laughably crazy.

With the larger part, though, I thought my child was not only hateful and trying to kill me but a demon as well. Now was my last chance to stop her and save my home. I thought it in those crazy terms, which seemed entirely sane; then I rose up to do it with as much resolve as I'd have had for peeling potatoes to cook in pure water. On the top of the bureau was a large pair of scissors. I've always wondered why they caught my eye and not the knife Fern had given me years before—it was in the bureau drawer. Anyhow I took up those scissors and took three steps toward the door in Dinah's direction.

She heard me and paused in her low singsong. Then she said "Mother, *quick.*"

I've never known what she meant by *quick*. But as I heard that single syllable, I looked to my right in the bright hallway.

A tall mirror hung there, an old pierglass that had been my mother's. When I saw my whole self bound on harm, something stopped me. It was not my will but some outside power, more than half merciful apparently. I turned back to where I'd found the scissors, laid them down very carefully and called Dinah to me in my gentlest voice.

By the time she got there—her face still addled from her own long nap—my mind had closed its halves together as silently as clouds cross the moon. I couldn't touch my own lovely daughter, not directly, for the best part of an hour. But I knelt beside her. And with Muddie's ivory hairbrush, I slowly stroked Dinah Slade's brown curls, fine as spider silk.

I well understand that to anyone who's never experienced a similar fright that will sound like the cheapest TV. It does to me now. But in late October 1942, I repeat I was forty-two years old, a woman whose body still seemed to work. I menstruated for another twelve years. I had no visible signs of illness. And that brief craving to stop my own child, a beautiful girl who has blessed my old age, was only the starting gun of a long siege of punishment.

I've mentioned how much people today talk on about depression. So I won't go on for much longer here about my own experience in the next four years after that day with Dinah. But to have the rest of my life make any sense, I'll need to lay out the chief events of that hard later time—hard for me and at least as hard for my loved ones. And I'll try to boil down into one sentence what those years felt like from inside my mind. Maybe the truest way would be this.

Imagine that every time daybreak strikes your eyelids and wakes you, you have three seconds of normal time to think some average trivial thought—"Time to wax the kitchen floor." Then your mind strikes a note like thumping the side of a big dead animal. And the voice in your head says "One more day you've got to live through, and you almost surely can't last ten minutes." And by "every daybreak," I mean every day that breaks over you, not one exception. The dark wind clamping your eyes never quits—not entirely, not for me, not once in four years of endless days each followed by its night.

When that wind blinded and smothered me, it was thought by everybody I knew to be a terrible trait that you were personally responsible for having.

You tended to look on the dark side of everything, you were sadly ungrateful for life's simple gifts, you were selfishly choosing to shut the window and doors of your mind and refuse air and light. You could choose to quit on a moment's notice. The other common thought was visible in the eyes of almost everybody in my part of the world including even Palmer finally—*You are scalding in the hands of God.* At my own worst I'd open the Bible many times a week and look at that hardest verse of all in the tenth chapter of the Epistle to the Hebrews—"It is a fearful thing to fall into the hands of the living God." All I could ever say back was *Amen.*

Whatever you believed, whoever you were in the 1940s where I lived, medical science had no cure for you—just the eventually exasperated faces of however many doctors you saw. Your church had very little more to offer except to say "Most everybody will be as bad off as you before they die." They also had to add as a postscript "Don't kill yourself. You'll go straight to Hell"—and all that when you were sitting by the absolute instant in a private Hell you'd gladly have swapped for Satan's worst grill.

That was the atmosphere. Here's what I did. I bought the groceries and cooked every meal my family ate except on the rare occasions I had a doctor's appointment, maybe three times a year. We never went out to eat, though by then the town had a decent cafe run by four sisters ugly as elbows but sensible cooks. I couldn't stand visiting other people's houses however well-meaning. I made at least three beds every morning and changed them once a week. I cleaned a sizable house with two porches and never heard one single complaint.

I did what I could to continue the job of raising my children. I wrote to August once a week when he was in England, France and Germany. And I think I concealed the great part of my burden. I know I strained not to tell him bad news when he was facing the Normandy invasion and hand-to-hand combat. I kept Dinah Slade as clean as any rock in a mountain stream, I kept her clothes neat (we'd had a good woman we took our wash to), I answered Dinah's childish questions to the best of my knowledge, and I gave her whatever love I could find in a heart as dry as any baked leather. I'd go to the meaningless meetings at school that showed I cared. I also took deep secret care every hour of the day not to think about Dinah's welfare too much. I was scared if I dwelled on her loneliness, I'd find some other common household tool and set out to save her by stopping her life. Bald as it sounds that is nothing but the truth.

I watched Palmer drift away from me by the inch, though his eyes stayed concerned and though his voice would offer me daily—every few days at least—the firm assurance that he'd take me anywhere I needed to go, that he'd spend his last penny to save my mind if we could find a cure and that I was all he loved on this Earth except for his own mother and our children. I slept beside him in the same bed nightly. Given the nature of men in general, in all I've seen or read about them, one of the most remarkable things was how Palmer managed any sexual feelings he might have still had for a body as cloudy and distant as mine.

It wasn't that he'd turned repulsive or filthy. I could still see he was a well-formed man who might be attractive to a number of others. And I tried to agree when he asked to join me at reasonable times. But then I reached the point where I could no more respond to his body than to anything else. After a few weeks of hoping to persuade me, he quietly put that out of his mind—for all the trouble he caused me at least. I understood that he thought he was showing me continued love. But I mostly had to refuse him for the time being anyhow. I remember using exactly those words the first night I stopped him. And he seldom tried to touch me again beyond a light kiss when he went to work for years thereafter.

I know that it's common in some quarters now to see every husband as his wife's chief rival or at the very least her suffocator. I've had my causes, great and small, for anger at Palmer and resentment of the thousand times when hopes of mine were the last thing on Earth he seemed to notice, even when I finally brought the hopes up and requested attention. You might expect that, when I was scouring the floor of my mind, I might well have turned on Palmer as a possible cause of my pain. He was no more innocent than anyone else who'd crossed my path.

But I honest to God don't recall ever turning round and letting him have a piece of my mind. Maybe there were too few pieces to share. There were times to be sure, hundreds of times, when Palmer looked and felt like a high gray boulder that was blocking my path and sometimes even pressing its grim weight down my bruised mind and body but never intentionally. You don't blame a rock for being heavy. Oh a few times I'd stand with my back to Palmer in the kitchen or bedroom and wish in silence that I could just look around in two seconds and discover that he'd evaporated from the world entirely and would never be back.

Sooner or later in the long ordeal, I wished the same thing about everybody I used to love. But after I pulled back from Dinah that time, I never again tried to speed that process with anyone in particular, though many times the air around me might well have driven off the strongest polecat. And sometimes my poor husband's growing deafness helped me feel a little pity.

It may not have been much more than pity, but pity was a feeling, and I had few other feelings. Sometimes I'd shed actual tears, just longing to *feel* some human sensation like the good smell of bread or the brush of the hair on the back of a man's neck when he bends to kiss you and you reach to hold him a second longer than he intends.

One of the small-sounding things that may have saved me was the fact that Palmer never seemed to hate my skin. On the contrary when I was at my worst, I'd sometimes stand at the bureau mirror and tell Palmer that even my *hair* hurt badly. I could hardly bear to pull a wide-toothed comb through my hair. It hurt right down to the farthest root and on into my skull. The first time I mentioned it, Palmer didn't speak but came to me slowly, reached out for the comb and with a touch as light as a baby's, he combed out the tangles, then brushed it as long as I could stand there and let him.

Even then, unhinged as I was I knew I'd just witnessed love as strong as humans get this side of the grave. I know it today and I miss it still, though I regret bitterly that Palmer possessed so little that I could actually use when I was turning on my long spit.

Maybe it's not strange looking back, but it's always seemed unexpected to me—the only two people who offered real help on a steady basis were my sister Leela and my brother Ferny Dane. I've mentioned that Leela had finally married Clarence Rooker and had a son Wilton in '42. The Rookers lived just four miles away. And at least once a week, Leela drove herself and Wilton over and spent the shank of the afternoon with me. She'd been acquainted with my blues all her life, she understood this siege was far worse than ever, and she never once said the idiotic hollow things that made you want to gouge out other people's vocal cords and fling them in their face when they came at you babbling Christian tripe.

Once a week Leela would just walk in and say, as the most natural thing on Earth, "Anna, it's time we washed your hair." Taking care of myself was the last thing that mattered, though I tried to stay clean enough for my family at least to bear. I neglected my hair though, so every Friday morning Leela would turn up with the shampoo and towel, and I'd let her take me like an upright baby and scrub me clean with fingers as kind as a year-old child's.

Or she'd sit still beside me and work at something—she'd taken up needlepoint—and if I began to wring my hands (as I literally did in my worst moments), she'd just lean forward far enough to tap me once. Then she'd say "You've got to trust this pain will pass on." For that little moment I'd almost believe her.

And though young Wilton was still a near infant, he'd plainly chosen me from the world—right from his cradle—as a primary pet. I couldn't look at him and not cause a smile on his winning face. I could almost tell myself he was falling in love with me as August had with Muddie, like a blessing from the skies. But I couldn't let myself quite believe it. When I wanted to take young Wilton and hold him close up against me, I'd stop myself and think *You'll be dead before this boy can talk. Don't break his heart early. Stand back. Let him run.*

My dear brother Ferny came once a month from Raleigh for Sunday dinner and then a drive, just Fern and I. Palmer would take Dinah up to Miss Olivia's for the afternoon, and Fern would take me riding through the country. He knew I understood about his dope-taking and never brought it up. He knew I'd always assumed he had some other private life that he kept secret and I never asked about. And he knew neither one of us cared one whit for the news of the past week or the years to come. So he and I would sit apart in his aging car and pretend we were studying nature, by the leaf and the smallest feather.

The main way you could tell when Fern was on his medication was his power of attention. He'd always been a focused child, but now he could stop the car and stare at a horse in a field for as long as you let him as if it bore a message he'd waited years to get. Even when we were moving, he'd put his hand up every five minutes or so to point and say "Look yonder" at a tree or a crow. Fern's eyes would be almost brimming with that simple joy or bottomless pity. I never knew which.

But far the greater part of the time, we sat through our trips in absolute silence inches apart, though nourished by the other's nameless desperation. I'd glance his way at least once a mile and recall what Muddie would say about people who were prematurely ill. She'd frown and say "Poor Albert Parker's *neck* is so frail, and his hair in the back is standing out like taffeta ribbon. He can't last long." Poor Ferny's neck was shrinking by the month, and his hair was lifeless as any doll's hair.

In the fall of 1944 on one of our rides, Fern suddenly felt the need to tell me why he hadn't been drafted. He said "You remember my childhood asthma?"

I told him I did, though in fact he'd never had it, not that I'd ever heard of.

In any case that broke the ice sufficiently for him to say "Is it Larkin you're still missing so badly?"

I could smile for the first time in what seemed years and tell him "No." I wanted to say "If it only *were* that, Fern, I'd weep for pure gratitude." I suspected, though, that the loss of Larkin still burned Fern's mind. But I was too trapped in my own misery to seek his out and aim to calm it.

He drove awhile longer in silence. Then he only said "But that would do it, wouldn't it? The sight of Lark would ease your pain. It's Lark, I mean, that you've been missing?"

Despite the fact that everything he'd said on the ride had come in the form of sidelong questions, still I thought I knew what Ferny meant, for himself if not for me. And lost as we both were, sealed in his car way out in the country, it didn't seem a childish thing to ask. So I told Fern "Yes, Larkin's drowning would be big enough to cause most any sorrow."

The whole way back home, we scarcely made a sound — just the breathing of two familiar animals who trusted each other in the same dry stall. I can isolate that single hour even now and recall it as the most peaceful time of those bad years. Sick as I was, and drowning in my sickness, I could tell myself for that brief stretch that Ferny Dane was worse off than me and that there was no chance on God's green Earth he'd ever improve. That was only pure truth.

He'd been truly abandoned by life itself; there was none left in him. I was falling too fast to offer him help. Leela and our cold elder brother had given up long since, and Fern was all but dead. He hung on however till August 1945, the end of the Second War right after Hiroshima and the bomb that melted people. On the day old stuck-up General MacArthur accepted the Japanese surrender, Fern's landlady found him laid neatly on the bed in his one rented room apparently dressed for that day's work, though he never got there. Since our elder brother was the senior kin, they called him first at his home in Charlotte.

And he made the choice, not asking me or Leela, to seek no autopsy but to bury Fern fast next to Muddie and Father.

He lies there still way out of place. And as for him having any private life, not one stranger showed a face at the funeral, male or female. If I'd had any say at all, I'd have wanted to know what killed the kind boy. I suspect his heart just gave up, daunted, as Muddie's had done. And I'd have suggested that his grave be up by the Roanoke River in that bright strip of ground where he and Larkin and Palmer Slade had paused on what must have been the pitch of Fern's life before they launched on the race back toward me when Larkin drowned.

I'd known—everybody in the world had known—that the war would end eventually and that our side would win. I'd even let myself believe that somehow the final surrender day would be the start of my recovery. I was hoarding the strength to grab onto that day like an iron bar and start to haul myself up to light. With the exception of Ferny's death on the day the great bomb made peace a necessity, the Second War was kind to my family. I'd like to think that even Fern died of happiness. The landlady said his radio was on when she found him and that his face was pleasantly composed.

No man from my generation of kinfolk had to go. None of the younger cousins and nephews suffered real harm, even my elder brother's two boys who were stout and wide enough to be perfect targets failed to get hit by German fire. And Augustus Larkin Slade as well. He got all the way to downtown Berlin before Hitler killed himself underground. August said he'd been near enough at the time to hear the Führer's pistol shot. But of course he didn't. There was serious noise on every side, and August has never avoided the chance to improve a story with a harmless lie.

In fact, sad to say, August has shared his father's hereditary deafness in which war noise may well have played a part. And good as he's been to me through the years, he's increasingly lived in that same world of distance ever since he got back home in '46. That was way too young for a lovable man to succumb to an ancient family trait. And inappropriate as it may seem, I've always held it against the Germans that my son's dazed and uninformed smile was brought on early by their vicious hatred.

Since August stayed in the occupation force—he wound up in Frankfurt—we knew he'd be gone another few months. I told myself that might give me time to grasp the mood of the whole peaceful world so my son might recognize me. I'd kept my troubles out of all my letters and had begged everybody else to do the same. Since August never alluded to it in his letters home, I had to trust he was unaware. I also began to think in earnest of bringing myself to life again before the boy was back.

So in the extra fine days of October '45, Palmer took me to Duke for yet another hopeless session — hopeless for me when we left home anyhow. The doctor I'd seen periodically for three years received us kindly, seemed sorry to hear that my condition persisted and recommended more tests than I'd undergone before. He wanted to know if we could stay overnight and see him tomorrow when he'd have the results. Palmer wanted to stay and I agreed.

We knew Dinah was safe with Leela and Clarence; then Palmer called his mother and she was agreeable to not consulting him for one more day. So late that afternoon we checked into the old Washington Duke Hotel, a likable place that was long since demolished. It had been a little more than twenty-two years since Palmer and I spent a whole night away from home together, since our Wilmington trip in 1923. That may sound incredible to restless modern ears. But it truly wasn't all that rare a thing in American lives back then, even lives like ours that had a decent income.

As we stepped into the elevator with a uniformed bellboy and our slim baggage (we'd packed an overnight kit in case of this happening), I waited for that first upward whoosh that old elevators made — your heart stayed behind for two more seconds — and my mind said *It starts this minute.* At once I wanted to ask what *it* was, but that seemed plain as my pale hands beside me. I would come back to life and be of some use to the ongoing Earth and the people I'd loved back when I had feelings.

It was the first trace of hope I'd felt for a very long time, and it almost stunned me, so I kept it from Palmer. I thought it was cruel to give him the smallest good expectation. But in fact that night in the hotel dining room, I ate for the only time in my life something called planked steak. It consisted of a cooked beefsteak laid on a seasoned plank of wood, surrounded by mashed potatoes and browned again. Palmer mentioned that I hadn't eaten that much in years.

And the doctor's tests all came back negative, a choice of term I've never understood. If you're well they give you a *negative* report, which has always scared me till I stop to think. Anyhow Dr. Menafee sat me and Palmer down in his office, gave us all the results and said that — apart from slightly low blood pressure and the need to gain weight I was in grand shape for a woman aged forty-five. Even my tenderest inner parts showed no significant damage from the passage of three children in labor.

Grand was the last thing I'd felt for years. And hearing it now it sounded as foreign as a horse dialect from the wastes of Mongolia. But Palmer beamed to hear it—I always watched him when he was present, more than any doctor—so at that my own mind lifted again one further notch up off the ground.

Then the doctor pushed on to the part you waited for in those less harried days, the part where the doctor didn't hesitate to give you the fruit of his whole adult common sense. Though I hadn't dwelt on my long depression when we'd met the day before, and though he hadn't talked privately with Palmer, Dr. Menafee took my right hand firmly in both his own hands and met my eyes. He said "Roxanna—let me call you that please; we're near the same age—you're in far better shape than you want to believe. With what you've told me about your parents and with what I've seen of the husband you've got, you could live another fifty years in full possession of your mind and the strength to walk about and do your work. My profession can't explain what's troubled you for so long. I don't low-rate your pain one iota. It's lasted longer than most such pain, but try to believe one fact I *know*—if you'll ride out this ache awhile longer, it'll pass you by. Or you'll pass it. Don't ever give up hoping, not for one hour. You are meant to live, to enjoy enough time to make life worthwhile and to treasure your family."

At the sound of somebody being that careful with simple words, the upward moves my mind had taken in recent weeks were dwarfed by what felt like a huge breath of air rushing into my body as I sat there, the doctor still holding onto my hand and his brown spaniel eyes locked on me. Then he bent, set a quick dry kiss on the back of my wrist and said to Palmer "You'll give me that much, won't you?"

Palmer said "Very gladly" and came to lay his own hand on my shoulder.

My eyes were brimming for the first time in years. What felt like relief came on me so strongly that it tasted like a *rupture*, as if some wall had suddenly collapsed in my heart and was spilling its long-held all-but-frozen contents. If these two good men were to be trusted, I'd be a human one more time, a wife to Palmer and mother to Dinah and August again—and in plenty of time for August's homecoming.

There was nothing left between me and healing but to drive back home, open the shutters, raise the shades, wash all the curtains—even now this late in the year—maybe repaint the kitchen, outfit Dinah from stem to stern in the new belongings she'd deserved for years and give my husband the go-word finally to put in the plumbing he'd delayed for so long.

God or Fate or my private chemicals utterly forbade me (and didn't God *make* my chemicals?). No Hebrew prophet on a cold bed of nails ever searched his soul more meticulously than I would be forced to in weeks to come. Despite my not being noticeably pious, I've never spent five minutes doubting God's existence or the truth of Jesus' claims that God is a loving father to us all. But what was I—what is any human being—expected to do when you think you're pardoned and saved from Hell, when you're shown the black clouds clearing above, the glare of clean daylight and then the sky clangs shut again and you're thrust deeper down than you've been?

Does God just turn His back and let Fate or Satan or blind dumb chemicals rule the road? If so in what way can that amount to true *love*? If so what would you suggest was *hate*? Wouldn't a father who behaved that inexplicably be cited today for unspeakable child abuse and rightly jailed for decades to come? And as for my being a subject worthy of punishment, I'll grant my many failures through the years. But we're not speaking of Hitler here or some cankered slut that's cheating her husband and mauling her child.

Even when I was deep in the pit, I'd rake my soul like a deep gravel yard. And I never found one sin or felony that any sensible human, man or woman, would have paused beside for more than five minutes of hot reproval aimed at my eyes. Even the day I took those scissors and walked toward Dinah—I stopped, don't forget. I'm as clean of that as you are.

In any case after three weeks at home and steady small improvements on all sides, I set my face toward the oncoming Thanksgiving meal I'd planned for Leela and Clarence and Miss Olivia. I'd invited them freely to help celebrate my recovery. And it was then I began to feel the ground that was firming under my feet start to soften and shift aside. I still can't point to any one moment when the slide recommenced. I know I got through the holiday itself with all the company and cooking and washing.

Leela's son Wilton was big for his age, and he was smart enough to take the day in and laugh along with us. I recall there were moments when I felt shaky at the dinner table, and I'd look to Wilton and find his eyes on me. I'd feel a little guilty that I loved him so much, so then I'd look to Dinah, and she'd be fixed right on me too. I could see straight into the floor of her mind. And young as it was, I could see I'd given her so very little that she was near starving and would always be.

She was six years old and, whatever I thought I saw and knew about her soul, I was wrong. Thank God, I was desperately wrong. However hard a time she'd had, trapped in a house with a mother like me, Dinah Slade was growing up undeterred with a heart as steady as any great clock with its inner works wound unfailingly by some benign invisible hand. I've never forgot what a handsome part Palmer must have had in keeping Dinah human — and a human with a spacious soul. In those days no part of child rearing was considered *man's work*. But Palmer did it with no audible sigh.

Despite the thousands of words I've used here, I don't know how to proceed in credible words to what comes next. I've said that the ground broke under me again from Thanksgiving onward through fall and winter. So it did and so I made it upright and working somehow till Christmas evening. Though the day had been as exhausting as any Christmas yet, that endless cold night I never shut an eye. Unlike some whom I've watched in deep melancholy, I'd slept a few hours most nights through the bad years. And I almost always slept without dreams, no dreams I recalled on waking anyhow. Till that final night, December 25th of 1945, I'd never been a victim of discouraging pictures and horror stories. I'd never heard voices that weren't truly present.

In fact the big problem for most of my time was that all my mind was seeing was *blank*. By far the greatest share of my time was spent as if I were walking through endless unfurnished rooms that were filled with an air that was one gray liquid which by special arrangement with Hell my lungs could breathe. That last Christmas night as I lay by Palmer in our same bed, I made every effort not to bother his sleep.

But as I lay on staring toward the ceiling at nothing but a total dim gray *blank*, I soon began to feel a deep howl forming in my throat. I gathered all the force I could muster to strangle it down. And for a long time I succeeded. Then at maybe four a.m., it started again to swell in my mouth. So I got up thinking I'd heard Dinah coughing and that maybe the short walk to her room would calm me down.

I didn't walk straight in through Dinah's open door but stood outside on the doorsill listening. She moved an occasional arm or leg. But no, her breathing was calm and healthy. If she'd coughed it was only a passing thing. I may have stood there fifteen minutes. And toward the end of that long wait, I'd reached a state that was almost peaceful. Not happy, not feeling I was suddenly cured but not harrowed either—just a momentary mercy. It (again, whatever *it* was) must have been preparing me for what came now.

I mentioned far back having only one vision in my early life, the night when drowned Larkin Slade came to show me he was alive and content and that Palmer might need me. That was truly a vision. My real eyes saw it, not the eyes of my mind but the two round jellies that sit in my skull either side of my nose. The thing that came on Christmas night 1945 was—what?—more like an *audition*, I guess. No satisfactory word exists. I stood on there in my young daughter's doorway and heard—just beyond her narrow bed between her and the window as if that were all the remainder of space—the individual voices of the damned.

Not one of them ever spoke a personal name, though I could hear both men's and women's voices and—dreadful to tell—even the voice of a child now and then that I was all but sure was somehow my nameless dead infant. They were not speaking English nor any other language I'd heard (I'd studied two years of French in high school), but somehow I understood every word. That was part of the horror. I quickly realized that, if their words were reaching me and making clear sense, then I was one of them and must join them soon.

What was worse, or worst, was the fact that—while they spoke no names—I could recognize for certain at least four voices among them. To this very day I've never told that to a living soul. Even now I can't make myself say who they were. Or who I knew I recognized, though not one of them was an enemy of mine. I'm still not sure they weren't truly there, beyond sleeping Dinah, in perpetual flames. And I'd never thought of any one of them as deserving endless torment.

Toward the end of their voices, they almost pressed on forward into sight. As their words grew weaker and farther off, it seemed I was starting to see their shapes—that there was this dull black screen stretched from floor to ceiling just beyond Dinah and that the dying voices were pressing hard to reach me. I almost saw the outlines of fingers thrusting from the other side. I know I saw the pitch-dark shapes of whole arms, shoulders and profiles of howling faces but never a thing I could call true sight.

I couldn't doubt for a moment they were *there* and that they wanted to reach me now, whether to fend me off or seize me. But for the present they lacked the last ounce of strength they needed to burst through toward me and lead me down. Next time they'd succeed. They made that clear before they faded.

That saved me for seven days longer, an endless week of gorgeous weather. In those times, merchants like everybody else seldom took holidays. So New Year's Day of 1946 was like most days in its air and purpose. In our part of the state, you were supposed to eat black-eyed peas and hog jowl on the first day of the year. I usually kept the custom and cooked both, though it had got harder and harder to find hog jowls anywhere except the few groceries that catered to blacks. At breakfast that morning Palmer said "I'm looking forward to those black-eyed peas." And then I realized that, for the whole week, I'd put off buying more than the urgent quart of milk or loaf of bread to see Dinah and Palmer through the post-Christmas purge.

From my bad night on, I'd scarcely eaten a morsel, though nobody seemed to have noticed the fact. So now I had to reveal my slackness. I begged Palmer's pardon—there'd been so little I could offer him lately— and I said "In that case we'll have to drive to Henderson."

"Why so far?"

I think I said "It's that far off," not knowing entirely what I meant.

In fact even that near the end of the war, our little downtown had begun the shrinkage that would kill it dead in twenty years. The man who'd run our one real grocery store had died in Guam from a sharpshooter's bullet in the war's last week, and his wife had promptly shut the store and moved to Georgia, so all we had was a sorry curbmarket. The two real stores were twelve miles away. We'd have to go there. And since I'd always resisted driving lessons and was one of the last white women left who couldn't run a car, I'd need to be driven.

Since Palmer's work was pretty much at his own discretion, he said "All right, get your coat and hat on—it's *cold* out there."

That was the instant I glimpsed my destination. I could plainly see that I hadn't planned this. Nobody living could ever look back and say Roxanna Slade planned what happened. It was handed to her by Fate or mere circumstance relating to a New Year's meal. Whether some hand was shepherding Palmer to make his request and likewise making me guilty enough to agree to ride to Henderson for peas and pork on a freezing day—I've often wondered how much of it had any prior meaning, kindly or vicious. In any case with Dinah still at Leela's house (Leela had seen, with no word from me, how bad off I was and had taken Dinah home with her two days ago), I had nothing to do but ready my lone self.

Three years before in a well-meant effort to lift my spirits, Palmer had given me a lavish Christmas present—a sealskin coat so long it almost reached to my ankles. It was a curious color of light brown. And it had genuinely come off a seal's back, not one of these wharf-rat-dyed-mink frauds that are still so common. Unfortunately for the seals, in those days their fur was not expensive. Even so I knew that Palmer had splurged way past our means. Furthermore the coat had half-dollar-sized bone buttons carved in the likeness of a young seal's head.

The day I opened the gift-wrapped box, I tried to pretend that the coat gave me pleasure when only the buttons did. I liked to read their surface with my fingers, like the real blind woman I was fast becoming. At least I didn't blame Palmer for waste, and somehow I went on prizing those buttons when I liked little else in the world. I'd had few occasions to wear it in the meanwhile. But this New Year's Day as I opened the closet, I saw the pale sealskin and thought "That's *it*." Again I've never known what or who made me say the words—I had no clear idea of what *it* was—but the curious fact of saying the words played a big part in what happened two hours later.

By that time it was past mid-morning, and the clear sun had yielded to clouds that made the cold air even harder to take. The fields on either side as we rode home were still locked in the frozen dew of last night. The brief sun hadn't been strong enough for a serious thaw. And the dead cornstalks were especially stark like a tribe of newly invented weapons stuck upright in the ground and waiting for soldiers who'd know how to use them.

I was almost tempted to speak out to them in the language I'd heard a week ago from the actual Hell beyond Dinah's bed. I think I even took a breath and opened my mouth to say one sentence. The mysterious words had already formed in my head.

But Palmer stopped me. He glanced over, smiling, and said "This is *it*."

As so often in my life, I wondered again what was this *it*? But I only waited for him to explain.

He said "This year—darling, I *know* you'll be better. By the time we go for New Year's food again, you'll be your old self."

I watched Palmer till I could finally say "Who told you so?" I had no reason to think he was fed by anything more than empty hope, a feeling I'd lost
entirely last week when Dr. Menafee's lies fell off me like a rotten blouse.

Palmer knew right off. "*Inspiration*," he said. "It just came to me."

I gave him a short little smile and nodded. That was the trigger, his word
inspiration. Two or three minutes before Palmer said it, I'd noticed that the
bottom hem of my coat was caught in the car door. That had meant nothing to me. I couldn't have roused myself to retrieve it but for Palmer's one
word *inspiration*. I heard it as an idea aimed at me more keenly than any
flaming arrow, and it lit my body with a kind of hot joy I hadn't known for
years. I looked ahead and saw the sharp curve we'd enter just before the
outskirts of home. I looked to the panel behind the steering wheel. Palmer
was always a fast safe driver, and we were going fifty.

I counted the seconds till the car got well within the grip of the curve.
My left hand was stroking one of the big carved buttons on the coat, but my
right hand went of its own accord to the cold door handle. I took a last
glimpse of Palmer who was watching the road, and I thought of no other
person or thing—live or dead.

Then I opened the door and, taking a last warm breath through my
teeth, I hurled myself with every ounce of force I had into freezing air. I
seemed to spend whole minutes in the air. So before I hit I had time to
think "Oh Christ, I haven't prayed one single word." But no prayer came.
There was no more time.

The back of my skull hit the road first and terribly—cold concrete. I
thought "That'll *do* it." But then my whole body rolled two complete turns
backward. I wound up on my hands and knees with the seal coat thrown forward over my head which meant I was trapped in a dense dark tent. A piece
of the collar was somehow clamped between my teeth. I was chewing dry fur.

Oh God, that proved it. I'd *made* it at last. I was at my rightful destination. This had to be Hell. The second jolt of unmitigated pleasure that flew
down through me from my wrecked skull was potent as lightning.

From then on I have no recollection of the next several days. From the
next two weeks in fact, I only have the faintest pictures of small quiet
moments and visits from Dinah. Palmer always said that when I jumped
there was no other car in sight, ahead or behind us; so he stopped as quick
as he could in the midst of the road and ran back toward me. By then, he

said, I'd sunk down to where I was almost lying flat on the concrete. The coat was still all over my head.

And when Palmer carefully lifted it back, he said my bloody face was calmer than he'd ever seen it and was smiling slightly. He never guessed why, I never confessed; and for the rest of his life whenever he told anybody the story, he stressed the fact that I'd fallen by accident, just freeing my coat. I never corrected him in public or private.

I was wrong to be smiling anyhow. Far from being in deep damnation, I landed in rescue. The only doctor in town was young and had no more than a two-room office. To be sure, in Henderson they had the hospital where Dinah was born. Palmer had never trusted it because his favorite cousin died there of apparent negligence. But the day I split my head like a melon, there were no such things as emergency squads with sensible help for many miles and years to come. And I was plainly hurt very gravely.

Palmer could never again describe it without going gray as ash all over. He said my head looked like some porcelain cup you'd prized and were holding most of the pieces of but could not find the rest. So what came to him on the spur of the moment was to pick me up, lay me gently in the car and get to Leela and Clarence's fast.

Leela was home when we got there, and a further blessing was that Clarence had taken Dinah fox hunting with his numerous well-bred cheerful beagles. (It was no real hunt. They'd turn the hounds loose, stand by the road and listen to twenty dogs chase a poor fox for hours through impenetrable woods till they caught him or gave up.) Leela instantly called the doctor, then quickly made up a downstairs bed. And again Palmer carried me in his arms.

As I said I have no memory of this. It was told to me many times in later years. So I see it still through the eyes of people who wanted to save me and wanted me to live. I wonder if, in my own stunned mind, I wasn't begging to slip through their dumb bumbling hands and go my way. I hadn't prayed for pardon when I jumped, but I'm almost certain I prayed now to die.

I do know that my first realistic memory is of Leela's boy Wilton who was almost four. Everybody said I spoke to Wilton first, though any number of family and friends and the pitiful doctor had trooped in and out. I recall I was propped up on several thick pillows, that my head was still aching very badly and that Wilton's hair was straight as hemp fiber—a pale cap of tow hair that made him look almost like a star in the dark sky when he'd steal in to see me. Where had he got that powerful shine? Both his parents were dark brunettes.

The thing I remember first is him coming in and handing me a fan he'd made by folding red paper into neat narrow pleats. And in fact I was over-heated with fever from various infected scrape wounds on my body and limbs. He must have heard his mother say as much and acted on my need with something he knew how to make. Sore as I was I tried to fan with my left arm. The right arm was broken and in a hard cast.

But then Wilton asked what nobody else had the gall to ask. "Why did you do it?"

When I'd looked out from my helmet of gauze and seen there was nobody else nearby, I answered him true. I said "I was trying to fly on off."

Wilton laughed high and clear, then shook his head and said "People *can't* fly."

Then I think I laughed for the first full time since before he was born. It hurt my skull like hammer blows, but I let it roll as long as it lasted.

And Wil laughed with me—his childish, not-quite-understanding laugh that bound my heart to his more closely than ever before.

By then I was saved. The boy was going on four years old. He'd outlast me. He'd be in the world as long as I lasted and way beyond. I could count on him the next time I failed. I almost knew I'd been truly saved.

I've hinted that anywhere God is concerned, I always wind up with far more questions than satisfying answers. In my darkest days when you might have thought that somebody from the church I'd belonged to since child-hood would step forward to help me—even a fair-weather member like me—I got precisely nothing. Since I was reared a Methodist, I was subject to a trait of the Methodist church. If you've got a minister you like and respect, he'll almost surely be moved by the bishop before you can thor-oughly focus your eyes on him. So maybe I'm being way too hard on plain human beings, but I did keep hoping that one of those highly trained men behind the pulpit might notice the bleak face I brought to church and vol-unteer to bring me the promises that he'd been particularly fitted to offer.

For instance in my second week at Leela's, I found myself mildly hop-ing for a visit from my pastor. I'd only met him three or four times on the very rare Sundays I turned up to hear him. His name was Alec Campbell, he was in his mid-thirties, and he had the kind of tall sharp face that looked at first as if he had honed it for years against the pages of hard wise books and the rocky walls of a normal life. The very fact that I now felt rescued made me all the more curious to see him. In sight of real healing, I may have felt strong enough to ask for the answers I'd feared to get in the valleys and troughs of the past four years.

And after a few more days, Mr. Campbell phoned Leela and asked if I were well enough for company. If you didn't want a dead-straight answer from Leela Dane Rooker, then you kept your mouth shut. I could hear Leela's end of the phone conversation. She said "Reverend Campbell, I thought your duty was to visit the sick, not wait till they're well." So I had to admire him for turning up as he did that same bright afternoon in the teeth of such a blast. Leela ushered him in, offered him a glass of sweet spring water, then left us alone.

The preacher had gently pressed my one good hand before sitting down. Then he took a straight chair in reach of my bed and waited silently for what seemed hours. I had to conclude he'd guessed the facts of what I'd done, and I thought *In a minute he'll lead us in prayer*. Maybe I truly did need to say, in the hearing of God and one of his servants, that I was deeply sorry for harming my own body and risking the minds and hopes of my loved ones. But when he finally started to speak, it was what I'd have called mere chatter in a woman—what so and so had said last Sunday, the weather, the news on soldiers from our congregation who were still abroad.

After a long ten minutes of that, when he took a brief pause to drink his water, I sat up slightly and said "You know what happened, I trust."

He gulped and said "Ma'm?"

I said "You attended college, I believe."

He nodded eagerly. "Duke Divinity School, yes ma'm."

"Then you know I caused this whole event?"

He said "Beg your pardon?" and looked genuinely baffled.

I said "Mr. Campbell, I wanted to die after years of mental agony. I threw myself out of my husband's car going fifty miles an hour."

I'll give it to him—that didn't throw him far. He met my eyes. "Is that so?" he said.

I wondered briefly if he thought I was crazy still. I'd show him I wasn't. I said "That's as true a claim as you'll ever hear."

He said "I believe you."

Then I shocked myself. I'd had no idea of being so bold, but it felt like a last credential I needed before I could go any further with this one man. "May I ask why you didn't fight in this war?"

He said "You mean this one that's just ended?"

I nodded to him. "—Called the Second World War."

He lowered his voice and spoke just to me. "Mrs. Slade, I had tuberculosis when I was in high school. My lungs are badly scarred. Please keep that information to yourself. I'm no longer dangerous to anyone else, but I wouldn't want to alarm our members."

I assumed he was truthful. I knew he'd impressed me. I told him his secret was safe. Then I said "You'll have an answer ready then."

"To what?"

I said "Is there more than one question?"

When he looked puzzled I said "Why were you and I singled out for torment?"

He said "Are you absolutely sure we were?"

It came to me slowly in a long quiet pause that nobody in my whole life had treated me with this much respect. This boy was assuming I had good sense and was pitching me balls as fast as my own. So after a while I said "I am, yes. I was recently shown the contents of Hell."

"In a vision?"

"Something like that. Entirely real. I mainly heard the groans of the damned in their weird language."

Mr. Campbell nodded. "I've heard that."

"You agree with me then?"

He nodded. "I do, oh yes. Every human suffers at one time or other if only at birth. Some suffer every minute that they draw breath. I've known two of those. One was my mother. Some live almost entirely happy lives and die in their sleep after eating their millionth home-cooked meal. Then a few like you and me are somehow teased out of the crowd by a long hot finger and *fried* in anguish. You and I are apparently safe now. Some of our partners are burned to mere cinders. There's no explanation available on Earth."

I'd asked for it, hadn't I? I couldn't complain. It was only a brisk clear statement of the truth. Maybe I should have corresponded with the Duke Divinity School years earlier. But then I saw that I had another question, maybe the last of all. So I said "—In which case, why are you working for God? Why haven't you turned your back and run to the end of the *stars*?"

Mr. Campbell looked as if I'd struck him. Then he burst out laughing. "*Somebody's* got to pay me."

I laughed with him but then had to lower my own voice and say "No, answer me please."

He actually got up—I thought he was leaving. But he went to the window and faced the late day for at least half a minute.

By then I was feeling as if I'd pressed him too hard. I started to say "I'm being discourteous—"

But he looked round, hot as a panther by night. Then he came back, stood behind his chair and gripped the top rail. What he said was "It may be a terrible thing to fall into the living God's hands. But oh Roxanna, imagine falling *out*. He's the only hand there is."

That was some twenty years before younger people in America felt licensed to call you by your first name on slender acquaintance. I hate to admit it ruffled me slightly, but the fact that he hit on the one verse of scripture that I knew best and that he'd tried to imagine an answer—that smoothed my feathers. I'm glad to say I thanked him. None of which meant I believed him entirely. I was already well enough, though, to be mannerly.

Medicine back then largely consisted of your lying down, being fed bland food and taking naps till you'd either died or your jellyfish body produced an imitation of life sufficient to cause your doctor and kinfolk to raise you gently to your rubber legs and beg you to walk. Except for eventual trips to the toilet and a wobbly few minutes upright on a chair some days, I stayed in bed at Leela's for five weeks.

Earlier here I may have suggested that Leela was not my favorite family member. And in our girlhood she was a real pesterance as often as not. Her young mind was tied up in clothes and boys in a way that seemed flighty to grim old me, and I gave her far less credit than I should have for what was lurking below her silly surface. I've mentioned her patient attentions to me throughout my bad years. But what she gave me in those five bed-ridden weeks is still beyond praise.

Leela's bound to have guessed that I'd left that car intentionally. I could tell by looking at people's eyes that nobody but pitiful aged dogs ever believed mine and Palmer's explanation of cracking the door open to spare my coat and then losing control. But where some others would glance above my head at each other when I told that tale, Leela never so much as rolled her eyes. She never alluded to my poor coat which it turned out Palmer had burned that same night, blood-caked as it was.

Toward the end of the second week though, as I began to swim up to consciousness, whenever Leela and I were alone, she'd make brief references to what she'd read about *shock* and the good results it was having—insulin shock for dementia praecox, electro-shock convulsive treatments for melancholia. By the time I could actually take in more than two spoken sentences and nod in response, Leela was saying "You invented your own shock treatment. I know it in my bones. Things are very *changed* now."

For whatever reason I believed she was right. The awful blows my skull and brain took, the brutal scrambling of veins and nerves, the unbroken rest of those days with my sister and her peaceful son and maybe the choice (by whatever had driven me) to lift its hand and let me breathe—in the third week at Leela's, I began to believe that all those things had fallen in place at the final moment and that I would heal now straight down to the core. I saved that belief to tell Palmer first.

When he and Dinah came to see me that evening, Palmer wound up alone with me for a minute. And while he didn't reach for my hand, I offered it to him. He took it almost reluctantly, looking tired and puzzled and hoping I wasn't about to pitch another wild curve. Then he rubbed his broad thumb along my fingernails, and that freed my mind to know what I meant.

At first I couldn't speak. My throat nearly closed so I had to look away. I faced the window which was nearly dark that far into winter. And I said to my husband "Excuse me having to turn away. But after what I did to you, I'm not strong enough yet to meet you head-on. What I want you to know is, I'm *going* to be. From this night on, my Hell is over."

Palmer reached out lightly, took my chin and turned me toward him. All he said was "God willing."

That galled me at once. I lowered my voice to spare the others who weren't far off, but I whispered fiercely "God did His goddamned best to kill me—" The word *goddamned* had never passed my lips before, not out loud.

Palmer smiled but put up a broad hand for silence. When I accepted the brake he requested, all he did was nod one time and say "I'll be looking forward to tomorrow."

Not till then could I see, in clear late light, how much wear he'd taken in these years. Oh I could recognize him; he was plainly himself. But his eyes had very nearly died. If there was any trace of hope left in him, it was dim as a candle on a flat field miles off. And there on the brink of my own rescue, I had to start dealing with the fact that my one partner alive on Earth was mostly gone. While I wasn't watching anything but myself, he'd slipped on away. Could anything reclaim him?

I'd quoted our wedding vows to him that single time he bruised them so badly with Roebuck Pittman. Could I start back now where I left off and begin on my old promises again? It was part of the wonder in my mind that—weak as water, still in a sickbed—I thought I could. I said "Do you think you could carry me to supper?" Leela would come with my tray in a minute, but what if I tried to sit at the table like a sane human being?

Palmer said "I could carry you to Birmingham and back if the need arose. You think you could sit up and hold a fork?"

I said "We won't ever know till we try."

So he went to Leela, Clarence, Wilton and big-eyed Dinah with that odd news. And none of them tried to stop the gamble.

I could hear them all through my open door.

Leela was always good at giving orders, and she didn't miss a beat. She ordered Clarence to bring a strong armchair from the living room and brace it with pillows. She ordered young Dinah to set me a place. She lowered her voice and ordered Wilton to be extra sweet.

So once I'd got my new bathrobe and slippers on, my husband carried me through half the house and set me down safely. I could see from all the others' faces how frail I looked, but—though I think I may have taken a catnap or two—I managed to sit upright in that chair for a good twenty minutes and eat baked chicken with buttered rice, corn pudding, home canned squash and English peas with excellent biscuits followed by Jell-O.

Leela was the world's chief Jell-O provider. She claimed it was still made from baby calf's hooves, all of which kept her fingernails strong as any ox horn. She did have the longest nails in the upper South, unbreakable as leather and painted Blushing Pink till the early 1960s when she switched to Jungle Drums, a lazy deep red.

Dinah's and Wilton's faces were all eyes and, for now at least, not entirely happy.

If I hadn't known I was Roxanna Slade alive and tasting food again, I'd have guessed they were seeing an actual ghost.

SIX

That was fifty years ago. And I lived through every minute of the time as my family did near me. I only slept when the others slept in the dark at night. And even in sleep I went on facing life in my dreams. So does everybody in the world of course. I'm not requesting an ounce of pity. I only mean to stress the fact that, though those decades were calm as my hand, I wasn't conscious of being bored for more than a few short stretches of minutes.

But I'm also aware in telling my story that there have been only five more happenings of any serious interest to others—till now at least. And it scarcely seems likely that any woman well on in her nineties is scheduled for thrills. I assume the sixth thing will be my departure for whatever comes next. That will be of great interest to me but very likely nobody else, give or take a funeral tear or two.

Somebody else will have to write my ending, if anybody sees a need. Nobody will of course and that's fine with me. I wouldn't have used all this much expensive ink if there were a chance that some young scholar eons from now would dig Roxanna Slade's small life back out of the dust and make her a model of wrong wrong wrong to ages unborn.

I'm perfectly prepared to discover that death may turn out to be *extinction* as plain as blowing out a match *or* some agreeable form of reward like meeting a few choice souls gone before me. (Wonder if you get to choose which souls?) I'm tired enough to let it be either, though of course I'm aware I have no choice in the matter as in so many others. Or does some distant switchbox in the universe make a decision after learning the hopes of your old age?

Maybe Hell is only the opposite of what you'd prefer—not thumb screws and brimstone but an endless low-grade headache or abscess, a sin-

gle middling disappointment that lasts forever like a friend's promised visit
that never comes. Some days I think that mere oblivion would be the highest bliss. Other days I find myself already talking with my long-gone parents in their fresh-ironed clothes and all of us at our youthful best in lawn
chairs with glasses of cool grape juice and my father playing the old mouth
harp that he'd bring out on long summer nights to *sadden us down* as he
always called it before bedtime.

The five real things, though, are worth a brief look. The first thing centers
on Leela's son Wilton. As I've mentioned he was a very smart four-year-old
when I fell from the car. When the doctor said I was strong enough to leave
his parents' place and go back home with Palmer and Dinah, I *was* nearly
strong enough to live a new life. Of course mornings were the danger spots
as always. But if I told myself to take a firm grip and say a quick prayer for
living water to refresh my mind, I'd almost surely have a passable day if not
something better. The problem again, though, was how to pass time.
Palmer had absolutely insisted on hiring a woman to do housework till I
was restored to full capacity.

With my head wounds still subject to pain and wooziness, I realized I
needed the help. So I told Palmer Yes but begged him to find an older settled white woman for the job. With all my old reasons, I still couldn't bear
to bring in a black maid and watch her patient acceptance of her fate. So
from out in the country Palmer found a white woman named Henrietta
Burwell. She was seventy-two years old as she never ceased telling you,
stronger than a mule team, and she'd had a busy life — two husbands and a
total of eleven children.

The children were scattered to the far winds now, and her second husband had recently killed himself in two awful stages that she relished
describing. First he put a shotgun to what he thought was his heart but
only managed to blow off his left arm. After eight months when he'd
healed from that — and "him as cheerful as a fat jaybird" — he went to the
smokehouse, shut himself in with his gun and a quantity of fresh-smoked
pork and that time he managed to hit his target. Henrietta would say several times a week "I know he was suffering in his mind mighty badly, but I
wish he hadn't made bacon too painful to eat again. I used to love bacon,
and now I can't touch it."

But she'd cook it for my breakfast and watch me eat it. And before I could wash myself and dress, she'd be in the parlor with the paper waiting for me. She'd tell all the news (getting badly mixed up) before I could read it, then want to ask me intimate questions about my past till time for dinner. Still I somehow liked her and I answered every question to the best of my knowledge—all the secrets such as they were of my love life with Palmer, every dream I'd ever had, every man I'd ever glanced at, all the problems I'd had with our sex's perilously designed private equipment.

By the time Henrietta had been with me for less than a month, she knew more than I did about my road through life. All but one thing. In some kind of silent delicacy, she never mentioned my fall from the car. You might have thought I crushed my head on a low door frame. Otherwise my story, through Henrietta's eyes, would be a lot more fun listening to than my own version if you have no serious interest in the truth.

She was no fool though. In under a week she understood my situation better than anyone else had yet. And in the third week when we had a premature spell of lovely spring weather and she found me on the porch looking grim in the sunshine, she stood square before me and said "Can I tell you what both of us need?"

Till she asked, I wasn't aware I was gloomy. So of course I said "Tell me."

Henrietta said "Bring that child of your sister's over here to stay with us."

For a minute it floored me. I said "Oh *no*." She'd hardly seen Wilton more than four or five times since she'd been with me. But then I pulled back and asked her why?

She said "Several reasons." Then she counted them off on her powerful fingers. "First his mother is *whupped* from nursing you so long. Second he's lonesome with no children round him. Third you love him like a rose in the desert."

I had to laugh. "Are there roses in the desert?"

She nodded. "Rose of Sharon—read about it in the Bible. Anna, I'm not *joking*."

She'd called me Mrs. Slade up till now, so the *Anna* surprised me, but she was old enough to be my mother. Then I knew she was right. Dinah was away from the house in school from eight till four o'clock. The house was too quiet. In ten more seconds of careful thought, I saw how Henrietta's idea might work on all our behalves.

Leela took to the idea with little persuasion. When she consulted Clarence and Wilton and they said Yes, I understood I was counting on a child—my nearest nephew—to brace my recovery when I had a sweet needy daughter of my own. By then though, Henrietta had strengthened my will to the point where I forged on ahead to take what I thought would brace me best. I was like a sick dog hunting the right grass out in the woods.

When Palmer asked me how long Wilton would stay, I said "No more than a week, I expect." He looked a little glum. I assume he would have liked to be my main prop, but we don't make those choices for ourselves. Palmer said nothing else though. And Dinah showed no reluctance whatever. She loved Wilton almost as much as I did, and they'd literally never had a cross word between them.

Wilton stayed till Easter which was late that year, the 21st of April. His parents would visit us frequently. He even went home and spent two weekends. But in those days white people hadn't bit down as hard as they have now on the idea that children belong with their own blood-parents every minute of the day and night. In big old families children were reared by numerous hands of sisters, aunts, old bachelor uncles. And mostly I think they benefited from it. They didn't get hipped on two lone creatures who might suddenly fail them as modern parents so often do—divorce, death, drugs or drunkenness.

Wilton had greeted my invitation with open arms, and he never showed a trace of homesickness in his weeks away. I could see that Leela and even Clarence would look a little hacked when they'd pay us short visits and watch their son wave them blithely away as they headed home. But they were too smart to show real jealousy, and Leela let me know she understood how much her boy was helping me onward.

There was no secret to it, no peculiar hunger or weird craving. I've said that Wilton Rooker was a fine child to look at, fine to touch and smell, to listen to. I know that, so far as my pure love was concerned, he had two powerful traits from his past. He looked very much like baby pictures of Ferny Dane, and he had his mother's natural grace. Even when Leela set my teeth on edge in our childhood, I never once doubted she moved like a beautifully trained slow dancer through space. And ordinary air was far more flattering to Leela than any space I knew.

Without a trace of girlishness, young Wilton could walk straight toward you through a room and make you thoroughly grateful for the sight. He also spoke in a voice that was unlike anyone near us. In those years well before television, educated Americans still didn't all speak alike. People in our part of North Carolina then spoke with the soothing tidewater roundness (*aboot the hoose* for *about the house*). It was easier by far to bear than the piedmont twang or the mountaineer whine. Wilton had somehow invented himself a means of speech that was low-pitched for his age and that always invited you to answer him fast.

His voice also had the tidewater tendency to curve up gently at the end of anything he said like a finger luring you to answer soon in your smartest best words. It seemed a welcome form of courtesy—seemed and was. And long before usual Wilton had things to say worth listening to. They were smart observations, not the childish jokes so many people keep making till they're eighty. One night when Palmer was reading a history book in the parlor, Wil bent down beside him to study some picture of the Revolution. Then he tapped Palmer's cheek and, clearly into his hearing aid, Wil said "Could you take me to meet General Washington?"

Palmer had the sense not to laugh but to tell him "Son, I wish to God I could have that privilege."

And Wil said "You can. He'd like to meet a child."

It was only a fact that Wil had gathered by watching the world. He saw everything that happened around him if he had sufficient light.

But I won't continue this hymn of praise. Other people's children are of little use generally in strangers' minds. I must record though that, in those weeks of his mild company, he taught me (too late for my own son and daughter) what actual springs of healing water children can be if you get very *still* and love them at just the perfect distance and temperature, not asking for what most hungry parents crave—which is full reward for all they've lost, among other things. And I will just add one true story to explain my certainty that one child's presence in the midst of my life was a gift from Fate when I mostly needed a trustworthy guide back into the world from where I'd been in the dim core of torment.

The week before Easter at Leela's request we made the plan that Wilton would spend Easter Sunday with me. Then he'd move back in with his parents the next day. Leela had been very generous as I mentioned, but she

let me see she missed the child badly now and was calling him in. I'd suspected for some weeks that I was all but safe to be on my own again. So I
told her I'd have Wil clean and ready on Monday morning. What I didn't
say was I planned to outfit him very handsomely for Easter. That seemed
the least I could pay in return for his goodness. I'd already cleared that idea
with Palmer.

So on the Wednesday I gathered myself for my first trip to Henderson since
I fell. Dinah was in school, Henrietta was driving and Wil and I were on the
front seat beside her. To my knowledge still, Wil knew very little about my
fall or where it had happened. But several times in recent days, he'd asked
me questions about Jesus and Easter. He couldn't yet understand why it had
been necessary for Jesus to die so God could forgive the world. More than
once I'd told him that I couldn't comprehend it either, but it seemed to
intrigue him. Children started early back then on the really hard questions.
He'd also mentioned his mother referring to how the blood of the sacrificed
Lamb could cleanse us all (Wil used the word *wash*).

So when Henrietta drove us into that same long curve where I'd made
my lunge, Wil looked at the side of the road where I'd wound up on my
hands and knees stunned blind in Hell. I had no idea what his mother had
told him about my calamity. But as he stared at that concrete pavement
and the roadside scrub, he said "Everybody's all spic and *span*." When he
turned back to me, his eyes were mischievous as any feist pup. And he
burst into laughter so fine and silvery that I had to follow as did Henrietta.

To this day I've never known what Wilton meant. I haven't asked either
(maybe Leela had told him about the blood I'd left at that curve). I'm sure
he didn't know himself and wouldn't today. He was acting that instant as
an angel of light. And I've felt cleaner every day since he spoke.

I somehow knew I would, even the moment his simple words reached me.
I could almost *see* it in his endless eyes that could go whole minutes without a blink. So through two more years when he entered public school,
Wil served unknowingly as my central hope for staying healed and enduring the time that came my way. He'd pay me short visits, just a night or two;
and few days passed without his calling me on the phone or sending a postscript to Leela's letters. Close as we were, Leela still wrote me letters like a
pioneer mother on the dim far side of impassable mountains.

And though school took up most of Wil's time and though adolescence came on him early and broke his focus on his one aunt Anna, he's gone on all his lucky life repaying my interest since the day he was born. I assume most women even today can understand that—how a child, especially if it's not your own child—can throw out lifelines and haul you in from some strong whirlpools. Not every child but some. I wonder how many men are left, alive above ground now that men have got so *mannish*, who can enter that brand of perfect trust and selfless devotion.

Palmer Slade could and did. He had the watchful good sense to see, even when he couldn't hear, Wil's good effects. And once I was firmly back on my feet, Palmer let himself share the child's good graces. He'd loved August dearly in early childhood. But I'd seen his love drift and hide for long stretches as August started telling us in everything but words that he was not *all* ours and needed room to swing his own cats. That coolness warmed a little when the boy got home at last from the war in the fall of '46. He and his father went out bird hunting several times and would otherwise sit on the porch after supper and swap long funny stories.

One last link they had was August's voice. Since he was fourteen he'd had a bass speaking voice, not a froggy boom but a dark walnut sound that I still love. And that one voice reached Palmer when almost nothing else could, even on those days when the atmospheric pressure was so low the poor man could barely hear lightning strike a tree (his ears obeyed the barometer). But after a month with us at home, August set out for Winston-Salem and found a decent job there, selling life insurance. And that let Palmer turn back to Wilton and lavish on him what affection was left in his nearly drained heart.

I could do little for my lonely husband, though he never seemed to blame me. Once the pall had thoroughly lifted from my mind and I began to have some confidence that I wouldn't wear it soon again, Palmer and I had a few excellent quiet times. Sometimes when I'd see him just staring at a wall, to show I was with him I'd say "Let's get outdoors."

He'd say "You're sure you want to?"

And once I said I did, he'd ride us around till he chose some spot we'd never seen together before. Then we'd climb down and spend an hour trekking through briars and brush. It might be pasture as empty as Mars or a stretch of woods deserted by birds. It was always a quiet deserted place. But Palmer would tell some tale about it. For instance he might claim that if he remembered correctly Major Slade had fought a cavalry skirmish here in the final years of the War. On his way north from Georgia, Sherman and all his maddogs had passed our way.

Palmer's eyes at least had never lost their keenness, and we could be walking along in dense growth that looked to me like nothing but compost when Palmer might stoop and tease a bullet out of the ground. If the bullet was whole, he'd know it had spent its force on the empty air. But if it was flat or at all lopsided, he'd tell me "This might be the one that got Major's leg." I'd tell him that might well be the case, and Palmer would carefully store it in his pocket. Then he'd always smile as if to say "I know this is foolish," but he never put a single bullet back down.

And we must have wound up with fifty on the mantel. In any case Palmer never failed to thank me for keeping him company on his lonely jaunts. And the best thing I remember from our trips is the time he found the rusty blade of a Union bayonet. He held it up toward me and said, of all things, "If Mother had been the soldier instead of Major, we'd be living in a separate country now." Palmer laughed but he meant it and I half agreed.

Then once in the late spring of 1948, we stopped on a dirt road I didn't recognize. Palmer didn't wait for word from me but led me inward in silence so peaceful I was halfway dozing when he pulled us up short and pointed ahead. My own eyes were still good and sharp—they're good today—but I didn't see anything I'd seen before. Still I didn't want to disturb the calm air and raise my voice to ask Palmer what and where this was. I let him lead me, and we had practically walked into it before I saw this was what was left of the old Montezuma gold mine. It had been more than twenty-seven years since our last visit here. And as I looked closely, I could see that very little of the cliff face anyhow had changed at all. There were just more tangled vines covering the mouth.

Palmer didn't face me but he finally said "You scared to walk in?"

I laughed and put my mouth to his good ear. "Never, dear friend. I've been in far longer tunnels than this. You lead the way."

Palmer met my eyes at last and said "This may be risky. I haven't been in there since you and I were married."

I thought of who would suffer if it caved in and trapped us forever. Dinah was nearly nine and, sweet as she was, she'd long since had to master the skills of flying alone. August was socketed in his life with a steady girlfriend. Wilton would miss us but he had his full mind to keep him company through any loss—he could imagine his way through considerable torment. Leela had Wil and Clarence. So I said to myself "Let it cave in now," and I took the first step pulling Palmer behind me.

I still don't understand quite what I meant to accomplish. But I'm almost sure it was one last peak in my love for my husband. I knew how unchangeably sad he'd become. I must have thought that death for both of us here on a fine day would solve more oncoming problems than it caused.

Turned out neither one of us heard a thousand violins or harp strings as we pushed through the young vines and entered the shaft. Palmer hadn't brought a flashlight this time. So once we'd gone two steps past the reach of daylight, we were in deep darkness for the whole long way till we saw pale sun creeping through the far end. I think I can speak for Palmer's no-nonsense view of things. I can surely speak for mine. So it's all but certain that neither one of us had any thoughts of what our walk represented. It was nothing near as tacky though as a last Dark Stroll Toward the Light of Easy Death.

At the far end we came out again on the plain that I'd called the *sea* except that now it wasn't a plain but a curious stand of tall thick trees that seemed much older than the twenty-odd years they'd had to grow in. They were mostly pines and between them lay wide spaces of ground under deep pine straw, no grass or weeds. Why hadn't Palmer offered to buy them years ago when they were young pulpwood? Again I saw no hidden meaning in the trees or in the quick change they'd made in this place where—more than any other surely—I'd chosen this broken man beside me when he was a lean eternal boy who'd buried his only rival brother and faced life alone, less likely even than ignorant me to last and thrive. Our hands were still joined.

Palmer took mine up and studied the fingers briefly. Then he slipped off the thin gold band he'd placed there in 1921. It had literally never been off my hand since our wedding. In my three childbirths and all through my sickness, I'd never removed it for any reason. Then still holding mine Palmer slipped off his own and showed me the two. They were nearly identical except for their weight on his palm. Finally he said "How long has it been?"

By then a cold fear had flushed up in me. As I've mentioned before, divorce in our world was scarce as gold ingots. But people sometimes separated and went in opposite directions. Was Palmer bracing me to ask for that? Where would he go now, tired as he was? Who would take him in? First though I had to answer his question. I said "If you're asking how long we're together, it's twenty-seven years this coming November."

Palmer said "How old did Larkin live to be?"

"You remember," I said. "He was twenty years old when I first saw him—the day I met you, my own birthday."

Palmer said "We've outlasted him at least. By a good long way." He was studying the wedding rings still.

And I was still fearful.

But then Palmer faced me and broke out a smile that was broader than any I'd seen in years on his long face. He closed his fist tight around both rings and said "Can I do anything I want to?"

I somehow managed a smile of my own. "I vowed to obey you, yes sir—go to it."

So he waited forever, then turned toward what I'd once thought was the sea and flung both rings east as hard as he could.

I can still hear the dull little *pock* they made as they each struck trees and dropped to the ground. And I tried to see where they might have landed but saw no trace. They'd been truly swallowed up.

Palmer's smile grew wider still and then he laughed.

I said "You telling me to walk home alone?"

He didn't hear me and after a long time he tapped on his ears as if I'd never known of his deafness.

I lowered the pitch of my voice and said "You've ended *something*. I need to know what."

"*Ended?*" he said. He was genuinely stumped. "Christ Jesus, Anna, I was just discarding what we don't need—*I* don't anyhow."

All I thought I knew at the moment was *I've never heard Palmer take God's name in vain. Whatever he's done, he's in dead earnest.*

When I didn't speak again, Palmer reached for my bare hand and turned back to lead us through the mine again. I must have pulled back slightly for an instant, so he stopped and said "Not a damned thing's changed. We're in this for life."

I still had no clear idea what meaning he saw in the thing he'd just done. I don't today. But I never asked him for any more. What he'd thrown away was just a few dollars of a common metal. The rest of his life, like most of all our time together, was a demonstration that he'd kept his promises and planned to continue. He did, to the grave.

His grave was four years off, sad to say. If he'd gone that evening after Montezuma, he'd have died as near to peace as he'd ever been. What he had to go through between that day and the final end was more than hard on him, and it gravely damaged another human being. No way to tell it but straight through and honest. For two more years from the day at Montezuma our life went on very much as before. Both of us worked hard every day but Sunday. And once I was strong and Henrietta (my babysitter) was gone after two long months, of course I cooked on Sunday as well. August married his girlfriend in '49. And we attended the wedding in Roanoke, the bride's hometown.

Her family were some of the well-known Shiflets of Virginia—well-known in those days anyhow for exceptional meanness. They did seem unusually sullen at the various wedding events. The bride's mother asked me if I was married when August was born. Turned out she meant was I Palmer's first wife and not a second choice, but still the family were remarkably odd. All but Daisy the bride. Daisy was only nineteen at the time. Still her even temper and the loveliest laugh in the Southern states won everybody's love, not to mention a mind as strong as a bear trap which—given August's tendency to slowness in the upper story—have come in handy many times through the years.

Dinah was a bridesmaid at ten years old. She'd quietly gone on making herself a priceless treasure (she was never less than her father's darling); and I went on just taking that for granted through decades to come, though in feeble defense I can say truly that at least I never treated her harshly for one single moment once I was my self after the torment.

What happened to Palmer, and all of us plus more than one stranger, came late in the summer of 1950. For a good many years, Palmer's main helper in the timber business was a light-colored black man from up on the river— Simon Walton. He was younger than Palmer by six years exactly. But like so many of his dauntless people, Simon had refused to age and was still a healthy giant when Fate struck hard. He was more than six feet tall, entirely bald all over his fine head and gentler than any spring butterfly. He and Palmer had not only worked together forever, they'd hunted and fished and gone on timber scouting trips as far off as Asheville and the Blue Ridge Mountains northwest of there.

It was liquor that did it—that and the blight on all white men of my generation in our part of the world where Negroes were concerned. And it happened on Saturday, the worst day for liquor in all local towns. I'd noticed in the winter of 1950 that Palmer was drinking more in the evenings. He'd casually mentioned that his sciatica was giving him fits. And he'd had arthritis since late in his thirties, not to mention the deafness.

So I didn't say a word when I'd see him head out the back, open his truck door, reach down deep in the glove compartment and bring out a pint of Kentucky bourbon. He'd take a seat on the passenger side with the door still open and drink off one or two long swigs, then wipe his mouth with his ever-clean handkerchief and come back inside. That was the only way country gentlemen drank till after the Korean War, and many men still won't drink today in the presence of a woman or a lady anyhow.

On the Saturday in question, I'd seen Palmer take a drink twice at least before I called him to dinner near noon. As ever I didn't say a word. And with me and Dinah near, he was his best self—no trace of trouble. He lay down briefly in the heat of the day. It was sweltering hot, first week of September. When I went in later to offer him some cold tea, Palmer sat up and said "Oh Anna, I promised I'd meet old Simon in town." As I said Simon was younger than Palmer.

Nothing seemed remotely wrong with their meeting on a Saturday. They often had weekend business in Henderson—some tool to buy, a truck to repair—but I warned Palmer not to get overheated and to be home in time for the good cool supper that Dinah was going to help me fix. She'd recently showed great interest in cooking, though if she had an ounce of fat anywhere on her body, I could never see it. Somehow as the afternoon went on, I felt uncertain about Palmer. In all our years he'd never once come home drunk or more than mildly tight. So I had no reason to suspect he was drinking. And certainly not with Simon.

It had always been a matter of strict principle with Palmer not to give any black person alcohol. In fact I never saw him offer so much as a sip to anybody *white*. He truly believed that few people should or could handle alcohol. And he'd once explained his theory to me, one he'd put together from his reading. It started like everything else with the Egyptians who'd been the first to ferment grain and manufacture beer. That clearly hadn't stood in the way of the Pyramids and Sphinx. Then the Greeks had learned to press wine from grapes and still invent civilization, so those skills had moved across the lower side of Europe in a few thousand years. It was only much later—all but modern times—when fermentation reached the frozen north of Scandinavia and Britain and later still before it reached the center of Africa and the Indians of America.

So all those nations who discovered it late had still not developed the blood that could handle any strong drink calmly. I have no idea how crazy or sound the theory was. It seemed to make sense when Palmer explained it to me on a map. A day seldom passed without his opening the atlas for some reason. But he at least—as a man of English, Welsh and Scottish blood—included himself in the class of the alcohol-belateds who had to be careful. And so he'd been, for that and no doubt other reasons which he felt I never needed to know.

Anyhow Dinah was ready to serve the first chicken salad she'd ever made when a sheriff's car pulled right up under the kitchen window and sat still a long time with nobody moving.

After maybe five minutes I arranged my face and stepped out onto the back porch to see if anybody was lost and needing help.

A rabbit-eyed young deputy got out and tipped his hat to me. When I said I was Mrs. Palmer Slade and could I help him, his big Adam's apple went out of control and he croaked out "Ma'm, the sheriff in person is driving your husband home in you all's car. I'm just waiting to drive Sheriff Phelps on back."

To my lasting regret I said "Is he drunk?"

"The sheriff? No ma'm."

"Mr. Slade of course."

"No ma'm, not that I heard any mention of. No, his nerves are just all tore up, it looked like. So me and Phelps are helping him a little."

Nerves had never been a problem of Palmer's. Whatever failings he had I never once saw him shiver or flinch at any surprise the world spun at him. Naturally I couldn't imagine what this might mean. I said "Can you tell me exactly what happened?"

The young man took his hat off entirely then and said "My name is Foster Pickens. I'm pretty new at this. But see, your husband has damaged a nigger. Bad."

I could only say "*Seriously?*"

He said "I'd estimate the answer is Yes. The nigger's left eye was busted all open by the time I got there."

Of course I was stunned. *What Negro and why?* I couldn't help thinking of Roebuck Pittman, though I had no idea if she was still alive. I asked the young man if he needed a glass of tea. When he declined I went back in and tried to get Dinah ready for whatever hard news was bearing down on us.

Ten minutes later the sheriff himself, in Palmer's truck, pulled in.

And Palmer stepped right out strong and straight.

I was just behind the curtains at the window.

The sheriff got out and, though his round face and little bright eyes were somber at the least, all he did was shake Palmer's hand and then go on to the deputy's car.

Palmer stood and watched them leave. There was no apparent blood on his white shirt or khaki trousers. His hands looked clean.

When he entered the back way, Palmer didn't so much as pause at the kitchen. He went straight to the bathroom, shut the door and stayed there a long time.

When he didn't come out, I walked to within two steps of the door. Water was running and I meant to knock and ask if he needed anything.

But his voice stalled me. "I'll be out in a jiffy."

Jiffy was the last word Palmer Slade was likely to use. He must have heard it on the radio.

The sound of it scared me worse than a sheriff's car and the news. So I just turned and Dinah and I set out the food in the dining room and took our chairs. I'd only told Dinah everything was all right.

In a minute Palmer was with us, same shirt and trousers, but his hair was wet and freshly combed. He looked oddly younger and, once he'd said grace as ever, he heaped his plate with the chicken salad and my famous hot rolls. Then he said "Anybody mind if I dive in?"

I saw he'd removed his hearing aid but I smiled. "Be our guest."

Dinah was a few weeks short of age eleven, so she was boiling with natural questions. I tried to hush her with discouraging looks, but she wouldn't be stopped. She hadn't touched the food on her plate when she said "Sir, are you in trouble?"

Palmer wasn't looking and at first didn't hear her.

That slowed Dinah down. She looked to me.

So I lowered my voice and clearly said "Please tell us what happened."

In thirty years I'd never seen Palmer's eyes water up, much less spill tears. But now he set his fork down, faced Dinah and me and let us watch him grieve for maybe half a minute. The water rolled steadily down his cheeks, and he never raised a hand to stop it.

I guess I'd lived through worse sights before, but I can't recall any. Neither Dinah nor I could speak a word.

Then at last Palmer said "You know I went in to meet old Simon on the courthouse bench as usual. He was late getting there which in itself was strange. But I waited peacefully for half an hour and then saw him coming. From fifty yards off I could tell he was drunk, more than tight anyhow. Twice he waved to me which he'd never done. So I was standing up when he got there. I decided not to mention his condition but figured I'd test to see what shape he was actually in. I said 'You ready to help me load this saw?' — our biggest circular saw had been in for sharpening. Simon said 'I got one question first.' I said 'Name it.' Simon laughed outright — 'Named money, named green-back dollars, boss man. You owe me, white man.' So my brain just clamped down tight on itself. And I hauled off and struck him cold in the face. My ring hit his right eye and popped it like a grape." The tears had gone on pouring while he talked.

I touched the back of his hand by his plate and said "All right. It's done at least." I wasn't trying to deny the gravity of what had happened. I was trying to put out the nearest fire. The major's signet ring was shining like a fresh-lit torch.

But Palmer wouldn't let me. He pulled his hand from under mine and said "The sheriff just happened to be nearby. He and I drove Simon to the hospital bee-line." By then Palmer's eyes were set on Dinah as if he were begging her to take up the story and finish it somehow.

Brave as she'd always been, Dinah said "You blinded Simon —" It didn't sound remotely like a question.

Palmer said "I did. We got him straight to Henderson, but they had to remove the eyeball then and there. He's in the ward right now. I need to go back." He consulted his watch and ate a little more. Then with an awful frown in his eyes, Palmer raised his own napkin, covered his mouth and spat out the whole chewed cud in silence. Then quick and quiet as any killer, he was out the back door and gone on his own.

Till he got home at ten, I wondered every instant if he'd drunk more whiskey and might wreck himself. Surely that was why the sheriff drove him home. But no, he was safe and sober when he joined us again.

By then Dinah had worried herself to sleep, full dressed on the sofa in the living room.

The hours he was gone—four cast-iron hours—I'd also kept reminding myself that Palmer had never said one word of chastisement to me in my bad times, not even a whisper of disappointment. I was in our bedroom folding laundry and rolling his socks.

Palmer walked up behind me so silently that, even though I'd heard him at the back door, I was shocked when he said "I appreciate you still being here."

I literally laughed. The idea that I might have left him and our home was so preposterous. But when I turned he was standing there slack with both hands open and empty at his sides, and he looked three or four times smaller than before.

He said "May I sit down?"

I said "It's your chair. This is your *house*, Palmer."

So he went to the rocker that had been Major Slade's and sat down heavily. When I'd asked if I could get him a sandwich and he'd refused, he let me go back to folding clothes. And then he said "I know you respect colored people."

"Some of them," I said, "just like the whites and reds and yellows."

Palmer said "Simon asked after you just now."

I said "I hope you told him he's in my prayers."

Palmer nodded. "I took that liberty, yes."

"How's he doing by now?"

That normal question seemed to free Palmer slightly. He got to his feet, reached up for the cord and started the ceiling fan. He'd put what he always called *ice cream fans* in most of our rooms only that past spring, big wood-paddle fans such as ice cream parlors invariably featured. Then he stood in the midst of the floor and spread his arms to let the breeze wash him. Finally he sat back down and said "Simon's begging my pardon every second breath."

It slipped out of me. "You didn't accept his apology?" These years later that sounds like a question from the old middle ages.

Palmer stalled a good while and then said "Interpret that please. You're speaking in tongues."

I sat by the edge of the fresh stacked laundry at the foot of our bed. Then I explained that, while I didn't blame him one bit, I also couldn't feel that Simon needed even a trace of pardon.

Palmer seemed to take it calmly. He said "You're assuming I owed him money—"

"Why else would money have been what he asked for?" Maybe that was too sudden a question to face Palmer with, but I'd known Simon for twenty-odd years. Simon had helped me with odd jobs a thousand times in the house and yard, and I'd never heard him breathe one vicious syllable.

Palmer sat back and raised his chin to the ceiling as if he'd find his answer spelled there. What he found was "See, I've owed Simon two hundred fifty dollars since late July."

I'd known that, at Simon's peculiar request, Palmer only paid him quarterly. But that much money was a lot back then. I said "What's been the hold-up?"

Palmer said "Poor business. I haven't wanted to worry you with it, but I've been short since right after Christmas."

I said "Darling, *we've* continued like normal." The last way I meant to sound was sanctimonious. I was just baffled that Palmer hadn't warned me to trim my spending in nearly nine months—not that I was ever lavish.

But he shut his eyes still facing the ceiling and said nothing more.

So I had to ask the one thing left before we could even try to sleep. "Are you in any legal trouble?"

"Of what sort, Anna?"

"For blinding a man."

That made Palmer look at me. And in the next minute before he could speak, this trail of feelings passed through his eyes like clouds on a March day. At last he seized hold of half a smile and said "When was the last time you heard of a white man going to jail for harming a Negro? My father lost a leg in his twenties just so we could *own* them like pickup trucks. And as you well know, that four years of war barely scratched the surface of slavery. It's *with* us. We *won*."

As I was hearing that sentence, word by word, it seemed to last about an hour. And I kept praying that Palmer's tears would start again just to prove precisely where his heart lay in what he said.

But he'd cried himself dry. It was ten minutes later after he'd washed his hands, stripped to his shorts and pulled back the bedspread that he spoke again. He said "I'll put this in writing tomorrow; but so you know in case I die in my sleep tonight, I'm setting up a small fund that'll pay Simon's doctor bills and his wages till the day he dies. And so you can sleep or try to anyhow—I didn't accept his apology, no ma'm. I begged *his* pardon and he gave it to me freely. If sometime between tonight and the grave you can understand *that*, you drop me a line or tell me outright."

I told him I would and thanked him gently.

In under a minute, like a hard-pushed child, he was deep asleep.

I had a good many dreams after that, all of them ending in bloodshed and noise committed by me in a light gray dress. I never mentioned them to anybody, not even Leela who'd become the person I confided in on the rare occasions when there was anything to confide (generally some minor complaint from the outskirts of menopause where I lingered for several years with no big trouble). And I never mentioned Simon's eye to Palmer again, not in any way, though what felt almost worse to me than the blinding itself was the fact that—three weeks later to the day—Simon drove his old truck up toward the kitchen door.

When Palmer went to meet him, Simon said he'd like his old job back if nobody else had it.

I was listening near the open window. And while Palmer had visited Simon almost daily in the hospital ward and then back home, I could hear that he was both shocked and glad to say he'd kept Simon's job open, sure—it was nobody else's.

I could gauge the miles and valleys of complications that my husband had had to crawl and scratch his way through in order to say that. And though Palmer Slade was fifty-one years old and looked much older in many ways, I recall thinking of him—that moment then with Simon in his eye patch standing in the backyard—as *young* and helpless in a way he'd never been before, not in my mind at least.

The two men worked together one more year. To me it seemed that nothing had really changed in their way of being together. And lately with all that's happened in racial matters, hopeful *and* horrendous, I've come to think there was one simple reason—one reason only—why Simon could ask for Palmer's pardon and then turn up with his dry eye-socket three weeks later and recommence work as if nothing had happened. And that reason was *Truly nothing had happened and maybe never would* to smash through that glass jar they were in—Simon and Palmer every day of their lives.

Whatever, I know that when Palmer's final sickness began, it was Simon Walton he wanted around him most times. And Simon rose to the challenge as unquestioningly as he'd performed every human duty that Palmer requested through their long friendship—or more likely, love. Friends almost certainly couldn't have survived the gaps and troughs that afflicted both men, but any two people bound by love are forced to live on burning ground every day of their lives and still keep moving.

Any human who can't stretch his or her mind to understand such a tangled and unjust blessing between two races or sexes or kinds almost surely should never try for love in their own life—and *certainly* should give up all idea of ever being married or having a child. After one single terrible fight, Palmer and Simon anyhow learned to occupy the same space patiently. And they taught the skill to me—or the fact that such a kinship is possible anyhow, however I've managed to use that knowledge in my life since then.

It was a brain tumor, cruel in every way but one, and that way was *speed*. It went like a brush fire right through Palmer's head and into the night. Simon noticed it first. He and Palmer were estimating a tract of timber in the coastal woods way east of home. And as often happened they got separated in the woods and spent awhile apart. Simon got worried finally and began to call out for Palmer—they had a low whistle call they used; it generally managed to pierce Palmer's deafness. No answer whatever. Eventually though, just before dark, Simon stumbled into a small clearing.

And there stood Palmer blank-faced and trembling.

Simon told me he was so surprised by the sight that he stopped ten yards from Palmer and said "You getting a chill?" It was early October; there'd been an early frost.

Palmer said "I am." Then Simon said Palmer's face went "ashy as *ashes*." And Palmer said "Simon, what the hell is my name?"

For more than a month, Simon kept that to himself. Then after I'd noticed a number of moments when Palmer seemed confused, I had to do something. At home what he showed me and Dinah was the same he'd shown Simon, the loss of names. I was old enough myself to understand that names are the first things most minds lose.

I remembered mentioning that to Leela when Palmer forgot my name and Dinah's more than once, and Leela said "That's natural. Names are the first words people learn—Ma-ma, Da-da—so they lose names first."

That seemed sensible and I tried to hold onto it as an explanation of what was overtaking my husband, but then I'd find Palmer standing in the darkest corner of our bedroom with his face to the wall like a school boy caught in some mild mischief. The first few times I let it pass and crept out without speaking. But finally it looked so sadly forlorn that I went up behind him and said "Old friend, can I *help* you?"

For a minute he couldn't turn around. But at last he faced me looking almost as young as the first day I met him. And he said "You can get me on to my home as soon as possible please"—when there he stood in the midst of the only home he'd known since leaving his mother's.

That was when I managed to speak to Simon privately one morning before he drove Palmer to work. I told him exactly those pitiful words.

Then Simon finally told me about finding him adrift in the woods down east. He said "Miss Anna, we got to take him down to Duke's soon now." *Duke's* was what black people quite sensibly called Duke Hospital (because it had been endowed single-handed by J. B. Duke who all but invented cigarettes).

That did it for me. Without consulting Palmer or anyone, I called our family doctor first. And he set the grim last march into motion.

The very same night I calmly told Palmer that he and I had a doctor's appointment the next afternoon. Palmer just nodded, then rolled over and slept like a rock in his usual place beside me. Next morning he dressed without a word of complaint and got in the car with me and Simon when the time came to leave for the drive to Henderson. After that our doctor sent him on to Duke. Simon drove us down there the week before Thanksgiving 1952.

Augustus came from Rockingham where he and Daisy had recently moved with their first son and met us for the first day of tests. For most of that day, Palmer seemed to know August and even managed to laugh at a few of the boy's old jokes. Then August's job called him back, but he phoned us each evening and calmed me a good deal.

*   *   *

Our family doctor had offered us no diagnosis, but he'd made the Duke appointment with a neurologist. As soon as I saw that final doctor's seamless face—he was young enough to be our child—I somehow knew we were on a downhill chute and wouldn't land safely. Not that the doctor was short on training or the skills that troubled nerves require, but I knew a face that smooth and untroubled would somehow bring us harder news than an older man who'd suffered himself and wasn't sapped still by youth or a sealed heart.

It took three days of painful tests but, after all that waiting in the presence of sad and stove-up strangers, it turned out I was right. Leela and Wil had come to our house to stay with Dinah while we were away. Palmer and I spent the nights at a widow's home near the hospital—a neat rented room. One of the black orderlies let Simon stay at his mother's house, but Simon would come to the widow's and fetch us at dawn and stay right with us till we finally got the results late on the third afternoon we were there.

The young man—Dr. Harrison Root—ushered us into a pale green cubicle and said it as straight as a shot to the forehead in any stockyard. "Mr. Slade, you almost certainly have a rapidly growing mass in your brain."

Why is the word *mass* the worst word of all in any hospital? Most people I know would rather hear *gangrene* or *perforated ulcer*. Anyhow when it hit me that instant, I know I let out a high little sound like some creature caught by the leg in a trap.

And the doctor looked at me with a frown as he went on reeling out his few options.

After the first words Palmer just folded in on himself like a withering leaf.

Simon, who had been upright behind him, put out his enormous left hand and held Palmer's shoulder.

Not looking back Palmer reached up his own right hand and set it beneath Simon's palm.

The options were exploratory surgery to see how much of the mass could be removed, a course of radiation or no action whatever.

When Dr. Root finished, Palmer and Simon both were looking at me. So the doctor faced me too.

I suddenly thought *Lord, Palmer doesn't understand and can't answer. Simon won't. I've got to speak now.*

But no, Palmer finally said "Number three" and held up three fingers.

I think we all believed he was deluded. But again before I could know my thoughts and speak, Palmer shook three fingers in the doctor's face and said "Number three."

It was Simon that saved us, though what a salvation. He looked to me and said "No action, Miss Anna. He's picking the third choice." Simon was clearly ready to head home.

That at least gave me something final to ask the doctor. I said "What exactly are our chances with this—with each of the choices?"

Dr. Root said "I'd be lying if I didn't say 'Slender or none' in every case." He was speaking straight at me. Palmer might as well have ceased to exist with the last word the doctor had said in his direction. "Mr. Slade might get a few extra months with surgery or radiation. If he just goes home, he might have a year."

With all the hardness I'd lived through, it was still way past incredible to me that one trained human in the business of mercy had said such words to live and breathing other creatures from the very same species. I didn't doubt his honesty, just the composition and purpose of his soul. And I sat there dumb, forcing that news down my own mind's gullet.

While I waited Palmer took his hand out of Simon's giant shelter and traced a design on the back of my hand. It seemed to be a circle with a small repeated dot in the center. He drew it again and again, no more words. Then he stopped and pointed behind him to Simon.

So I said "Simon, help us out of here now." I don't know what I meant except maybe *Pick up my poor husband and me this instant and fly to the moon, the farther side.*

Even that cold doctor looked up into Simon's half-blind gaze.

Though Simon had long since discarded his eye patch and though his doctor had finally stitched the empty socket shut, the huge face boiled with careful strength and the power to flatten whatever it chose to remove from its path. When he'd held the doctor's attention long enough, Simon said to him softly "We're going to take Mr. Slade to his own home right now, thank you, Doctor. One of us three will call you as soon as we know what's the right thing to do. That may take us awhile. This is one good man." He'd never lifted his hand off Palmer. It was Palmer he meant. For whatever knotted incalculable reason, Simon Walton meant to save him.

*   *   *

But it turned out to be the third choice after all. The doctor had called it *no action whatever*. There was no cutting, there were no burning rays, but there were real acts, and they went on for months in Palmer's own home with his people around him. I hesitate to call the invention of television an unmixed blessing, though it's been my personal college education; but Palmer's last months came just when TV sets were getting affordable. Completely on my own I made the decision to invest in one at an after-Christmas sale, and it brought Palmer—and all of us really—a good deal of peace in those hard months.

It appeared that Palmer's deafness hadn't got any worse and that his eyesight was fair for a man his age. So once Simon got him washed and dressed every morning, the two of them would sit in front of that big old cabinet-TV and stay till you'd have thought they'd go into fits or start screaming. But no, they'd laugh a good deal and point at the screen frequently, though Palmer almost never said words now.

The Jackie Gleason show was his absolute favorite. He'd watch that with me and Simon and Dinah, and he'd always beam with silent contentment. When I'd say that I hoped Jackie did my favorite of his many characters— the Poor Soul—Palmer would nod at me fiercely without a word.

The only show I recall him actually speaking about was Liberace. One night when Liberace's boneless hands had played through a lovely piece by candlelight and he'd turned to the camera with that creepy cat's smile of his and started talking to the audience in his slick mortician's voice, Palmer faced me as if he were utterly normal again and said "Anna, can't something be *done* for him?"

It was the last time Palmer called my name. And he'd done so while making a kind inquiry about an unfortunate fellow creature, a fact I continue to think about.

That happened at the frozen end of February. From then on the only words he would say anywhere near me were "Where are my mother and father please?" Miss Olivia was alive of course up by the river. Dinah would sometime pay her short visits when I couldn't get away, but the major had been gone forever.

So I'd tell him "Palmer, they're all right without us. They send you their love." And that would mostly calm him—so much so that soon he'd gone entirely mute. After that it was only another few days before he lapsed into frequent long naps and finally one deep unbroken coma that slid into death so painlessly we never heard him pass nor knew he was gone till Simon woke me at four one morning.

By then of necessity Palmer and I were sleeping apart. After Christmas when he'd really ceased to know me steadily, he found it hard to sleep in our usual bed. Maybe by then he thought I was a stranger or maybe he needed the extra space to think his last thoughts, mute though they were. So Simon and I had fixed up August's old room—Palmer in August's bed, low to the floor, and Simon on an iron bed of Muddie's in the farthest corner.

Not long after that, when Simon woke me on a warm night near dawn, the first thing I thought was "Spring starts today." And so it did. It was March 21st, had been since midnight.

But what Simon said as he pointed toward the other room was "Oh Miss Anna, Palmer's cool to the touch."

I'd noticed weeks before, when Palmer got too blind and weak to walk safely and Simon carried him most everywhere, Simon had gone back to calling his old boss-man and boyhood friend by his first name—*Palmer*, the name they'd used in a thousand country baseball games up by the river. Though Palmer was not an old man by any means, he'd been such a sober responsible soul that there were very few people left who addressed him familiarly, and Simon was the last one.

Tired and stunned as I was so close to daybreak, I understood that *cool to the touch* was Simon's try at telling me gently that Palmer was *gone*. I found my robe and slippers, and we went back toward him.

Cool is what he was, though his limbs were soft and movable still.

I looked at him a long time till I'd finally convinced myself he died calmly. Then I put his clenched fists under the cover and kissed his long-lashed eyes that Simon had already closed. I fully realized that he'd died on the morning of his mother's birthday. But I didn't mention that.

And Simon bent to kiss Palmer's forehead.

Then I went to the hall phone and called August Slade. I let Dinah sleep as long as she could. She was near fourteen and didn't need one more deep sorrow any sooner than morning.

As I said that happened at the spring equinox. Shrubs, trees and bulbs were well on their way to full leaf and bloom. I noticed the fact most plainly at the funeral when I first realized that spring this year was more than usually welcome. I and the children could deal with their father's death in longer brighter days than if he'd died in winter. Neither August nor Dinah had showed any signs of inheriting my tendency to dark depressions, and I'd been stable for seven years.

Still I watched us all, and the sky, for signs and omens we should try to anticipate and nip in the bud. Again there was no real treatment for depression except electric shock followed by awful seizures that sometimes broke your neck or limbs and always wiped your memory out. But awful as the shocks and seizures were, I'd have taken them gladly to escape the tunnel I'd known so well. The thought of my son or daughter in that darkness was a constant worry.

They made it very strongly through the next weeks however and took many burdens off my tired shoulders. It turned out Palmer had eased most burdens before he died. He must have had some premonition of the mass that killed him. For some reason anyhow six months before his diagnosis, he'd secretly made a detailed will and left a long letter to August in his lockbox. It contained a full set of suggestions for his funeral and some other advice. So August arranged the funeral with the slim comfort of knowing he'd done his father's wishes.

A little to my surprise, Palmer asked to be buried at the old Slade place by Larkin and Major and all those other vanished ancestors including the three children his mother had lost too early. His older half-brothers were buried elsewhere by then with their distant wives. He'd scarcely seen them since early childhood.

Miss Olivia was on the front steps to face us as the hearse pulled up the now overgrown alley to the tall immortal house itself. One match could have ended it centuries ago, and there were no dogs to greet all arrivals. But here it stood with its main present occupant, immortal herself.

She was ninety years old, had turned ninety just two days ago as Palmer died. But she stood there straight as a young green tree, and she had no need to hold the stair railings to her left and right. Her hair had whitened in a few scattered strands. Still as we stepped out of the car to face her, it looked dark as ever in the fresh March light.

For an instant I thought *I can't bear this. Now this can finally kill me.* But I knew that was wrong. In recent years Miss Olivia and I had kept our ties in clean cool order, partly by almost never meeting but mainly by a silent understanding that—as Palmer aged—he needed both of us, not one or the other. So I went on toward her.

And when she leaned her dry cheek down to meet my lips, she said "You know you had the world's best boy?"

August was holding my left elbow, but I knew the boy she meant was Palmer, and I said "Yes ma'm. I did. I know I did. And I'm thanking you for him."

All the pallbearers had been picked by Palmer—six Negro men he'd known since birth. They each looked big enough to carry the coffin in their sole arms, but Simon was bigger than all the rest. Our young little preacher read the burial service. And as in olden days when people were stronger than they've been since, we didn't leave the grave till two other black men—both old but able—had shoveled enough sandy dirt in the hole to cover the coffin lid.

When I finally had to look away, I glanced to the house. It had changed not a speck since the day I first saw it, despite the toll of years and deaths. For a moment that felt too hard to bear—the fact that dry unpainted boards could outlast Lark and Major and Palmer and all their outright gifts and cravings. I think I might have gone straight to the car if my eye hadn't suddenly found relief.

There in the absolute center of the porch to my real surprise stood Mally Shearin in an immaculate blue and white maid's uniform.

She'd long since moved up North, I thought. Had she come just for this?

In any case when Mally met my look, she gave a slow deep nod with her head and then a calm smile as welcome as dawn on troubled seas. After that we entered the house for one more ceremonious meal, bountiful and splendidly cooked by Mally and Miss Olivia herself who'd still not surrendered a single chore to age and old bones.

I spent the next few weeks tending to business too small for August and straining to keep Dinah cheerful and upright. It initially shocked my sister, but one of the first things I undertook was clearing all Palmer's clothes from the house. I well knew that the garments of a lost loved one are generally treated as holy or haunted anyhow for years to come. But practical as Palmer was and eager as I was to sidestep melancholy, I convinced myself it would be a sin to let good clothes hang slack till they wound up in some moth's belly. What I could, I gave to men Palmer's size whom I knew he respected. Since Leela seemed so sensitive about them, I wrapped all the rest (shoes included) and sent them to the Salvation Army in Durham post-paid. Sad to say all of it was too small for Simon.

Palmer was never a sentimental man, so his personal effects were two slim handsful. August took the gold pocket watch and the hearing aid. Major had carried the watch through his war, and it still kept good time. Dinah asked for the little white bust of George Washington which I'd bought Palmer at Mount Vernon on our honeymoon. It was five inches high, made of powdered marble and had quietly dissolved through the damp long decades till now General Washington looked jowly but smiling, more like his chubby Martha than his own stern self.

I thought of asking Simon to drive out to Montezuma for me and find those two gold bands that Palmer had flung to the wind—I'd have worn his band on a chain near my heart—but then I recalled again that Palmer had made the choice to fling them. So there they are still unless some wandering hunter has found them.

The only sizable article left was his personal knife. It was surely not gold, probably not even silver though it was sided with mother of pearl. But Palmer had used it every day since the major gave it to him at sixteen. It opened out to a really serious implement nine inches long and always a little scary to me. So I gave it to Simon, silently hoping he'd use it as peacefully as Palmer mostly had. Beyond that, Simon of course had his small fund to draw on; but he hadn't yet touched it, just lived on the wages Palmer paid him quarterly for work and that I gladly paid for the faultless final care he gave to the boss who'd required his whole left eye for some mysterious reason three years ago.

It turned out Palmer had quietly done better than I knew with his timber. And I had a fund as well, certainly not riches but enough to see me through to the grave and Dinah through college if she wanted college and we managed wisely. It was not a trust exactly but a combination of life insurance, government bonds, some electric power stock, certificates of deposit and—neatly stored in Palmer's bank lockbox—to my amazement a five-pound sack of modern gold coins that he'd invested in, in case of disaster. It seemed entirely typical that the son of a Confederate officer would gravely distrust all subsequent currency but gold. There were also the deeds to hundreds of acres of timber land that Palmer had partly inherited and slowly acquired through the years of his own hard work in all weathers.

So here I was at age fifty-two, strong apparently as any grown bear, decent to look at if still no beauty, the mistress of a spacious house that was clean as any hospital operating room and in sole charge of a good deal more than I'd dreamed we owned or ever would. August joked that "the widow Slade" would be a nice catch for any man on the loose at middle age with a taste for good cooking. I allowed that was true, though I was too old-time in my ways to spend more than three seconds thinking of any man to fill the place that Palmer had vacated in my mind.

—Heart and body as well. If anything I've said anywhere here gives the impression that Palmer Slade didn't earn my love every day of his life (with the stated exceptions) and that I didn't feel and return that love from the depths of my being, except for the years of blank torment, then I've badly misstated myself and I'm sorry. Not of course that love has to be *earned*.

Isn't that the whole point of mankind's inventing such a scarce and costly trait? The sight and presence or just the mental odor of some other person presses love from your heart, and you donate it freely whether your object wants it or not. I've had the great fortune all my life not to have felt real love for any person that didn't seem to want it—my brother Ferny, Larkin and Palmer, my children and Wilton. Not only did they *want* what I offered, they all but ran to take it from me even at times when I felt parched dry.

I'm not especially speaking of love that has a powerful physical side, though I confess that in every case I mention above there were instants when the lay of a strand of hair on a brow or the dry little tuck in the midst of a lip seemed like the total of what they were and demanded some direct form of honor from all the neighboring flesh in the room, then and there that moment. I loved, and love, every one of those names but Palmer Slade's in the coolness of kinship that was still strong enough to lift granite blocks if a block had fallen and trapped their leg. It was only with Palmer that I knew, and recall with increasing plainness the older I get, what women of my time and place simply never discussed. We even lacked the words to convey it.

And forty-odd years of watching television and reading occasional risqué books haven't taught me how to describe one of the better things Palmer and I built together. But to do any justice to him and our marriage, I need to try. In telling about our honeymoon in Washington and our one trip to

Wilmington, I've already tried to suggest the careful way Palmer helped me into the most private part of a woman's grown life. I've also told how at the time of our marriage all I knew about what sex was for was children. I just thought it was God's very peculiar invention for providing more humans to fill the ranks of the old and dead. Plus it did seem a little funny.

In fact to this day I still wonder what people think they are *doing* when they have sexual relations using birth control. Not that I think such relations are wrong. By no means. Deep at the core I'm one of the least prudish persons I know. But what are two grown people of the opposite sex—joined naked together—*making* for themselves, for their partner and the big world around them if it's not a baby? Is it anything more than a game, a dance or a private inexpensive pleasure trip? I've never known anybody in person who has thought out a sensible answer. And the only impression you get from TV and reading is that it's a way to have a quick patch of fun and in the process gain some kind of upper hand in whatever comes next in your time together.

Without going into more personal detail than the world could use, I will say that the physical pleasure part was never uppermost for me. I don't know whether that was the result of Palmer's not being a perfect rider. No young woman that I knew in my time had ever been told to take an active part in the whole process, so Palmer may well have felt the same thing about me. If so he never mentioned it. And if he did have that one spell of using a woman other than his wife, he never once suggested that it was somehow caused by coldness from me. If he hinted at any cause at all, it was him having more in the way of *need* than he could ask one woman to bear.

No, what I think Palmer Slade and I built with our bodies—and it was a building long years in the making, a home as real as any Mount Vernon—was a kind of separate life that we lived in the dark with no other watchers. It was a life with its own foreseeable motions and with a language that, even if my husband and I spoke scarcely five hundred words in all the years we shared each other's bodies, could calm our daytime grudges and fears and make our normal daylit faces not only easier to meet but to welcome. And even in the early stages of my torment before my body hurt too much to touch, the nearness of a soul as good as Palmer Slade's—a soul I could feel—sometimes served as a momentary balm.

And once I'm dead I want both August and Dinah to know that their father and I went on meeting, even once or twice in his final weeks when all I really had left to give was my aging body that he still seemed to want. Even the final time he walked into my bedroom in the dark, when I wasn't certain he knew my name, he had the same kind hands and bones that had come to me first in the upper reaches of the old Slade house when I was as innocent as any spring leaf and he'd just lost a younger brother that all the world had loved more than him.

I hope I managed to wipe that feeling out of Palmer's mind before he died. I surely worked at it. By then Larkin Slade scarcely existed in my full memory. It was Palmer whose every touch earned what I gave him, if that was anything to his stunned mind.

So no, though I had more than forty years left, the thought of yoking up again with some old codger, slack in the hams, barely creased my mind. In fairness I'll state that no old codger or any other man ever showed that kind of interest in Roxanna Slade again. It didn't surprise me nor turn me bitter toward all humanity as it has with one or two older women I've known.

What it's mainly done is make me wonder how some of the creatures I see on real-life television—women way into their seventies and eighties—will trek to Florida or fly to Las Vegas, put polyester pants on their withered legs, glue on eyelashes and cake their wattles with clown makeup just to win a year or so in a mobile-home retirement village with some parched scoundrel and his loose false teeth whom they never so much as glimpsed in his naked youth when he might still have been steered by nothing but the sight of you and your clean smell or the promise of your hair.

When I'd lived through the shock of Palmer's departure and had laid all the business matters to rest, I very slowly began to see that a sizable job had been left for me to do. Palmer had partly left it to me, but I had mainly postponed it for myself. The job was Dinah our only daughter and the one soul who still needed me for more than occasional visits. I mentioned her being nearly fourteen when Palmer died. With Simon she was my main other standby through that hard time, a quiet strong help with a man she'd loved as much as daughters ever love their fathers.

Toward the end Palmer had entirely forgotten who she was and often responded as if she were some attractive maiden to whom he might have paid some court if he'd been younger. He understood that he was old, so he never was less than a thorough gentleman in her presence. He would call her Maylee, a name I'd never heard in real life. I suspected he'd got it from one of those country music stations he'd learned to like on the radio. At first I thought the name was wrong for a child as quiet and back-standing as Dinah, but Palmer persisted in calling her that, and I let it go. At the supper table he'd urge her to eat—"May, you eat like a bird."

She'd say "Birds eat every minute of the day worse than pigs."

He'd laugh and say "Like a *wren*. You eat like a wren." Then he'd draw what he remembered of a wren on the tablecloth with just his finger. It had long since ceased to look like a bird.

Palmer's eyes were affected by then. He could see TV if he sat back from it. But without his bifocals, he scarcely knew his daughter. If anything, Dinah was large for her age—already five foot eight and well filled out, though not the least plump. By then she was in the first year of high school, the ninth grade. I never kept her home, not once, to help me out. And she brought back gratifying report cards that proved her diligence. So with everything else I had to do, I naturally thought she was on a safe track and could manage without my full attention as she'd had to for so much of her life. Busy as I was though, I was wrong not to guess that—at her age and hungry as she was for serious care—Dinah might set out to find attention on her own. Or to take the first likable offer she met with.

That came from a neighbor, a boy who'd spent his entire life—and Dinah's—a quarter mile up the road from our house. He was nearly two years older. But because of rheumatic fever in childhood, he'd stayed home a year and was in Dinah's grade. His name was Harley Beecham. He was tall for his age, and across his brown eyes was a kind of invisible band of mist. He wasn't literally retarded, but maybe the early fever had slowed his mind and left it slightly stunned and retiring.

In any case at sixteen, Harley hadn't developed a child's normal speed. All the same he'd never been less than the soul of courtesy to me, and through the years he'd helped Palmer with numerous chores around the place. You just couldn't ask Harley to move heavy weights—his heart had also been weakened by the fever.

That alone had roused sympathy in Dinah. From the time she could sit up and take solid food, she'd shown a bias toward any pet or person with less than the regulation set of skills. Even as a young child, five or six, she'd get up numerous times in the night—when all other children were dead to the world—and check on a cat that had fallen from a height; or she'd stroke our decrepit dog that was dying blind and in pain.

I knew all that and I'd seen that, once Palmer entered his final weeks, Harley was taking up most of Dinah's slack. He already had his driver's license, and they went to Henderson two nights a week at least—movies mostly or so they reported. And after school they'd study at Harley's house or ours—depending on what state Palmer was in, calm or disturbed. I had so much to think about that frankly it never crossed my mind to see how these two children had bodies equipped for adult life regardless of their innocent minds.

Yet when they came to the kitchen that June—a week after their school shut for summer and a little more than three months after Palmer's funeral—the instant I saw their serious faces, I knew the story they'd come to tell. Harley asked me if I would please sit down. I took my chair at the kitchen table. They sat to right and left of me, and they both met my eyes. I'll give it to them—they were fearless as bear hounds, though they looked as lost as the last two orphans alive on Earth.

Harley had set both hands palm down on the table. He looked to Dinah smiling and said "You want me to start?"

Dinah thought about that, then finally said "Let me just say two big things first."

Before she could go a syllable farther, I felt all oxygen fleeing the room. In another few seconds I at least would be suffocating. But I tried to show my care and patience.

Dinah spoke to her own hands mainly, not me or Harley. She said "Mother, I'm pretty sure I'm pregnant. I want you to know that Harley loves me. And if a baby is truly coming, we plan to get married."

It slipped out of me automatically. "Dinah, thirteen-year-olds can't be married in North Carolina or anywhere else in the civilized world without their parents' permission which I can't give."

They looked at each other. This hadn't crossed their minds.

That pause and that bald sign of their innocence flushed down through me as a hot taste of anger. And somehow anger helped me catch a quick breath.

Dinah knew me so well, she could see I was on the verge of an outburst. She touched my arm and said "*Wait* please."

That did it. This child that I'd been forced to neglect in my torment and had then skimped on while her father died—how could I ever redeem myself in her present life that was now so blotched? But before I could think or speak another word, I'd run entirely out of breath. You'd have thought I was in a tank at the bottom of the deepest ocean, all air expired. I actually felt I'd die in an instant, and the only thing I could think to do was face Dinah Slade and let her see I didn't die mad.

Harley had already got to his feet and taken a brown paper bag from the trash. He came back to me, opened the bag and said "Breathe into this, Mrs. Slade. This'll help."

I'd never heard of any such idea, but somebody dying is prone to experiment. I took the bag and to my amazement was breathing amply after four or five tries.

Harley said "I learned that at football practice." When he saw the blood return to my face, he said "Tell us what you think would be right. We're over our heads."

I could feel that the anger had leaked away. I could also feel a great wave of sadness heading toward me. It came straight onward and in its wake I understood two things I'm not sure are true but have never forgot. First I thought that what had caused this sadness in me was my own loss of a child thirty years ago. And second I knew that Fate was punishing me justly for that long moment in Dinah's childhood when I took the scissors and headed her way in our quiet house with nobody near to halt me or shield her. Of course I couldn't discuss such matters with Harley and Dinah, not that night anyhow. So I tried to start with the first entirely practical thing that came to mind. I said to Harley "Well, for a start, have you begged Dinah's pardon?"

Dinah stalled him with a hand. "He's tried. I won't let him. If I'm old enough to start a baby, I'm old enough to take charge of it." Her voice was rising like a child drum major in a silly parade.

That oncoming tall wave broke over me then, but no tears came—thank God—just an odd relief to watch these children in terrible trouble behave so calmly. What anyone younger than the three of us that night might need to know is this—the last thing a white girl from decent surroundings could do in 1953 was have a bastard child and keep it. Oh I'd heard of rich girls being sent off to private clinics in northern Virginia for what would be called a weak chest or a nervous breakdown. They'd stay however long it took to have the baby and give it away and then come home looking healthy as weeds.

To be sure I'd also heard of abortions being done for money by women on poor back streets—women with no more training or equipment than I myself had. I'd even heard that their main method involved the use of either a straightened-out wire coat hanger or a slippery elm stick, greased and pointed. Also of course there were reputed to be occasional legal doctors with sufficient sympathy and fear for the health of the unlucky girl.

That last possibility seemed the best hope. So blind as I still felt, Harley drove us the next afternoon to our family doctor. When Dinah and I went in together to Dr. Balfour's office, I told him flat out the nature of our worries. But I didn't say one word to suggest what I hoped he might do to solve our problem.

For the first time in Dinah's life, the doctor politely asked me to wait outside while he examined her. I tried to object. But he just said "Mrs. Slade, my nurse will be here to assist me and your daughter. I'll call you when we're ready."

So what could I do then but go back out and sit by Harley who was gnawing the knuckles of his huge left hand till they were near bloody before I could stop him?

In maybe half an hour, the nurse came out and called me in and asked Harley to join us. I wasn't convinced that Harley's presence was appropriate at this moment, but he'd already stood up, so we went in together.

Dinah's eyes were swollen from crying which was no real surprise.

The doctor sat us down. The nurse left the room. And the moment he started to talk, I knew he wouldn't solve the problem, not the clean quick way I'd hoped. But he sat at his desk and thought a long moment before he started. Then at once he confirmed Dinah's pregnancy and said there was no way he could stop it. He acknowledged that people often sought help from unlicensed women and men. He even mentioned Raleigh, Norfolk and Richmond as places where he'd heard of such events. Right to this moment I can see his young face when he said "Death lies in that direction far too often." Then he stopped and watched his immaculate shoes for a while.

Harley finally asked him "Sir, do you know for sure if the law forbids a fourteen-year-old girl to get married?" He was cheating by three months on Dinah's real age.

The doctor waited long enough to have searched every law book ever written before he said "I can't help you there either. I'd only say that both of you seem to me far too young to try this on your own."

I'll give her credit—Dinah braved her way through the only other question we could ask in this room. "Are you saying I should keep this child?" When I was thirteen I couldn't have said that sentence aloud for a guarantee of Heaven.

Dr. Balfour spoke with the dead-shot honesty of people in those freer times. Doctors today would be terrified you'd sue them at the mere whiff of honesty. "I'm saying that you should thank your stars your fine dad's gone on to his deserved rest. That's as far as I'll go." Then he turned to me. "You'll need to ask your pastor for any further guidance. I'll be here every day and at my home every night if any one of you needs the services I can give you." Then he got to his feet. He was done with us now.

When I was the last to leave his office, he lowered his voice and said "Mrs. Slade, all three of you have got my real sympathy but you understand?"

I managed a smile and told him "No sir, I doubt I do." But I also thanked him for his honesty.

Of course I understood his reasons. But as we drove away from the curb, I suddenly knew that my heart and mind were in danger again. I know it sounds selfish to anybody who's never known long melancholy, but I sat by Harley on the broad front seat with Dinah behind me and thought of nothing but where I'd wash up from this latest downpour. I was so absorbed that I didn't see where Harley was headed till he'd stopped us in front of the Methodist parsonage.

There stood the minister's wife in the yard already walking toward us in a summer print dress that looked like something made from fertilizer sacks. She was Lucy Myrick, her husband was Chambers Myrick, and they'd only been at our church six months. I scarcely knew them, though Chambers had paid two visits to Palmer in the final days.

Harley opened the door and was standing outside before I could stop him.

Dinah said "Mother, please get out. Harley's planned this."

In another two minutes we were in the pastor's study, and Chambers had closed the door. With the exception of a single framed picture of Jesus looking fresh from the nearest beauty parlor, it might have been yet another doctor's office—a doctor that read books and wrote on long lined yellow pads in a child's blue script (next Sunday's sermon was already underway). By the time we were seated, it seemed that Pastor Myrick had already guessed the problem. He may have got more such visits than I knew. Before any one of us could speak, he said "Let's start here now with a little prayer."

It wasn't so little. He went on awhile thanking God for everything down to dust mites, but he finally said "Please guide us out of this corner your humble servants are in."

At that point Harley had got out of his chair and knelt beside it with both his hands propped under his chin like a praying infant.

I'd put a hand on Dinah's knee to keep her seated.

But she'd closed her eyes so I'd followed suit. When we heard the *Amen* we all looked up.

There were tears all down the pastor's smooth face. He rubbed them away and said "I'm a *tender* heart, I can tell you truly. This may not be the job for me."

I'd never heard that much truth from any one minister, and I smiled his way. I've always wondered why more of them don't quit while they can.

He said right off *"That's* the ticket! We're brave and honest anyhow—all of us, aren't we?"

By then we felt about as brave as shot chipmunks, and none of us spoke.

So Chambers said "You want the Lord's will from me, right?"

This was still before preachers had become TV comedians and beggars, so I was both shocked and amused by this lurch into such a flip tone. I said "I think we all know that—we're, generally speaking, decent people. We all own Bibles. Dinah's glows in the dark. We're here because Harley wants to speak with you."

Harley was scarcely back in his chair, but he took right over. "See, Dinah and I are wondering what to do with a baby."

The pastor finally said *"Your* baby?"

Harley said "Nobody else's, no sir."

And Dinah said the one clear word "Mine."

I've never known why but that syllable alone set my mind free of fear for myself, and I knew we'd come through this somehow in fairly good shape. We'd wind up human beings still. So I said "Harley, is that your only question? If so let me tell you we're *having* this child."

I won't deny that the sound of it stunned me—it plainly stunned everybody in the room—yet when I looked to Dinah next, she was smiling a little. And Harley had clasped his big hands together and was shaking them right and left of his face like a champion boxer. But his face, however flushed and sure, was as blank as an infant's just before a wail. And Dinah looked about nine years old. Still something deep in me said they were right.

So after I'd talked in private with Leela and called up August in Rockingham, I knew what seemed like the one path open. My sister and son had surprised me—I don't know why—with their gentle patience (and this again was a situation by no means common in the world we knew). Odder still was the fact that Leela and August independently had the same suggestion. I should get the doctor to give Dinah a medical excuse to withdraw from school for as long as it took and then move her up to Miss Olivia's by the river till the baby could come and arrangements be made for what happened next.

None of us were ready to think our way ahead to parting with the child by legal adoption. For a couple of days, I kept the suggestion to myself. By then I'd realized I couldn't send Dinah to Leela and Clarence; I couldn't put Wilton through such ordeal. But I've mentioned that Miss Olivia and I had done a lot better with one another in recent years.

She was ninety years old now and finally troubled by her joints and her eyes. Colored Mally Shearin, though, worked for the old lady still and had long since proved her near perfection as companion and help. The kindness Mally showed me eleven years before when I'd gone up there at the start of my torment was a clear memory still. And any question of who might have been Mally's actual mother or father had ceased to concern me.

Leela and Wilton drove me up to the old Slade place, and they had a picnic down by the river while I slowly broke my news to Miss Olivia and asked for her advice. At first I thought that she and I should sit in the parlor and keep things secret as long as we could. But again Mally Shearin greeted me so kindly that I realized she'd have to be a big part of any solution that involved the Slade house.

So I just sat at the ancient kitchen table and asked Miss Olivia to sit for a minute while I told her something. She did, with Mally still working behind us. Odd and evil as it sounds today, I have to add that, however much I'd need Mally's help, it just didn't cross a white mind back then to ask a dark woman, however young, to sit down with us and participate. Still Mally was present and Miss Olivia and I proceeded as if she were invisible or had no ears and tongue to tattle.

I told every fact with nothing concealed, and then I said what was merely the truth. "I'm at the very near end of my rope. Help me please."

By then Miss Olivia's old eyes were so hooded she looked like some kind of antique serpent that had long ago known human language but was slower and slower in receiving it now. When I'd finished my story, she shut her heavy lids entirely for maybe ten seconds.

The silence was long enough for Mally to turn from the sink and check on us both.

Then Miss Olivia looked out again, though not quite *at* me. She said "Pardon that silence. I felt compelled to pray for assistance."

Till then I'd never heard her refer to the Lord or to prayer even at funerals, so I figured she was either moving onto new ground or I'd startled her worse than anybody before. Considering what she'd borne and done, that didn't seem likely. So I said "I know just how you feel."

She let that enter her brain, then shook her head fiercely. "*Nobody's* ever known how I feel. That's a superstition, that we understand each other. We're all as separate as peas in a pod."

Behind her Mally smiled toward me.

But I had to acknowledge Miss Olivia's point. At bottom it was true.

That freed her up to ask some questions. "How decent is the boy?"

"A modest set of parents—the father is a splendid car mechanic, the mother fades to nothing in the sunshine but gets her work done, all the children are polite."

Miss Olivia nodded. "You have no intention of seeing them married?"

"That's illegal still without my permission, mine and his parents'. But no, they're babies."

Miss Olivia's eyes had stayed as open as they could. She was pushing on fast now past all nonsense as if it were thick ice and she were a steel prow. "You don't want to pay some Negro woman two hundred dollars in Norfolk, Virginia to end this tomorrow?"

I couldn't imagine where she'd got details on where and how much an abortion might cost, but I said "No ma'm. None of us wants that."

Miss Olivia waited till I thought she'd lapsed into some state unconcerned with me. Then slowly she roused and looked round to Mally. She said "Mally, I've got to take her in—don't I?"

Mally said "Ma'm?"

"I've got to bring this grandchild up here to hide in the country and help her have this child and then place it."

Mally was no longer smiling at me. So far as these two tough women were concerned, I'd ceased to signify in this big choice. Mally said to Miss Olivia "It'll be hard on us — harder you than me — but there's nothing else to do."

It was that simple then. And I of all people should have known that no human business could solve itself without a few swipes from the unforeseen. But I'd been in such a high state of alarm since the children first told me that, for one long moment, I leaned way forward and laid the side of my face on the table where Larkin and Palmer, Major and his all-but-superhuman wife had shared a few thousand bountiful breakfasts. I felt rescued one more lucky time.

Miss Olivia even laid her frail right hand on the crown of my head and said "Ease up. You've always taken things too *hard*. The world doesn't end."

But when I sat up and faced her, she no longer looked as strong as she had.

For an instant she loosened hold on herself and let me see how every day of nine decades had gouged and scored her but left her still breathing and ready to serve whoever could claim to be her family. Why on Earth had the two of us — both sensible women — spent so many watts of power over so many years taunting each other like rival geese just because we shared one ample young man (a son, a husband) who was long gone now?

Compared to some of the losses she'd taken with scarcely a pause, I told myself this was minor business for Olivia Slade. Surely she'd longed to shut down her life so far as calls from her kin were concerned. Still I told myself I'd make it up to her in weeks to come with anything a younger woman might have to give her. I was still fifty-two for a few months longer — what could I give?

As it turned out, a fair amount. But first I had to convince the children that the plan was right. When Leela and Wilton drove me home, Dinah and Harley were waiting in the kitchen planked down in front of Palmer's TV like souls in a trance. It was the first time I truly realized what television would do to the country, the young minds anyhow.

I quietly made myself a pot of coffee strong enough to eat through tile and sat beside them. When the next advertisement came on the screen, I asked Harley to stop it please. Strange that, with all I've forgot, I can rerun that whole commercial plain tonight. It was for Frosty Morn pork products, and it showed a cartoon line of plump pigs dancing a French cancan. In a squealing chorus they were singing

> *The height of a piggie's ambition*
> *From the day he is born*
> *Is the hope that he will be good enough*
> *To be a Frosty Morn.*

Why is that as clear as a papercut today when I can't remember the names of old cousins I meet in town?

Anyhow against their better will the children finally turned to face me. Big as their problem was, the pigs had them grinning.

I said "I've made a plan that seems right to follow. Don't stop me till you've heard it."

They looked to each other, still not quite themselves after living inside that television all afternoon.

I said "Dinah, your grandmother Slade has asked you to come stay with her up on the river. Mally Shearin will be in the house too. She's there night and day now. We'll get you a school excuse from the doctor, and you'll stay there till the baby comes."

Dinah and her grandmother had always liked each other, and Miss Olivia was certain that Dinah had polished the moon. But the first thing Dinah said now was "Mother, you'll be with me, won't you?"

I hadn't thought that far ahead. So I said "I'll take you up and stay till you're settled, then come up every few days and every weekend. But no, I think it'll look more natural if I stay here and run this house. You can't leave houses too long—they die." That last was just an idle remark that I hadn't planned.

But when Dinah heard it, she nodded fast and finally said "This house has been dead since my father died, and there's nothing you or anybody else can do about it."

That puzzled poor Harley. He still didn't break his usual silence, but he looked over at me, and his little mouth wrenched up. He was back into being a child again, his mental age, and on my side.

It bothered me too. Was Dinah out to hurt me? For the time being anyhow, I chalked it up to her age and the genuine weight of sadness she had every reason to feel from more than one cause. I'd need to watch her closely now and try to keep her from aiming downward into whatever tendency for depression I might have passed into her bloodstream the night I conceived her.

Again these arrangements were made in June of 1953. From Dinah's memories and the doctor's report, the baby seemed likely to come in early February. In that case Dinah would miss one whole year of school at least. It also meant that she would be in the hardest part of her pregnancy in the very gloomiest days of winter—endless dreary rain, a snowfall or two—and though Miss Olivia had put oil burners in three of the downstairs rooms, the old Slade house was far from an ideal place to visit in less than bright weather.

Harley drove us up there with Dinah's things. I'd thought of course that Leela would drive us. But Dinah said "Mother, Miss Olivia needs to know Harley better. He'll be hoping to visit me as often as he can, and we need to know right off if Grandmother means to be spiteful and shame him."

I told her it was my sense that Miss Olivia could digest anything an alligator could—an alarm clock, a butcher knife—but sure if she wanted Harley to be judged at the start, then let him dare it. It was my deep wish then that Harley would simply wither away on the vine of Dinah's mind, but I knew not to say so.

Miss Olivia had said we should get there for the midday meal, and we pulled up to the house on schedule. Harley rushed to set Dinah's bags and boxes on the porch till her room was assigned. And since nobody came out to meet us, Dinah and I went on in the front door, calling "We're here" all the way to the kitchen before they heard us.

Miss Olivia and Mally were each at work—Miss Olivia at the squatty woodstove that only she would have fired up on such a hot day, and Mally slicing hard-boiled eggs over by the sink. Neither of them said a word when they saw us.

But Dinah walked slowly forward to her grandmother and kissed her pale lips.

Miss Olivia took Dinah by the wrist and held her still for a long searching moment. Then she said "This is your house as much as mine, darling girl. Let's eat this feast." She gestured around herself to the number of tureens and bowls of fresh produce, smoked ham and bread.

When I didn't speak but stood on in the doorway, Miss Olivia faced me and said "Honey, you planning to fly back home on angel wings before you eat sweet Mally's harvest?" Her eyes had almost shut again, owing to a broad smile—her rarest offering. She was literally that glad to have her granddaughter near for a while whatever the reason.

I said "Moths ate my angel wings and, yes ma'm, I'm hungry." To my almost certain knowledge, Miss Olivia had never called me more than *Anna* before in her life and surely not *Honey*.

By then young Harley had come up beside me. I hadn't known it but it soon turned out that he'd met Miss Olivia on more than one occasion in the past, times when he drove Dinah up here to visit in the months her father was so sick. He said "We're both very grateful to you, ma'm."

Miss Olivia gave him a look that was either peaceful or as hard as hailstones. Her eyes were so pale it was hard to tell. Then she said "Grateful? Yes. You both ought to be."

When I looked to Mally, she was smiling again. Some genuine beauty was swimming down in her, way beneath the skin.

I felt like it was somehow headed for me with some kind of news that would brace my heart. And I thought *We're all going to get through this.*

Well all of us did, not the way we expected but that seldom happens in any department. One of us took the longest way of all through the problem— on out of the world. Or maybe it's the shortest, depending where you land. But I still think what happened to all was almost surely for the best and showed the hand of Fate in one of its more seemly moments. Harley drove me home late that June afternoon, and I did what I'd told Dinah I would.

I stayed at home, kept the vegetable garden and the house on their routines, answered occasional questions about my daughter by telling as much of the truth as the questioner could use. Mostly I'd say her grandmother Slade was growing feebler and needed help and that Dinah herself needed country rest for a nerve condition. It was my nerves I meant but nobody knew that.

To the best of my knowledge, it satisfied people. At least I never heard vicious rumors or unkind laughter. Why should I? The only people other than the children who knew the full facts were Miss Olivia, Mally, I, Leela and Harley's parents (if he'd told both of them—I was never sure whether his father knew). Black Simon was bound to have figured it out on his own, but I told him only as much as I thought he needed to know, and it didn't alter his loyalty or his natural good nature by a notch either way.

*   *   *

So through the whole summer, I was on my own alone in the house for most of the time. Leela's son Wilton was eleven by now and was not as wrapped up in our old games as he'd once been, but he stayed over with me numerous nights. And we sometimes managed an hour or so on the dark porch late, just us and the sky when the seamless utter trust we took in each other's nearness could rise in us again and ease any pain the day might have brought.

Like a good many married women with children, I'd halfway dreaded the day when I'd be a widow with grown *gone* children and nothing left in the house but me, tribes of mice, an attic of bats and every now and then a black snake to chill any blood that might have overheated. But through those months I slowly came to prize the silence. The loneliness slowly turned into solitude, a condition I'd known precious little of in my crowded life.

Nobody knew the first thing about solitude in those packed years of endless kin, not unless they were hermits way back in the woods gnawing on half-cooked songbirds and turnips. You might not be married or anybody's parent, but your chances of getting twenty minutes' solitude were nonexistent unless you changed your appearance entirely, vanished in the night and dug you a cave with at least two exits in the Blue Ridge Mountains or points farther west.

And on many nights when Wilton was home with his own parents, I'd sit on my front porch like the last soul left on Earth, telling myself that the passing car lights were meaningless mineral bodies in the dark and that, at least, I was left with the full reward for years of tending other souls. The *reward* was this *needlessness* pouring up through me. I even allowed myself to think more than once that if my time should run out now—this given instant—and my cool remains in this clean nightgown be found next morning by the paperboy, then I'd have died a happy woman despite the discouragements I'd fought through.

Leela or Harley would drive me up to the river for a visit or an overnight stay when I felt duty calling or when any of Dinah's or Miss Olivia's letters gave cause for curiosity. Generally speaking right on through August, they both seemed almost alarmingly fine.

I can truthfully claim that jealousy has played a slim part in my life. But on some of those visits, the dry hand of jealousy would sometimes rake the back of my neck when I'd watch how Dinah had fitted her life to Miss Olivia's tall outline—still plain to trace as a granite cliff face—and I'd see Miss Olivia's old-ivory eyes (that had watched five of her own children die) follow Dinah's swelling form through a room and then boil down their ebony pupils to coal-dust-black in sheer contentment to know that she might be an old woman with agonized bones but was leaving behind this piece of herself and—inside Dinah—a still younger piece on its way toward daylight.

All through the first three weeks of September, summer put on a mean fling for itself. It was over a hundred degrees in the shade for a number of days. Even in those times before white people were spoiled by air conditioning, that much damp heat was hard on everybody. You hated to fire up the whole kitchen just to cook yourself the merest morsel, so you tinkered with your windows and shutters to see what combination of open and shut worked best at what time of day, and then by bedtime you found yourself haunting different rooms of the house in search of a breeze and a dry place to lie.

Alone as I was I wound up sitting out on the porch most nights till past bedtime waiting till the house had cooled as much as it could, then sleeping on a pallet on the floor of whatever room felt nearly bearable. Even at two and three in the morning, the floor would be warm as a human pressed too close against you. An occasional treat would come in the form of a thunderstorm. Since my early childhood I'd been the only woman I knew who loved real lightning and thunder loud enough to shake the whole house.

One night that summer with Dinah gone, a bolt of lightning struck right by the house. And a ball of blue fire the size of a child's head rolled out of the light socket by my bed and passed through the hall door. Fireballs were common enough, with antique wiring. Still I halfway wondered whose ghost it might be. It caused no harm in any case and gave me a little entertainment in the swelter.

More than anything in years, that summer's meanness made me feel my age. I'd pause every minute or so and think *I believe it's bound to be two degrees hotter than it was just now.* That kind of thinking is strictly adult. In those days anyhow children and young people scarcely noticed the heat. They'd just shake their heads to fling off the water and go right on with their furious lives. But the heat wave of 1953 nearly did me in. So much so that I phoned Miss Olivia's place daily at least to check on everybody's health up there.

If Miss Olivia answered she'd call me a goose for worrying about them. "Anna, I was born in the fires of Hell. I'm headed there eventually. Fire's my *home*—I thought you'd noticed. Go fix yourself some cold lemonade and find you a weaker soul to pamper." When I'd ask to speak to Dinah, Miss Olivia would sometimes tease me by saying "Dinah's out chopping cornstalks" or some such foolishness.

If I insisted and got Dinah's voice, she'd also claim to be doing fine. Once she told me they'd waked up deep into the previous night—Miss Olivia, her and Mally—and walked to the river and stretched out on quilts on the pavilion there and told ghost stories till sunrise sent them back inside. Dinah laughed at the memory. So I didn't ask if Larkin or Ferny, Palmer or Major or anyone older had showed up or touched any one of their hands.

But the visits I paid them increased my concern. Miss Olivia was pale as a peaked child's hand. Mally had lost a good deal of weight bending over that blistering woodstove for three full meals plus the extra attentions to a pregnant child and a ruined old woman. And while Dinah went on growing as expected, her eyes were taking on a hollow look that made me fear that the baby was somehow turning against her from the depths of her womb. They can choose to do that. I'd seen that look in many pregnant women's eyes through the years. And I'd learned to dread or welcome it, depending on whether the mother's life seemed ready for a child at that time and place.

Meanwhile I'd gone on quietly gathering whatever information I could find on the matter of unwanted infants. I'd mentioned the fact to no one but Leela, and she'd suggested I write around to the nearest orphanages— Oxford and Raleigh—and the State Health Department. Everybody answered with startling promptness, and every answer was bleak as a sleet storm. Yes, they all accepted such children under certain conditions. And they seemed to feel they could place Dinah's child in a "loving home" in a matter of days.

I'd visited the Oxford Orphanage years ago when a distant cousin and her husband were hell-bent on adopting a daughter. They'd had a son long before, and then my cousin went barren. The prospective parents were so full of feeling on the subject that they asked me to accompany them as a cool-headed referee to help them choose. The man in charge at the

Orphanage was alarmingly fat to be responsible for so many children, all scrawny as dog paws. But we'd come in time for the twice-weekly line-up when would-be parents were trooped along the dormitory floors where the children, sorted by age, would stand at the foot of their cot and let you ask them questions and feel their arms and legs for strength.

The infants were all in one big nursery in cribs like orange crates, and you were allowed to lift them and try to make them smile. A fair number of the children looked attractive to me, but way too many of them had the bluish thin skin that so often meant tuberculosis, and they all had mercilessly close-cropped hair to discourage outbreaks of head-lice. My cousin picked a three-year-old girl who could play the harmonica and was sweet as a pup but turned out to be a sweet helpless thief in later years.

So I'd been trying to brace myself to pass my findings on to Dinah, and through her to Harley, when the weather turned hot. Dinah was nearly halfway through her term, and I really felt we had to choose a plan more or less immediately and get our minds and hearts into line to bear the separation when it came. I'd convinced myself that separation was the kindest course for a girl as young as Dinah. Leela agreed and I strongly suspected that Miss Olivia would stand behind me if Dinah objected. I take no pride in recalling that today. But anyone thinking I was curt and coldhearted should try to remember the tone of those times when bastard white children were scarce as white tigers and were cruelly treated in the outside world by young and old alike.

Despite the decision I'd made in my own mind as days went on, I felt a rising sense of the awfulness of having to make a decision at all. And the nights filled up with more and more desperate dreams, all featuring pitiful children. I couldn't discuss my concerns with anyone but Leela.

And on a broiling Saturday morning in the midst of September, it was Leela who said we should just visit Dinah tomorrow and face all our fears. Under the pressure I'd made for myself, I accepted the offer. And in midafternoon after church and dinner, Leela came to collect me.

At the old Slade place once we got out of the car, the sunlight struck us like a slammed iron door. The shutters on every window were closed, and nobody stepped outside to greet us. When we tapped at the front door and stepped on in, nobody answered our first *Hello*. That scared me at once, but Leela pushed on toward the kitchen and beckoned me to follow. All down that hallway I couldn't help thinking how little this house had changed since the first day I came here thirty-three years ago. No color had faded, nothing had darkened, every face in the pictures was still the same solemn age. Every splinter, every dust curl would outlast me.

In the kitchen Mally was sitting in the green straight chair leaning forward on the table in a nap. The air was entirely still and damp. Both stoves gave off scalding rays still, but Mally didn't seem to hear our footsteps.

So Leela bent forward and touched her on the arm.

Mally came up looking beat and baffled. Then she said "I'm dreaming I'm a Santa Claus elf in a big freezer locker right at the North Pole."

Leela laughed. "That's the only cool job left." Freezer lockers were just then invading the South, but none of us had one.

When Mally offered to pour us iced tea, it scared me even worse. What was she holding back? So I had to ask where Dinah might be.

Mally lowered her voice to a whisper. "She and Miss Olivia stretched out in yonder." She pointed behind her to the back bedroom (that opened off the kitchen) and lowered her voice still softer to say "Miss Olivia been trying not to buckle in all this heat—not doing too good."

"And Dinah?" I said.

Mally said "Dinah stronger than *me*."

No sooner did I feel slightly relieved when there stood Dinah in the bedroom doorway yawning but smiling. She gave a little wave to me and Leela, then raised a hushing finger, stepped forward and began to shut the door behind her.

But Miss Olivia's voice said "Dinah? Company?"

Dinah said "Grandmother, you need your rest. It's just my mother."

Miss Olivia said "*Just?* Anna Slade's the one daughter-in-law I've got that I'd cross the *road* for." I truly think that was the one time she sent a whole word of praise in my direction, and it was not exactly a *reckless hymn*, was it? Still it came on the last day it could have, so I've always been grateful.

To the best of my knowledge, this is what happened. With help from Dinah, Miss Olivia got herself up and slowly joined us at the kitchen table. I've mentioned her looking frail before. She hadn't recovered any of the flesh she'd been steadily losing, but then she didn't seem any frailer today. And once we'd all drunk a little iced tea and talked about odds and ends, I felt compelled to bring up the subject of my explorations—the matter of

what to do with this child once it came to life. I know I expressed it in just
those terms, *Once it comes to life.*

Miss Olivia said *"It's* a boy or girl, Anna. *It's* alive this minute. It lives
here with me." She looked round for Mally who was combing her hair in a
mirror on the kitchen mantel. "Lives with *us,* don't it, Mally?"

I could see Mally wince. She hated being cornered but she said "Lives
anywhere you are, yes ma'm — correct."

Miss Olivia faced Dinah then. And I wished I could have dropped off the
Earth, for starting trouble on a punishing day. Miss Olivia waited for Dinah
to agree; and when Dinah stayed quiet, Miss Olivia said "I'll take out legal
papers if you want me to. No kin child of mine will go for an orphan." She
said the word *orphan* slowly enough to let us all hear that it was one of the
saddest words in the English language. And she said it straight at me, no
one else. The blaze that would have burned in her eyes in the old days when
I was a young bride was a low shine now but a *shine* all the same.

I thought I'd just withdraw and wait for a cooler calmer opportunity to
talk with my own daughter about urgent business. Leela had already given
me several hushing looks. So I turned to Dinah and tried to show that my
present silence was a mark of respect to this old lady. It was far from total
surrender to the lady's old ideas. In any case I didn't know Dinah's feelings,
not her present feelings, on the baby's future.

But Miss Olivia saw us sharing a glance and said to Dinah "You're still
with me, aren't you?"

That struck me too hard. Dinah was my own blood-and-bone daughter.
If anybody did, I had rights here in this grim house and for numerous reasons. No way would any grandchild of mine wind up under this vicious
roof in the country with a woman ninety years old, however headstrong. I
reached out my right hand to Dinah, and she gave me hers. All I said was
"Darling, we'll do the right thing."

I'd watched Dinah age and strengthen in the past months. Anyone living
near Olivia Larkin Slade would strengthen fast or be ground to paste by the
first sundown. The fact I had to remember, though, was — this was a child
nearly fourteen years old with no husband, no prospect who could promise
her more than Harley Beecham, a child himself and no boy-genius. Yet I'll
have to grant that, this awful day, Dinah Slade looked smart and sober
enough to make any choice her life could hurl at her.

So when she told me "Mother, *I'll* do it when the right time comes," it shied me badly.

I said a true but cruel thing. "I'm glad to hear you know who your mother is."

Dinah was too kind to answer that any way.

But Miss Olivia took it right up, nothing wrong with *her* ears. She gave the last of her scary smiles—smiles like the one God saves for great battles when the crows all gather from miles around and wait in trees for the stinking meat of the wrong *and* the right—and she said straight at me "Roxanna, you forget who delivered this child?" She nodded toward Dinah.

It was the second time in thirty-three years of knowing me that my mother-in-law had said my full first name. But I also realized she was confused. She was mixing up Dinah's birth with August's. She and Coy had helped me give birth to Augustus, but Miss Olivia had been nowhere near Dinah's birth. Still, regretting my meanness just now, I went along with her mistake. I said "You helped me have her, Miss Olivia. I've always thanked you."

Miss Olivia said "*Helped* you? If I hadn't taken this girl when I did and breathed life into her, you'd have strangled her dead. She was blue when I took her from your tight fork." While the old lady waited for that chill poison to spread through the room and on through the walls, she turned back to Mally. "Ain't that so, Coy? You were there right with me."

Mally said "Yes ma'm" and when I caught her eye, she wouldn't smile.

At the sight of Mally's grave honest eyes, the one kindness anywhere in sight, I well knew—even before the dam of all this pressure broke—that I'd done the worst thing done in this house in the hard decades since my first visit here.

When I left I could scarcely meet Dinah's eyes. They were no more than righteous but they burned.

SEVEN

I had just come in alone from the pitch-dark porch when the telephone rang. The clock had nearly made it to midnight. Who did I know that would call me so late? Ever since I'd left Miss Olivia's in late afternoon, I'd felt both awful and stubborn in my wrong. Hell-bent I'd pushed a serious question that could have waited for a break in the weather—and all just to show who ran Dinah's life or thought she did. I'd made my aged mother-in-law, who was helping me and mine, mad and confused.

Yet in the eight hours since I'd left her, I hadn't been able to make a simple phone call and beg her pardon and say that we'd talk when the hot spell broke. Wasn't I a woman nearly fifty-three years old, and wasn't Dinah Slade my daughter? Apparently not. So as I picked up the ringing phone at midnight, I thought *Dear Lord, don't let it be them.* I was already thinking that Dinah Slade had slipped off from me now and gone her own way. I also knew I'd earned just that—desertion by a child I'd left on her own in a sad part of childhood long years ago.

It was Dinah's voice. At first she seemed pleasant, so pleasant I knew something had to be wrong. And what was she doing up this late?

But I kept calm and let her tell me how the land lay.

Dinah scarcely mentioned mine and Leela's visit but went on to describe, as she mostly did when biding her time, every detail of the supper they'd eaten with special emphasis on the dessert which was buttermilk pie (much better than it sounds).

I accepted her lead for as long as she let me, just saying "How nice" and "That sounds good" till finally she broke.

Not tears exactly. She was like her father in having few tears. But her throat tightened up, her voice got thinner, and at last she lowered to a whisper and said "Mother, tell me one thing absolutely true please—"

I swore I would.

Even then it was hard for Dinah to bring it out in words. But she finally said "Tell me my father is Palmer Slade, not Larkin his brother."

Before I could even wonder how that question arose I told her "It *was* Palmer, darling. But he's left us, you know."

Dinah said "I'm not *crazy*. I know he's gone but he was truly my father, wasn't he?"

I couldn't imagine where this was headed. But I told Dinah "Yes, I'd be the one to know. Go look at the dates on Lark's tombstone. I can guarantee your father answered to *Palmer* Slade every time I called him. Why on Earth though is that a problem this late in the night?"

It took her awhile to say "You saw Grandmother getting mixed up today. It's gone on getting worse all evening. And when I helped Mally get her to bed an hour ago, she'd got so bad that she told me I was Larkin's child and not to forget it—that you'd lied to me from the day I was born."

Somehow I'd managed almost to recite the words with Dinah as she hauled them out. I'd somehow known Miss Olivia would get to that in time if she truly wanted Dinah and her baby. So I spent a careful minute on the phone then and there, explaining the facts of the matter—that single bright day up by the river ending in death. I even told her for the first and last time about Palmer coming to my bed that night two weeks after Larkin's death. I'd never told another soul, and I was scared it might throw Dinah badly to hear her mother's secrets. But when I was done, I could tell she believed me.

Dinah said as much and then in the voice of the full-grown woman she'd seemed toward the end of the afternoon, she asked me not to mention the baby's future again around her grandmother.

I said "But darling, those plans must be *made*. Or this child will come here, and you'll cling to it, and where will that leave us?"

Hearing myself this many years later, I sound like a heartless witch of a mother. I'm all but ready to believe I was, in short stretches anyhow. But once more, 1953 was a whole world ago; and all I could think of was ways to save the remains of Dinah's childhood when I'd already torn the biggest part from her in my long torment. Still I pulled back in hopes she could get some sleep between midnight and dawn. I told her I'd get Simon to drive me up as soon as the heat broke. Then she and I could take our own walk down to the river and think our way through whatever we faced.

And that seemed to ease her. I could tell she was still concerned for her grandmother's health—and with reason. Miss Olivia's mind had been rock-steady until today. The worst thing about her cruel stretches years before was, you always knew she was sane as George Washington. You couldn't just tell yourself you faced a lunatic. So now there was little I could say to guide a fourteen-year-old pregnant girl in tending the speaking ruins of a creature as powerful as Olivia Larkin Slade, but I told my daughter I loved her, and I knew I did. God knew she'd earned it.

Through the remains of that stifling night, I dreamed short snatches of one plain story. I was in a big house with the young fine Larkin. We were holding hands and watching each other with the curious longing we'd felt that one day; but we went no further toward sharing our bodies—which is to say that, so far the dream was entirely realistic. Then it began to invent its own history, for in the same big house above us there lived a baby that could just barely walk. It somehow lived entirely alone, no parents or nurse. And it was hunting us down, red-eyed, like a starved grown wolf. We knew it and knew it was bound to find us.

Two mornings later a little after six, the phone rang out of season again. The heat had broken toward three in the morning with a cool hard rain. I'd sunk into deep sleep then, the first time in more than two weeks. So the phone startled me in the grip of one more scrap of that dream. My shocked mind told me it was Dinah in trouble or somebody telling me she was bad off or was bound to the hospital right away.

It was Mally's voice. She said "Miss Anna," then went straight to her point. "Dinah asked me to call you and say Miss Olivia took sick in the night. She fell out of bed about five this morning. We both heard her and come running fast. She already had herself upright again, but she can't make a sound, and her left hand can't seem to do much moving."

Anybody would have known she'd had a stroke. I said the one word "Apoplexy," which was what old people called strokes in those days.

Mally said "Dinah said that much already. I told her she don't know Miss Olivia's mind. Ever since you were out here two days ago, I been thinking she was planning something *strong* and here she's done it."

I couldn't follow this. "What's her plan then, Mally?"

"I don't think she's sick, Miss Anna. She just quit talking."

"What good would that do her?"

"Nobody can't argue, not with her no more. She shut her mind and her mouth down, both."

I'd watched Mally there with Miss Olivia for years. They'd built as close a web between them as the finest net any fisherman owned, and I'd never heard Mally say one hard word to her tough old boss. In fact Miss Olivia had said to me, not a month ago, that Mally was the only woman left— black *or* white—who'd never showed her a trace of meanness. But Mally's tone this morning was making me wonder if she'd turned against the old woman and was now seeking favor and shelter with me? So I tested her once. "Mally, Miss Olivia's been shut down forever against me and mine. She tried to kill me when I was a girl."

Mally had clearly been informed on that old history. "She told me, Miss Anna, she drove you too hard. Your nerves couldn't take it." A long pause followed, so long I thought we'd disconnected. Then Mally said "She been good to me as anybody's mother *I* ever heard of."

That was strange to hear for more than one reason. I let it ride. "Where is Dinah right now?"

Mally said "By her grandmother's side. She asked me to call you."

"Dinah's bearing up, you think?"

"Dinah strong as you."

I actually laughed. "God help her then." But I asked if I ought to come up there today. I'd kept Palmer's Chevrolet, and by then I'd persuaded Simon to get a telephone. I could have called him, and he could have driven me up there within the hour.

But Mally said "Hold off a day or so."

I asked if they'd even thought of trying to get her to a doctor. Simon could drive up and take her to Henderson or anywhere else. But I knew the answer.

Mally said "You know she's not leaving here. Hasn't left this place since Mr. Palmer died. I buy every grocery come through this door."

"But she's not in pain?"

"Miss Anna, you know Miss Olivia won't answer that. Won't even nod her head. Pain and her are old-*time* companions."

I granted I knew that and hung up, again feeling I'd brought this further weight on my daughter, not to mention what suffering this old veteran was enduring to be silent and halted, if just in one arm. I felt very strongly the ebbing out of the last life from that generation that had made me from dust and then shaped the child into who I was now. No sense of grudge or blame but a sadness like none I'd felt since the last day Palmer Slade spoke my whole name.

I waited three days with no further word from anybody at the old Slade place. On the second day I tried to phone Dinah, but Mally answered and once more said that Dinah couldn't answer right then—she was with her grandmother. That was why, late on the third day, I got Simon to drive me up there unannounced. For all I knew my only daughter was working herself unmercifully hard and would need some relief. When we got there at six o'clock, I told Simon to wait in the yard till I at least checked on the indoor weather.

Simon knew me well enough to say "Miss Anna, don't go in yonder now and scare that old lady."

If he hadn't been my main adult friend left alive, apart from my kin, I'd have taken offense. As it was it came as a useful warning, though I did say "A circular saw going ninety miles an hour pressed right on her face couldn't scare Olivia Slade." But I tapped the door gently and just as I opened it, there was Mally, lean and troubled. Right off I said "I've been badly worried. Where is Dinah, please?"

Mally didn't look mad but she didn't speak either. She gazed up behind her and pointed upstairs.

So I climbed quietly, paused to listen at the top and—when all I heard was unbroken silence—I stepped on toward Miss Olivia's own room. Five feet from the door, I could see the old lady plainly, fully dressed in her usual chair as straight as a rail.

She seemed to be facing her bed in the corner, and her eyes were open. But if she heard me, she didn't turn or nod.

So I said Miss Olivia's name clearly—still no response. Then I said "Dinah Slade?" and silence still reigned. So I went on, stopping again just short of the door. It had been long years since I entered that room. And still Miss Olivia gave no sign of knowing I was anywhere near. What she was watching was Dinah on the bed lying flat on her back and apparently dozing in a white cotton nightgown that had once been mine.

Dinah's arms were straight at her sides, and the longer I watched the more I could see she was utterly motionless—no trace of her breathing. Then I went cold as hailstones. *What in God's name has gone on here? Is this child sick or, as it looks, even worse?* Her belly was still full. The baby was still there. I knew I must step up and try to wake her, but the fear made me detour. I went and stood in Miss Olivia's sight directly before her, and I whispered "Is Dinah sick?"

She met my eyes with no flinch or falter.

And meeting Olivia Slade's naked gaze was a challenge to every atom of your being. I managed to pass it for maybe ten seconds. Then I looked back again and pointed to Dinah. "What's happened to her?" By then the fact that Dinah hadn't roused to my normal voice had me rushing the limits of sanity. I'd actually let myself consider that this old woman with Mally's help maybe had somehow drugged my child and killed her outright.

Miss Olivia didn't make a sound, though she did take her right hand and lift her other arm and hand which looked genuinely lifeless.

My next thought was *All right. She's truly had a stroke*, and that began to clear my head. In another minute I went to Dinah, sat lightly beside her on the edge of the mattress and held her wrist.

It was cooler than the room but not cold and dead. When I squeezed it gently three times, her face turned toward me. And after a slow rush of blood to her face, her eyes half opened.

For the longest moment they didn't recognize me. But at last Dinah said "I was scared it was you."

That was sad news, to say the least. I'd long since known how badly I'd ignored her when I was in torment, but I couldn't recall a single instant when I tried to scare her or bring her down to where I was huddled. So I changed the subject and whispered in her ear "How's your grandmother doing?"

Dinah beckoned me toward her own pale lips. "I'm praying she's not too long for this world."

That came as a shock too. No one surely in all Miss Olivia's years had loved her more unquestioningly than Dinah Slade. I'd have guessed the girl would have crawled through acres of broken glass to keep the old lady breathing moments longer. What I said was "Is she in any pain?"

Dinah said "*Terrible*. Look at her eyes."

I nodded. "I just did. Has any doctor seen her?"

"You know she wouldn't hear of that."

I said "You think I caused this, don't you?"

Dinah turned to the blank wall beyond the bed and stared at that. Then still faced away she said "I do, yes."

I said "Me too. Please say you forgive me."

Dinah looked around then, no trace of a smile. And she said "Any pardon is not my business." She pointed past me to her grandmother's upright body. It seemed like both a corpse and a bonfire.

At that I put my sick head down on the edge of Dinah's pillow and lay there for what felt like a week, planning (first) whether I could beg that pardon and (then) in what words—how far back to go in my old records with this one woman. When I thought I had it right, I sat up and slowly turned my head backward.

Miss Olivia might have been hammering granite with both her eyes as she braced for a second round with my presence.

At last I said "Beg pardon, Miss Olivia. I was mean as a snake—and have been for years—where you're concerned. Please go on now and turn me loose so I can tend to my child here once you've gone to God." No sooner had I said it than I heard my mistake. Nobody living could tell Miss Olivia she was at the point of death. She meant to live as long as a younger drop of her blood was left in the world in any descendants needing her care.

And as I expected she gave me nothing whatsoever, not so much as a blink of her eyes. She had heard my awful plans three days ago. She made whatever response this was—this sight of her ruined in her special chair. But however wrecked, she was fully in charge here and had been forever. *Who in God's own name was I?*

I even stood up and straightened my clothes, brushed back my hair and went on waiting.

Nothing. Not one whiff of forgiveness. Miss Olivia knew I'd killed her or was killing her now. She was bound and determined that I pay every penny and bear every penalty for crossing her will to save her blood-kin, which I was not, not in *her* way.

My mouth locked up. I didn't know one other syllable to say, so I looked back to Dinah.

By then she'd moved to the edge of the bed and was sitting up and looking past me. She said "Grandmother, please answer my mother."

I couldn't help hearing that she still hadn't asked Miss Olivia to *forgive* me, just to answer my offer.

I turned to see if Miss Olivia could obey even someone she loved as much as Dinah.

The old lady had flabbergasted me more than once in our previous lives. She could run twisted paths like the finest fox in the woods and lose you, and now she gave me a look that might have sawed a shaft through the Great Pyramid. Then she shut her eyes and held her right hand out toward me.

Was she offering me touch? And could I take it?

Still behind me Dinah said "Mother, move."

I moved on toward my mother-in-law then and took the one good hand that my meanness had left her. Neither one of us grinned, shed a tear or offered more warmth. But then we'd known each other forever and could scent the slightest clearing of the bloody air between us. When I spoke I just said "Miss Olivia, I've got Simon Walton downstairs strong as Goliath. Let him carry you gently to the car, and let's ride to Henderson for you to see a doctor."

Miss Olivia's eyes cut back to Dinah.

And Dinah said "We're set against that. She'll live on here." Again my daughter sounded like a pioneer wife that had brought her family through the Cumberland Gap past rocks and rapids. And once I thought that much, I had to grant that some of those tough wives must have been no older than my young child here behind me now but long miles gone.

Simon drove me home so I could think. In the cool of the evening, I telephoned Leela who said there was nothing left to do but wait Miss Olivia out and then talk common sense to Dinah about her coming child. We both understood that *waiting Miss Olivia out* meant waiting for death. With that old champion's dauntless strength, she might outlast us. I knew that waiting was the only course, though, unless I was ready to go back up there with Simon tonight and seize Dinah Slade against her own will. No question of that of course. By late in the night, alone as I was, I felt like a person pinned at the elbows from behind by something at least as powerful as melancholy and stronger even than the hopeless sadness of Palmer's last affliction.

But you live on, don't you? There comes a time in most people's lives, I seem to have noticed, when—unless you accidentally pick up a knife or a loaded gun in your household chores when you're feeling off stride—you're forced to conclude that you're going to *last*. Your endurance is all but endless, and you're nothing that matters more to Fate than a middle-aged house-wife from the northeast corner of a humble state. But Miss Olivia was one of God's *exceptions* to human rules. I learned that again for the billionth time as I sat in the kitchen in early light and ate a substantial breakfast of buttered cinnamon toast with bacon and a world of black coffee.

I was on the verge of walking uptown to post a letter to August and Daisy when I heard a mild hand knock on the back door. Turned out to be a young boy, the color of Mally and with her hair and eyes. I mentioned the resemblance and the boy nodded "Miss Mally's my auntie" (black people here still pronounce *aunt* as *ont* in the British style). Then he said "She made me drive down here to tell you something."

I said "Son, you're too young to drive." He was maybe twelve.

"Yes ma'm, but Miss Mally say the phone is broke and to tell you, gentle, to come up yonder."

Of course my mind raced at once to Dinah—miscarried, hurt, dead, what? I asked him "Is Dinah Slade all right?"

He nodded hard. "Doing fine, last I saw her. She the stout one, ain't she?"

I had to smile. "She's expecting, yes. But what's the trouble?"

"Miss Mally told me not to tell you."

I hit him a low blow, figuratively speaking. My purse was in my hand; I offered the child a crisp dollar bill which was real money then.

He shamed me. "No ma'm. But the trouble's Miss Olivia."

I said "Is she worse off?"

He nodded. "Cold dead." Then a big grin took his helpless face. He turned full around and pointed northeast—the Slade place precisely. Then he said to the air "I touched her too. Lord, cold as *scissors!*"

That she was. They had found her at dawn when Mally went in to help her rise and dress for the day. They said she'd seemed unfazed by my visit, had eaten a little soup in the evening and had lain awake while Dinah read selections from Miss Olivia's chosen book of the Bible—Ecclesiastes, the one about fools, her favorite subject. Dinah had kissed her good night then, left a low light on and gone to her own room. Dinah had fallen asleep at once, worn out by the day. So neither she nor Mally had heard the least sound of trouble in the night.

When Mally saw Miss Olivia next, she was neatly composed flat of her back and facing the ceiling with both eyes open, entirely natural. Mally even spoke to her while she raised the window shades. And she later told Dinah, "I knew she was lying there waiting for you like she always did. I was trying to stall her and give you a few more minutes to sleep, but then I felt of her hand and knew. She'd met her match finally."

Both Mally and Dinah were pitiful. Even some two hours later—when I'd packed an overnight bag, finally found Simon and got up there—they sat at the kitchen table like actual souls of the lost. I'd have thought that Mally could manage a spewing volcano or a big earthquake (and she could have, every instance but this as time would show). But that one morning Mally looked like the child she must have been before that strong old woman took her in and raised her. Aside from smoothing the bedcovers slightly, they'd done nothing else with Miss Olivia.

So I had to step in, call the undertaker that had buried Palmer and make those arrangements. None of her stepchildren were alive, and their scattered widows and children had paid her so little mind in recent years that I felt no pressure to track them down at once. The people Miss Olivia had truly mattered to—Negroes from up and down the river and the bad back roads and her old tenants' widows—all found out by their own country grapevine and wandered in through the next two days with cooked food and other offerings.

One old woman I'd never seen before brought a beautiful stark-white linen pillowcase she'd embroidered through the years for her own coffin. She wanted it to go with "Miss Livvie" now, and I didn't refuse it. I well understand that many people today, black and white, may find that hard to believe or stomach. To them I can only say that it's been my observation through life that people will choose out *someone* from the world to love and honor, or maybe just honor, no matter what that person's standards may have been.

Not many souls can live without that much, however odd their choice looks to others. I actually saw and heard that old woman, black as pitch with hands so wrenched they looked like crab claws, when she told me "to be real sure" it went on to Glory with her "mistus." I understood that her word meant *mistress*. Later I even put the slip on Miss Olivia's favorite pillow, and I cupped her mighty skull in my own hands and lowered its heavy weight onto the linen. There were still only scattered white strands in all that rich dark hair that had never thinned.

Near sundown the next day, Mally and Dinah, August and Daisy with their two boys, Simon and Harley and I, Mally's nephew Princeton and a small clutch of neighbors buried her. Miss Olivia had paid no serious attention to church in the years I'd known her, less so even than me; so I asked our minister to say the least he possibly could. After the meeting those children and I had with him back in June, I didn't want to give him too much rope and have him rattling on about somebody he'd never known and what a stalwart Christian she'd been. Any unfinished business between Olivia Slade and her Maker was no doubt underway at that moment, which very likely explained the splendor of the sky; and I've never felt comfortable lecturing God on his available choices.

I listened to the sweaty young man make his way through Paul's great promises in the teeth of death. Then I signed off and stood there counting the times I'd been here beside the earlier dead. Young Larkin was first, then Major, then mine and Palmer's stillborn child, then Palmer himself. There was maybe room for two more bodies if they hunched up close and gained no weight between now and the end.

Looking around me I realized that almost surely the next would be me, and then I'd be the last. Whatever happened with Dinah and Harley, Dinah would lie wherever her husband finally led her. Augustus would have no wish to lie here. For all his sweetness he was very *progressive* and had his eyes on a life in Charlotte or—pray God—Atlanta if he could just climb out of the job he was stuck in in Rockingham.

For the first time since my own worst torment, I let myself think all the way down to the time of my death. In a few more weeks, I'd be fifty-three. According to the mirror, I was holding my own. I could finish my trek anywhere from tonight till fourteen years from now. I was gauging my possibilities from Muddie's life span; she died at sixty-seven. I hadn't the slightest intention of living as close to a century as I have. In fact returning to the world there before me, I saw my children (strong as they were, even Dinah in her trouble) and knew that if I vanished this instant they'd pause a few days and then do what the world in general does—head out once more on their own hike.

Flawed as I'd been and absent and dark in my bad years, I'd kept my

marriage vows to Palmer and his dust. I'd reared my children almost as well
as I knew how. I'd fed a very few of the hungry, as many as knocked on my
door. I'd tried to lighten the load of a very few black people that came my
way. With no delusions that such a slim total entitled me to Heaven, still
when the gravediggers stepped up to lower Miss Olivia, I actually felt a
slow instant of pride in who I'd been till that complicated moment—an
evening as fine as I've ever seen with early stars big as furnace mouths all
burning clean.

I was all but right. Looking back I see how you could claim that my life
truly stopped at that funeral. By far the majority of white women in my
time and place were forcibly retired, flat out of a job when their husbands
had died and their children were grown. Their lasting for another four or
five decades sometimes served as a well-earned rest. More often it was slow
time, day after long day of nothing to do that anybody needed, no other
mouth to feed, no spirits to raise and urge on forward—a billion hours of
television, telephone chatter and doctor's visits down toward the end. Just
last night I watched a program about baboons. A male or female baboon
that lasts beyond the mating age is welcome to hang on with the family,
grooming others for fleas and passing on pieces of useful knowledge. Few
human families allow for that now.

For me, to be sure—after Miss Olivia went back to the Earth—there was
still young Dinah and her growing baby. I'd spent long months agonizing
over that with no good plan accomplished. Yet the last thing I'd told
myself, before we watched the dirt hit Miss Olivia, was *I'll give her her last
wish. I'll see it through to safety. Her* was Miss Olivia and *it* was the unborn
child in our midst. And by that I meant I would never mention adoption
again nor urge Dinah Slade to do anything but cherish her body and all its
purposes and bring a healthy child to the world for her and me to raise.

We did exactly that. I stayed in the country a few days more with Dinah
and Mally. And though the three of us never sat down and spelled it out,
we gradually understood among us that Dinah and Mally would stay in the
Slade house till near Dinah's due date. Then the two of them would move
in with me in time to get to Henderson for the labor. Then we'd look at
the future one week at a time.

When I didn't bring up adoption again—and Lord knows they never mentioned it to me—Mally came up to my bedroom the last night I spent in the old Slade house (Dinah had moved into her grandmother's room). She was in a flannel nightgown and a wool bathrobe as if this were snow-time. Even so she still looked frailer than usual and trembling—very slightly trembling, her chin and hands.

I told her Miss Olivia had left her a hundred dollars in the will—a nice sum then, especially from a woman who had very little cash at her disposal.

Mally already knew that. She said "I'm not here to beg for money. Money don't mean *nothing* to me, never has. I just want you to know that I mean to stay right next to Dinah and her baby as long as she'll have me—long as you'll let me stay."

That surprised me greatly. I don't know why. Maybe because, even that long ago, it seemed old-timey past believing. When I faced Mally's eyes again, kind as a doe's, I had the only answer I could think of. As it reeled out of me naturally, it felt like something I was hearing from an angel, not saying myself. The news was that good—and that good for me. I said "Come when you will, Mally. Stay long as you can. You can see old me on into the grave if you think you could stand to watch for that long."

Mally was solemn but she thanked me and turned to go. At the door, though, she looked back and said "That's an offer that could *last*, I know. You a strong woman still. Just let me take it one step at a time. I'm safer that way."

Before I could nod Mally was halfway down the stairs. All my grown life, as I've mentioned before, it had been against my conscience to work black women on a regular basis in my house. I don't repeat that here to win special credit in this modern world. In those active years I never mentioned my conscience to anyone, not even when they called me an utter fool for hauling water and cooking year-round with no other help when Negro women were thick on the ground and begging to work. But before Mally's steps had faded off, I felt that soon I'd be taking strange steps into something new. Thinking that only, I slid off into peaceful sleep—a far more peaceful sleep that night than I'd ever known in this *thrumming* house. Even with Miss Olivia gone, it was live still (in every wall and floorboard) waiting for its next drink of blood.

Our plan worked out with very few hitches. Either Harley or Simon and I would drive up and bring Dinah down for doctor's appointments. I'd stay up there most every weekend, and Mally and I slowly worked our way through the mountains of Miss Olivia's remains—hers and every one of the Slades for five generations at least. We even found the original land grant by which Lord Granville, of the Lords Proprietors sitting in London in 1668, had bestowed a wide parcel of riverside woods on Livingston Slade, the major's great-great-grandfather. It sported Granville's own signature, and I had it framed for August's Christmas.

There were whole barrel-top trunks stuffed with old letters, schoolbooks made by the pupils themselves (all young Slade boys) in elegant eighteenth-century script bound in tan homespun cloth, plus the major's stacks of cavalry papers—his commission, various citations, his written parole at the end of the War which let him bring his riding horse home in April '65 to start the spring plowing, however late. I grieve still to admit that, with Dinah and Mally saying they had no use for any of it, I burned many more of those papers than I saved. I'd asked Augustus by mail. He only wanted the major's war papers.

Even now I can think of snatches of memorable words I saw in the letters as I burned them. Major's mother had written to him when she heard of the wound that cost him his leg. At the end she said "Son, you must never fear that you have lost *anything* in my eyes. Now you stand a commanding head taller." Or something very much to that effect. And when Major had gone to Spottsylvania in March of 1896 to sit by the deathbed of a cavalry friend, he wrote a brief note to Miss Olivia who'd only married him two years before—"Dearest Liv, This awful sadness of Tom's—he's out of his mind and scarcely knows me—doesn't weigh an ounce compared to what I know I'll receive in reward from you as soon as I bury what's left of his bones."

Lacking as I did any personal contact with a serious library or college, I couldn't imagine how else to save such traces. So all those pounds of witness to vanished lives—urgent to the writers—went up the chimney and are no doubt drifting still toward the stars as particles of smoke which may be as good a fate as any. Almost certainly no later human being would have learned anything by reading the passions and secrets and boredoms of the nameless dead from a corner of the world that since the Civil War has barely ruffled the local newspaper much less the big world. Maybe the greatest loss of all, though, was the first loss I noticed.

                    *   *   *

The night of Miss Olivia's funeral when I couldn't sleep, I went out to the Office where Palmer and I had started our marriage. I spent hours threshing old books and drawers, hunting the volumes of Miss Olivia's diary. They were gone from the shelf where they'd always been. When I asked Mally at breakfast, she had no memory of ever seeing them or knowing their whereabouts. I seemed to recall that Miss Olivia had still written in the latest volume as recently as the early 1940s when Dinah and I paid her that sad visit in the hope of cheering me and heading off my torment. She may have burned them for her own secret reasons. They've never turned up in any case.

What a sizable pity to have no remnant of what that ceaseless mind thought of itself and the life it was caught in. Painful as some parts no doubt were, surely she couldn't have left a better legacy to Dinah and the world. Recalling it now I suspect that such a big loss was part of the reason I got the idea of writing down *my* story in time—no substitute for Miss Olivia's, I'm sure, but still an honest voice left over from a whole other world where women especially (but some men as well) labored through every day of their lives with far more careful intelligence and judgment than the beasts of burden they're widely considered now to have been.

We also burned a ton of ruined clothes that moths had long since turned into lace. For myself I kept Major's gold braid epaulets that were tarnished half black and the shawl Miss Olivia had worn to my wedding. The light paisley wool had somehow escaped destruction. When it came to clearing out the high oak bureau in Palmer and Larkin's old bedroom, I nearly flinched. They were still too much alive as boys with blood and warm breath. They still felt that young and unfinished in my mind. To save my feelings I asked Mally please to take that job. But she said "those boys' clothes" was my rightful chore, and I shouldn't shirk it. So I gritted my teeth, and it took a whole morning. Turned out Miss Olivia had never discarded a thread that touched either one of her sons.

Packed as dense as cotton in a bale, there were everything from christening dresses to school graduation suits that seemed to have shrunk to boy-doll clothes—little sawed-off-looking drainpipe legs on the skimpy trousers, little coats and vests that could barely have shielded a starving widow from the cold, much less a man's chest. In general I couldn't tell what was Palmer's and what had been Larkin's. But there was one blood-red baseball cap still pretty much intact. I recall Palmer saying how Larkin had been the finest unsung pitcher in American history, so I still have the cap.

Maybe each of them wore it in separate games. Palmer was after all the elder by one year. Inside the sweat band some hand has written *Sladie* in black ink—a nickname I never heard for either of them, though it sounds more appropriate for Lark than his brother. Every year or so still, I take that out and think about it when I weed my own closet. I'll leave it for somebody else to burn when I've absconded with the last human mind that knows the cap's meaning.

With all our aching diligence, we had that relic of a house stripped to its bones by the first real cold spell in mid November. Everything left was something useful to Dinah and the oncoming child or to Mally. When the clean-out was finished, I spent more of my time back at home. That was partly natural and partly my private plan to get my mind and soul as calm as possible before standing by while my young daughter bore a child outside the safety of marriage. All through those mostly solitary days, I prayed a lot more than I'd ever done in my past concerns.

It was not on-your-knees, well-laid-out pleading. That kind of show-off had never felt right to me even when supposedly educated preachers stood up every Sunday of their lives and issued want-lists to God. No, my private way was something on the order of semi-constant *radio* contact. I'd always enjoyed those gospel songs that sprang up all over the South in the early days of the telephone—

> Got a little telephone in my bosom;
> I can get Jesus on the line. . . .

and the famous "Royal Telephone" hymn—

> Central's never busy, always on the line,
> You can talk to Heaven almost any time.

Tacky as those were they bore more relation to my own practice than most other descriptions of prayer. I'd be sweeping down spider webs on the porch and hear my mind, of its own will with no prod from me, say *Keep Dinah's spirits up today* or *Whatever you do keep Mally safe and healthy—we'll sink without her.* Most of my little dispatches in those days anyhow were about people near me. But several dozen times a day and more so at night, I'd be washing a fork or plumping a pillow and hear my mind beam out a brief hope like *Let me fight down anger and my big fear of humiliation.*

Did I think the God who made this maybe infinite universe sat somewhere and waited to decode such notes? And if so did my particular voice have any weight? Well all I can say now is—given what I hear and read every day about the wonders of computers—it strikes my feeble mind that, if a man-made computer can keep many billions of facts in its heart and act upon them instantly, then couldn't there be a mind somewhere that's at least as responsible and ready to listen as any old idea of God?

And if it listens, then surely it wouldn't resist leaning in now and then and tilting a crossroads or weighting some scales. If there's no such mind anywhere, then why has the human race through history so far as I know insisted on bowing to someone on the heights? Speaking for myself again I've never enjoyed regular bowing. I'm aware of course that the plea for *help* which so many of us broadcast turns out way more often than not to be answered with a silent *Forget it* if not a flat No.

I'm still glad to say that, heard or not, my requests were all but perfectly answered. When Dinah and Mally moved in with me in late January, none of us tried to keep their presence a secret. We didn't conceal Dinah's physical condition, but of course we didn't march her down Main Street at high noon either. Harley was in and out of the house at frequent intervals, the minister paid us more than one call, and several people at the post office felt sure enough of our friendship to ask if Dinah's health had improved and would she be back in school this spring?

I thanked them politely and said she was better but would need further time to get back to normal, none of which was any kind of lie.

I'd been convinced from nearly the start that everybody in a ten-mile radius was bound to know the true story. It had to be known to the whole school full of teachers and students old enough to have heard what a baby was. As for other adults I could sit down with our thin telephone book and literally pick out the names that would be sympathetic and those that would laugh or shake their blue-rinsed hair. Of course it pained me to know that much.

But since I'd never really had a woman friend apart from my sister and a few black women whose judgment didn't count with anyone but me, all I truly worried about was the child itself. Dinah had borne enough already to bear this next round. I kept reminding myself that young children, prior to adolescence anyhow, are more elastic to knocks and cruel words than modern parents want to believe. But that didn't stop me aching fairly steadily at the thought of the meanness my next grandchild might have to weather.

The child was a girl. She arrived on schedule, was strong and well; and her mother came through with less in the way of drawn-out pain than I'd have guessed for a first delivery by so young a parent. I'd secretly hoped for a boy, with the notion that a boy might take the meanness better. Girls in those days hadn't yet started taking karate classes. Also I had serious doubts as to whether a bastard girl would ever get noticed by a decent husband. But then the Second War had done so much for sex in this country—spreading it around, making it public and humorous. Maybe by the time this girl was grown, the rules and feelings about illegitimacy would have long been eased.

So when the nurse came out and told me and Mally and Simon that it was a girl and weighed seven pounds, I nearly broke down in genuine relief. Somehow I knew that, though I solemnly vowed on the spot to let her mother raise her so far as a teenager could, this child would be my last long happiness. I didn't shed tears but Mally did (she'd borne the greatest burden of anyone but Dinah herself), and Simon hauled out the cigar I'd bought him. It cost me half a dollar and smelled like tar rags burning in the night.

Harley had just left home for school when the labor started. His mother and I had spoken on the phone and decided not to call him out at that moment but to let him join us at the end of classes. When he got to the hospital at just past four, the nurses were almost ready to roll Dinah back toward her own room. So all of us went in together. And when Dinah's bed came through the door, she looked older still but no worse for the whole slow day. She kissed Harley first, then me, then Mally. Then they both shook hands with Simon.

After that Harley stood at the head of the bed, and together he and Dinah announced their private decision. The girl was named *Olivia Roxanna*. It turned out Harley had also insisted that he be named on the birth certificate as the child's father, so Beecham was the baby's family name from her first moment.

But since I'd mostly been called *Anna*, everybody tried to call the girl *Roxanna* from the start. That made me happier than I'd have guessed. And when I'd held her and said her whole name, I soon began to feel that something was getting completed somehow here in my arms. I'd always wanted the use of my whole lovely first name, and I'd been denied it as I said before by almost everybody but Ferny. So much else that still felt incomplete in my life would work out in this girl, I suspected. I knew that grandmothers tended toward such unrealistic hopes. But as time demonstrated I was one *accurate* grandmother in that respect.

She was nobody's beauty—Olivia Roxanna—but she had a healthy goat's appetite, and she grew like a weed in the house that Palmer and I had bought with Betsy's money nearly twenty-eight years before. We fixed up the back bedroom off the kitchen for Mally who'd silently chosen to live with us now and to take a modest salary. So as much as we tried to let Dinah make her own decisions, the baby had three mothers from the start. And together—with almost no pouting matches—we brought her through the early months of colic, ear infections and a stubborn case of whooping cough with about as much luck as you get with babies.

It was while she was coughing so badly that for some odd reason all of us, me included, began to shorten her name to Rox. I guess it came from the hopeless tenderness we felt for a little thing tortured by a dangerous illness that we couldn't spare her. We didn't call her *Anna* since that was me; but we needed something short to get her frail attention when her eyes drifted off or froze, terrified, in the midst of her spasms. So *Rox* is hardly a charming sound, but *Rox* it's been pretty much ever since—*Rox* and *Livvie Rox* to friends her own age.

In September Dinah went back to school. I've said she was in the same grade as Harley which was some reassurance for anxious me. And then I knew how much time she'd spent reading books in the months she was gone. The only thing of value that Dinah had really missed was first-year Latin. Otherwise her good mind took the leap like a squirrel to its perch. And with Harley beside her in all their classes but football practice, she got less mean talk than I expected.

Or so Dinah claimed and Harley backed her up. The two of them went on dating like children on Saturday nights, more *careful* children. And in general the school months went so well that late in the summer of '55 when the baby was eighteen months old, I offered them a weekend trip to Wilmington and tagged along as a pointless chaperone. All of us got brown as biscuits and came home rested and ready for more.

The *more* was the children's last two years of high school. They went along with the usual tizzies and one completely uncalled-for sermon from a vicious old-maid algebra teacher but no other big troubles. Oh also in their senior year, their calculus teacher—a forty-year-old bachelor with rat's hair and one wall-eye—made some remark in class about *scarlet women*, and the whole room snickered till Harley just stood up silent in the midst of the room and waited for silence. Given Harley's muscles, silence *descended*.

Of course I wanted to go up and snatch the fool teacher bald, but Dinah just laughed and sang it like a song—"Dear Ma, he's nothing but a miniature pebble in the rocky road of life." And in no time she and Harley had their diplomas, age seventeen and eighteen. To that point believe it or not, none of us had ever sat down again and talked out their future. Everybody had *thought* about it endlessly but never called a meeting.

Turned out we didn't need to. The children had their plan well set. They graduated on a Friday night. I went to commencement while Mally stayed home with the baby. And though I noticed when four or five old hawk-eyed women tried to let me see they were snubbing me—the youngest one all but dislocated her neck to show me how fast she could turn away from me—I just took a prominent aisle seat and clapped hard every chance I got. Sang all the hymns too, every one of them "Christian." That was well before the multiethnic days such as now when Christians scarcely get mentioned in public.

The next noon—Saturday—Dinah and Harley walked into the kitchen and asked if I was feeling all right.

When I told them Yes, they said in that case they were bound out right then for South Carolina. They'd be back Monday morning. In those days there was a thriving marriage mill in Dillon, S.C. You didn't have to wait for a blood test or license, just turn up male and female together with the money to pay for some old bird to read the civil vows in your presence while his wife stood as witness. I was hoping they'd eventually take church vows for the seriousness of the undertaking.

But as later months passed they chose not to with no ill effects that I've ever noticed, so who was I to insist? In short they've been married for nearly four decades—far longer than Palmer and I got—and they've never lived more than eighteen miles from me. They've likewise never let me feel overlooked or of no use to anybody else alive, which (believe me) is more than a great lot of parents can expect.

Harley hasn't burned up anybody's stock market making big money. With no inclination for a college education, he's had a succession of small-town jobs down through the years. In recent years he's wound up running his own land-scaping business with a handsome new store that sells not only trees and shrubs but nursery inventions my mother never dreamed of like knee pads for kneeling gardeners. Last Christmas was Harley's first since the new store opened, and he looked forward to a bumper business. He took Simon with him up to Pennsylvania back in late August to place advance orders for his holiday greens, wreaths and Santas. When they got back Harley told me he was going "strictly plastic" for that first year. He said "I can't fail with plastic, can I, Miss Anna?"

I winced within but said No to please him. He was so proud of being on the verge of a boom. And sure enough there was not a real leaf or actual berry anywhere near his shop from Thanksgiving well on past the New Year. To help him out I even bought an artificial tree myself that I've been ashamed of ever since despite its safety and the cedar-smelling spray Harley threw in to make it more natural. In any case Harley sold every plastic Santa and Rudolph as fast as they arrived. Still he made a small killing for himself and Dinah which always relieves me.

Dinah works with him at heavy rush seasons. But otherwise she's been what's now called a full-time homemaker as if that were any less an achievement than chairing the board of Ford Motor Company. Of course at Dinah's age, her mothering duties are long since over.

I asked her once maybe two years ago if Harley paid her a salary at Christmas when she worked in that shop twenty hours a day.

She waited, frowned awhile and then said "Mother, Harley's paid me a good dog's loyalty for you-know-how-long. I couldn't ask him for another plugged nickel."

I felt rightly chastened and have never mentioned the matter again. My concern just came from the fact that I have so little in the way of funds or property to leave the children, and what little there is is complicated in a way I'll speak of later. That fact sometimes has me scared in the night that they'll starve without me when I've passed on. Not likely of course but very few mothers of my generation—who've gone through the various wars, depressions and Cuban missile crises of our lifetime—can ever really believe that their children are fit to go outdoors on their own alone.

Dinah raised young Rox as well as anybody that young could have. Once she and Harley were married, they lived with me for the first two years, Mally helping right along. When they moved on into their new place, I was more than ready to spread myself again into too many rooms.

And as much as she loved Rox, Mally was ready to settle back into a calmer situation with no child pulling on her by the minute. She and I had done all the nursing while Dinah finished school. Mally was a great deal younger than I but was still past thirty with no visible boyfriend and clearly no children of her own. I even risked asking her one time, when she and I had been living alone together for over a year, if she didn't have any hopes of her own—her own house, a family.

She said "Miss Anna, when you want me to leave just say the word *leave*. I'll be gone in ten minutes. But don't try to drive me into no man's hands. That ain't going to happen to Mally Shearin, not for you nor nobody."

Needless to say I've never mentioned the subject again. And Mally is fifteen yards down the hall in her own bedroom as I write this line. In many ways that I'm glad and thankful to acknowledge her presence near me is the last substantial blessing of my life. And yet with all the turmoil of the past decades in matters of race, and with victories for tolerance that I couldn't have imagined, Mally's in her own space *alone* as I am in mine. That's not merely the normal result of a younger woman's putting an elder to bed and then relaxing in her own quiet space. It's more or less the iron unchangeable pattern of our lives, set in a time and place where the tint of your skin may still be the main thing about you and may never relent, not even in death (you'll be forced to spend eternity in separate graves).

At ninety-four years old with the average amounts of rheumatism and brittle bones (I broke a leg last year), I don't move through the house as freely as I did. So I often eat from a tray in my bedroom. But on those days when I go to the dining room or even the kitchen to eat at the table, Mally will very seldom sit with me even when I ask her. Of course she's seventy herself by now and has her own problems with "the high blood" and dizziness.

But once I sit and unfold my napkin, Mally will mostly discover some brand-new chore she's got to perform that instant or die. And though we're both slaves to three soap operas and the morning, noon and evening news on color TV, we tend to watch our separate sets at opposite ends of a house that's emptier now than the dried-out Ark once the Noahs left it.

I sometimes tell myself—I've even told Mally—that her and my habits were not formed by brown and black skin as much as by our age and long acquaintance. We're like two old mules that have plowed in the same yoke for near forty years and are ready to put some distance between them, provided we hear each other sneeze every hour or just breathe. A cross word between us is heard no more than once or twice a week—always about some trifling business like Mally not raising my window shades when she comes in at dawn (I love early sunlight) or me not leaving my knife and fork in the right position when I've finished my dinner. Mally's a member of the Etiquette Police, trained by the finest Chief of them all, Olivia Slade.

It was just recently, eight months ago, that Mally brought up a matter that I'd buried deeply long years past and had no notion that she'd ever heard of. My burying it so long may seen incredible to anybody not bred up in my world. But take it from me straight—Roxanna had that question *underground* well past her own reach. Then for a change one evening I'd begged her to sit with me in the shank of the evening and hear those famous three tenors sing on television.

Mally is devoted to the stout one whom she calls *Papparachi*. And I'm partial to the taller of the two Spaniards, the one whose name means *Placid Sunday* according to Dinah, always so soothing. Mally accepted and we scarcely spoke through the whole two hours except to agree that we wished they'd stop imitating the Three Stooges in the lighter moments and just trust their God-given voices. Once they were done, though—and I thought I'd be asleep in ten minutes—Mally looked over toward me and said "Miss Anna, you feeling all right?"

I told her I was *tol'able*, my father's old word.

She said "Well this won't take but a minute."

The face that she had managed to keep from the rough hands of time, a generally pleasant face that had plainly once been beautiful, was frowning so hard that I felt a quick chill. Mally was on the verge of saying she had to leave me, move out on her own. And that would send me to the nursing home fast. But a sly smile took her, and then she said "Do you know who my father was?"

I was so overjoyed that she hadn't mentioned leaving, I couldn't hear the hardness of her question. I answered truthfully at once and told her No, I didn't.

For the only time in all our years of acquaintance, she waited and then said "That's the God's truth? No lie?"

I said "God's truth" and finally heard what a grave glimpse of the past might be concealed in her brief curiosity. So I got the best grip I could on my mind, and I said to Mally "Has somebody told you something mean?"

"No ma'm, not lately."

And then I did a thing odd as June blizzards. I said "Mally, call me *Roxanna* please—us two old women."

She frowned more deeply, shook her head hard but grinned. "Let me think that over. I'll get back to you on that any day"—an expression she'd recently got from TV. She revises her sayings every month or so as she hears them on our programs. I may well do the same, though I notice Mally more.

I said "Are you asking if you're kin to Palmer Slade?"

She said "Yes," leaving out *ma'm* for the first time ever.

I'd known for years now, not only that Coy had been Mally's grandmother but also that her own mother was Roebuck Pittman, who was still alive though out of her mind far worse than before. How Mally came to have the last name *Shearin* I still don't know and declined to ask. Maybe she was married briefly. I hadn't failed to learn either that Mally was born in 1925, not long after Palmer had known Roebuck in very close quarters. I'd also known for a great many years that, if Mally was right about her birthdate, then she was conceived well over nine months after Palmer had promised to do his best to focus on me. This moment, though, I gave Mally no more than the utter bare-bone truth as far as I knew it. I said "I wondered about that the day I met you, but I never asked Palmer."

Mally nodded calmly. "Miss Olivia says the answer is Yes."

"*Says?*" I asked her. "You in touch with her still?"

"No, I'm talking about the month she died. Seemed like Miss Olivia felt her time creeping up on her. She was doing a lot of things, careful and right, for the very last time. So one night when I was washing her feet—remember how I had to soak her feet to cut her old toenails, tough as whitleather? Anyhow I'd finished and was standing up when Miss Olivia said 'You know you're my granddaughter, don't you?' " Dinah was fast asleep a few yards away.

The news was not exactly a shock, but the echo of that old strong woman's voice was chilling. "Was that news to you?"

Mally weighed my question. "I'd heard it two or three times from Mama Coy long before I was grown, but I never asked questions. Roebuck was already more than half crazy; and so far as I knew, I'd never lived with her." Mally stopped there but didn't stop watching me.

For a change I was left with nothing to say. But this came to me next. "You believe Miss Olivia then?"

"I think I do. Now."

"Why now especially?"

You could tell by the calm in Mally's eyes that she'd rehearsed all this a dozen times. "Because of what the old lady said next. She touched the crown of my nappy head and told me 'You know I ain't got a cent to leave you?' I told her I knew that. Far as cash was concerned, Miss Olivia was badly strapped by then. But you know that. I didn't want none of the land or timber, sure didn't want that old piece of a house."

Coming in a rush, that was way too hard for me to think my way through, morning or night, and it was well past my bedtime now. Miss Olivia had indeed died strapped, though August and Dinah would eventually have a little cash from her timber. But the first thing to say to Mally was "You're bound to feel cheated—a grudge anyhow."

Mally did something I'd never seen her do. She put her long hands over her face, bent down to her own lap and laid her head on her knees for the better part of a minute. When she looked up she made Miss Olivia's clearing-cobwebs gesture across her eyes, and it left her looking beautiful in a way I'd never seen before. She was not the least like Miss Olivia. There was none of that obstinate heat and hardness but instead a far-off kind of strangeness in Mally's eyes and in the gentler set of her jaw—a strangeness that seemed on the verge of becoming at least as familiar as the taste of my own mouth. Then Mally said "I gave my grudge up when Dinah's baby come here safe."

"How was that?" I said.

"I'd made God a deal. See, I'd been dreaming about Dinah dying and strangling that child before it could breathe. I told God if he would spare both of them, I'd lay my bitter heart to rest."

"And you did," I said. It was no kind of question. Though I silently knew how much of a miracle that would have taken—to sweep Mally's feelings clear of regret if nothing worse—I had good reason to know such things happened every so often. Hadn't God or some indwelling angel swept Palmer's record with me as clean as a creature could manage? When I'd thought that much, I sat another moment. What happened next was as slow as my own efforts to walk but also as real.

I watched Mally Shearin's broad calm face go very slightly hazy before me and then Palmer's strong face move up behind it as if through water, not breaking the surface but barely showing its print from beneath. No question at all it was him near his best. He was there more plainly than in any of the others—August or Dinah or now young Rox. Palmer lived on in this aging child who'd saved my life so many times since he left the world. I thought it would but the sight didn't pain me. Then less slowly Mally's face firmed back to its usual state. The last thing I'd said had confirmed her refusal of hatred.

Mally surely didn't owe me thanks, and I didn't expect it, but she nodded at least and then smiled again—this time an oddly complicated smile that dawned more slowly. She said "If what Miss Olivia claimed is so, you know what else that makes me, don't you?"

I honestly didn't at that full moment. "No, what?"

"Your stepdaughter."

It hit me so hard I couldn't speak, not pain but as big a surprise as I've ever felt.

And in my long silence, Mally just said a single word "Maybe. *Maybe's* all I'm saying."

I hadn't had to think this fast in years, a great flood of thoughts, by no means all of them troublesome or sad. One of the first things came from my watching TV so much. I understood that tests could be done now on Dinah and Mally that would show if they were sisters—half-sisters anyhow depending on their blood. If it turned out Yes, we could wind up in court with Mally claiming her rightful share of Palmer Slade's leavings down to the very bed I slept in. Of course she'd got her small salary from me plus room and board for forty-one years.

Was Mally bringing this up now for fear I'd make my will and shut her out? Till now she'd never mentioned so much as a penny more than I paid her with a bonus twice annually, Christmas and the Fourth of July. Had she held off till now to slam me broadside? After what seemed like six weeks of silence, I finally knew I had to meet her straight. I said "Are you telling me you feel like this is part yours now?" I gestured to the whole house around us.

Mally said "*Been* feeling like that ever since I came here."

"You want me to leave it to you in my will?"

That shocked her near as hard as she'd shocked me. Then she laughed outright. "Lord God, the Klu Kluk would burn me down the same *night!*" Local black people had called the Klan the *Klu Kluk* even when it had real life. I'd heard nothing about it here for twenty-odd years. There was plenty of loose hate to go around, though.

I had to smile with her. "Yes," I said, "they'd likely turn bitter."

She said "Doctors now got that test—that blood test. You seen it, I know, on the TV."

I acknowledged I knew. "You want to ask Dinah to take it with you—the test, so we'll know?"

At last Mally said "Too late, don't you think?"

"Too late for what?"

"You bound to know it would stop Harley's heart if his wife come up with a nut-brown sister. August's wife would take to her bed, even far off as Rockingham; and those Shiflets of hers way up in Virginia would be jumping off bridges. Dinah might even disrespect her dead father. And what'll Rox think, even old as she is, if old brown Mally turns into her auntie?"

"They've all had to deal with rough turns in the road. They'd likely survive."

Mally said "You think that's me—a rough turn?"

"Maybe more like a cliff," I said. "Nothing wrong with a cliff—stand high up and see the whole world." By now my thin blood had warmed and waked me.

But Mally stood. "Let me put you to bed before you keel over."

I'd had to pay such strict attention to my own little bits and pieces of business since Palmer died that my mind didn't want to quit tonight with a big outstanding question on my plate. And I told her as much. "Mally, you know I won't sleep ten seconds if you'll be truly left out when I die."

"Say *pass*, Roxanna. Don't never say *die*." Old Southerners, all colors, avoid the word *die* in all its forms.

By then I could see that Mally was the tired one. Her whole face was almost ashy with exhaustion. She'd come a long way in the last half hour.

So I said "*Pass, pass*" just to ease her mind. And then I said "Let's settle this tomorrow."

"If we both *alive* tomorrow," Mally said. But she laughed again. Whatever else has been battered in her life, Mally's laugh has stayed as sweet as any creek in the heart of the woods back in our girlhoods when water was clean. Even with her under my own roof, I've often woke up in the midst of the night and wished I had a whole tape of her laugh to haul me up out of fearful dreams.

I say *my* roof. That night after Mally had helped me put my aching bones to bed, I thought till I saw my own way clear to who would own this roof when I left it. I thought I could make *my* way the right way for all involved. I still think I have. Mally and I had watched the three tenors on a Saturday night. On Monday morning I shut my door and called the lawyer that Palmer had trusted in Henderson. I'd dealt with him several times since Palmer died.

He was Charles Rose, well on in his eighties and dressed accordingly but practicing hard and, according to all reports in the paper, still saving unlucky boys at the final moment from Death Row in Raleigh and redeeming women from the Hell of vicious mates, in addition to winning every land fight any of his clients ever entered. On the phone I told Mr. Rose a little of what I had in mind. Right off he said he'd drive out to see me the next afternoon. Good as his word he was there on the minute.

Mally had never seen him before, but on my instructions she brought him into the parlor and left us there. I asked Mr. Rose to shut the hall door (I didn't recall it ever being shut). And then I told him the true details so far as I knew them. I went so far as to say I was sure Mally had to be Palmer's offspring and that I wanted a hidebound will that no one could break with an iron crowbar. Till then I'd just had a short handwritten will leaving everything equally to August and Dinah. The new will, though, would leave this house to Mally Shearin plus a third of the proceeds of selling those gold coins that Palmer left and I'd never had to touch.

I told Mr. Rose I meant to explain it to my children before I signed. They would get their favorite pieces from my own belongings—furniture, souvenirs, a few small pieces of family jewelry. Through the years the children and I had sold off the old Slade place to pay local bills. But I still owned a fair amount of good timber land. How did a lawyer think I should handle that?

Mr. Rose said "Dear lady, you sure about this? Can Mally Shearin, if that's a legal name, prove her paternity?"

"It's my word," I said.

"Ah, dear madam, time has grown teeth since you and I were young. Your children could at least *try* to shred any will that leaves their father's property to an outright stranger, not to mention a Negro, mulatto or not."

It had been many years since I'd actually heard anyone say the word *Negro*. He pronounced it the way Martin Luther King and all the rest of us used to—*Nigra* (today that pronunciation is considered an insult). But I told Mr. Rose that my children were, none of them, broke. "They'll agree to my wishes when they know the reason."

Mr. Rose then set in explaining various ways to handle the rights to the timber land. It confused me of course till he said he could simply set up a trust that would hold the land itself and divide the proceeds from timber sales in an equitable way amongst legal claimants. He thought the trust should include all the children and any grandchildren. With August and Dinah, Olivia Roxanna and August's two boys plus Mally Shearin that made six portions of equal size.

I told him it sounded fair to me.

He urged the blood test on me again for Dinah and Mally (or August and Mally if Dinah objected). He could arrange it in absolute privacy anytime we wanted at a laboratory in Raleigh.

I told him that I'd very much enjoyed relying on my own instincts for nine decades and meant to do so still. No blood test would be necessary. I trusted my eyes to recognize Palmer Slade in all his leavings.

Mr. Rose had heard me out calmly. Now a great smile took his whole broad face and nearly shut his eyes that are morning glory blue.

It didn't bother me but I did ask him what was funny.

He said "I'm compelled by human decency to tell you that you'll be paying me a fair amount of money to draft you a will and a trust agreement that may not keep out the gentlest spring rain once you and I are gone. Are you prepared for that?"

I told him I understood precisely, had never expected guarantees from life and that he should proceed.

He opened his briefcase and shuffled through a fistful of Palmer's old papers as though they might contain some form of rescue. Nothing apparently. He faced me, grinned again and shrugged his wide shoulders. Then he said he'd start drafting the will tomorrow but suggested that I not tell a soul till we'd signed and sealed it. Then if anybody pouted once I was underground, the courts would no doubt sort out the claims as they generally did.

I told him I doubted any such eventuality.

Mr. Rose laughed, said he'd pray for us all and then finished up "With your leave, madam, I'll strain to hang onto life itself to defend your wishes in any such feud."

I laughed too and told him that his far greater youth was why I'd called on him and no other.

Despite the lawyer's warning I disobeyed him in one respect as I'd warned him I would. That night I wrote the following note and copied it six times in crystal clear script—

Dearest Children and Grandchildren,

If this comes as a shock, you will learn to live with it.

Your father and grandfather, Palmer Slade, is also the legal blood father of Mally Pittman Shearin whom you all know and have every reason to feel grateful to for her flawless kindness to Olivia Slade, Dinah Slade Beecham and to me, your mother.

I am ninety-four years old as you know so well; and I know the above to be a firm fact, though Mally never received a cent from Palmer nor me, beyond her earned wages. In preparing my last will and testament, I have chosen to do the only fair thing by my own lights and by God's above. Mally will get an equal portion in all Palmer Slade's remaining land and timber. And since each of you has your own house, or will never think of living again this deep in the country, my house will be Mally's as well along with a share of other things I possess.

I have thought this through and am sure you will agree. Please make each of yourselves a copy of this letter, sign your name at the bottom in real ink (no ballpoint mess that will fade), have a witness sign and date it in the presence of a notary and send it back to me post haste.

Your loving and earnest,
Roxanna Dane Slade

Within ten days I had all the answers and everybody signed to indicate agreement—not a word of complaint, though I'll never be certain that everybody's happy with my settlement. Nobody said that they were or weren't. I mailed the signed agreements directly to Lawyer Rose, he drew up the final draft of the will, Simon carried me out to the car in his arms—still strong enough to bear me in his own late eighties (my old hollow bones barely tip the scales now).

Long as I'd known him, and good as he'd been through sun and hail, we were more than halfway to our destination before I could make myself face Simon's profile and say "Who is Mally Shearin's real father?" The words were scarcely out before I prayed he didn't know or wouldn't answer somehow.

He drove a good while and never turned toward me, but he finally said "You don't want me putting my old mouth on your family business."

I said "You've never lied to me yet."

"No ma'm," Simon said. "That far, you right. But you ain't asking me to say *wrong* or *right*. You asking me to guess what happened in the night long ages past."

It sounded as if we were talking about the tombs of the pharaohs, and I had to smile. But I said "I'd respect your opinion as always if you'd let me hear it."

But through another silence Simon showed no trace of a smile nor any temptation to say a word further. The strong right wall of his face gave me nothing. He was plainly pretending I hadn't said a syllable more.

So in another minute I let myself believe this was wisdom from a careful old friend or, if not wisdom then at least good sense in drawing no lines in the air between us—lines we neither one could ever forget nor maybe forgive. In ten more minutes we'd covered the few miles left to Henderson.

And there on Garnett Street in an office like something from a silent movie version of a lawyer's office in the wild-west days, I signed three copies of the hopeful arrangement. Two young dyed-hair secretaries stood by to witness my sanity, and Lawyer Rose looked both proud and anxious to have finished our business. At the moment I thought he looked like a president signing the peace to end a great war—his face still knew everybody concerned was armed to the teeth. But once I was safely back in the car, I told myself my wish would prevail.

The whole way home with Simon telling me some long story about his oldest boy in prison and how he's becoming a mail-order preacher while the eldest daughter is moving up the rungs as a social worker down in Savannah, I felt I'd shucked off a burden that had been on my back for seventy-two years.

In the depths of my mind, I'd carried that load every day of my life since I learned that Palmer had a Negro woman in addition to me. Now I'd set it down on the ground on the literal Earth. It felt truly splendid to *do* one more thing that had some weight before I depart. I hadn't really done a thing that mattered since Dinah's last weeks before Rox's birth. So there beside Simon I felt even lighter than I am on the scales, which is practically airborne. Hereafter, which is where I'll be soon enough, I can only trust in whatever decency I managed to press into my two children and their live descendants. I'd estimate they're decent enough to do what they promised. But old as I am who am I to know?

I thought I'd reached the end with that sentence. Reading through the whole story now days later, though, I feel I owe—owe *who?* God only knows—a few last ownings-up and corrections. Now that all those memories have cooled, what bothers me most in the pages above is how chilly I feel as a human being but especially as a wife and mother. Maybe that feeling is truer than I think. Maybe there's a deep core of chill down in my brain as a part of whatever made me subject to the killing blues till I was nearly fifty years old and had to fling myself from a car and crush my skull before I was more like a normal person.

But I owe it to myself to say in all honesty that when I was well I loved Palmer Slade like the night wind in summer. I loved August and Dinah as much as any mother I've watched has loved and attended to the voices of her children. It's only fair to complete the truth and say that, like a fair number of aunts and grandmothers, I loved my nephew (Leela's son Wilton) and Dinah's Rox even more if that's possible. And I wouldn't swear on anyone's Bible that I haven't come to treasure Mally Shearin as highly as any other soul. I say *treasure* since she wouldn't let me use the word *love* on her behalf.

The other night she was in my room. We were watching some television story about love and how it drove everybody wild from ants in the ground to the finest old-money billionaires in Newport. And when I was almost sick from the TV sweetness, Mally turned to me with the gravest face and said "Love is just what you feel till you get to know the person."

I laughed. So did she. But late in the night, I thought she'd got hold of one big secret. A secret that runs the early lives anyhow of way too many people. By *love* of course I take it that Mally meant *romance* and *passion*. As I've said, Mally and I have never discussed her relations with passion. I, though, have always been short on romance. That and passion were more in Leela's line from the start.

I could never quite manage to rouse myself sufficiently to dust a person with gold in my head and stand there and wait for the sun to adore him. Much as I liked the presence of Larkin the day I was twenty, he never seemed anything like a god till he came in that vision after his death. And though I enjoyed his brother Palmer's face and limbs as much as any white girl of my time could—more so than most—I always felt he was needier than me which prevents awe and worship.

So whether I loved my kin sufficiently will have to be decided by them. And who has ever felt loved *enough*? As I said the only thing resembling a complaint I ever heard from Palmer was the news of his woman. I grant that once August got himself back from the Second War and cleared his head, he streaked right off to the farthest edge of the state and has only visited three times a year except in emergencies. That may have been a silent comment on his mother. I've also considered whether or not my failures with Dinah, when I was not *there* for so much of her youth, somehow caused her a few years later to seek out Harley too soon and start a bastard child just for something to hold that was warm and could talk back dependably.

If such was the case, then I think I can say that—since the last days of Dinah's pregnancy—she and I have been as close as we ought to be, very dear to each other. Dinah's not one of those in-bondage daughters who has to phone her mother five times a day and get permission to wash a lettuce leaf or say the word *No* to any live man. I know women who can't sleep at night till they've had a long talk with their mother or daughter about what each one served for supper and how the family liked it.

But I've never once doubted I mattered to Dinah as much as anybody except her husband and child, and isn't that exactly what Christ intended when he gave his opinion that a man must leave his father and mother and *cleave* to his mate? I assume he spoke for men *and* women—he usually did or so I believe.

*   *   *

Wilton has gone his way in the world to Boston where he works in art design and has a wife who can scarcely speak her name for shyness. But he sends me fairly regular pretty things he's drawn—mainly trees and clouds (I spend a mint on frames)—and he calls me monthly, every first Sunday of his life.

Rox has generally lived closer by with a few jaunts away after one man or another. It's especially hard to believe that she's over forty now. She's had a difficult time in her dealings with the world outside her own room, especially the male half. She's come much nearer than anybody else in the family to inheriting the melancholy that I likely inherited from my own mother. Rox has never sunk as deep in the dumps as I went at my worst, though she's suffered greatly and had whole years of her life bent double by that same dark arm clamped over her mouth and aiming to kill her. It's led her to drink far more than was wise and to seek, in men, some reward that's not to be found in other humans of whatever age and sex.

Still she's had a good doctor in recent years and been on helpful medication as well, and now she's living with her third official husband. I once asked her why she had to marry every man that spent the night with her. Couldn't they just keep on staying as friends or whatever without the legal papers? Her answer was "I'm your granddaughter, darling. That's a real load to bear." I'm not altogether sure what she meant, but I left it alone and am still doing so. None of Rox's three spouses could be accused of having good sense, but this latest one seems at least to respect her. It's been more than a year since she's come by my house wearing dark glasses to hide a bruised eye.

The other grandchildren—August and Daisy's two boys—were so scarce in their childhood that I never really got to know them, and now they're past grown too. That was their mother's choice, and I never fought it. Now both of them send me a Mother's Day card with the names of all my great-grandchildren on it. Between the two of them, there are five offspring. With a few minutes' warning, I can call the children's names. But as far as feeling close, we're frankly as distant as continents. Well-*wishing* continents but far out of sight. They've had their mother's mother to love them, I very much hope.

I've said before that in my generation women's lives ended when their husbands died and their children scattered. Then they either went quietly

crazy with loneliness and slugs of cooking sherry, or their minds dissolved
in premature senility in front of a TV showing Perry Como all hours of the
day. Or they got obsessed with their poor grandchildren, carrying pictures
of them everywhere and boring kind strangers, not to mention the children. I've literally never known a white woman from a self-respecting family, born back when I was, who got herself a useful paying job when her
husband passed. I'm sure there've been some, but I never met them.

The ones I've known were kept by their children or by old-age assistance
or they died in what used to be called the County Home, a polite name for
the Poor House. And of all that number, I don't know more than two
who've offered to donate so much as ten minutes a week to the homeless
and desperate. My kind of woman—here in my homeplace and always
claiming to be a sworn Christian—has seldom borne the least resemblance
to Mother Teresa in any connection outside her own family. I include
myself in that sad majority.

I know that's been a practical tragedy for a great many of us, and again I
don't exempt myself from judgment. I've outlined the few achievements
I'm even half proud of since Palmer died when I was fifty-two. With the
limited education I had, there was very little in my part of the world that a
woman could have done in the way of honest jobs but stay home and clip
her inheritance coupons and wait for her Social Security check like light
from God.

In my little town to this late day, there are still no hostels for the dazed and
hungry. The nearest was in Henderson and since I don't drive I couldn't
get there to make jelly sandwiches and smile at the wretched. I'm not making fun. Far from it—I know there are saints alive on the Earth and I'm not
one. But neither is anybody else known to me. So here I've sat in what has
amounted to more than four decades of talking to myself. If that hasn't
driven me crazy for the last time, I doubt God could (in any case I never got
truly low again).

And speaking of *crazy*, Rox and Dinah sometimes have wondered aloud in
my presence if the biggest part of my trouble in life didn't come from the
simple fact of being a woman, a *held-down* woman with insufficient air to
breathe and all but no roads to take that hadn't been trod by every woman
since Eve at least. Because I honor my female kin, I've tried to give them
honest answers. But I'm afraid they aren't highly satisfied with my honest

claim that No, in my particular case I don't think my womanhood has
been any sizable curse. Oh I can recall whole days of my childhood when
I was half sick because my older brother could do something or go somewhere forbidden to me. There were even doors open to poor young Ferny
that I envied and sometimes dreamt of walking through.

But as my brothers grew up on either side, and I watched my father sup-
port us the best he could by working thirty hours a day nine days a week, I
had fewer and fewer opportunities for self-pity. I can say now a big thing
that I knew then but held in silence. I had by birth a keener mind than any
of theirs, and I'd taken more pains to soak up the little our country school
offered. Leela could have said the same and frequently did.

Anyhow by the time I pledged my life and obedience to Palmer Slade, I
was on the way to being equipped with eyes that saw how few real privi-
leges he or any other man could flaunt at me. Again it may have been
because I loved him so steadily that—more often than not, when I'd felt
overburdened to the point of screaming—I'd notice some way Palmer had
moved his exhausted eyes at supper or stroked his worn wrist, and I'd wind
up sorrier for him than me. Or at least as sorry.

Which is not to say that I think modern women in America have been at
all wrong by asking in no uncertain terms for absolute fairness in money
and all else, wherever they work, and for more dignified attention from the
men in their path (not to speak of the hope that no man will ever even
touch a woman or child again in anger, not to mention uncontrolled
desire). All things being equal I also think women should get to be Marines
or public executioners or any other hard jobs available to men that they
might want.

I suspect, though, that when they've won those positions they'll probably need to grow suddenly blinder. I've mentioned that most human
beings in my world have seemed to be *blind* for the greater part of their
waking hours, but the men of my acquaintance have been blind for more
of their time than the women. I still don't know why, maybe just because
most children are entrusted to women's care. Men's feelings are just as
complicated as ours; they just walk past them more often than not. But that
hasn't made me want the steady presence of a few men any less in the
midst of my life.

I realize as well that if I'd had different early chances for college, say, and jobs outside the kitchen and bed—yes, I might have won the Nobel Prize by now and be on TV hourly admired by the children of the Earth and receiving huge boatloads of praiseful mail for having learned how to keep hate out of young minds. (When I think of the hate that boils in young men now and many young girls—I know how much they've borne from their fathers, yet I also know you can say one true thing about every human—*they each had a mother or some woman who raised them*.)

But I also know I can't find it in me to wish that my youth had had such choices in it. Modern women after all, despite the real gains they've earned, are missing out this instant on some boon the mysterious future will bring—like the final victory over cancer, which is surely not more than twenty years off, and the promise of upright sane lifespans past the century mark. So doesn't it seem a form of greed to demand everything the world can afford at any given time? Coming along where and when I did, I'd estimate I've had some real luck and nowhere near as much heartbreak as many women known to me. I think that ought to give my kinswomen pleasure or relief anyhow—but of course it doesn't, and they may well be right. Maybe I've been a blind galley slave and my main miseries were caused by men. I continue to doubt it. And if so, well I only say Thank Christ for blindness.

Once I've admitted to that much thinking, I owe the very paper I write on at least a final attempt at saying what I think my life's been and where it might take me when I head out of here. The first thing I find is, to my considerable surprise, I've thoroughly enjoyed it which is likely the main reason I'm writing this. Among a lot else it's an overflow of pleasure and thanks. Most days lately I feel I'd do it all over again, even the torments, especially if I could start out next time in the confidence of living through nearly a century with a mind and body that worked for all but four years. What kind of a challenge would that be, though, with a promise at the start?

I'm not claiming I have no regrets. Regret stacked behind me at a regular rate in my active years, less frequently since I "took the veil" at ninety-three, the year I broke my leg. I think most of my sorrows and guilts are owned-up-to here. In my mind at least, I've been as capable of cruelty, waste and physical harm as any felon in our vicinity. And the mind's where cruelty counts above all. To make a near-deathbed confession, though, I'm bound to admit that—if I could do it all again—the one thing I'd try hardest to improve, to have more *of*, would be sex with my husband.

I'm not smart enough to say why exactly. I hate to repeat the only thing that's ever troubled me about it, but I think it's a problem that so many people overlook and then get damaged by. Again in all my TV-watching time—from the worst soap slop to the Mind Extension channel—again I've never heard anybody say what sex is *about*, what it's *for*. And again that's not to say I think it's just for baby making. If the dark truth be told, I think I always felt sex brought me closer toward God or Heaven at least than anything else I did with my husband or anybody else but you can't say that in the Christian church, not any I've known.

That was one more reason church has meant so little to me. I've seen better sights and felt stronger feelings elsewhere—*well-intentioned* feelings—than any church in my experience can offer. And more than a lion's share of those good things passed into my mind and body through Palmer Slade as he worked above me, almost always in the night when I couldn't see enough. I know that's the happiness I think of most in what amounts to my present lone state. If that seems wrong or hard to hear from a speckled crone, I'll take the penalty whenever it's applied.

So owning up to my worst and best, and trying to look as far ahead as these dim eyes can see, I think the memory of me will last out the span of my kin who are presently alive plus Mally and Simon. More than not, I truly believe they'll remember me somewhere along the scale from gladly to pleasantly. I've amounted to that much anyhow, a likable memory in a handful of minds, give or take a few natural reservations. Isn't that the best most people can claim? Mally and Simon of course could bring the deepest-dyed indictment against me and all I represent—I and all my kin and neighbors with our semi-pink skins. No way any legacy or modest trust fund can wipe the slates of any white person in any black eyes.

But the greatest wonder of that remarkable race is how slender a grudge it's held against us. Oh I understand that millions are rightly and violently mad and millions of others so stunned by history that they scarcely see plain sunshine above them. I've watched all the fiery riots and massacres. There are half-starved pot-bellied black children up many a gulley in the county I live in. So why aren't all of us pink souls flat-dead in our beds with throats cut ear to ear?

And by *us* I don't just mean me and my kin, my Southern neighbors, but way the bigger part of white America. And in case I seem to have claimed some premature wisdom on the subject of racial relations, let me say that the little I've done to swim upstream against the current of blind white fear doesn't amount to so much as a single handful of dry dust thrown on those wild waters.

As it is, Simon Walton has keys to all my doors and my car to boot. And Mally Shearin cooks every morsel I eat, not to mention her merciful attentions to my body where one slight slip could kill me on the floor. Once they and their kind memories are dead—theirs and several of my blood kin's memories (say, thirty years from now)—for practical purposes Roxanna Slade will be dead as King Tut and with no hill of gold to mark her corpse. Therefore gone *entirely* except for those few peculiar strangers who haunt country graveyards and read lost names on mossy tombstones.

Will that truly be *it* for all this effort? Have I and mine struggled on as we have just for an endless blind unbroken rest in the common dirt? All through these pages I see I've mentioned God and Fate a lot, both Hell and Heaven. Am I headed either place? Are there any such places? I certainly claim no authority whatever. But I have what feels like two real pieces of evidence, however private to me and my eyes. First I'm aware that my lasting to be near a century old is no guarantee of wisdom or foresight. Many turtles live longer than that, and I just saw two nights ago that a healthy elephant in the jungles of India may well live to be 125. (Elephants of course and maybe some turtles are far superior to human beings as are all whales and dolphins.)

But the point is that I'm as old as humans get to be with rare exceptions. And the main hint that I've picked up on the subject of immortality has come with my age in the past ten years. I've watched a few dozen people through their long lives and I see that, unless they go crazy or are addicts, they just stay who they were from the day they were born. I'm speaking of friends live and dead like Leela and Simon, Mally and Palmer, even poor Ferny Dane who's been gone so long I can barely see his face. I don't mean that people learn nothing from life, but the hearts and souls they bring here with them as they leave what Miss Olivia called "their mother's fork" are extremely *persistent*. With a naturally good soul, that's excellent news, not so with the bad.

The fact that our inner depths are fairly unchangeable sounds not only scary but like a promise of something to me, something far more durable than one set of bones. We come here from somewhere that shaped us already. After so many years we head out again for maybe that homeplace or somewhere else that keeps on *lasting*.

The other hint has stayed with me the whole way through my life. Long before I joined the Methodist church at age thirteen, I knew there was something in the world but me. I'd felt it keenly from the age of five, mainly when I was outside the house in the garden or the woods and when I was alone or with Negroes who could always get still enough to let nature speak and be partly heard. The thing that I knew had caused my feeling never seemed like something especially good or monstrous.

I never felt like the thing was spying on me to catch me out in some dirty dealing. But it did feel enormous, and it felt *like me*. It was so huge in fact that it constituted everything seen and unseen. And I was a small part of its complicated makeup—among the smallest cogwheels but a working part still, not vital maybe but working still. I could choose not to work by killing myself or shirking my duty. But the bigger thing would go on without me, though it hoped for my service and could hear my requests.

With all the pain and waste I've known in my own life and lives that touched mine—not to mention the horrors of this whole century, one slow bloodbath—I've never been able to shake that knowledge that came with my childhood. Children seldom are fooled, I've found, about main things like truth and what's right. I haven't discussed it with anyone since Palmer died. He was the only person I've known who could hear me out and not laugh or run for the nearest exit. But however hard I've slashed away in my bad times at what I knew, I haven't succeeded in felling the trunk of that certainty that came into the world with me, straight out of the box like batteries with a flashlight. Even TV religion, all of it calling itself some brand of *Christian*, hasn't quite shut me down. To be sure it's bolstered my weak blood pressure to dangerous heights and sickened my stomach with its hatreds and lies.

But once I get myself calmed down, if I lie in my own bed in the dark and look straight up at nothing at all beyond the ceiling, I can almost always start to feel again that calm first fact from my childhood. And then the whole great hoop of whatever *is*, gorgeous or dreadful as it may be, starts turning in the night sky above me bearing everything that has ever been or is—from Dinah Beecham's frail perfect fingers the day she was born, to Olivia Slade's meanest effort to drive me down or Roebuck Pittman's raving in the road, plus the men and women who torture children daily, plus Gandhi and Eleanor Roosevelt and the true living saints.

Once I've glimpsed that for the length of one more night anyhow, I can tell myself that the only axle which matters is turning with all its weight of trees and waterfalls, plagues and fire storms, souls in torment and me in some surviving shape no doubt huddled out toward its rim holding nothing in hand but my strong memories and the hope to keep breathing so long as I know my family's names and can smile when they touch me. The hoop itself may never fail. If I'm dead wrong then I'm no worse than *dead*. And by the time I'm numb and cooling, whether tonight or years from tonight (there's a woman in France who's a hundred and twenty and talks good sense), I'll likely be tired enough for sleep, though if what's called for is music and dance, I estimate I'll be prepared, if only to hum and sway in place.

REYNOLDS PRICE

Reynolds Price was born in Macon, North Carolina in 1933. Educated in the public schools of his native state, he earned an A.B. summa cum laude *from Duke University, graduating first in his class. In 1955 he traveled as a Rhodes Scholar to Merton College, Oxford University to study English literature. After three years and a B.Litt. degree, he returned to Duke where he continues in his fourth decade of teaching. He is James B. Duke Professor of English.*

In 1962 his novel A Long and Happy Life *received the William Faulkner Award for a notable first novel. Since, he has published nearly thirty books. Among them, his novel* Kate Vaiden *received the National Book Critics Circle Award in 1986. His* Collected Stories *appeared in 1993, his* Collected Poems *in 1997; he has also published volumes of plays, essays and two volumes of memoir* Clear Pictures *and* A Whole New Life. A Palpable God *in 1978 contained translations from the Old and New Testaments with an essay on the origins and aims of narrative;* Three Gospels *in 1996 contained his translation of* Mark *and* John *with introductory essays. His tenth novel* The Promise of Rest *appeared in 1995 and completed—with* The Surface of Earth *and* The Source of Light—*a trilogy of novels entitled* A Great Circle *and concerned with nine decades in a family's life.*

His television play Private Contentment *was commissioned by "American Playhouse" and appeared in its premier season on PBS. His trilogy* New Music *premiered, with a grant from the Fund for New American Plays, at the Cleveland Play House in 1989. His sixth play* Full Moon *was performed by the American Conservatory Theatre in San Francisco in 1994, and in 1995 he began to broadcast regular commentaries for "All Things Considered" on National Public Radio.*

He is a member of the American Academy of Arts and Letters, and his books have appeared in sixteen languages.